I0771889

Foiled Stars

FOILED STARS

JENNIFER ASCIENZO

Stag Beetle Books

PART ONE

Arrival

CONQUERING forty-seven planets in fifty-three days was a record for Dante. The faster he worked, the faster he could return home.

As he surveyed the planet he occupied, dirt soiled his black-gloved hands, tumbling onto the ground below. Body beading with sweat, his fitted armor suctioned to his skin. It'd been a while since he last endured such a vigorous workout. Over a year.

Fortunately, Universe 2 lived up to its defenseless nature. Until that evening, the planet crawled with free lower life-forms. Now they existed under his control.

Wind gusted and howled through the ruins from the battle that occurred hours before. The hopeless begging and piercing screams of his captives rang through his ears. Dante ran his fingers through the strands of his damp hair. He conducted one last survey of the terrain, kicking up ash and copper dust with his heavy boots. Dante couldn't wait another moment. He wanted—no, *needed* to get this mission over with.

Desperate to go home to his own world, *eleven Universes away.* But at the same time, endless curiosity consumed him.

He had one more planet to visit. One more until he could embark on the long, treacherous journey home. One more and he would be *free* until, of course, his next assignment rolled in.

A minuscule planet, the rich hue of sapphire and emerald, with a mere population of eight billion. Earth: it promised to be a fruitful acquisition indeed.

* * *

Dante sat in the cockpit of his ship while the emergency functions blared. The interior lights flashed bright red, indicating obvious distress. Maybe it was a result of a passing asteroid shower, or perhaps something more than that.

His warriors sat nearby, shaking their heads, eyes widened with disbelief. Dante couldn't afford any mistakes, considering he'd been traveling through the deepest depths of space for well over a year.

He anticipated returning home triumphant after the successful completion of his mission, as he'd done countless times before. After all, he, Dante Martyne, was not known for experiencing failure or setbacks of any sort.

Dante slammed his fist against the arm of his seat, leaving an indentation. Everyone jumped at the vibration echoing against the metal cabin walls.

He leaned forward in his seat. "Pilot, what seems to be the issue?"

The pilot's teeth chattered so loud Dante could hear them from where he sat. The pilot's body trembled as he tried to summon the words. "There's a—" He grasped the steering panel for dear life as everyone knocked around and the ship descended lower, lower, lower from space. "Crystal liquid fuel leak."

Dante gritted his teeth, blood pressure boiling to a steady rage. His eyes darted suspiciously around the room.

"Whose task was it to secure the crystal liquid fuel lines before we entered Universe 1?"

As anticipated, *nobody* came forth. Dante couldn't entirely blame them. He wasn't certain he would own up to a mistake of this magnitude if he was in their shoes.

"I ask you a second time. Who was it, or shall I select one of you at random to bear the blame?"

Simultaneously, everyone pointed to a young man at the back of the room Dante identified as "tech." Throughout the voyage, Dante never bothered to learn his name. First, because the tech was beneath him, and second, because he didn't care enough to ask.

The tech's eyes widened and wavered on the verge of tears. The color washed from his youthful ruddy face.

"So, it was you then?"

The tech leaned forward in his chair; hands cupped tightly around his mouth. Dante was certain he meant to vomit all over the floor, but hoped he didn't. The stench, together with their sweat-stained uniforms, was more than his stomach could handle.

To Dante's surprise, the tech sat up, face pale. "Yes, Sire, but I—"

"Silence," Dante said. The tech shut his mouth tight, trembling. Having no tolerance for failure, Dante was disinterested in hearing his pathetic explanation.

"I'll deal with you later."

The tech buried his head in his hands, while Dante concocted a punishment for his crime.

The ship jolted violently, and everyone thrust forward in their seats, choked by their restraints before smacking against their chairs. Groans erupted through the cabin including his own.

The ship descended, and Dante had an inkling they were in for a nasty landing.

"Pilot, where are we headed?"

"Earth, Sire."

This isn't the most terrible news, as we're headed there regardless, on a secondary mission. Dante beheld the glowing sapphire and emerald sphere. However, the idea of being stuck on a planet crawling with human life forms longer than he initially intended irked him to no end. He preferred to operate on a regimented schedule.

Dante's stomach flipped and turned as they descended, and the pull of gravity set in, suctioning him to his seat.

"*Everyone brace yourselves,*" were the last words Dante heard before he was ripped into the darkness.

Two

AUTUMN TOSSED and turned in a fitful sleep. Nightmares invaded her mind, growing darker and more twisted at every corner. A screech. A skid. The burning heat of twisted metal. Her eyes sprang open, and she shot up from her bed.

A dream. Her heart thundered in her chest before her eyes drew to the corner of her bedroom. For a moment, she could see the fading dark silhouette of her late mom. It had been three weeks since she'd passed. When Autumn blinked, the image disappeared, rippling into nothingness.

Autumn's eyes teared up. Her mom was gone, *really* gone. Her heart cracked once more in two.

When the bare soles of her feet connected with the floor, a tremor knocked her to the ground. She winced as she skinned her knees.

A second, more violent tremor struck not more than a moment later, followed by the soul-crushing shattering of her precious snow globe collection, in a distant corner of the room. Glass smashed, glitter, water, and all, spilled in a jumbled mess.

Another loss. She choked under her breath. *Another painful loss.* How much more could she suffer through until she finally gave up? Although incomparable to the loss of her mom, it was still a blow. Many of the globes were birthday gifts from her late mom and grandmother.

Autumn wobbled to a stand, her vision out of focus. Stretching her arm, she reached for her black metal cast Eiffel Tower lamp stationed on her night table. The light didn't turn on.

Her smartphone vibrated beneath the bed, falling during the commotion. Kneeling, she grabbed hold of it. It read 1:55 a.m., with the only notification being a lone message from Caleb Cortez that made her clench her jaw and dig her nails into her palm. *The jerk.* She couldn't believe how persistent he'd been. Couldn't believe he thought she'd forgive him.

"What the hell does he expect?" Autumn deleted the message and inhaled a shuddering breath, willing back more burning tears from welling in her eyes.

Not tonight, I don't need this tonight.

Her heart raced. Dad. She forgot about her dad. She slid her feet into her pink fuzzy slippers and fastened a bathrobe around her waist. Carefully, she maneuvered around the mess on the floor, using the pale stream of light from her smartphone as her guide.

She flung open the door, darting across the hallway. Pulse pounding in her ears. She hoped and prayed he was okay. If he was hurt or worse, she'd be all alone.

Bursting into his room, she shouted, "Dad, Dad, are you all right?"

A tangle of sheets and comforter led to the opposite side of the bed. Frantically, she cast the light around the room, but found no trace of him. No trace of anybody, except for her mom. Her last ironed blouse hung from the handle of the closet door. A bottle of her favorite Versace perfume on the dresser beside the final vase of flowers her dad gifted her. Red roses and baby's breath wilted to dust.

A groan erupted. She sprinted, tripping over her own slipper clad feet, to find her dad tangled in the sheets on the floor. Autumn gasped and knelt to help him. The whites of his bulging eyes were visible even in the pitch darkness. Short, wavy, umber-brown hair frazzled. Coarse beard hairs prickled against her arms.

Summoning every ounce of strength, she pulled him to a standing position. But it proved to be a daunting task, considering she stood at a grand total of five feet, and her dad was a few inches taller, but more than twice her weight.

She missed her mom more than ever. Who would take care of him if she didn't?

"Thanks, I'm okay." He brushed himself off, grabbed his simple silver metal frame glasses from the night table, then pushed them onto his whiskered face.

"What was shaking before?"

"I think we had an earthquake." He ambled over to the wall to try the switch. "Dammit."

A buzz rattled through the room. Autumn jumped to grab his phone as it danced along the edge of the night table and handed the device to her dad.

He slid the screen up before pressing the phone to his ear. "Hello? Okay, yes, yes, I see. I'll be there in a few minutes."

She stared at him in silence, wondering who called.

"The fire department needs me," he offered.

The call wasn't out of the ordinary. Her dad had registered to be a volunteer firefighter years ago. He regularly served their native town of Monroe, NY. But still—the earthquake laid heavily on her mind. She'd never experienced one before.

Stomach churning, she didn't want him to go alone. Deep down she felt if she went with him, she could protect him from harm. And often, she wondered if she could have protected her mom as well.

Autumn stood there quietly as he threw on a sweatshirt and a pair of tennis shoes.

"Can I come too?" She fidgeted her hands.

He blinked and inhaled deeply before exhaling. "All right, but only if you promise to wait in the car."

"Okay, I promise," she repeated his words, knowing it was the answer he wanted to hear.

"I'm serious." He placed his hands on her shoulders. "I don't know what I would do if I lost you too." He choked on the last word, a single tear rolling down his cheek.

"I promise, Dad. I promise."

* * *

When Autumn and her dad left the house, the neighborhood was in a state of frenzy. People stood on their front lawns; bathrobe clad. An emergency vehicle roared in the distance. The faint scent of smoke filled the air, and a coal-black cloud drifted beneath the luminous glow of the crescent moon. The stars sparkled in the sky, coloring the grass the lushest shade of green in the spectrum.

It would've been an otherwise beautiful evening in their small town. A picture-perfect July night, if it wasn't for all the commotion. The air was tight with fear and uncertainty. But mostly *fear*.

After checking in with a few neighbors, Autumn and her dad loaded into his silver Jeep. Fortunately, nobody had suffered serious injuries, except for a few minor bumps and bruises. Autumn loved this aspect about her hometown. Whenever someone was injured or distressed, neighbors stepped up to aid one another. They'd been exceptionally helpful after her mom's passing, offering her family endless sympathy casseroles, support, and company.

While she rested her head against the seat, her dad turned onto Lakes Road. Her heart swelled with pride. No other parents she knew held down a full-time job, and dedicated their sleeping hours to volunteering for the town whenever it was in need. Her dad was secretly her hero.

Streams of light on the roof of his Jeep swirled blue and white. Ambulances, fire trucks, and state trooper cruisers were the only other vehicles on the road in the dead of night. Radiant lights twinkled and glowed in the distance.

That's when Autumn spotted it. The *pole*. She slammed her eyes shut, unable to face it, even though it'd since been reconstructed. The location where her mom was discovered. Injured and hobbling, drenched in rainwater and blood. She couldn't bear to think about it. Didn't want to ever see it again.

She blinked away her tears, not wanting to worry her dad, and stifled her breath. Although the faintest sniffle came from his seat, she kept her mouth closed out of respect.

* * *

When Autumn and Guillermo Ramon arrived at the scene, emergency vehicles clumped together along the street. Sections of the street were blockaded off with yellow metallic dividers. The fire raged at a popular hiking site known as Farrah Falls. In years past, Autumn had spent many warm summer days here swimming, hiking, and exploring with her friends.

Her dad parked the car and turned to look at her. "I'm not sure how long I'm going to be, but under *no* circumstances are you to leave this car. Put on the air conditioning, adjust the radio. Do whatever you need to, but *please* stay here."

Autumn nodded and once again promised she wouldn't

abandon her post. She watched as he joined a uniformed group of emergency responders. They hiked into the dark forest, flashlights waving in hand.

Yawning, she rested her head. Her fluttering eyes closed.

Her phone buzzed one, two, *three* times. Caleb texted her *again*. This time she peeked. Each message was more desperate than the last. So pathetic. Autumn hit the block button, her patience at its end. He had some *nerve*, really, he did. Texting her at this hour. She hoped he would stop contacting her all together, come college in the fall. Hopefully, he'd find a new girl to harass and disappoint. But Caleb was thick and persistent. He didn't understand the magnitude of what he'd done. Autumn had rarely hated before, in her eighteen years of life, but she hated him almost as much as the person who struck her mom and killed her. All Autumn wanted was a normal drama-free life and for everything to return to the way it once was. She strove for this goal every day.

Frustrated and exhausted, she turned up the heat, and her body relaxed. Sounds muffled and her head grew heavier, her breathing deepening.

* * *

A few hours passed before Autumn opened her eyes again. The neon blue digital clock on the Jeep's dashboard read half-past three. She inspected the surrounding area, surprised her dad hadn't returned yet. It didn't make sense. How could he still not be back from his call?

Heart speeding in her chest, her imagination raged. What if he was hurt? What if he disappeared? What if he was eaten by a *bear*? Holy crap.

What if, what if, what if? She had no way of knowing.

Separating her trembling fingers, she reached into her pocket and grabbed her phone.

Are you okay?

Her text message to him was followed by a vibration. Her blood froze in her veins. *He forgot his phone.* Her dad had a habit of either never having his phone or forgetting to turn it on.

Against all logic, and in a definite breach of her promise, she opened the car door, placing her fuzzy slippers on the concrete. It was empty outside, except for a few straggling EMTs fiddling around on their phones.

Autumn walked over to the trailhead, using the light on her phone as her guide. She peered out as far as her eyes could see. The entire forest was shrouded in blackness, and a thin layer of smoke drifted through the night sky. She inhaled before entering the stretch of trees.

It was quiet, save for the crisp chirping of the crickets and the babbling water crashing over rocks. The occasional sparkle of a lightning bug illuminated the air, shifting away the darkness. But there were no people at all. Not even footsteps.

"Dad?" she called out, her voice echoing above the moonlit trees. "Dad? Where are you?"

Three

DANTE WOKE from the brief void of darkness that engulfed him. Against his will, his heart sank to the floor; more desperate than he was before, more desperate than he'd ever been.

Temples throbbing, he balled his fists and slammed them into his seat. "Someone is going to pay for this!" he roared, struggling for a moment to compose himself.

Carefully, he moved his body. To his good fortune, it was intact. All ten of his fingers and toes unbroken, and his limbs fully functioning.

Undoing his harness, he glanced around the cabin, surveying the damage. The same stroke of luck didn't hold true for his soldiers. Broken bones protruded with bruised patches of skin. Fresh crimson blood flowed from noses and mouths. A few necks were snapped, others bent the wrong way.

"Shit," he murmured. "Shit." This was going to be one expensive expedition. A screw up like this would most certainly come out of his pocket. He'd never hear the end of it.

Rising, he waded through the pile of broken bodies for Ronan and Armienti, his only two relatives on board.

In the cabin's rear, he spotted them immediately. Armienti's head hung forward, golden wavy mid-length tresses tousled about his face. Armienti looked ridiculous, and he would say so himself if he were awake. Ronan sat next to him, plugging his nose with black-gloved fingers. Dark droplets of blood dripped, staining his lips and armor.

Dante approached an unconscious Armienti and slapped him across the face. Relief flooded through him as he roused them from the ether.

Armienti blinked his crystal blue eyes repeatedly before focusing his attention on Dante.

"Have we landed?" Armienti groaned.

"Yes," Dante affirmed. "It appears so." He offered them each a hand. "Can you both stand?"

They nodded, and with a firm tug, rose to their feet. A bit wobbly at first, but gradually steadying their weight.

Dante stomped his boots with a growing panicked rage against the cold metallic tiles, as he advanced on the pilot who lay comatose in the control seat. He cracked him across the back of his onyx helmet. The pilot gasped upon impact then stood and fell into a trembling bow.

"Oh good. You're alive," Dante's mouth flattened. "Have we landed on Earth?"

The pilot performed a hologram computer scan of the surrounding area. Buttons clicked, and gauges swirled until the profile reached completion.

"Yes, Sire," The pilot's limbs trembled. "It appears we've landed on planet Earth. The area bears coordinates 41.40116 °N, -74.32058 °E."

Upon hearing this information, relief flooded through Dante. At least they occupied the correct planet.

"Excellent." Dante's lips curved. He glanced at his cousins, whose faces glimmered with excitement.

Dante cocked his head to the side. "Nonetheless, pilot, now that I think of it, I'm perplexed as to how you failed to notice the ailing crystal liquid fuel lines. I do believe that was your responsibility as well."

Beads of sweat dripped from beneath the pilot's helmet. Dante tapped his boot on the ground and folded his arms across his chest, impatiently awaiting an explanation.

"Well, answer. I don't have all damn day."

The pilot gulped. He fell onto his knees, pressing his hands together, gaze averted to Dante's feet.

"Sire, please," the pilot begged. "Have mercy, I have a family waiting for me back home." He lowered his head fearfully.

Dante's eyes widened at the miserable man who groveled before him. He scruffed the pilot by his collar, yanking him to his feet.

"That's all you have to say?" he roared. "You imbecile, because of you, over half my crew is dead and we're stranded here!"

Dante's gaze darted around the room. More soldiers awoke, groaning in agony, but many more laid still, never to open their eyes again in this lifetime. His dreams of returning home early, triumphant, shattered before his eyes.

Dante recalled the other responsible party who openly admitted his failure. The tech, oddly enough, was quite untouched from the wreck.

He snapped his fingers. "Tech, come over here at once."

Compared to Dante's well-defined form, the tech had an odd, gangly body. He obediently approached his master.

The tech's mouth quivered, but no words came out. *Words won't help him anyway.* With a wave of his hand, Dante signaled to Armienti, who next wrapped his capable arms around the young man's torso and dragged him from the cabin. Dante followed, holding the pilot firmly in his grasp.

"Ronan," Dante said, "dispose of the injured and the deceased. There's no room for useless warriors on this ship."

"Are you sure, Dante?" Armienti began. "I can—"

"Save your time and energy."

With a single nod, Ronan obeyed his instructions. Blood-curdling screams and gurgling from men choking on their own fluids resonated from the steel walls. Slamming bodies vibrated against the floor followed by the stillness of death.

Dante and Armienti left the ship, terrified prisoners in hand. Both men sagged limp with fear, and a growing wet spot stained the pilot's crotch. Dante and Armienti tossed their captives onto the ground.

Dante scanned the area. A full circle of cracking trees on fire set ablaze above their heads. Thick smoke churned. Through the chaos, the stars twinkled in the sky like specks of glittering dust. Dante allowed himself but a moment to admire the crescent Earth moon. To him, every phase was more beautiful and less deadly than the full moon.

The steady chatter of human life-forms ensued close by, but he paid them little mind.

"Gentleman…" Dante cracked his knuckles. "You have five minutes. Run for your lives."

The condemned pushed themselves back onto shaky feet and fled the area as fast as their legs would take them. Armienti snickered.

To "thank" the prisoners for his spoiled mission, Dante caved to his love of sport. He found the thrill of a hunt invigorating. And why shouldn't he? He *always won*. Dante promised them five minutes, but only four had passed before he grew bored of dallying. Besides, he was generous enough allowing them a head start when he could have killed them on the spot. *They can't have gotten far.* Even if they *had* managed to put some distance between them, the enhanced speed he shared with his cousin would close it easily.

Zipping through the woodland, Dante and his cousin spotted several humans in passing, holding lights in their hands. Based on the tone of their voices, he assumed they were the ones he'd heard talking earlier. It was the first time he'd ever encountered humans in the flesh; he'd only ever read stories.

Everything else was ingrained in him. He was told they were stupid and possessed archaic technology. They were essentially useless and helpless. The worst excuses for lower life-forms. That's what made their planet the *perfect* target.

In the distance, Dante spotted a commotion, and assumed it was somehow connected with the raging fire they encountered earlier. He guessed it'd been initiated by his ship, and the speed it collided with Earth. Crimson, alabaster, and cerulean lights whirled, causing shadows to dance through the trees. And then—time ceased.

He encountered a ghost. A distant memory. Dante's heart thrummed.

What little of it he had left.

For an enchanting sight, stumbled around with the faintest stream of glowing light in hand. She was fair, possibly the fairest girl he'd ever seen. But also—strangely nostalgic.

Dante never imagined a human female could possess such loveliness. The girl reminded him of a spirit from his past, and how he hadn't encountered a beautiful girl in forever and a day, in the loneliness of space.

Before he could make himself known to her, she stumbled in her own little world and ran in the opposite direction.

Armienti elbowed him, snapping him out of his starstruck gaze. "Did you see what I did?" He licked his lips, watching the girl. "If she's any sign of what the girls look like on this planet, we're in for a real treat."

"I beg to differ," a disembodied voice whispered. "That human girl is average."

Dante frowned at Ronan materializing from behind a tree. Clumps of gore tumbled from his hair. He reeked of stinking perspiration and fear.

"I'm afraid your opinion doesn't matter. You wouldn't know a beautiful girl if she slapped you in the face." Which was true. Beautiful girls were not his cousin's type.

"We should go collect her," Armienti added.

"Turn your attention elsewhere." Dante folded his arms. "I saw her first. Find your own human."

The nerve of his gilded haired cousin, staking a claim over his beautiful find. If they weren't related, he would have beaten him for making such an utterly preposterous assumption.

Dante strode to the area where he'd last seen the girl.

"You can't possibly approach her in your current state." Armienti chuckled, correct as usual. His mouth tilted in his natural form.

Dante hadn't bothered to factor his appearance into the equation.

"Thanks." He shook his head at his disastrous oversight.

Dante quickly assumed a form that was a little more *human,* concealing his natural born features from plain sight and abandoned his mission of executing the offenders.

He found the girl humming to herself, sitting all by her lonesome on a stone. Legs crossed, back turned to him. The little beauty fixated on a computerized device she held in her palm. Perfect timing on his part.

Placing his hand on her shoulder with the lightest touch, he spoke.

"Hello."

Four

AUTUMN SAT ALL BY HERSELF, scrolling through her phone. The breathing forest thrived behind her. Emergency lights swirled, and there was still no sign of her dad. She figured all she could do was wait for his return. It was better than stepping on a snake. She shivered, cringing at the thought of slippery scales beneath her feet.

She shook at the slightest pressure on her left shoulder, then jumped at the faint whisper spoken in an unfamiliar voice and language. Perhaps she'd breached exhaustion and was imagining things.

Waves of adrenaline rolled through her limbs as she turned to face the person who sought her attention.

Before her stood a guy a few years her senior, but no more than college aged. He towered a clear foot above her head, clothed from head to toe in obsidian, with jaw length strands of silken midnight tousled around his face.

Autumn carefully studied his features, her gaze shifting from his pronounced cheekbones to the cleft on his chin. The pair of amber eyes that regarded her through the shadows were attached to a handsome face with a golden olive complexion.

But—

There was strangeness about him, though she had difficulty pinpointing exactly what it was. Perhaps because he sneaked around startling unsuspecting girls in the dead of night.

"Can I help you?" She tightened her fuzzy pink bathrobe.

The guy didn't answer. Instead, he stared at her, examining her face. His pupils dilated. For a moment, when he blinked, she could have sworn they shifted black. Autumn's cheeks heated against her will.

"Don't you have something to say?"

He responded to her question with a smile so luminous it blinded her in the dark. Autumn couldn't help but return the favor.

"*Autumn!*" A group of people emerged from the forest, flashlights flickering in hand.

Her dad ambled with a less than thrilled expression on his face. The screen of her phone faded and died.

Autumn glanced at the quiet guy through the dark and said, "Goodnight, I guess."

She waved at him, but he never moved or responded.

When Autumn reunited with her dad, he removed his glasses and wiped them over with a clean edge of his sweatshirt. He hugged her tightly. "I asked you to stay in the car."

"Sorry," she muttered. "You were gone so long I got worried."

"We had an agreement. What if you had gotten hurt or lost?" His voice trembled.

"I was talking to that guy over there. I never left the street." It was easier for her to lie to him about her whereabouts. He was already nervous and didn't need to know she had been searching for him in the forest.

He glimpsed. "What guy?"

Autumn turned to look, but the guy had vanished into the night.

"Never mind. It was no one."

* * *

Autumn and her dad drove home, leaving the excitement behind for the night. She faded in and out of consciousness, lying in her reclined seat.

As they hit a bump in the road, she glimpsed into the side-view mirror, and could have sworn she saw a shadow trailing the car at every pass and turn. She blinked hard, figuring she was more exhausted than she thought.

Inevitably, she drifted off.

When she woke, the car was parked in the driveway.

Stumbling, she followed her dad into their bi-level house. When he tried the light switch, relief washed through her to see the electricity worked. *Thank goodness.*

She examined the interior of their home post-earthquake, and her excitement for having the lights back deflated. The house was a mess. Her dad stormed around, cursing up a storm. She frowned, on the verge of tears for the third time that night.

The walls that were originally decorated with framed photos of her mom holding her as a baby were now hanging at haphazard angles, while some of the frames had fallen to the floor, shattered pieces scattered across the carpet and beneath the couch.

Shards of an antique Japanese tea set now smashed to oblivion littered the kitchen counter. Its delicate silver pieces shattered. It sucked. At this rate, she'd never get to sleep. The clock read 4:30 a.m., and she had work at 8:00 a.m. sharp.

Autumn grabbed the broom and dustpan, and her dad seized the vacuum cleaner. Together they tidied up the house.

Her mind couldn't help but wander to her mom. If she'd been there, she would have been joking and smiling. Maybe even singing *Castle on a Cloud*. Three weeks without her felt like a lifetime.

Afterwards, Autumn gulped and walked up the stairs mentally preparing herself for the devastation in her room. Her precious snow globe collection littered her bedroom floor. All eighteen of them destroyed. Autumn's lips quivered. She fell to her knees and sobbed her heart out.

What laid before her was a lifetime of memories. It was customary every year for her family to gift her with a new globe on her birthday. She held her favorite globe from *Alice in Wonderland;* Alice's head was severed from her body, and the accompanying caterpillar detached from his mushroom. It was the last gift from her mom. This one stung the most.

She wiped her tears. *"Get it together, Autumn,"* she murmured.

Solemnly, she cleaned, reminding herself they were inanimate objects that could not substitute her mom.

After a long heart-wrenching night, she collapsed in bed exhausted and dreamed. Not of car accidents or death or twisted metal, but of brilliant amber eyes watching her, and the handsome face she'd seen in the shadows.

Five

THE NEXT MORNING AUTUMN STRETCHED, wiping her weary eyes after barely three hours of sleep. She dragged herself to the bathroom, moaning and groaning the entire way. *Man, I wish I didn't have a double shift.*

Autumn brushed her teeth and showered, lathering herself with a lavender body wash. The scent always reminded her of her mom and the times they used to garden together when she was a little girl. It was a beautiful garden filled with Japanese maples, moonflowers, sage, and lavender. Sometimes, they would spend summer days on end mulching and weeding or searching for fairies, which she now knew didn't exist. No magic did. Only *pain*. Her eyes warmed with tears, and she wiped them away at the recollection of simpler, better times.

A few minutes later, she dressed in her diner-issued uniform: a sun-yellow apron, ink-black jeans, a pressed white polo, and of course a pair of black low-top Converse. Her favorite sneakers. Autumn had been working at the diner since summer's start, and all though she found the work miserable and grueling because of a *certain* somebody, it was money in her pocket for college.

When she left the bathroom, her gaze automatically fixated on the wall where her shelves hung, and she stopped. *No, no, this can't be right.*

Autumn reached out with the most delicate touch imaginable and rested her fingertips on the smooth glass of her resurrected snow globe collection. Alice's head re-affixed to her body, and the caterpillar blew Os from his mushroom. Glittery water swirled in a tornado, and the windup tune cranked, each note more haunting than the last.

Unsure of whether she should smile or scream—she cupped her hands over her mouth. There was no logical explanation for this. Unless her mom had intervened. Maybe she was looking after her. Or maybe she had been so tired the night before, she'd imagined the whole thing.

Regardless, Autumn mouthed a silent "thank you," to her mom, wanting to believe she had sent her a sign from beyond. She glanced at her phone. *Crap, I'm late.* She no longer had the luxury of time to dwell on this mystery, at least for the time being.

The sun had barely risen in the early morning sky. Orange and golden-yellow rays peeked over the horizon in a glittering display of light. As she passed through the driveway, her eyes fell longingly onto the apple-red Neon parked beside her dad's Jeep. She sighed; it seemed that everything in her life would serve as a reminder of her recent loss. Autumn had missed her driver's test because of her mom's funeral, and on top of that, she was woefully out of practice. No matter how much she wanted to drive herself, she would have to reschedule the test again soon.

The Monroe Diner was only a ten-minute walk from her house. She arrived, sweat-drenched and breathless from running to be on time. A quick survey of the parking lot filled her with a touch of dread. It was way *too* crowded, even for a Saturday morning.

The welcoming scent of pancakes fresh off the griddle greeted her. Silverware clinked on plates and people chatted, sitting at packed booths and tables.

As she made her way through the swinging kitchen doors to clock in, she realized she was an entire *fifteen minutes late*. Autumn hoped upon hope her manager wouldn't see her, but when she reached to punch in her numbers, a firm finger smashed into her shoulder, feeling like if there had been any more force behind it, the fingertip would break skin.

Autumn whirled around. *Busted again.*

Marcela Sanchez, her manager whom she unaffectionately dubbed *Marcela the Menace*, glowered at her. Lips pursed, causing her nonexistent chin to wrinkle. Marcela leaned over, and her spectacles fell to the edge of her greasy nose. How did she find her so fast? *Dammit.*

"I'm so sorry, Marcela, I—"

Marcela raised her palm, interrupting Autumn's poorly contrived excuse. She tapped a finger against her functional, *not* fashionable, leather watch.

"Autumn Ramon, how nice of you to finally join us," she said sarcastically. "I know you're still relatively new here. But as you know, in this diner, I require my staff *to be on time.*"

Autumn nodded mechanically.

"You've earned your first strike." Marcela struggled to hold back a smile. "Three strikes and you're out."

Autumn lowered her head before meeting Marcela's gaze.

"I'm really sorry. I had a late night." *And a terrible last few weeks.*

Marcela shook her head, bangs sticking to her slicked brow. "Spare me your explanation, Ramon."

She grabbed a pile of laminated menus and shoved them into Autumn's hands. "Get your pretty little face out on the floor. Time is money, and we have a shortage of both around here."

Autumn turned on her heel, rolling her eyes so far back into her head it surprised her they didn't get stuck. She went about her duties for the day and tried her best to ignore the discomfort creeping through her subconscious.

* * *

Dante waited patiently, sitting crossed-legged on a tuft of green, near the human eatery where he saw the girl enter earlier. Careful to keep his distance, and careful not to be seen. He'd been admiring her *all* night long. How he enjoyed the way she slept. The way she mumbled in her strange language to herself, and the sweetness of her scent.

Seldom in his life had he been caught under-prepared. Yesterday evening was one of the rare times he'd been made to feel a fool; unable to sleep after everything that transpired. Although familiar with the human species, he neglected to learn their dialect. A blatant oversight on his part.

He palmed his communicator, studying desperately not one, but *all* the languages on planet Earth. French, Italian, Spanish, Click Talk, although he doubted the last one. In any case, he wanted to be prepared. Dante figured such preparation would optimize his chances of speaking with her, and clearly stating his intentions.

Peering from his active module, he noticed many attractive girls walking by the double watering hole he sat next to. Armienti was correct. They were gorgeous.

They smiled, cheeks flushing crimson when they noticed him. It was painfully apparent they found him attractive. And why shouldn't they? He was quite the catch, if he said so himself. Accustomed to the attention, he flashed them a brilliant grin.

Eyes drifting, Dante admired his girl, wandering in front of windows draped with wispy alabaster cloth. She wore a uniform, the golden shade of the sun, her dark coiled hair beautifully arranged in a ball atop her head. The girl's skin mirrored his human disguise, and her cheeks were pink. But by far, her eyes were her most magnificent feature. They were wide and innocent like a doll's. The shade of the pale moon glow. Mesmerizing, yet nostalgic at the same time.

As hours passed Dante grew bored of studying the array of human languages and ambled along the walkway to waste some time. The single Earth sun blazed high in the sky. Clueless as to how long she would be in the facility, he wondered, *what could she possibly be doing other than eating and looking sweet?*

If this was the case, she was the slowest eater he'd ever encountered, but also the fairest. He planned to welcome her with open arms upon her exit. Hopefully she'd be receptive.

An idea dawned upon him like a spark of electricity. What could a practice run for their second encounter hurt? He'd also be confident his human disguise was working.

Dante eagerly scanned the green and settled on a girl who sat beneath the shade of a tree. Bronzed wavy hair cascaded midway down her back. She palmed an archaic computerized device identical to the one he'd seen his girl with, except she spoke instead of typed.

Dante advanced, hoping his hours of studying would pay off. The corners of his mouth curled with wicked delight when he identified the language as English.

Excellent.

He strode over, chest puffed and folded his corded muscular arms. Dante watched, but she remained unaware of his presence. A few minutes had passed when her emerald eyes finally met his. Humans were *not* observant creatures.

A stupid grin overtook her lips, *exactly* as he expected. Dante crouched beside her, cocking his head to the side.

"Hello, pretty." He extended his hand. "What might your name be?"

Stars twinkled in her eyes as she shook his hand. "Kayleigh."

"Kay-le-igh. Do you mind if I—"

"No, not at all. Please."

Dante slid to the ground, crossing his legs. "Now, what might a beautiful girl such as yourself be doing all by her lonesome?"

Kayleigh's cheeks flushed pink. "I'm just relaxing," she said and paused. "Don't I know you from somewhere? School maybe?"

That was highly impossible, but he played along. "Precisely. I'm glad you remember me."

"I do," Kayleigh said jovially. "It was gym class, right?"

"Correct again." Dante leaned closer, staring into her eyes. She wasn't his girl but would have to suffice.

Kayleigh blinked. "What are you doing?"

"This—"

Dante pressed his lips to hers. Their mouths mingled together briefly before he pulled away. Kayleigh stared at him strangely before attacking him with a stream of kisses, knocking him onto the green. They rolled around, lips locked, limbs tangled, grabbing at one another, their clothing shifting downward.

She pulled away; strands of Dante's onyx hair lay over his face. He pushed them behind his ears.

"Let's go somewhere private," Kayleigh suggested. "I know the perfect place."

Dante grinned wickedly and rose to his feet. *What an easy species. She's doing all the work for me.*

Kayleigh grabbed his hand, leading him across the green, over the blackened travel way and into the forest.

* * *

When Dante returned, his body radiated with relief, all thanks to *whatever* her name was. It had already escaped him. *Foolish human*, but he couldn't blame her for falling for his charms. She wasn't the first, nor the last. He chuckled, recalling her scrambling to dress herself, and throwing shoes at him, uttering obscenities.

Once again, he scanned the eatery to see if his girl had emerged. She raced around frantically, surrounded by large groups of people. *What the hell could she possibly be doing?*

The sun had fallen halfway in the sky. Tempted to go inside and collect her, he knew it probably wouldn't go over well, considering he was a stranger and all. "Why must she take so damn long?" he mumbled.

He sauntered about, keeping an ever-watchful eye in case she emerged. Dante's stomach twisted and turned from hunger. It was then that it dawned upon him: he hadn't consumed a morsel of food since before the crash.

Reaching into his pocket, he discovered a bar of freeze-dried meat and ate it whole, licking the wrapper clean.

After he was satiated, his frustration peaked. Not only was he stranded on this pathetic excuse for a ball of mud for who knows how long, he chased a girl around, like a complete and utter fool. A destructive need brewed deep inside of him, char-acteristic of his warrior race. This was unheard of. He'd never waited for anyone this long in his life.

Dante snapped. He stormed up to a red metal bullet affixed to the gray rubbly ground and kicked it clear across the field with his inhuman strength. It plopped into a nearby pond at the center of the green with violent force. Water rose from underground spraying everywhere, including his clothing, enraging him further. In retaliation, he stomped into the earth, forming a crater, rock and rubble spewing everywhere.

Dual sirens from emergency landcrafts blared as he tugged the smooth strands of his hair, massaging his strained temples. A headache threatened. What the hell was wrong with him? He, Dante Martyne, wouldn't let this human best him, nor would he fall victim to this unfortunate situation.

* * *

The girl took longer than Dante had hoped. Seconds turned into minutes. Minutes turned into hours. And before he knew it, the entire day escaped him. The sun lowered in the sky, as Earth's singular moon in crescent phase rose through the close-knit shadows.

Thank the gods! He couldn't handle the change he suffered because of the full moon. Not after everything he'd been through.

Dante admired the stars shining brightly overhead. Oh, how he longed to go home.

The brisk swing of the eatery door interrupted his self-pity. Finally, his girl ambled from the building. His mouth curved. When he went to cross the travel way, he stopped short.

His girl laughed and talked with two other human girls, one with gilded hair as bright as the sun, and the other with rich umber-brown tresses. They gathered near a half circle of docked land crafts. From where he stood, he could detect the melodic sound of his girl's voice, but he also made out the word *party*, from the loud girl next to her. And "party" was universal in any tongue.

Party this, and party that, and party, party, party, party, from the golden girl's mouth, clearly the most talkative of the three. She flapped her gums like there was no tomorrow. He wished he could silence her so he could hear his girl speaking, but he didn't want to call attention to himself.

"Ah, shit," Dante murmured. The three females piled into a land craft and rolled away.

Dante took a few steps to follow them, frustration and disappointment brewing, when an idea dawned upon him instead. They headed to a party, and parties were perfect for socializing. Perhaps all wasn't lost. There were guaranteed to be throngs of beautiful females present. That's all he'd seen thus far on Earth.

He called Armienti. "Round up Ronan and the remaining soldiers and meet me at 41.33366°N, -74.19214°E immediately. We're going to a party."

They arrived within seconds and teleported into the night.

Six

AUTUMN RODE SHOTGUN in her best friend's Corolla. The air conditioning on full icy blast, radio humming.

She stared out the window as Lauren drove, unable to comprehend the terrible day she suffered through. Not only was she operating on three hours of sleep, Marcela didn't leave her alone, even to the point of following her into the ladies' room. Autumn wasn't given a single moment of rest throughout her double shift.

Her manager had it in for her the minute she walked through the door.

She stretched and yawned.

Autumn sensed Lauren's sky-blue eyes scanning her in the darkness. Grinning, Lauren twisted a golden lock around her finger, and tossed it toward the rest of her blonde tresses.

"We're going to have so much fun tonight," Lauren said, peppiness saturating her voice. She bounced in her seat as she drove, nostrils flaring with excitement.

Autumn forced a smile despite her exhaustion and melancholic disposition. If she was honest, she was in no mood to go to a party, but maybe it would be good for her to get out of the house. All she had done lately was work, cry, sit at home reading by herself, and cry some more.

Autumn had initially declined the invitation by ignoring Lauren's texts and yet Lauren showed up in the diner parking lot anyway. Bubbly personality and all. It was almost like she gagged, bound, and tossed her into the car.

Autumn sighed. Maybe she'd made a mistake. Maybe she should have put her foot down harder. It would have been nice to lie in the comfort of her own bed, with a peppermint iced tea on her night table and a good book, which she could never get enough of. But then again, summer was almost over, and she'd be heading off to college. Unsure of when she'd see her friends again.

Autumn tensed as a foot pressed against her seat. Followed by a series of giggles. Her other best friend, Ellie, sat behind her, texting. She tossed her phone into her lap to secure her dark-brown waist-length hair into a high ponytail. After the beep, Ellie threw shimmer on her freckled cheeks and glossed her lips.

Lauren glanced through the rearview mirror. "Oh Ellie, you're silly. Who are you trying to impress? There's nobody there but high school guys."

Ellie shrugged. "You never know." She put on the finishing touches of her makeup. "Tyler Sanchez was looking pretty hot at graduation."

"He's such a player." Lauren snorted.

"Who's he again?" Autumn drew a blank. She lost track of the number of guys Ellie had dated so far.

"How could you not remember him, Autumn?" Ellie tilted her head. "You only went to school with him for the last *eight* years."

Autumn blinked. She supposed she didn't find him particularly memorable.

Ellie continued, "Seriously, how could you forget his delicious muscles and gorgeous face. He was captain of the football team. This is *his* party!"

Autumn rolled her eyes.

"Did either of you feel the earthquake last night?" Autumn rerouted their conversation to a more *meaningful* topic.

"Yes." Lauren nodded. "On the news they said it was a magnitude seven."

"It was intense. My Dad and I were first responders. Did you feel the tremors, Ellie?"

Ellie shook her head. "No, I didn't. I'm the deepest sleeper ever."

"Ellie!" Lauren chimed. "What are we going to do with you?"

"How's that possible?" Autumn laughed. "It threw me to the ground."

It also destroyed her snow globe collection she found resurrected, but Autumn made no mention to her friends. They'd think she was crazy. Maybe she was, or maybe her mom was looking out for her.

That's what she secretly wanted to believe.

Or she was so delirious from lack of sleep she had imagined it all.

* * *

They arrived at Worley Heights, a housing development on the outskirts of Monroe. The neighborhood sparkled with dozens of orange-gold glowing streetlamps and overflowed with bi-level housing.

There was no mistaking their correct destination. Throngs of teenagers fumbled around in the humid night air, swinging colorful glow sticks. They trudged in a singular direction.

Lauren parked amidst a sea of vehicles. Before leaving the car, Autumn glanced into the visor mirror, horrified by the reflection. She looked even worse than she imagined.

Taking the cosmetic emergency seriously, she performed a quick touch up, shaking out her bun, allowing her coils to fall freely over her shoulders. Autumn smoothed her hair behind her ears and rustled around in her jeans pocket, searching for her lip gloss. Swiping her lips with a watermelon tint, she removed her disgusting soiled apron and realized this was as good as it was going to get.

As Autumn finished fixing herself, Lauren and Ellie stood outside of the car, tapping their sandaled feet against the concrete.

"Come on." Lauren flung open the door and took Autumn by the hand. "You look great."

"Yeah, you look amazing," Ellie added.

As they walked, a cool breeze drifted through the late summer air. Autumn shivered, breaking out in goosebumps, unsure of what she'd gotten herself into.

Seven

ACCOMPANIED BY LAUREN AND ELLIE, Autumn walked over to a pale blue house with the front door ajar. Guys were passed out on the lawn, with permanent black markered mustaches and eyebrows, in various stages of undress. Autumn even spotted a naked one with his ass crack in the air. She snorted. *What an idiot.*

On the way inside, they stepped over a chunky puddle of vomit. She and her friends plugged their noses as they maneuvered around it, sparing their shoes.

Gross.

Inside, Autumn surveyed the living room. People grinded on each other, made out, and played beer pong in the darkness. Techno music pulsated, and everyone held a glow stick. It reeked of musky body odor, mixed with alcohol breath.

Autumn sensed a change in proximity. Her friends vanished. Lost within the crowd, she threw a finger into her mouth and chewed her cuticle down to a nub.

She scanned the room, for any sign of them. *Crap.*

Autumn whipped her phone out and called Lauren and Ellie, dismayed because her calls were directed to voicemail. It didn't matter, anyway. She could barely hear their answering messages in combination with the music ringing in her ears.

Tears welled up and burned in the corners of her eyes, but she willed them away. She had done enough crying over the last few weeks and refused to let the situation get the best of her. Autumn waited and waited and waited for a response, but none came.

Autumn roamed through a few different rooms; darkness and neon lights melded together in a kaleidoscope of color. People danced and swapped spit. At one point, she was sure two people were doing it on the couch, their noises muffled by the commotion.

After a while, all the roaming made her parched. Autumn battled her way to get a drink, stumbling into the kitchen. She sighed. She didn't see Lauren or Ellie there, either. How could they do this to her? Especially in a terrible place like this?

Across the counter, there were several bowls of red punch with fruit bobbing and melting ice cubes. Autumn knew better than to drink from them. Who knew what concoction existed within their sugary exterior? Sweat, backwash, alcohol, or even vomit. Her skin crawled.

She ventured over to the refrigerator. The blinding light briefly shined in her eyes as she selected a sealed bottle of water. She chugged it, quenching her thirst.

Upon her last gulp she looked up to see a familiar face emerging from the shadows.

"Caleb?" Autumn's heart pounded. "What are you doing here?"

* * *

Dante and his entourage arrived at the door of the abode where his girl and her companions had entered earlier. It was truly a repulsive sight. Pathetic humans laid inebriated in puddles of their own fluids and vermin all over the green. The humans couldn't so much as hold their drink. *How ludicrous.*

Cringing, he plugged his nose, choking back the bile threatening to rise from his gut. Dante carefully avoided their disgusting bodies with his immaculate boots. Anywhere was cleaner than walking around this place.

Why would his girl come to this gathering? Surely, she had class.

The group accompanying him didn't seem to mind, though. Upon entering the stinking gathering, all twenty-two of them, including his cousins, were fascinated by the male and female humans.

"Run along and play." Dante urged them with a flick of his wrist. "You've earned it."

Dante promised them excitement and delivered. *What a wonderful and generous master I am.*

They disappeared into the darkness. How they conducted themselves was none of his concern. All he could focus on was finding his girl. She had to be around somewhere.

Offhand, there was no sign of her. Only the faint floral scent she bore.

He slithered through the crowd, maneuvering between the spaces where the humans stood, but often fell all around him. What fools they were. What useless fools, conducting themselves so carelessly.

This gathering, by no stretch of the imagination, resembled any party he'd attended before. Dante was accustomed to events being far more *organized* and *sophisticated*. This place reminded him of a cheap brothel. Humans kissed and rubbed all over each other. Legs exposed and breasts bounced. Hoarse noises radiated through the crowd. The occupants were little more than beasts.

Dante did a double take. He spied one female his girl traveled with earlier that evening. She sat on the lap of a guy laughing her head off; slender neck exposed as she bit her bottom lip.

Dante's mouth coiled. If she was here, the other couldn't be too far off.

* * *

Autumn couldn't believe she bumped into Caleb. *What rotten luck*. Why here? Why now? Reluctantly, she embraced her ex-boyfriend, trembling as they made contact.

She hoped not to see him at the party. If it was up to her, she'd prefer to never see him *again*. The mere sight of him induced vomit from her already unsettled stomach.

Stepping away, in more of a stumble than a step, she stared up into his sapphire-blue eyes. Caleb twisted his signature red baseball cap over his unruly ink-black curls. The strands of his hair shined in the glowing light.

"It's nice to see you, Autumn." He ignored the awkwardness of the situation. "I tried texting you a few times."

"I know. I blocked you."

"Oh." He grew quiet and shook his head. "Um, how's your summer been? Other than your mom..."

That's *all* he could think of asking her? No apology...

"Fine, I guess." Disappointing was more like it, devastating even, and this situation didn't help.

She folded her arms, still in disbelief she'd bumped into him. "What are you doing here, anyway?"

Caleb leaned in close, resting his palm against her shoulder. She inhaled, realizing he reeked of alcohol. Crinkling her nose, Autumn wanted nothing more than to disappear.

Caleb blinked, long lashes grazing against his cheeks. Autumn became painfully aware of the stubble on his face, his strong jaw, and just how cute he looked. Caleb had a Latin

American beauty about him, which at one time she found irresistible, but now made her heart burn.

"Same as you," he smiled. "Enjoying the party."

He lost his footing and fell into her. Autumn moved over, propping him up against the counter. What an idiot, and he's *drunk* too.

"Did you drive?" she asked, somewhat concerned. Even if he was a jerk, he had no business on the road in this condition.

Caleb grinned. "No, of course not, my DD did."

She glanced around, but found no trace of his supposed DD. Maybe he was off wherever Ellie and Lauren were hiding.

"Where is he?"

He shrugged. "Who knows?" He paused and continued. "Who did you come with, by the way? I know this really isn't your scene."

"Lauren and Ellie, but I lost them."

"That's a real shame."

Caleb wrapped his arm around her shoulder, and she went rigid. He hung his head, lips grazing against her lobe.

"Did I tell you how pretty you look?" Warm alcohol breath drifted over her ear. "I wish you could forgive me. I didn't mean any of it. What happened between me and Misty —if only you'd let me explain."

Autumn watched in horror as he pressed his mouth to hers, filling it with the sour taste of beer. She shoved him away, wiping her lips. Caleb fumbled and slammed against the tiled floor.

Autumn turned on her heel and rushed out. He was a disgusting, selfish pig who deserved to be alone. She resumed the search for her friends, more desperate than ever.

* * *

Dante moseyed through the darkness. He stepped over, under, and around the humans, lost within a never-ending maze of filth.

As he growled frustratedly, he spotted his girl sprinting, head down and arms crossed.

Dante pursued her with stealth and precision. There was no way he'd let this opportunity escape him again.

Eight

AUTUMN ENTERED a room undetected and closed the door. Leaning her back against the wall, she attempted to relax herself, taking deep, controlled breaths. What a night it'd been. All she wanted to do was climb into bed and sob her eyes out.

The nerve of Caleb. What the heck was wrong with him? So selfish and self-centered. Such a jerk. Although she hadn't seen him in a little over a month, pain overwhelmed her all over again. The last time she felt this terrible was the disastrous night of prom.

Autumn reached into her pocket to check her phone. There were no texts or calls from Lauren or Ellie. She could have throttled them for abandoning her.

Autumn sighed and glanced around the cozy, quiet nook she'd wandered into, cast in darkness, except for the cerulean fish tank glowing against the far wall. She pressed her fingertips against the glass, admiring the clownfish and sea horses floating through the water without a care in the world. For a moment, she wished she could join them. Life would be so much simpler. Anywhere was better than where she was.

Even more intriguing, however, were the objects behind

the tank. Autumn's heart fluttered. There were hundreds of books of all shapes and sizes. She'd wandered into a secret library.

Autumn pressed the spines, and they creaked beneath her weight. She closed her eyes and selected a book at random, pulling it from the shelf. Her mouth curled when she recognized it as *A Midsummer Night's Dream*. Sinking to the floor at the first sign of comfort that night, she lost herself within its pages.

An hour into her reading, Autumn detected faint breathing. Peering from her story, her eyes took a moment to focus in the darkness. The door never opened. A dark silhouette drifted back and forth in the corner. Autumn's hands trembled, the book landing in her lap with a gentle thud.

"How long have you been there?" Autumn struggled to stabilize the tone of her voice.

She squinted, failing to get a better look. The figure jumbled its words in a series of whispers before speaking aloud. Autumn was certain English wasn't the person's first language based on the distinctive foreign accent.

"Why, for however long you've been reading." The shadow choked out. "I've been admiring your beauty beneath the lamplight."

Autumn was certain she was speaking to a masculine stranger. His voice was soft-spoken, but unmistakably male. The hair on the back of her neck rose as she stared into the void beside her. She wished she could decipher his features but felt rude shining her smartphone light in his face.

"My name is Dante. Dante Martyne." He extended his hand.

She shook it, the calluses on his palms scraping against her smooth skin. His body temperature spiked.

She flashed an uneasy smile. "Nice to meet you," she said, his hand still in her grasp. "I'm Autumn, Autumn Ramon."

Dante inched closer, still concealed by shadows.

"I find this party excessively boring." He raised his voice a notch. "Vulgar even."

Autumn chuckled, fidgeting her hands. "So do I. I came with my friends, and they ditched me." Perhaps not the smartest detail to admit, but it was the truth.

Dante laughed; a hint of his too-white teeth visible. "What a coincidence. My friends abandoned me as well," he said and paused. "Would you like to leave with me, Autumn Ramon?"

Autumn tensed when Dante grazed a finger against her arm, unable to believe how forward he was. The creeps were out in full force tonight.

However, this jerk didn't reek of alcohol like Caleb did. Instead, he smelled of ground cinnamon. Which Autumn found appealing, but *not* under the circumstance.

"No, thanks." Autumn grabbed her book, crossing her legs on the floor. She thumbed her way back to the page he rudely interrupted her on. "Now if you'll excuse me, I'm reading. Go find somebody else to bother."

The shadow of his head cocked to the side, and he didn't budge. Autumn stared at him.

"Perhaps tomorrow," he suggested. "When you've finished reading."

Autumn's jaw tightened. This guy could *not* take a hint.

"I'm afraid I'm busy," she said. "I'm busy every second, minute, hour, and day until the end of time."

Dante froze. Autumn assumed her words hit home. Rejection was never easy for anyone to deal with. He murmured incomprehensibly and jumped to his feet with a single fluid leap—startling her. He sauntered out the door. He could go find somebody else to hook up with.

"Autumn! Autumn! Why did you run off?"

When Autumn glanced up, Lauren and Ellie stood in the doorway.

"What!?" Autumn's mouth fell open. "You guys disappeared on me. Where were you?"

"Searching for you!" Lauren shouted, racing into the room. She grabbed Autumn's hand, pulling her to her feet. "Come on, someone called the cops!"

Autumn ran with her friends. She didn't need an arrest on her record. They sprinted through the deck door and into the yard, people swarmed and scurried around them. They made their way to Lauren's car through the commotion.

They climbed inside of the Corolla and clicked their seatbelts into place, flashing lights sped through the street. Autumn caught her breath. Adrenaline crashed through her body.

Lauren drove, her blue eyes sparkling with concern. "Autumn, seriously, why did you disappear on us?"

"Yeah, not cool," Ellie added.

Autumn glowered at her friends. *Seriously?* "You guys left me. I called and texted. What were you doing?"

Lauren placed a hand on Autumn's shoulder. "You walked away as soon as we arrived, so we made our own plans. We figured maybe you saw someone you knew."

Ellie reached into her pocket, checking her phone. A faint ding arrived. "Sorry, it just came through." She paused, cheeks reddening. "While you were gone, I hooked up with Tyler."

Autumn rolled her eyes. It figured.

"I talked to a few guys, too," Lauren admitted, turning the wheel of the car onto Route 207. "There were some really hot ones there tonight. I'm guessing a fraternity from Jersey. I was totally shocked."

"Did you meet anyone?" Ellie asked.

"I ran into Caleb."

"No, you didn't!" Lauren gasped. "Don't tell me he's the reason you left."

"Guys, I didn't leave." Worry laced Autumn's voice. "Anyway, he was drunk and stupid."

Lauren patted Autumn on the shoulder. "What a loser. You were the best thing that ever happened to him."

"Yeah." *Of course she was.*

Her thoughts slowly drifted to the guy lingering in the darkness. The whiteness of his teeth, the spiciness of his scent, his soft-spoken voice. And how she inspected the room before entering and was sure she was all by herself. She hated to admit she found the shadow lurker intriguing.

Nine

IT WAS WELL past midnight when Dante strode back into the central corridor of his inactive ship. The palms of his gloves were stained and drenched with dark crimson blood. His mouth curved with wicked self-satisfaction as his tail twitched around his waist. Nobody made a fool out of him and got away with it.

After a long chase, he slaughtered the pilot whose pathetic oversight would leave him and his men stranded on this useless planet for almost one Earth year. What a horrifying amount of time to be stuck on this desolate ball of mud. Even worse, this news was cast upon him after a miserable wasted day and an even worse night.

One down, one to go, he gently reminded himself. Oh, how he looked forward to butchering the gangly tech once he located him. Somebody needed to pay, and he refused to take responsibility for this oversight.

Other than that, he had little to look forward to at all. Before this mission, he was so close to going home. The chance now squandered.

Dante meandered through the hallway and into the

common area, where his men sat around scattered tables and ate. The standing members of his crew reverently cleared a path for him.

As he rounded the room searching for his cousins, he overheard tales of conquests from earlier. The irony of it all. He went to such great lengths to attend the ridiculous gathering, and he didn't even secure his girl.

Autumn Ramon, with her piercing moonlit eyes and full, pink lips he wanted all over him. She had some nerve turning down his advances. He wasted an entire day learning her language, practicing until he had it perfect, and she scorned him.

Him.

What made her think she was so damn special? She was a human.

He plopped down and took a seat at a vacant table, scowling. He massaged his throbbing temples. Fabulous, just fabulous, he had three hundred and sixty-five more days and counting of this hell. Dante buried his head in his hands, pitying himself.

Ronan and Armienti sat at his table. Ronan cleared his throat, breaking the silence. "I heard a nasty rumor that we're to be stranded here for one Earth year. Is it fact or fiction?"

"Unfortunately, it's a fact." Dante smoothed the strands of his obsidian hair. "To my knowledge, the Emperor dispatched a replacement ship shortly after our crash."

Armienti slammed his fist against the metal table, leaving an imprint. "That's the most unwelcome news. I'll surely be missed back home."

Dante sighed. "Indeed, we all will."

"How ever will we pass this death sentence?" Ronan added.

Armienti grinned. "The same way we always do. We'll explore and make sport."

"The females here are certainly skilled in the bedchamber," Dante blurted, deflecting his growing insecurity.

"Forget the females," Ronan said. "The males are well endowed."

"I agree with you, Dante." Armienti chuckled. "They threw themselves at me the whole night through."

Armienti surveyed himself in a nearby mirrored panel, running his hand through his flawless golden locks. He grinned and winked. "Can you blame them?"

Dante rolled his eyes. He'd never encountered a vainer man in his life. Armienti's high opinion of himself was borderline disgusting. Sure, he was attractive and all, but come on, really? Who among them assumed the highest rank?

Hearing them speak freely about their intimate encounters fueled his ire. His face warmed at the recollection of Autumn Ramon's rejection. The first time he could understand; he approached her foolishly, speaking in his native tongue. The second attempt's failure remained a mystery. Perhaps he should've gone about it differently and tried to impress her.

He had a mind to march over to her home, pluck her from her bed, and toss her into his. How easy it would have been if he were back home... But Dante regarded himself as a man of standards. A unique set of standards. There were some things that had to be taken by force, and other things that had to be given freely. The affection of his girl fell squarely into the latter category.

As he listened to his cousins yap away about their "prolific" experiences with humans, an idea dawned upon him. Perhaps he could catch her attention another way. Dante stood up from the table.

"Where are you going?" Armienti's voice echoed through the large chamber as Dante ambled off.

He sprinted upstairs to his private quarters to conduct some necessary research. Although he was familiar enough with the human species, there were still some finer details left to uncover.

The walls of his plain undecorated cabin were laden with dark steel, and the silver tiles of the floor glistened beneath the dimming lights. A long rectangular window along the back wall overlooked the forest.

Rays of pink and golden twilight sprayed through the glass.

"Show me Earth currency," he muttered into his communicator.

The handheld device beeped twice before flashing a series of translucent green 3D holographic images. They rotated before his eyes. There were various currencies, some paper, others coin. Why was the human species so complicated? Throughout space, he dealt exclusively with credit and gemstone, but here, the currency changed depending on the area of the planet one resided.

Dante snorted. These humans... He needed to be more specific in his search.

"Show me Earth currencies in connection with coordinates 41.40116 °N, -74.32058 °E." He recalled the location off-hand. How could he forget? This area would be his prison for the next year.

Dante discovered humans dealt in a monetary unit known as the dollar bill. These bills were housed in public facilities known as banks, and could be easily obtained by manipulating an archaic piece of machinery known as an ATM.

The corners of his mouth coiled when he recalled seeing this exact device not too far off from the eatery. Powering off his communicator, he sprinted back to the common area. Armienti and Ronan were precisely where he left them.

"Where did you go?" Ronan raised a brow.

"Never mind." Dante dismissed his cousin's concerns. "I'm tired of the bland food on this ship, and I wish for both of you to accompany me to a local eatery I happened upon. I crave a freshly prepared meal."

"It could be fun." Ronan shrugged.

"Sure, why not?" Armienti concurred.

* * *

They entered the quaint township of Monroe by foot. Any other means of travel would've drawn unwanted attention, which Dante wasn't in the mood to attract, considering the length of time they'd be stuck here.

They passed the double watering hole, where he'd wasted half a day trying to learn to communicate with Autumn Ramon. The singular Earth sun glowed and cast faint shadows around the stunted buildings.

Dante crossed in front of dozens of rolling land crafts in search of the ATM he was positive he saw during his previous visit. The humans sounded their irritating alarms. It took every ounce of self-control in his body not to clear them, between his lack of sleep, the situation they were in, and his *first* rejection.

In the near distance, his gaze settled on a facility titled M&T. He spotted the machine. It glowed green and white, which Dante hoped signified it was active. The trio circled the contraption.

"What kind of machine is this?" Armienti's nose crinkled.

"Yeah, it's ancient." Ronan crossed his arms. "It looks like a piece of trash."

Dante snorted. "It's filled with human currency."

"Why do we need money when we can—"

Dante raised his hand, silencing Ronan. Sure, they could dine and leave, but that would be counterproductive.

Examining the machine, Dante pressed his fingers against

buttons and drawers. No matter what he did, he couldn't seem to get the device to activate.

In a last-ditch effort, he balled his fist and whacked it across the front utilizing a sliver of his true strength. Wires sparked, and metal sprayed everywhere in shards. Fortunately, so did the dollar bills. He scooped them up and shoved them into his pocket in a wad. The humans and their *useless* technology.

* * *

When they arrived at the Monroe Diner, Dante was beyond mortified. Humans swarmed around. Young humans, old humans, tall, slender, short, and stout. They were everywhere.

Their incessant chattering irritated him. The air, however, trailed with the exotic scent of food. His stomach grumbled. Once again, he found himself famished. Another day had passed since he had last eaten. Even worse, he waited. Waited for humans to come and show him to his seat, waited to be noticed.

After five minutes, which seemed like eons to him, the most hideous life-form he'd ever encountered during *any* of his travels approached him. The name on her shirt read *Marcela*, and she reeked.

Dante was ready to pluck his eyes out at the sight of her. And the smell… He feared if he regarded her, even a moment longer, his appetite would vanish and never return.

Hesitantly, he followed her, Armienti and Ronan accompanying him. Judging by the look on their faces, they were clearly unimpressed. They were seated at a table near a window overlooking the travel way, and the docking station containing an array of land crafts.

"Your waitress will be with you momentarily." A foul odor

wafted out of Marcela's mouth. Dante gagged. *Repulsive. Absolutely repulsive.*

Waitress, waitress. He couldn't quite recall what the word meant. He figured he'd find out soon enough. For a simple-minded species, they sure had a complex language system.

Dante glanced out the window. There she was—Autumn Ramon in all of her human glory. She fumbled to the building, tan satchel in hand, silver-gray eyes wide.

His lips curved. *Look who finally joined us.*

Ten

AUTUMN SPRINTED to the Monroe Diner. Her heart thudded in her chest; lungs raw from shallow breathing. She desperately clutched her crossbody bag.

She was late again.

Autumn blamed her tardiness entirely on her friends. If only they hadn't suggested the stupid house party at Tyler Sanchez's. She hadn't arrived home until 5:00 a.m, and though her mind reveled in the four hours of sleep she had, that meant Autumn was an hour late for her Sunday morning shift.

Naturally, oversleeping on the busiest morning of the week meant that Autumn rushed to the diner without so much as a shower, let alone deodorant. Her trusty watermelon lip gloss would do very little to mask how disgusting she felt showing up with unbrushed teeth, a messy bun to beat ALL messy buns, and a sour attitude. Her current state was a recipe for disaster.

After Autumn burst through the front door, her eyes darted around the diner. The restaurant was already packed. Every bar stool and table was occupied. People sardined themselves into the waiting area, nagging the hostess at the front register about when they could expect to be seated.

Autumn jogged through the swinging doors of the kitchen, and there stood Marcela in all her nastiness. A hand on the fullest part of her hip. Marcela's beady black eyes narrowed. Autumn gulped. She didn't need this right now.

"Refresh my memory," Marcela tapped her foot. "Wasn't it just yesterday we had a chat about your recurring lateness?"

Autumn fidgeted her hands. "Yes." She detested admitting her manager was correct.

"I see this trend of yours has developed into a nasty habit." Marcela shook her head. "This is strike two for you, Ramon; if you accrue one more, you remember what happens next?"

"Yes, I'm sorry again. I—"

"I don't care. If you can't be on time here, how can you possibly expect to be on time for college come fall?"

A valid question. Autumn opened her mouth to answer, but Marcela snapped her fingers. Without hesitation, Marcela walked Autumn back into the restaurant, and shoved a pile of menus into her hands. *Again.*

"Do you see those three gentlemen in the far corner?"

"Yes."

"I'm assigning you to their block. They've been waiting here for quite some time." Marcela's mouth twisted. "In case you were wondering, it's all your fault."

Her fault? Autumn's cheeks burned. She wanted to whack Marcela over the head and storm out the door. But of course, she didn't act on it. She needed this job to put away money for school.

Gritting her teeth into a forced smile, she navigated her way through the crowd. Along her path, she ran into a group of giggling waitresses.

"You're so lucky, Autumn," one of her coworkers whispered.

Another girl with shimmering strawberry blonde hair elbowed her. "Enjoy."

Autumn shrugged it off. She was too annoyed to care what anyone was talking about. Given the opportunity, she could've fallen asleep standing up. Worst of all, she was on her last strike before termination. This day was shaping up to be another awful one.

As she drew closer, she saw the source of the commotion. *Holy crap.* Her mouth slackened. Sitting together in a booth were three of the most handsome guys she'd ever seen in her life.

The first had eyes as blue as the sky, and hollow, defined cheekbones. His wavy blond hair tousled to perfection over his muscled shoulders. His skin was gilded like he'd wandered off a California beach after an intense modeling session.

The second had eyes as green as fresh clover in a meadow on a summer's day. His hair cut short and spiky, and although his complexion was lighter than the first guy's, there was no mistaking he spent a generous amount of time in the sun. He had a well-built physique and a strong, square jaw.

Autumn did a double take. The third, and indisputably the most attractive of the three, looked familiar, but she couldn't place his face. She bit her bottom lip as he examined her with his brilliant amber eyes. His messy raven-black hair partially concealed his face, before he pushed a loose strand behind his ears.

Although they were gorgeous to behold, Autumn found them strange. They were all dressed in onyx long-sleeved shirts, pants, and boots when it was sweltering out. She supposed it was some kind of uniform. Maybe a fraternity?

Autumn's cheeks boiled. She'd been staring for too long. Not that it mattered—they must have been used to it.

As she distributed the menus, their curious eyes watched her.

She cleared her throat, trembling slightly. "Good morning," she said, trying her best to even out her voice. "I'd like to apologize for the wait. My name is Autumn, and I'll be your waitress for today."

The raven-haired guy chuckled. Autumn couldn't recall saying anything humorous. Her cheeks melted with shame.

"Am I correct in my assumption that a waitress is a servant of some sort?" Raven hair flashed his too-white teeth at her.

"That's what it sounds like to me, Dante," the gilded haired guy chimed in, his teeth equally dazzling.

"Same," spiky hair added, teeth glinting.

What is this, a Crest commercial?

Autumn stared at them, puzzled. She knew she had heard his name and his distinctive soft-spoken voice before.

Crap! It's the guy from last night. Dante. A wave of adrenaline crashed through her body, leaving her weak in the knees. Autumn hoped he didn't recall their awkward exchange. Maybe he even started drinking later if she was lucky.

Autumn cracked an uneasy smile. The conversation got a little weird. "I guess a waitress and a server are the same." She shrugged, not knowing what else to say.

"What a fascinating tidbit of information, Autumn Ramon." Dante raised a dark brow. "I was under the false impression all you do is read."

Autumn stiffened. 1000% sure he remembered her. Her face flushed.

"You three must be from out of town." She quickly rerouted the subject. "Or a nearby college, am I right?"

"What a perceptive conclusion you've drawn," Dante propped his chin on a fist. "What gave us away?"

"Well, for starters, I've never seen any of you before." She paused. "I'm pretty sure I've seen everyone in this town at least once."

Dante's midnight hair swayed. "You're correct in your assumption, Autumn Ramon. You're such a clever girl."

"Call me Autumn," she insisted.

"Okay...Autumn Ramon." Dante's lips curled.

She sighed. "Well, I hope you guys enjoy your visit to Monroe. It's a lovely town. Do you need some more time to look over the menu?"

"That it is." Dante smiled. "What's a menu?"

Convinced he was mocking her, Autumn began to roll her eyes, but forced herself to be cordial. Even if he was a jerk, he was still a paying customer.

"The laminated paper in front of you." She pressed her finger against the plastic, offering him a detailed explanation, like she would a young kid. "You know the one with the little pictures and writing all over it?"

Was he for real? What an idiot. He must have been angry because she'd rejected him at the party. What did he expect after creeping around in the dark?

"Ah yes," Dante said. "We'll take three of the largest breakfast platters you have on this so-called menu."

Autumn reached into her pocket, removing a pad of paper and a pen, and furiously scribbled.

"Okay, so three breakfast combos," she reiterated. "Would you like sausage or bacon?"

"Both."

"What type of eggs would you like?"

"Surprise us." Dante grinned.

Surprise them? Autumn couldn't imagine not selecting her own breakfast. She hated surprises, even more so after what happened with Caleb and her mom's sudden death. If she never lived to see another surprise again, it would be too soon.

"And to drink?"

"Red wine would be delightful."

Red wine? Autumn made a face she didn't expect and couldn't control. "This is not a bar."

"Cold water then."

Autumn nodded, completing his order. What was wrong with this guy? First of all, he never let his friends get a word in edgewise, and to order wine at a diner instead of coffee or juice? Weird.

She scooped up the menus and turned on her heel. She heard a soft chuckle and peered over her shoulder. The blond shot her an approving look. But Dante leaned over and whispered into his ear, putting an end to it. She couldn't help but wonder what he said.

Autumn returned to the table with three cold waters and distributed paper straws between them.

Just as she thought her morning couldn't get any worse, a familiar white Audi A8 rolled into the parking lot. Her stomach twisted so hard she grew nauseous. Out stepped Misty Beckett and Hazel Hernandez, here to grace the diner with their magnificent presence.

Eleven

THE OCEAN PARTED when Misty Beckett entered the room. The spoiled only child of a Wall Street businessman and a former Miss New York mother who always got what she wanted. Luxury cars, vacations, clothes, the latest in phone technology, a statue named after her. *Even other people's boyfriends.* Always by her side, Hazel Hernandez, reaped all the rewards.

Autumn recoiled as Marcela seated them in her block. It happened in slow motion, like a horror movie she couldn't control. *Why today? Why me?*

She approached her former classmates and placed two menus on the table. Neither Misty nor Hazel acknowledged her. Instead, they sat there texting away on their phones. Autumn cleared her throat. Misty glanced at her with her large cerulean eyes and smirked.

"Hey Misty, hey Hazel." The bile rose to Autumn's throat. "How's your summer been?"

"Seriously?" Misty clutched her phone. She examined Autumn, pin-straight honey-blonde hair tucked behind her ears. Her straight nose wrinkled her skin, tanned from the excessive time she spent in the Caribbean—or so she bragged every day back at Monroe Woodbury High School.

Autumn narrowed her eyes. Why did she even try to be polite? It was pointless. Misty was a snobby ex-cheerleader, captain of the squad, and super popular. They were polar opposites. There was really no point in being civil. Especially after what she did with Caleb.

Hazel finally placed her phone on the tabletop. She scrunched her pug-esque nose before smoothing the strands of her wavy, umber-brown ponytail. Hazel was the less threatening of the two, following Misty around like a helpless, lost puppy, desperate for her master's attention.

"Our summers are certainly going better than yours." Hazel stared at her blankly.

Autumn bit her cheeks. She refused to freak out in front of them. This had been the worst summer so far of her entire life. Under the circumstances, it surprised her that they were so insensitive.

"I agree," Misty chimed in and focused her attention back on her phone. It clicked as she pressed her hot pink gel set against the screen. "While you were busy flipping burgers for a living, my family and I summered in Saint Martin. We leave for Bermuda in a few days to stay on our other property for the rest of the season."

"And I just came back from Paris," Hazel added, although no one asked. "I still have major jet lag, but I should recover by the time I begin my academic career at Columbia University. It's Ivy League in case you were unaware."

Misty grinned; eyes partially focused on her phone. "I'm attending the prestigious Oxford University in London. Where did you say you were going again, Autumn?"

Autumn ignored her question. Where she attended college was none of their concern. "Are you ready to order, or do you need more time to look at the menu?"

Hazel rolled her eyes. "We've been ready to order for ages, but you distracted us with your boring conversation."

Autumn sighed, grabbing her pen and pad.

"I'll have a fruit salad." Misty tugged her tank against her flat, tanned stomach. Straightening her spine, she pushed out her breasts. "I need to look hot while I model my extensive bikini collection."

"And I'll have a plain bagel," Hazel added. "Heavy on the lox, light on the cream cheese."

"Oh, and one more thing." Misty toppled her plastic cup filled with water over the table's edge. It splashed all over Autumn's jeans and sneakers. "You better get that." Misty pointed her manicured nail to the cup, before returning to her phone.

Autumn huffed a breath, bitter tears threatening to rise. It wasn't enough that she endured four solid years of torment at their hands, but they attacked her at work, too? People stared, including the guys in the corner. Dante glanced at her briefly before returning to his own conversation.

Grinding her molars, Autumn went to grab a mop and bucket from the kitchen. Her sneakers squeaked. Although the restaurant was loud and crowded, Misty and Hazel's amplified snickering reached her nonetheless.

By the time she finished cleaning up Misty's mess, the orders were ready to go. She filled a tray with everyone's breakfast selections. Her stomach grumbled; she hadn't had a chance to eat anything.

Juggling the food, she distributed it to the tables. When she stopped at Misty and Hazel's booth to drop off their food, neither of them were there. She watched in disgust as they giggled in front of Dante and his friends, appetite fading away.

As Autumn ambled to Dante's table, Hazel squeezed the blond guy's biceps. He grinned and puffed up his chest.

Dante's spiky-haired friend crossed his arms and stared out the window with disinterest.

Poor Dante was subject to the Queen herself. Misty grinned, bending to give a clear view down her shirt. Flipping her flat ironed tresses, she flirted with full force. The same tactic Autumn was sure Misty had used to steal Caleb.

When she tried to touch his hand, Dante swatted her away, attention entirely focused on Autumn. Her cheeks heated as she met his gaze.

"Misty, Hazel, your food is on the table." Autumn gestured to their booth.

"Thanks." Misty hissed, and returned to Dante, jabbering away about her upcoming luxurious vacation. Apparently, nobody cared but her.

Dante rolled his eyes at Misty and Hazel and said, "Leave us."

It sounded more like a command than a request. Autumn bit her cheeks.

The two girls stiffened and ceased their conversation. In a robotic trance, they walked back to their booth. Autumn distributed the remaining breakfast platters.

"I hope you enjoy your food. I'll be back to check on you shortly." She smoothed her palms against her sun-yellow apron.

"Thank you." Dante's long lashes grazed against his prominent cheekbones. "I look forward to your return."

Autumn walked away, face and neck flushed. She was just as ridiculous as Misty and Hazel. One word from his lips, and she melted, even though, deep in her gut, she sensed he was odd. *Odd yet intriguing.*

When she passed by Misty and Hazel, she should have been paying attention instead of daydreaming. If she had been, she would've noticed Hazel's snow-white espadrille in her path. Before her brain could register, she tripped and fell front first onto the tiled floor, sliding into another waitress. Metal trays, dishes, and drink cups splattered everywhere.

"I'm so sorry," Hazel said in a honeyed voice. Misty snorted before hiccupping.

Autumn came to a shaking stand, thanks to a kind hipster couple with tattoos and dreadlocks.

She fought the intense urge to wrap her fingers around Hazel's throat and strangle her, but reminded herself about what her mom had taught her about forgiveness. Violence was never the answer.

Refusing to acknowledge them, she marched to the kitchen to grab the cleaning supplies. Misty and Hazel wouldn't get the best of her again.

When she reemerged through the swinging door, soapy bucket, and mop in hand, a silent group of onlookers surrounded the booth where Misty and Hazel dined, and the air grew thick with hysteria.

Twelve

AUTUMN SLOSHED the bucket and mop onto the floor and raced over to the standing crowd of people. She pushed her way through the gridlock bodies and gasped.

Both Misty and Hazel knelt together, frantically grasping their throats. Their bug-eyed faces shifted from tomato-red to purple, and finally deep blue. Saliva dripped from their petrified mouths as they gagged. *Why was nobody helping them?* People stood around, frozen.

Autumn whirled in a frenzy, jumping up and down, waving her hands through the air in desperate search of the manager.

"Marcela!" she shouted. "Marcela!"

Marcela barreled over and yanked Misty to her feet. Autumn followed her lead, grabbing hold of Hazel. Even though she despised her, she couldn't in good conscience allow her to suffocate. Fortunately, she learned the Heimlich maneuver in senior year health class.

She wrapped her arms around Hazel's stomach, applying pressure over her abdomen. Pushing with all her might, after several strained thrusts, mangled pieces of lox and bagel came spewing from her mouth in a mushy explosion. Hazel gasped for air in a violent burst.

Meanwhile, Marcela dislodged the fruit salad from Misty's throat. Half-digested pieces of fruit skidded across the floor. Raw coughs escaped her mouth before she breathed and fell on all fours.

Everyone in the surrounding circle suddenly woke up and applauded when they realized Misty and Hazel would live. Misty's red-rimmed eyes were tearful, and Hazel's face flushed beet-red from humiliation.

Autumn had never seen either of them embarrassed or looking less than perfect. For as long as she could recall, it'd always been the other way around. They were nasty girls who reveled in the suffering of those they deemed beneath them. Basically, *everyone*.

Misty, followed by Hazel, scrambled for her designer clutch, tossing cash on the table. They scurried away like frightened mice, leaving not even a thank you in their wake.

Autumn exhaled a deep sigh of relief. Dealing with her bullies for four solid years of high school and one bizarre incident after graduation was way too much for her taste.

Her hands quaked while she cleaned up Misty and Hazel's disgusting mess. Although she loathed them with every ounce of her being, she was in a hazy state of shock. How was it possible that both of her former classmates almost lost their lives from choking? What were the odds?

After all the weird drama, she returned to Dante's booth. The three guys were unphased by the events. Before gathering their plates, Autumn inspected them, surprised to see not a single crumb or trace of yellow egg yolk.

"I'm sorry for the wait." Autumn chewed her bottom lip. "I had my hands full, as you probably saw." *What a dumb response*, she scolded herself. *Of course they saw; they were a few tables away.*

Dante shrugged, and his two friends stared at her with blank expressions.

Okay.

She blinked. "You must have been starving."

"We were famished," Dante said after a few moments. "And we certainly haven't had a meal of this caliber in a long while."

"Agreed," spiky-haired interjected. "We're no chefs."

Autumn blinked. When she looked away from their striking faces, she noticed they were all wearing short onyx gloves made of a stretchy spandex material. *Strange.*

"I see," Autumn replied, understanding exactly what that was like. She was a terrible cook herself.

Leaning over the table, she assembled the silverware, neatly stacking it over the pile of plates she collected. "I'm glad you enjoyed your breakfast. Is there anything else I can get you?" They shook their heads.

She walked over to the register and printed a check. Slipping it into a leather envelope, she placed it on their table.

"Thanks for choosing the Monroe Diner. I hope to see you again soon." She smiled and walked away after her standard farewell. What an awkward day all around. She couldn't wait to go back home to shower, read, and get some much-needed rest.

She experienced a sadness though, deep inside that she hadn't said something more interesting or hadn't given them a proper farewell. They were fascinating in a small town like this. But what did it matter? She'd probably never see them again.

While tending to her next set of customers, she watched Dante and his friends get up to leave. It wasn't their handsome faces this time that captured her attention, but their flawless posture and fluid, graceful feline movements. As they walked beneath the lights, the bulbs flickered. They took more graceful steps towards the door and by a trick of the light or a problem with her eyes, the flickering lights seemed to follow them.

The phenomenon ended as they exited the restaurant. Autumn blinked hard, holding her eyes closed, positive she hadn't imagined it. She couldn't help but wonder why it'd happened to them and no one else?

When Autumn returned to their table to do a final wipe-up before another set of customers could be seated, she couldn't believe what they left behind.

Sitting tucked inside of the black leather envelope sat a stack of crisp $100 bills piled half a foot high. There was so much money, she could barely carry it with one hand. *Why would they leave this for me? Was it some kind of joke?* She could only think of one reason. They were trying to buy her off. Her initial regret of not speaking with him longer faded.

Grabbing the money, she shoved it into her apron pocket and stormed from the restaurant.

As expected, Dante and his friends hadn't gotten far. They ambled at a snail's pace, mere seconds from the diner.

"Dante!" Autumn barked. "Don't move."

Dante and his friends halted. A smirk graced Dante's beautiful mouth. "Autumn Ramon, why ever do you seek my attention? It was just last night you informed me you'd be reading until your dying breath."

She stood there, chest heaving as she steadied herself.

"Have you perchance come to thank me for my generosity?"

Autumn couldn't believe his nerve.

Rustling through her apron pocket, she removed the excessive number of bills. She pulled out enough money to cover the cost of their food, and a twenty percent tip for herself.

She placed a hand on her hip. "I'm not interested in whatever you thought this money could buy you."

Dante's mouth flattened. "I haven't the slightest clue what you're talking about."

"You're really going to make me say it, aren't you?" He remained quiet, and she continued, "I'm not going to hook up with you for money. I'm not a whore."

Dante's mouth fell into a tight flat line. He leaned closer and whispered, "What's wrong with you? Any other girl would be thankful to be in your position. What exactly don't you find appealing about me?"

Autumn's eyes widened. "Everything from your attitude to the smug look on your face. You're everything I hate."

She tossed the remaining bills at him. Money fluttered in the street and all over the sidewalk. Autumn's head pounded so badly it was ready to explode.

Dante stared at her; eyes narrowed.

"Ramon, get back here this instant!" a disembodied voice shouted in the background. Marcela.

"I don't have time for this." Autumn turned on her heel and headed back to the diner.

She glanced over her shoulder. Dante stood on the sidewalk in silence, arms folded.

Thirteen

DANTE WALKED to his ship with Ronan and Armienti in complete silence. Although his stomach hummed with fullness from the delectable meal he'd consumed at the human eatery, he was ill with dread. A heaviness crept through his chest he couldn't quite shake. A desperation. He tried not to focus on the feeling, because his cousin Ronan had been blessed with the ability to read minds. He didn't want to feel any more humiliated than he already did.

Seldom had anyone made him feel as foolish as Autumn. It reminded him of the miserable years of his childhood he spent residing in Universe 24, being schooled by the Grand Supreme Emperor and his cronies, Keyserike and Valdez. The three worst people he'd ever known.

This was different, though. He was frustrated because he was scorned by a girl. A servant, no less. He shook his head as they passed through the door, positively mortified with himself.

Autumn possessed intelligence, far more intelligence than he anticipated. Not to mention *beauty and sass*. She was perhaps even more beautiful than he was. She saw right through him and *hated* him. He couldn't help but wonder what else she noticed about him she'd left unsaid.

Who knew a human could be so perceptive?

As they made their way through the cold, dark ship, soldiers ambled by, bowing their heads out of respect. Instantly, Dante was reminded of how alone he was. Earth was his prison for the foreseeable future.

Armienti placed his palm over Dante's shoulder. "What transpired back there between you and that human girl?" Armienti muttered. A lucky break. His cousin had heard *none* of what they discussed, which was strange considering he was within earshot. Armienti had exceptional hearing.

"Yeah, Dante." Ronan stared at him, emerald eyes unimpressed. "I thought you secured her the night of our arrival."

Dante cleared his mind so as not to risk divulging his personal business to his cousin. He stepped away from them, in no mood to have this embarrassing discussion, although they typically shared everything with each other.

"I'm exhausted." Dante yawned and stretched his aching muscles. The lack of sleep had taken a massive toll on his body. "I'm retiring to bed," he said. "I suggest you do the same. We have many preparations to make."

When he arrived at his personal chamber, it felt wonderful to lose his *human* disguise. His complexion shifted to a cool hue as he ran a hand through his midnight hair. It was like shedding a second skin. Not to mention draining on his energy level.

It was simpler to blend in until the time came to perform his duty. There was always the off chance he might be recognized. Though he doubted anyone he knew would be this far out in deep space, he wasn't willing to take any risks.

Laying his weary head onto his pillow, he collapsed, allowing the darkness to pull him in.

* * *

He woke hours later, tangled in the crisp chains of his sheets, wrists wrapped with silken fabric. Pale moonlight in the first quarter phase and twinkling stars reflected through the glass of his lone window.

He rolled over to the opposite side of the bed. It remained cold and untouched. It'd been this way since Maeve had gone. He closed his eyes, dreaming of her, recalling simpler, better times.

Maeve crashed through the bedroom door, spinning on the balls of her toes. "Come here, come here, come here, I have something to show you."

Her long, curly hair framed her heart-shaped face as she pulled his hands. Dante sat up, every muscle in his body screaming in agony from his latest mission. He'd conquered a planet with one hundred times the normal gravity the day before. And had another mission scheduled in forty-eight hours.

His vision doubled, then cleared. "What's wrong? Are we under attack?"

"Yes." Maeve feigned a straight face but gave herself away, flashing pink cheeks and teeth. "Stop asking questions and follow me."

Maeve yanked him from the bed, bare feet pattering against the marble floor. Her short gossamer dress flapped in the heat.

A servant approached her, and she stopped running. "My lady, where do you think you're going at this hour, you can't—"

When the servant's eyes met with Dante, she stopped speaking and looked at the floor, trembling.

"Don't worry, we'll be right back." Maeve waved, reassuring her.

Maeve led him to the far end of the palace.

"Okay, are you ready? Are you ready?" She grinned; fingers laced behind her back.

Dante shrugged. "Um, sure." He could barely stand straight.

She opened the door and Dante stared at her and then into the yard.

"Can you see it?" Maeve hopped.

Falling rain and wet sand pooled along the ground.

Dante raised a brow. "It's raining?"

"Exactly," Maeve ran outside. "When's the last time you've seen rain? What are you waiting for? Come dance with me." She twirled around, falling into a courtesy. Her dress clung to her body, soaking.

Dante didn't immediately follow, but the way she looked at him with her pleading gray eyes, he found himself outside, holding her in his arms. They danced, body against body, and kissed until dawn.

Dante opened his eyes, a shiver traveling through him. He outstretched his hand through her memory, her smile fading into the air.

It made little sense to acquire a companion. He made that mistake once and hadn't recovered. Because of his demanding schedule, he attained women on a short-term basis. After having his fun, he was on to the next. But the void remained. *Maeve.*

For the first time in a long while, he couldn't help but wonder what it would be like to find a woman lying next to him. To see her smiling face and know her desire was solely for him. He trembled at the thought.

Dante stretched and yawned, refreshed after a much-needed nap. He ambled to the lavatory to take an invigorating shower. Underneath the warm, steady stream of water, he was bombarded with haunting memories of Autumn rejecting him. The hatred in her eyes, and the way she defeated him.

His previous embarrassment shifted to fiery *rage*, not only toward Autumn Ramon, but also at his own miserable situation. The nerve of *her* turning *him* down. He spat into the whirling drain.

She was difficult, wild, *untamed*. Gritting his teeth, he despised the power she yielded over him.

He wanted her more than *anything*.

Dante stepped into a full-body dryer and pulled on a fresh, fitted onyx armor. A flaming star emblem with deep hues of purple and silver lay stitched over his right breast. Dante needed a different type of release. A natural-born desire boiled through his blood characteristic of his warrior race.

He didn't have to search any further than the walls of his ship to find it.

Dante loved to fight, and refused to let his technique suffer because he was stranded on an alien planet. The innate need existed deep inside of him, intense and fiery.

As he strode through the common area, head held high, he scanned the room in search of his latest *opponent*. His men, try as they might, were no match for his superior strength. He even outranked Ronan and Armienti, who were both skilled warriors in their own respect.

His attention settled on one man who chatted with soldiers of greater rank. The person of interest had orange-red hair hanging beyond his shoulders in twists. Dante cleared his throat, ceasing all conversation. He gestured for the soldier to approach him.

"Sire." The soldier bowed. "You summoned me?"

"Come now. I wish for you to be my sparring partner."

His once bright countenance faded instantaneously from the man's face. His limbs quaked, but he fought to steady himself and maintain his dignity. Dante couldn't blame him for being fearful. If the roles were reversed, he'd be petrified as well.

He led the soldier, whose name was...irrelevant, into the

dark stretch of forest around the ship. They made idle chit-chat about the weather and the schedule of the replacement vessel that was to come and collect them sometime *next* year. Long, uneven shadows cast through the trees.

They stopped in a clearing. Dante removed the top of his plated armor, and it scraped against the surrounding rocks as he tossed it to the ground. The pale moonlight reminded him of Autumn's eyes.

Dante limbered up and assumed a fighting stance. The soldier followed suit, trembling from head to toe. Dante experienced a deep sense of self-satisfaction as his knuckles collided with a *crack!* across his opponent's jaw. The soldier attempted to block as Dante raised his fist again, once, twice, *three* times more. The soldier sputtered to the ground, screaming as he fell onto a pile of jagged boulders. Dante leapt at him in a heartbeat, throwing fist against bone.

The soldier finally went unconscious.

"How weak you are." He spat on the ground. "You're worthless."

He had heard the same sequence of words a thousand times before from *Keyserike* while growing up. An icy shiver trickled down his spine at the thought of being like one of the people he despised most in all the Universes. No, he didn't want to be like Keyserike.

Stretching on his top, Dante ambled whistling in the darkness. The haunting tune echoed through the humid night air. He spied a stray soldier lingering in the forest.

"Collect the fallen soldier over there," Dante instructed.

"Sire." The man bowed, following his orders.

Too bad a certain human girl wasn't as obedient as he was accustomed to.

Once back on board, Dante reentered his chambers and freshened up for his nighttime ritual. It calmed him so, relieving his mind of all of his worries and despair. After he took a second shower, this time ice cold, and threw on a fresh uniform, he bumped into Armienti in the hallway, golden tresses damp and combed.

"Where are you off to this early?" Armienti's brows rose.

"I'm going for a walk." Dante crossed his arms. "I have much on my mind."

"Would you like company?" Armienti suggested. "It would take me but a moment to prepare myself."

"Perhaps another time." For this activity, he preferred to be alone.

Armienti shrugged, and Dante departed.

* * *

He stepped into the cozy darkness of Autumn's bedchamber. It was rather simple and unimpressive, like a typical servant's quarters. An alabaster door concealing a closet housed her strange human shoes and clothes. Never had he seen more bizarre styles of attire than here on Earth.

He took a second glance. Her belongings were all over the floor and hung disastrously. He couldn't imagine treating his own possessions with such little care. He valued all of what he owned and liked to think he took nothing for granted.

There were the amenities as well. A simple sink, toilet, and shower. And all the way to the right, Autumn laid slumbering.

Dante approached her and knelt beside the bed, hand trembling. He knew what he was doing was wrong, but he *had* to see her.

He couldn't resist.

Autumn laid beneath a thin linen sheet, clothed in a silken fabric adorned with clouds. Unbound hair splayed across her pillowcase, she slumbered with a poise he'd never seen in any other creature. It captivated him, though he'd never admit it aloud, and would be humiliated if anyone discovered his secret.

Him. Pining after a human. He'd only heard of it in myths.

He removed his glove and traced a silhouette around her lips. They felt softer than he could have ever imagined. Dante moved his fingers over the rosy apples of her cheeks. Then to her hair. The strands were silky, yet wild. Twirling his finger around a coil and placing it among the rest of her mane, he inhaled her rich floral aroma.

Such an intoxicating creature.

Suddenly, he detected a disturbance…

Dante bolted behind the closet door in the blink of an eye and peered through the crack. Fortunately, his speed was superior to hers. If he was human, his secret would have been discovered.

Autumn wiped her eyes. Even in her exhausted state, she moved with beauty. Dante watched with curiosity as she ambled from her bed and left the room. *Where could she be headed?* He waited there instead of following, though, confident she'd eventually return.

She re-emerged with a glass of water. Autumn consumed half, making sweet little gulping noises with her delicate throat. Afterwards, she placed it on the table and drifted back to sleep. Her breathing became even and relaxed again.

Dante wiped his arm against his beading brow. He waited a respectful amount of time before returning, wanting to be sure she was out.

Maneuvering through the darkness, he approached her once more. Who was he kidding? What a fool he was, lingering in her room. Creeping around, when she said so herself: she *hated* him.

He sighed, chest aching.

What was he wasting his time here for? He should be

preparing for his mission, instead of spending every waking moment yearning for Autumn. If only he could win her over. It shouldn't be this difficult for someone in his position.

Unless of course...

Dante grazed his thumb and forefinger cyclically over her temples. This would do the trick for sure. The left corner of his lip curled.

Fourteen

EVERY NIGHT for the last two weeks when Autumn closed her eyes at bedtime, she found herself in a plain, blinding white room. There were no windows or natural light, only a stark artificial glow. She sat on a bed with a crisp snow-white sheet, as if she stayed in a hospital. The floor was tiled with silver plates, cool against her bare soles. She was clothed in a thin, plain white camisole and her satin cloud shorts.

Autumn shivered, skin prickling. She rubbed her hands together for warmth.

In the simple layout of the room, there was a single door, silver with no handle. Autumn couldn't help but wonder where it led.

The door slid open, followed by a puff of steam, and Dante strode in. He regarded her with his piercing amber eyes.

Heat pooled in her belly. There was no mistaking she found him *physically* attractive, but his attitude not so much. She'd been thinking about him non-stop since the morning at the diner; the *nerve* of him, and what a jerk he was. Somehow, she didn't think it was his first time trying to buy what he wanted, and she could imagine any girl easily falling for his charms.

But this was a dream and dreams were harmless. He couldn't break her heart, like Caleb had. So what if she wanted to have a little fun for once? *Dreams should be fun.*

Dante drew closer, his kneecaps brushing against hers. Tossing his gloves, his calloused palms scraped over her body. Fingers catching in her hair.

Bending over, he pressed his lips to hers, exploring her mouth with his curious tongue. Tentative at first, but more passionate with every stroke.

As his hands slid up her thighs, she bucked. Nobody had ever touched her there before, and often she wondered what it might be like. For a dream—*she wasn't disappointed. Why did it feel so real?*

With a single flick of his wrist, he slid her camisole strap from her shoulder. Nuzzling his face against her ear, between hot broken breaths, he murmured against her skin, *"Oh My sweet, sweet Autumn."*

And she woke up.

Autumn glanced around the quietness of her room, the central air droning. Rays of sunlight peeked between her blinds. Wrapping her arms around herself, she breathed, cheek pressed against the cool pillow. The scent of cinnamon permeated and followed every dream with him.

This obsessive thinking of him was such a waste of her energy.

Still, Autumn couldn't help but wonder why she hadn't run into him anywhere. Monroe was a quaint little town with a moderate population. She bumped into most everyone in ShopRite, walking the ponds, or at the Monroe Free Library. But Dante, she'd *never* seen. Not even once. He *did* mention he was only visiting.

She sighed, willing him away from her mind. Autumn

gave him more power than he deserved. She started college in two weeks, and she'd soon forget him.

Rolling over in bed, she grabbed her phone. Hmm. Several new messages from Lauren. How'd she guess?

Get up sleepy head! :)

...

Don't ignore me!

Autumn rolled her eyes. Lauren needed to *chill*. As she stretched and climbed out of bed, her phone pinged. She stumbled into the bathroom and washed up before throwing on a black tank, olive-green cargo shorts, and her low-top sneakers.

And then—she remembered.

A few days back, she'd promised to hang out with her friends. Sometimes having two best friends living right around the corner could be *exhausting*.

After she got dressed, another ping followed.

Here.

Crap. She popped back the blinds, and sure enough, Lauren's silver Corolla was stationed in the driveway.

Autumn dashed downstairs to the kitchen to find her dad tinkering at the table on his laptop. He often worked remotely.

"Good morning." Autumn grabbed her tan canvas crossbody bag.

Peering from his computer screen he replied, "Good morning, where are you off to?"

"I'm hanging out with Lauren and Ellie, they're already outside."

"Okay," he said. "Please, please, *please*, promise me you'll be careful, and wear your seatbelt. Will you be home for dinner?"

She nodded and waved as she turned the corner. "Love you, Dad." She hated leaving him alone after what transpired, but she didn't have plans to be gone for more than a few hours.

As Autumn strolled outside, the radio blasted from the car. Lauren and Ellie danced, arms flailing, to Katy Perry's *California Gurls*.

Autumn climbed inside and hugged Lauren, who popped her double mint gum. In the backseat, Ellie grinned, her freckled cheeks pink. Autumn figured she was texting Tyler or some other guy. She never knew anymore.

Lauren glanced at Autumn's ornamental apple-red Neon parked in the driveway.

"When are you going for your road test again?" Lauren smiled.

"Right before school starts." Autumn tossed her curls into a high ponytail to escape the heat. "Hopefully, I'll pass this time around."

Ellie stuck her face through the front seats. "Have you been practicing at least?"

Autumn shrugged. "Here and there I guess." Which was an exaggeration. She knew deep down she needed to prepare more than she had, but she wasn't exactly motivated after what happened to her mom.

"Well, you better practice, girl!" Lauren raised a finger. "If you don't pass, how do you expect to drive to college?"

"I know, I know." Autumn dismissed Lauren's concerns. She'd add it to the plethora of other worries she had on her mind.

"Enough logistics, you guys." Ellie smoothed her palms through her sleek ponytail. "What's the plan for this afternoon?"

"We could always go for a hike," Lauren suggested. "The weather is beautiful."

What? Was Lauren crazy? It was muggy and a million

degrees outside. Not the ideal weather for a hike. "It's too hot." Autumn frowned.

"I agree. Let's go to the mall instead," Ellie added.

"Come on, guys!" Lauren pouted, bottom lip protruding. "This is one of the last times we'll be able to go on an adventure for a while.

Autumn shook her head, realizing Lauren had won *again*. She was infamous for guilting her and Ellie into everything. She was right this time, though. They would probably see each other again a few more times this summer and then not until winter break, but there was no guarantee of that or anything beyond.

"Okay, okay, we'll hike." Autumn instantly regretted her words.

"Fine," Ellie caved.

Lauren grinned. "Awesome, we're going to have such a great time."

Autumn opted not to push the matter any further. It wasn't worth getting into a scuffle when the clock was ticking on their last summer vacation before college. They pulled onto Lakes Road, and Autumn still didn't have a clue where they were headed.

The three friends stopped to grab beverages for their trek. Autumn, Lauren, and Ellie left the car and went into Dollar General. A thick wave of heat radiated from the blacktop, baking Autumn's feet.

Inside the store, she welcomed a gush of cool air. They wandered to the refrigerated section. Autumn enjoyed every moment, knowing they would soon be sweltering in the forest.

As they reached for their drinks, selecting acai-berry, dragon fruit, and lemonade flavored sports beverages, a familiar face shone in the glass's reflection. No, no, no, she was *not* in the mood for this.

Misty's best friend Hazel stood there with her messy brown high-ponytail. Her pug-esque nose flared as she wound her designer wristlet over her hand.

"Hazel, what do you want?"

Lauren folded her arms. "Bitch, go haunt another store."

"Yeah, Hazel, we don't have time for your nonsense," Ellie added.

"Easy," Hazel said in a honeyed voice. "I come in peace. I'd like to speak to Autumn alone...preferably."

"Whatever you have to tell her, you can say in front of us. We're not going anywhere," Lauren said.

"Yeah."

"It's okay guys, really." Autumn's voice elevated. "I'm fine."

Lauren took Ellie by the arm, and they ambled one aisle over. It was quiet, a little *too* quiet, so Autumn knew her friends were eavesdropping, but she didn't care.

"What do you want?" Autumn placed a hand on the fullest part of her hip.

"Listen, Autumn." Hazel laced her fingers together. "I know we haven't always seen eye to eye."

"That's the understatement of the year," Ellie said, loud enough for everyone in the store to hear.

"Geez, Ellie, butt out!" Hazel shouted, throwing her hands up in the air. "This is none of your freaking business!"

"No, she's right," Autumn said. "Get to the point, unless you're here to trip me again like the bitch you are."

"Like I was saying, before I was so *rudely* interrupted." Hazel wrinkled her nose. "Thank you for saving my life. When Misty and I choked, nobody else lifted a finger to help us, but you did." Which was true. Everyone stood around, staring like zombies. It was weird.

This *wasn't* what Autumn expected. For the first time ever, Hazel behaved genuinely and contritely.

Autumn stiffened as Hazel hugged her, unsure of what to do in this situation. This didn't make up for the four solid years of torture she suffered at her hands, but it was a start.

When Hazel left, Autumn stood there, speechless. Ellie and Lauren scrambled from the aisle.

"What did she mean you saved her life?" Lauren's eyes widened.

"Yeah." Ellie's mouth fell open. "Tell us."

"Everything," Lauren added.

Autumn explained the events that took place at the diner two weeks prior, and both of her friends agreed if they'd been there, they would've let Hazel choke and die. *She's such a bitch, she deserved it*; they reminded her. Not to mention she was best friends with Misty, who ruined her life.

Autumn dissented; she'd made the right decision and knew if her mom had been alive, she would've been proud of her. She had no regrets.

Fifteen

AUTUMN STARED out the window as Lauren drove along Lakes Road, heart speeding in her chest. She knew it was coming; she knew it; she knew it; she knew it. *The pole.* Closing her eyes, she sucked in a breath. A vision of her mom limping in the rain invaded her mind for the thousandth time that summer. She kept quiet, not wanting to alarm her friends.

When she opened her eyes again, there was the calm familiar sight of Round Lake. People in their silver row boats glided around a central island of trees. Couples in white swan peddlers drifted, and the sun's rays glittered over the silent, still water.

Seconds later, they passed Walton Lake. Evergreen trees partially concealed the body of water, and there was an air of mystery about it. Autumn always wondered why it was so much emptier than the first.

Mid-text message to her dad, the car came to a complete stop. He warned her to be safe, and she put his mind at ease.

When she glanced away from her phone, Autumn saw they were at the trailhead of Farrah Falls. The lot was empty, the temperature already breaching ninety degrees.

They entered the forest, relieved by the coolness beneath the shade of the trees. Autumn hoped this hike would be at least *somewhat* bearable. They passed over a curved footbridge, no damage visible from the fire earlier that month. Autumn figured the fire occurred deeper inside.

Morning transformed into afternoon, and as Autumn feared, the heat caught up with them. Lauren had sweat slicked skin, golden tresses matted in a damp high ponytail. Ellie's tank was stained, wisps of hair sticking to her forehead, and Autumn could only imagine her own terrible state.

She caught a whiff of herself and gagged; her deodorant had failed her. She shot Lauren a murderous look, tempted to say, *I told you so*, but she kept her mouth shut for the sake of keeping the peace. She and Ellie were partially responsible for this predicament. Next time, she'd be sure to put her foot down.

They reached a field, tall grass swaying in the afternoon heat. It extended to another stretch of forest. Beautiful dragonflies and butterflies flitted, but Autumn was more excited for the sound of flowing water. They'd reached the waterfall at the end of the trail.

She sprinted as fast as she could, followed by her friends. *Enough was enough.* When she reached the waterfall, her breathing ragged, the water poured from more than a hundred-foot drop and flowed through to a naturally occurring pool.

Autumn placed her palms on her knees, tired of walking and unable to take another second of this heat.

"I'm over this." Autumn fanned her face. "I'm going for a swim."

"Good idea," Ellie agreed.

Lauren remained silent. Instead, she crouched behind a berried shrub and climbed out of her sweat-soaked clothes.

Autumn dashed behind a bush a little further away. She

tugged off her tank and cargo shorts, removing her undergarments as well. She tossed them to the ground in a heap.

She couldn't wait to feel the water against her skin. In the back of her mind, she was terrified of stepping on a snake again, but her overwhelming need to cool down took over.

Autumn covered herself with her arms.

"What are you up to?" Lauren chortled.

"I think she's going for it!" Ellie yelled.

"I sure am!" Autumn didn't care that she was about to go skinny-dipping. She'd never done it before, but the thought of trudging five miles back to the car in soaking wet underwear was horrifying. She dove into the water, creating a colossal splash. Lauren and Ellie screamed as they were sprayed with the aftermath. They raced around on the muddied sidelines.

Moments later, her friends joined her. They immersed themselves in the refreshing droplets. *What a relief to be out of the heat.*

When Autumn dunked her head and reemerged, she heard dragging sobs. Lauren's face grew drawn and solemn. And Ellie's cheeks were slicked wet with moisture that wasn't from the crashing waterfall.

Autumn waded closer. "What's wrong?"

"Yeah Ellie, why are you crying?" Lauren stumbled, feet sliding over the smooth algae coated rocks.

Ellie's lips quivered, tears streaming. "I'm really going to miss doing silly things like this with you guys. School won't be the same without you."

"We'll still talk every day." Autumn smiled warmly. "Don't worry about it, it's going to be a big change for all of us."

Lauren's mouth curved. "Seriously, we're only a text away. You know that don't you?"

"I know." Ellie buried her face in her palms.

"Let's stop talking about this." Autumn's heart clenched at the thought of first losing her mom and then her friends come fall. She sniffled but did her best to hide her own impending tears. "We still have a few weeks left. Let's make the most of it."

They spent the rest of the afternoon wading beneath the waterfall. Autumn hated to admit it, but Ellie uncovered a sore spot. She tried her best for most of the summer not to consider what life would be like without her friends. People grew up, and they went off to college. Time waited for no one.

The sun lowered in the distance, elongating shadows through the trees across the forest floor. Autumn's stomach grumbled from hunger. Dinnertime had arrived.

Lauren and Ellie climbed out of the water and went to find their clothes. Autumn did the same and concealed herself, hobbling over to the bush where she'd dumped her belongings hours before.

But they weren't there. Her pulse skyrocketed. She knelt on all fours, pressing her hands against the dirt and underneath the shrub. Maybe she identified the location incorrectly?

She darted to a neighboring shrub. And another, and another, and another. But no such luck. Autumn's breathing turned shallow.

"Hey, you guys, I can't find my clothes."

"Wait, are you serious?" Ellie pulled on her underwear.

"Hold on, we'll be right over to help you," Lauren added. "You can borrow my top."

"Thanks."

Whatever the case was, she couldn't go home like this. What would her *dad think*? Crap.

A round of violent snickering ricocheted from a patch of distant trees, followed by the crunch of fallen branches. She froze.

Sixteen

DANTE COULDN'T BELIEVE his stroke of good fortune, especially after the devastating setback he'd suffered upon his arrival on Earth. Nothing had gone his way.

Until *now.*

He, Ronan, and Armienti took a walk through the woodland to stretch their cramped legs. Bored and restless from sitting around all day, they toyed with the idea of exploring the remainder of this world. Dante didn't want to leave his ship, in case a message arrived for him, so he took advantage of the next best option.

While they strode through the forest, expecting to see the dense gathering of trees they'd grown so accustomed to, he heard the high-pitched chatter of human life-forms. Dante suggested they investigate out of sheer boredom.

To his delight, they discovered girls. *Naked ones.*

Thank the gods above, he thought.

The first girl had her hair swept high above her head, the second had a *loud* mouth that beckoned to be silenced, and the third one... He gasped. The third one was Autumn, and she was even more beautiful than he could have hoped for, with her supple breasts and youthful doll-like features. Leaving nothing to the imagination, droplets of water shimmered on her golden skin, reflecting the fallen rays of sunlight.

She conversed with her two companions: the dotted girl and the mouthy one. Dante narrowed his eyes at her irritating friends but relished her laughter. Being in her presence melted him to the core.

Dante longed to join her, but his yearning transformed to anger. He hated her for making him desire her so terribly and wanted to humiliate her the same way she humiliated him. Three times now; he'd kept a careful tally.

Three.

While she was preoccupied, he smelled her distinctive floral scent and slipped by with inhuman speed and seized her clothing. Ronan and Armienti watched him in silence, probably wondering what he was up to, and why he would go to such great lengths to pull a stunt as nonsensical as this. He didn't care who witnessed it. His previous good manners vanished, and only a desire for revenge remained.

Waiting for the fun to begin, his lips curled. Ronan and Armienti cupped their mouths to prevent themselves from being discovered, but inevitably, laughter seeped out.

Autumn's bare feet crunched against the ground. She crawled around, searching on all fours. Her quest became erratic, eyes shining like crystal glass. *Foolish human, she really has some nerve.*

Dante emerged from behind the tree, clothes concealed behind his back. A smirk plastered his face. He couldn't help but take amusement in her suffering.

"Autumn, Autumn? Is that you?" He descended a tree-covered hill.

Their gazes locked. Her eyes bulged, cheeks flushing deep crimson. She wrapped an arm around her dripping breasts and crossed her legs slightly. The joke was on her, though; he'd seen her naked long before.

"Dante!" she shouted. "What are you doing all the way out here? Are you stalking me?"

"Me stalking you? Don't flatter yourself."

She glowered at him. Though she was partially correct, he was too proud to admit it. He did, in fact, visit her chamber nightly, but in this case, he was enjoying a nature walk when he stumbled upon a most welcome discovery.

Autumn's cheeks glowed. Dante grinned at her well-deserved humiliation.

"Don't you dare come any closer!" Her voice cracked. "I'm warning you, I'm not decent!"

"And what will you do if I don't heed your warning?"

She stood there quietly, contemplating. "I'll think of something."

"I don't doubt it." His mouth curved. "I admit, I much prefer you this way."

"Seriously, stop right there!"

"If I were you"—Dante halted in his tracks several paces away— "I would adjust my tone. For I have what you so desperately seek."

"What?" She shifted her arms, allowing him a brief glimpse of her body. "You stole my clothes?"

"Guilty." He waved her garments through the air like a trophy.

"Damn you, Dante!" She stomped her foot against the ground. "Give me my clothes right now!"

Dante folded his arms. The nerve of this girl shouting orders at *him* and expecting him to obey.

"You're in no position to make demands of me," he reprimanded her. "Unless you give me exactly what I desire, you shall never see your precious clothes again."

"Autumn, what's going on over there?" A distant voice

shouted across the way. He looked and saw the mouthy human with golden, cascading hair. Her clear blue eyes thinned into slits as she stared at him from the opposite end of the watering hole. She needed to learn how to stop sticking her beak into everyone else's business.

Autumn snorted. "Okay, fine, enough of this. What is it you *desire* from me?"

Finally, her resolve caved. His throat ran inexplicably dry when it came time to vocalize his needs to her.

"Well, I..." He stuttered, actually stuttered. *Him.* Dante's heart raced as he smoothed his midnight tresses with his hand. "I wish to experience the pleasure of your company."

She bit her bottom lip. "Are you asking me out?"

Asking her out? There were so many of these human phrases he'd yet to grasp. Autumn, however, seemed perceptive of the idea.

"Yes," he said, regardless of whether he was familiar with the terminology, and he most certainly wasn't.

"Um, okay."

Dante's lips flickered with amusement. That was far easier than he'd anticipated. All he had to do was figure out what *asking her out* entailed.

"How can I contact you?" He cocked his head to the side.

"I'll give you my number *after* you return my clothing."

"I'm afraid that isn't how this arrangement works. You'll give it to me now."

Her mouth twisted. *Good*, he'd outsmarted her for once and defeated her at her own game. If he gave her back her clothing first, she'd more than likely deny him her number. Whatever it may be.

"Throw your phone to my friend, she'll type it in for you."

Dammit. He didn't have the phone she requested. He was screwed. Remaining calm and collected, he said, "That's entirely unnecessary. I'd prefer for you to recite the numbers aloud."

Autumn rolled her eyes. "Fine, Dante, you're ridiculous. It's 888-3535."

Eight, eight, eight, three, five, three, five. Perfect. Those were seven digits he'd never forget.

"Those numbers had better be valid." *For your sake,* he was tempted to say. But even if they weren't, he knew precisely where to find her.

"I promise they are," she said. "Give me back my damn clothes!"

She stared at him with quivering lips and large, watery steel-gray eyes. She was done with him. Unfortunately, he wasn't quite finished, especially after the way she humiliated him during past encounters.

Nobody had ever treated him like this.

"And one more matter, dearest Autumn." He smiled wickedly, smoothing a strand of fallen hair behind his ear. "Tell me you look forward to our meeting in your sweetest, most convincing voice. *Really* put some feeling into it. Your clothes depend on it."

"Ewww no!!" She scrunched her nose. "You can forget it!"

He shrugged and turned on his heel. "Suit yourself." He ascended the hill.

"Okay, okay!" she bellowed. Dante whipped around. He knew she'd come to her senses eventually. He folded his arms, watching and waiting, amused.

She swept her lengthened lashes over her rosy cheeks, pouted her full pink lips, and stared at him with her mesmerizing eyes. "I'm looking forward to our hangout together." Voice utterly melodic, it sent shivers trickling down his spine.

He grinned. "Well, why didn't you say so to begin with?" He rolled her clothes into a sphere and tossed them to her, putting her out of her misery. They tumbled into the ball of foliage.

"Until next time, Autumn Ramon."

* * *

When Dante rejoined his cousins, Armienti's eyes teared from laughing so hard, and Ronan's cheeks tinged crimson with amusement. They navigated their way together through the woodland toward the stranded ship. The sun descended in the sky. Amethyst, sandstone, and rays of gold danced through the leaves.

"What's the delay with you and Autumn?" Armienti quirked a brow. "I thought you ensnared her ages ago? I assumed that's where you've been running off to at all hours of the night."

Armienti was perceptive, damn him. But if he noticed his nightly absence, Ronan must have known as well.

"Well, obviously, you've assumed incorrectly," Dante snapped at Armienti. "I plan to seal the deal with her during our outing." Dante paused and continued, "I use my nights to clear my head."

"And cloud hers with dreams of what you wish to be," Ronan added.

Dante's face and ears burned. He hadn't thought enough to conceal his innermost thoughts, and Ronan easily tapped into them. He would trade his most precious ability with Ronan in a heartbeat to hear Autumn's thoughts, to understand why she despised him. But that privilege was reserved for those who were mated.

"How preposterous, and a complete and utter waste of my time."

"Then what's wrong with right now?" Ronan shrugged.

"If we turn around, we can still catch them. Humans are slothful creatures."

"I'd prefer not to have you two within earshot when Autumn and I make bed sport together," Dante grinned.

"I think that's highly unlikely. She doesn't care for you in the least," Ronan murmured, tousling his spiked hair.

Dante opened his mouth to respond when he saw the carcass of a seated man propped up against a tree, covered in a thin layer of slime. Decapitated head in the crook of his arm, contorted face frozen in a scream. Insects swarmed in a tornado of black speckled dust. It was one of his soldiers dressed in standard issue uniform. He'd died in his *human* disguise and maintained the likeness even after death.

Dante knelt to inspect. Judging by the way his blood clotted, he'd passed over the last hour.

"Nice clean kill." Armienti crouched beside him. "I'm rather impressed."

It certainly was a kill indeed. Or a statement of rebellion. Dante gritted his teeth. Somebody had stepped out of line. *On his watch*. Proof they needed to remain nearby. The kill was good. Maybe a little *too* good. Although the man was a weakling, it reminded him of the barbaric murder style he'd witnessed in Universe 24. The one he knew all too well.

Dante snapped to his feet. "Someone is going to be punished for this." He grabbed the severed head from its resting spot and traveled back to the ship with his cousins.

He stormed to the common area, flanked by Ronan and Armienti. But nobody acknowledged him. He took the head and slammed it onto the floor. Metal dented, bone crunched, and sinew hung from the neck with dried, sticky blood. The room fell silent. Everyone averted their gazes to the ground.

"Whose handiwork is this?" Dante snarled. There were no takers. *How unsurprising.*

"Heads don't go around ripping themselves off," Ronan added.

Dante nodded. "This is a business, an operation, and I won't tolerate any of this rogue bullshit. Now I never ask for anything twice."

Nobody stepped forth. Aware he'd already whittled down half his crew, and an example needed to be set. "Your arm." He pointed to the first soldier who dared make eye contact. At least with one arm, he could still perform his duty.

The man sank to his knees, trembling.

Dante stared at Armienti, who twirled a lock of his gilded hair around his finger, not wanting to bloody his gloves or uniform. As usual, the unfortunate task fell to the lowest ranked of the three. Dante gestured to Ronan and turned on his heel. Groans and shrieks ricocheted through the cabin.

He dashed to his quarters and into the wash closet. Falling to his knees, he vomited his guts into the toilet. The stress of this mission wore on him. How did it come to this? What was wrong with him? When did he become so far gone that when he looked into the mirror, he could no longer recognize himself?

He'd become exactly what was expected of him. *Ruthless.* A second wave of nausea hit, more violent than the first. What would Maeve say if she could see him now? For all he knew, she could. *Or Autumn, who despised him for good reason.*

He recalled the number he strong-armed from her and *needed* to understand its purpose. After cleaning up, he eagerly typed in the digits she provided him.

His communicator swarmed with too many results when he entered the number, the screen glowing bright green with 3D holographic images. From what he could gather, the numbers were specific to a human communication device. And it dawned on him. It must have been the archaic gadget

Autumn utilized the night of their first meeting. A night he would never forget.

He refined the results further. "Personal human communication devices."

"Ah," he murmured. She was referring to a phone. Dante was awed to see how antiquated the device was compared to his own. However, he became confident with a few minor tweaks, he could program his communicator to transmit to hers.

He popped open the side of his communicator, revealing transmitters, data chips, and crystals. After he swapped and rearranged a few pieces, he resealed the device. The speakers crackled with local human frequencies.

Carefully, he punched in the series of numbers she provided him with. Key by key. Stroke by stroke. And to his delight, it rang.

Seventeen

AUTUMN'S POCKET vibrated as she sat in the front seat of Lauren's car, still soaked from her swim. Despite her five-mile trek back to Lauren's Corolla, her clothes were still damp. And her skin was littered with mosquito bites and poison ivy.

Worst of all, Dante had her *actual* number. If she'd been thinking straight, she would have given him the number to a local pizza place instead.

Staring out the window, her cheeks burned with the mere thought of the incident that had occurred. Dante was a player, for sure. No decent guy tried to hook up, offered money, and stole clothing to get someone's number. He was a pompous jerk, but she had to give him credit where credit was due. He sure was *persistent*.

And for whatever reason, he was interested in her.

Autumn sighed. What she didn't need was the added stress of a guy after her mom's passing and Caleb's betrayal. She didn't think she could trust anyone else because of him.

Her phone buzzed for the second time since she'd been in the car with her friends, this time disrupting her thoughts.

When she glanced, she noticed there were no names or numbers flashing across her screen, rather the symbols [X] [X] [X] [X]. Probably spam. She clicked ignore.

Lauren and Ellie talked amongst themselves, and her mind wandered back to Dante. What are the odds she would run into him in the woods, of all places? Twice now she'd encountered him there. Still not believing he'd seen her naked, she pressed her palms to her warming cheeks.

"Autumn, Earth to Autumn." Lauren waved her hand in her face. Autumn blinked and stared at her friend.

"Did you hear a word we said?" Ellie watched her through the rearview mirror.

"No, sorry. I was daydreaming."

"We were asking if you're going to go on a date with that hottie Dante?" Lauren batted her long golden lashes.

"Well, I—"

"We think you should." Ellie bounced in her seat. "He's super-hot and so are his friends. And we were thinking if you do—"

"You could set us up with them!" Lauren grinned.

Autumn shrugged. "I'm thinking about it, I guess."

"What's to think about!?" Ellie exclaimed. "A guy like him doesn't come around every day, and he's obviously into you, to pull a stunt to get your number. You should be flattered. I know I would be."

"Well, um..." Autumn paused. "Fine, I guess if I go out with him, I can put in a good word for you guys."

What did it matter, anyway? In two weeks, her friends would be in different states, thousands of miles away. Unless, of course, they were just looking to hook up. Autumn wasn't sure she would ever want to hook up with anyone. Someone always wound up getting hurt in the end. And she was positive if one more painful situation arose, she'd shatter into a million pieces.

* * *

When Lauren dropped her off at home, her dad's car was missing, and the windows were dark. She figured he was at the supermarket, his *favorite* place, or picking up dinner for them. After her mom's passing, he did most of the cooking. Which really meant ordering takeout.

Autumn ran upstairs to her room, wanting to rid herself of the frightening stench of sweat from the day's adventure. Even from beneath the shower stream, the noise of her phone rattling on her bed drove her crazy. *Now what?* She ran out, water dripping all over the floor, and found the bizarre sequence of characters flashing across the screen. She hit ignore. *Annoying spam!*

The sound of car brakes accompanied lights trickling through her bedroom blinds. Her dad was back. And just in time—her stomach grumbled with hunger. She pulled on a pair of cozy cloud pajamas and ventured to the kitchen.

A brown paper bag from Plum House, her favorite sushi restaurant, sat on the counter. She popped open a pair of wooden chopsticks and ate a piece of rainbow roll.

Her dad grinned through his salt and pepper whiskers. "I know it's not what your mom used to make."

"Thanks, Dad, it's great." Autumn plopped another piece of sushi into her mouth.

"Thanks for texting me and letting me know where you were. Did you have fun hiking with your friends?" He wiped his whiskers with a napkin before eating another piece of his spider roll.

"I didn't want you to worry. Yeah, it was okay." Truth be told, she was hot, miserable, and sweaty. "How was your day?"

"It was just like all the others. We did, however, settle a few overseas accounts."

Autumn smiled. She barely understood how her dad made

his money. What she did notice was that lately he seemed jaded about his position, and his enthusiasm for life was diminished.

Since her mom passed, he was like a robot going through the motions. Autumn could relate, but at least she had friends to help her through her pain. Her dad's closest friend was his computer. If it wasn't for her, he'd be all by himself. And that was the most terrifying thought of all.

"How are you doing, Dad? You know, with Mom gone?" Autumn placed her chopsticks on a napkin.

A tear rolled beneath his silver frames. "I'm taking it one day at a time, but don't worry about me. How are you handling all of this?"

She glanced at the table, vision fogging. A hole burned in her chest.

Her dad continued. "She loved you more than anything in the world."

"I know," Autumn choked on her words. "I love her too, well both of you."

"She was taken from us too soon. This just goes to show how life can change in the blink of an eye. One day we're here and the next we're not."

Autumn nodded, processing his words.

"I don't want us to lose touch," her dad said. "I want you to know you can talk to me about anything."

"I know. Thank you."

"I only want what's best for you and our family."

* * *

After dinner, Autumn debated whether to tell her dad the breaking news. If her mom had been alive, she would have been privy to the information first.

It probably didn't matter, but it ate away at her anyway. "I got asked out today."

"Really?" His eyebrows rose. "Who's the lucky guy?"

"His name is Dante. I met him the night of the earthquake."

"And you told me you weren't talking to anyone," he adjusted his glasses. "Maybe he fell from the sky. Unlike Caleb." He rolled his eyes.

"Maybe."

"When *is* this date?"

Autumn laughed. "You know as much as I do."

It dawned on her how little she knew about Dante. Only that he appeared on four separate occasions, and she couldn't stop dreaming about him. She hadn't dreamed of anything else since they first met.

* * *

After dinner, her dad rested on the couch, streaming his favorite show. The news. Autumn realized she hadn't checked her phone for a few hours. It remained upstairs on her night table.

She made her way to her room and heard *Bzzz* as soon as she entered the doorway. The same set of symbols flashed across the screen for the *seventh* time. Annoyed to no end, and ready to give someone a piece of her mind, she swiped the green answer button.

"Who is this?" Her heart thundered in her ears.

Nobody answered right away, followed by the gentle lull of a low-pitched frequency.

"Good evening, Autumn Ramon."

"Dante?" Autumn made a face she was lucky he couldn't see. "*This* is your number?"

"But of course," he murmured. "Were you expecting to hear from someone else?"

"No," she reluctantly admitted. "Your number isn't registering on my phone."

He grew silent for a moment before his breath crackled against the speaker. "If you remember correctly, I mentioned I'm from out of town." Now that she recalled, he said something to that effect at the diner. He was visiting for a short while. Maybe he lived overseas.

"Where are you fr—"

"The reason I contacted you is to find out your availability for the meeting you promised me."

"I promised you," she snorted. "You stole my clothes and left me with no choice."

"And I'm sure I can manage it again if you try to back out of it."

Autumn busted out laughing. He sure was determined, she had to admit.

"What's so hilarious?"

"You are." She cupped her hands over her mouth, muffling her voice.

He grew silent on the other end.

"I'm free this upcoming Saturday."

"What's Saturday?"

"You know, as in three days from now." Was he for real? Her stomach muscles ached from laughing so hard.

"You're in luck, I'm free as well."

"How does noon at the Galleria in Middletown sound? Do you know where that is?"

"No, but I'm positive I can locate it." He paused. "I look forward to meeting you at our designated time and location."

"Yeah, it should be fun. I'll be sure to keep a close watch on my clothing until then."

He chuckled. "Good night, Autumn Ramon. Pleasant dreams."

Autumn placed her palms on her scalding cheeks. She couldn't believe she would see him in three days. Spinning around on the balls of her feet, she fell onto her mattress, staring at the ceiling. She was seriously hanging out with *Dante*. Which she assumed meant a *date*, but still with him, she could never be sure. It was probably the biggest mistake she'd ever make.

Eighteen

DANTE HAD METICULOUSLY COUNTED the three suns and three moons that had flown by, and Saturday arrived, according to human time. Humans naming their days was puzzling. For a simple species, they were unnecessarily complicated. In any other world, the day would have been numbered 224/365.

Lying in bed, he scrolled the screen of his communicator, pondering the unique predicament he was in. Not only was he behind on his mission, now he had to worry about the logistics behind *asking Autumn out*. He researched the phrase "*ask out*" relentlessly. Although he was well traveled, he never encountered a situation quite this complicated before. There were so many human rules and customs to adhere to.

With each word he digested, his anxiety piqued. He couldn't quite comprehend what about this girl made him so nervous. She should be fearful of him, *not* the other way around. After all, he was a direct threat to her planet, and he wasn't as human as he led her to believe.

To his understanding, she wanted him to pay court to her, and he intended to play along.

When Dante noticed the time, he climbed out of bed, real-izing he had many last-minute preparations to make before their scheduled encounter. Obviously, the first and most pressing was his appearance. There was no way he could meet her in his current state. Although he had human-esque features, two arms and two legs, five fingers and toes, it was crystal clear he was not of this world and could never be.

After he set his disguise in place, he left his room and passed through the common area. From a distance, he heard Ronan and Armienti bragging to the soldiers about their latest encounters. Dante was tempted to roll his eyes at the numbers they boasted.

Though his cousins were beautiful in their own respects, it was impossible they each secured a dozen guys and girls on this planet when he'd had *one*.

When the soldiers spotted him, they quieted. The atmosphere had been different after what happened a few days prior. Everyone was on their best behavior. He tried his hardest not to gawk at the one-armed soldier sitting in the corner of the room. A blank hopelessness filled his eyes.

He'd done what his training had taught him. Fear was the most powerful teaching method, and control was crucial in a situation like this one. Someone stepped out of line, and it didn't particularly matter who, if it didn't happen again. His crew was already bare bones, and he'd been charged with a mission beckoning to be completed.

Armienti stood up from the table and strode over to Dante, hair flowing over his shoulders in a golden wave.

"It's finally the big day." Armienti nudged his arm.

"Yes, I suppose it is, isn't it?"

"Perhaps when you're done with Autumn, you'll think of passing her off to me." Armienti winked. "She's such a pretty little human."

How presumptuous of his cousin. If they hadn't been

blood relatives, he'd be sitting next to the one-armed man at the wall.

"No, I think not."

"But why?"

"I want to be selfish with her."

Armienti sighed. "I wish you'd reconsider. It's not like she's your *mate*."

Dante grinned. "What's the matter, cousin? You couldn't find one suited for yourself, of the twelve you've already been with?"

Armienti went to respond, but Dante brushed past him, blood seething in his veins. The nerve of his cousin, challenging him for his claim. Perhaps he was overdue for a lesson he wouldn't soon forget.

* * *

Thanks to his inhuman speed, he arrived in the township humans called Monroe in mere minutes. However, the Galleria in Middletown he was scheduled to meet Autumn at was on the further side away, bearing coordinates 41°27'8.8776" N and 74°22'2.0532" W. Unwilling to draw attention to himself by using his preferred methods of transport, an idea dawned upon him.

He decided it was time to acquire a *human land craft*. From what he could gather, they were in excess, and secretly, he wanted to impress Autumn by being more human.

Sauntering along the walkway, he spied the perfect vehicle. Onyx with tinted windows. It had an appeal to it compared to the others, but still not what he was accustomed to back home.

He broke the door handle, and its wings shot toward the sunny, cloudless sky. He climbed inside. Its seats were dark and buttery, and its wheel and gauges were simplistic enough. Even a child could operate it.

Smack dab in the middle of his assessment, he received a most unwelcome distraction. A middle-aged balding male human with a rounded gut, short in stature, flung open the door in a frenzy. A tray containing cups filled with a sweet brown liquid came crashing to the ground with a splash.

Dante furrowed his brow and stared at the human man who dared to disturb him.

He screamed obscenities and dug his nails into Dante's shoulder in a pathetic attempt to remove him from his seat.

Dante didn't have time for this. He assured Autumn that he would meet her at 1200 hours, and he was never late for any engagement.

Raising his palm with lethal precision, he held it before the man's ruby-red face.

"Hush."

At Dante's command, the man's knees buckled, and he collapsed to the ground. The whites of his eyes exposed before rolling back into his skull. He lay there silent, his heart forever frozen.

Dante huffed. He meant to stun him, not stop his heart. Humans as a species were fragile, one of the many reasons Earth became a target.

He searched and searched for a key when he realized the land craft didn't activate via retina scan, thumbprint, or spoken word. He discovered a silver set of keys in the dead man's hand. *"Inferior piece of human technology,"* he grumbled.

The land craft ignited, and he took off.

Dante didn't count on how slowly the vehicle traveled. He might as well have walked. Still, he tolerated it for the sake of remaining discreet.

More than halfway there, *Drat!* He'd forgotten the most basic rule of human courtship. He'd failed to bring a gift for Autumn. Dante pulled off the travel way and ventured into a shop adorned with flowers. He reemerged with a bright, fragrant bush.

Dante considered himself to be intelligent, and it was in his best interest to keep her satisfied. If she was pleased, she'd more than likely return the favor. Then again, what he'd presumed of her thus far had been incorrect.

Her motives were a mystery to him.

When he arrived at his destination, the coordinates on his communicator beeped and flashed. In his not so humble opinion, the building where the Galleria was located was underwhelming. Filthy, flat, and a dismal greenish gray. Not like the magnificent buildings of his home world. He was unsure of why Autumn selected such a location.

It was so packed; he barely found a space to dock his land craft. Humans, both male and female, young and aged, stared at him. He inspected himself, and his human disguise was still in place. What was everyone's problem? He wasn't so used to locking eyes with anyone. They usually stared at his feet. If they knew who he was, they wouldn't dare look him in the face.

After entering the facility, his skin crawled. Humans swarmed around like insects. They puttered around with their foul human stench, bumping into him. He assumed it was because they were too simple to have proper control over their own bodily movements.

Dante scoured the area for a central location to meet Autumn, but everything blended together. Shop after shop filled with people, peculiar clothing, and other oddities. On the second floor, he discovered a substantial selection of eateries, where humans dined in a casual context.

Discreetly, he checked the communicator in his palm. Autumn was *late*, and lateness of any sort drove him crazy. The time read 1210 hours, and there was no sign of her.

Had she duped him? If that were the case, all bets were off. He'd report to her home effective immediately and demand an explanation.

Swiping his screen, he decided a call was his best option. He heard a familiar ring, indicating his communicator had successfully intercepted her device.

"Hey," she answered the phone. The sweetest voice he'd ever hoped to hear transmitted through the speaker. It was music to his ears.

"Are you still coming?" He hated to ask, breath catching in his throat as he waited for her reply. "Or did I miscalculate the date?" Which he knew was impossible. He'd tracked the days to perfection.

"I'm sorry." She laughed nervously. "We hit a bit of traffic, but we're walking into the mall now."

"We?"

"Yeah...I'll explain when I see you." Her voice wavered. "Where are you, anyway?"

"I'm where the food is."

"Great," Autumn said. "Well, I'll see you in a few minutes."

She disconnected the call.

Who the hell is 'we'?

Nineteen

THERE WAS NO TRAFFIC. Autumn's phone alarm failed to sound. It was embarrassing. Especially since she selected the date and time. And now Dante was waiting for her. She couldn't understand why he called instead of texting *twice* in a row.

Before this point, she hadn't talked on the phone in years.

She hated to admit Marcela was right. Maybe she needed better time management skills if she was going to make it in life. Tardiness would be unacceptable come fall.

Autumn passed through the first floor of the mall. The neon red AMC theater sign glowed, and fresh buttered popcorn fanned through the air in a cloud of deliciousness.

Her stomach tumbled with every step. She couldn't believe she was going through with this. And to make matters worse, her *dad* was with her.

When she arranged the date during the week, she failed to consider she would need a ride to the mall. To her everlasting horror, Lauren and Ellie already had weekend plans with their families. So, her dad was her fallback, and out of desperation, she asked him and he agreed. On one condition.

That he'd be introduced to her date.

Autumn cringed at the thought of the meeting. Not entirely sure what Dante's deal was. He was hot. Really hot. But he displayed to her on more than one occasion his intentions were *questionable*. The chances of him being a player were astronomical.

But she figured, *What harm could he do out in public?* That's why she was careful to select a crowded place. If a problem occurred, she could leave. No harm, no foul.

Fidgeting her hands, she rode the escalator. Like every other indoor place in Orange County, the mall was packed. A popular hangout spot, but this was unbelievable. Clearly, everyone had the same idea. Dozens of families walked around —holding plastic bags, sipping iced coffees, and eating warm soft pretzels with cheese dipping sauce.

Autumn's anxiety reigned supreme. It was frustrating her dad wouldn't just drop her off and leave. She wished she'd passed her road test at the beginning of the summer.

In the food court, people sardined themselves into tight seating arrangements. Everyone carried trays, bubbling fountain drinks, and fast food. However, there was no sign of Dante within the crowd.

Tired of scanning, she grabbed her phone, hands trembling with anticipation. Autumn sucked in a deep, shuddering breath, wondering if he'd wandered into a nearby store. There was only one way to find out. She texted the odd symbols that comprised his contact number. So many brackets and exes all at once.

Mid-press, a gloved palm rested on her hand. Her heart soared. Glancing up slowly, tentatively, her eyes locked with Dante's. Upon further inspection, although his eyes were primarily amber, this time she stood close enough to see flecks of green playing off the flickering lights above their heads. They glimmered, gazing down at her.

She couldn't help but wonder why that happened. She gasped as he pressed his fingers around her hand and placed a single kiss on her knuckles. Autumn's mouth fell open; she was rendered speechless, as if under a hypnotic trance.

Just like the people at the diner.

Her dad's eyes darted between them.

"You're Autumn's father, I presume." Dante approached him.

"Yes, and you must be Dante." Her dad chuckled.

"You are correct, sir. And I promise to take exceptional care of your daughter during our outing."

Dante's arm secured around her waist, and her cheeks melted. Autumn stood there horrified while he and her dad exchanged pleasantries. If she could shrivel up and disappear, she would have.

"So, you're aware, I'm going to hold you to your promise." Her dad smiled, almost painfully.

Dante's mouth curved.

An unreadable expression crossed her dad's face. "Have fun. I'll text you in a few hours."

"Okay." Autumn's cheeks set ablaze. He left them alone. *Finally.*

"I'm really sorry about him." She twisted her fingers behind her back. "My dad is overprotective. He insisted on meeting you." She paused. "Also, I don't have my driver's license yet. I'm going for a retest at the end of this month."

"That's quite all right." Dante's lips flickered. "He has every reason to be protective of you. If I had a daughter with even a single drop of your beauty, I would beat any man who so much as looked upon her."

He left her side and walked to a nearby table in the food court. When he reemerged, he carried with him an extravagant bouquet of cream, salmon, tangerine, and blood-red roses with a spring of baby's breath wrapped in translucent cellophane.

"This is for you." He passed the flowers to her, and she reluctantly accepted them. They crinkled in her grasp.

"What's the matter?" His mouth fell into a straight line. "Is my gift somehow unacceptable to you?"

It was just the opposite. Autumn bit her cheeks hard, resisting the intense urge to grin. Nobody had ever thought enough to give her flowers before. *Not even Caleb.* Once, he picked her a few daisies with the roots still attached, but it was nothing compared to this.

Considering all the other stunts he'd pulled off; this change of pace was refreshing. She gave him a hug, and he stood as stiff as a plank of wood. It was like he'd never been hugged before in his life.

"Thank you." A smile escaped her lips. "The roses are beautiful."

"Not a problem," he muttered. "When I saw them, I thought of you."

"I'm sorry I'm late." They strolled through a crowd of people who were now staring at them.

He smoothed a lock of fallen hair behind his ear. "I'll make a one-time exception for you."

She giggled.

"In any case, I'd like to thank you for meeting with me. I know your reading time is invaluable."

"Well, you didn't exactly give me a choice." She subconsciously bit her bottom lip. His gaze focused on her mouth before meeting her eyes again.

"In this matter, I'm afraid I couldn't take no for an answer."

They began a lap around the mall, and several questions popped into her head. She knew nothing about him. He watched her intently. Autumn couldn't help but fixate on the cleft of his chin and his pronounced cheekbones. He looked handsome, but as she knew better than anyone, appearances could be deceiving.

"Where do you go to school?" She tilted her head to the side.

"I'm no longer in school."

"Oh…" She paused, somewhat surprised. Looking at him, she assumed he was college-aged. "How old are you then?"

"Should it really matter?" He chuckled, exposing his too-white teeth.

"Yes, it does matter to me."

"How old are you?"

"That's not fair." Her mouth twisted. "You can't answer a question with a question. I'm eighteen, since you asked but I'll be nineteen in January."

Dante went silent, lost in his own thoughts.

"Wait, are you seriously thinking about your own age?" She snorted. What the heck was wrong with him? He was acting stranger and stranger by the minute.

"No, now that sounds utterly absurd." He laughed abruptly. "I'm two years your senior." That made him twenty. She was afraid he was going to say *thirty*.

"Do you have a job?" A silly question to ask perhaps, but she was interested in knowing.

"You're a curious one, aren't you?" He grinned. "Yes, of course I have a job, and might I add, I work tirelessly at it."

"What do you do?" She traced her fingers along the petals of her flowers.

"Well…" He sighed. "My position often requires a bit of travel. I specialize in law enforcement, but I dabble in land acquisition as well."

"So, you're a cop?"

"Military, actually."

"How exciting." Autumn pressed the roses to her nose.

"I've never known anyone who's had two careers so young. Do you like them?"

"They're all right, I suppose." He folded his arms. "Enough about me. I don't want to bore you with the mundane details of my life. Tell me about yourself."

Autumn immediately caught his drift. She might have asked him one too many questions, and he probably thought *she talked too much*.

"What do you want to know?"

"I want to know everything there is to know about you and more."

Dante's lips curled, penetrating amber eyes flickering to hers. Her heart accelerated, breath catching in her throat.

"Um, well, as you know, I work as a waitress at the Monroe Diner." She snorted. "I can't believe you thought I was a servant. Are there servants where you're from?"

His lips twitched and curved. "There are servants everywhere."

"Where are you from, anyway?"

He placed his hand on the small of her back, and she left it there. "Enough about me. Please do continue."

Autumn nodded. "In a few weeks, I start my freshman year of college. I'm majoring in pre-med."

"When you say start, do you mean you'll be leaving this area?" Horizontal lines crept across his forehead.

"Not anymore. I'm going to college in Rockland County, it's about an hour away from here." His facial expression slackened. She was in disbelief that he was already thinking so far into the future. They had only just met.

"Why the change of heart?" He cocked his head to the side.

"It's complicated."

"Well, we certainly have the time."

She stared at him debating, realizing she had nothing to lose by telling him. "I originally got accepted at UPenn, but then my mom passed away. So, I applied to a nearby college. I didn't want to leave my dad by himself." Her eyes clouded, and before she realized, a warm salty tear rolled down her cheek and onto her shirt. She was beyond embarrassed she'd cried in front of him. *On a first date.*

Before she could reach to dry herself, he brought his finger under her eye, wiping away her tears.

"I'm sorry for your loss, Autumn. It must be difficult to lose a parent."

"Thanks, um, it was a terrible accident. My mom was out on a morning jog, and she'd jogged along the same road hundreds of times. A car struck her. They never found the driver." A long silence followed.

"What interests you about medicine?" He rerouted their conversation.

A relief. She feared if she spoke another word about her mom, she might lose it. "Well, it's more of a recent interest, I initially wanted my major to be English. But now I want to help people when they're sick or injured." People like her mom who had nobody to help them, she omitted. "I'm hoping to be the first doctor in my family."

"A noble profession." He paused, contemplating. "Is that why you saved that choking girl? Even though she attacked you?"

Autumn sighed, cheeks flushed. She wished he hadn't been paying attention.

"I went to high school with her and her friend Misty. They weren't the nicest to me. The reason I saved her was because I always try to do what's right."

"What did they do to you?"

"It doesn't matter." Autumn vividly recalled instances where they stuck gum in her hair, drew on her clothing, broke into her locker to steal her books, and the fling between Misty and Caleb hurt most of all.

"Envy is a green-eyed monster," he said. "I don't know anyone who would extend the courtesy you did, including myself."

That was exactly what Lauren and Ellie said to her in not so many words.

He continued, "Forget about them. They'll get what's coming. Their kind always do."

Autumn pressed a smile, still in disbelief she spilled her guts to him. She felt weak, vulnerable, and stupid in front of a handsome guy who was still a stranger to her.

His arm wrapped around her waist again, offering her a strange sort of comfort.

"You were saying before that you're going to school." He backtracked. "When you're not studying, how is it you truly occupy your time?"

"I read." Her mouth bowed. "Anything and everything I can find. I also like to hang out with my friends and family and dream about traveling all over the world one day."

"So, it wasn't a lie." He chuckled softly.

"No."

Speaking of her friends, she remembered what she'd promised. Or rather, what they'd *begged* from her. "Are your friends single?"

"Why? Do you prefer them to me?"

She ignored his question. "My friends Lauren and Ellie want to know. The ones you saw me with in the forest."

"They're not my friends, they're my cousins, actually. And trust me, you don't want your sweet innocent friends around them." He rolled his eyes. "Especially Armienti."

"Which one is he?"

"The blond."

Lauren and Ellie were going to be so disappointed, but

honestly, she wasn't surprised, considering Armienti's handsomeness and how he undressed her with his eyes in the diner like a present on Christmas morning. Her friends were leaving for college in a few weeks anyway, and they deserved better than another hook-up.

"What kind of guy are you?" She batted her eyes subtly while maintaining his gaze. The lights curiously wavered with each pass of the mall they made.

"Well, Autumn, that's up to you to decide."

Before she could respond, her stomach grumbled loud enough for Dante to hear, twisting and turning in a painful mess. Her attempt at being cute was an *epic* failure.

"Are you hungry?"

She nodded, cheeks burning. "I'm starving."

"Well, why didn't you say so?"

* * *

They stood on the winding line to *Wendy's*. Autumn wanted cheese fries for lunch, but Dante was unfamiliar with all the restaurants in the food court. It was odd.

When she asked him if he wanted Italian or Chinese food, he said, *Italian and Chinese, what?* He'd never heard of them before like he was from another planet.

She found it bizarre that he refused to tell her. But she didn't press him any further on the subject.

Dante paid for their meal, which meant it was *officially* a date, even though she hated it when guys paid for her. It was like giving up a sliver of her independence.

For someone who claimed he had no knowledge of the food types, it was astonishing to watch him eat *ten* cheeseburgers and *five* boxes of large fries with extra ketchup. It was like he was starving and had never seen food before in his life. It was a wonder where he put it all.

Autumn's jaw lowered as he wiped his mouth with a napkin, paper and French fry boxes stacked high. "Wow, you must have been really hungry."

"You have no idea." Dante rose to his feet, palms smoothing against his pants. "I'm going for more; would you like some more food too?"

"No, thanks." Autumn's face warmed. "You go right ahead."

Throughout two rounds of lunch, he maintained proper table etiquette, even going as far as placing a napkin over his lap, and chewing with his mouth closed, which was unheard of with her friends. He was prim and proper, a far cry from the guy who lifted her clothes from the forest floor. By the time they finished, she felt her phone buzz in the back pocket of her shorts.

Downstairs near the theater. I'm ready when you are. She sighed. Her dad had come to collect her.

Autumn glanced at the time, and it read five. She was surprised to see how late it was.

"Your father is looking for you?"

"Yes," she murmured. "He's ready to go home."

"I'll return you to him, exactly as I indicated. First, I need to know when I might see you again?"

He took hold of her hand and squeezed it, gloves sliding against her skin. *Why did he always wear gloves?*

A flicker of adrenaline ran through her limbs. She wanted to see him again; the idea excited her to no end. But in the back of her mind, a voice screamed. She was terrified to trust someone new.

She sucked in a breath. "How about next week?"

"Perfect," he said sweetly. "We'll make another date."

Dante brought Autumn back to her dad, and they parted ways. Before he left, he flashed Autumn a gorgeous smile, and she disintegrated. *Not like this,* she reminded herself. It was too much too soon. When her dad rolled his eyes, she had an inkling he had something to say.

During the ride home, she sat in the front passenger's seat, holding her spectacular bouquet of multicolored roses. Autumn stared out the window at long stretches of forest, cellophane crinkling against her fingertips. She tuned out her dad.

"How old is Dante, anyway?"

She looked away from her reflection in the glass. "He's twenty."

"Well, he had me fooled," her dad muttered. "He looks at least twenty-four."

"He's mature for his age," Autumn countered. "He also works two jobs."

Her dad continued, "I don't like the way he hugged you on a first date. It makes me question his intentions."

"Dad!" Her cheeks heated.

"Yeah, he's a little too *friendly* for my taste. I can't quite put my finger on it. Call it father's intuition, but I don't care for Dante. He gives me bad vibes."

"You said that about Caleb, too. You say that about every guy." Autumn's heart sank.

"Well, I was right about Caleb."

"I don't want to talk about him." She crossed her arms.

But Autumn hated to admit, he was right.

"Just promise me you'll be nice to him, I kind of like him."

"Okay, I'll try. Your mom would have given him a chance."

Twenty

DANTE RETURNED TO THE FOREST, careful to conceal his newly acquired land craft. He had a feeling he'd be utilizing it frequently on this planet. Even if it was a sluggish piece of trash. But he needed a normal human way to transport Autumn around if need be. He wanted to impress her more than anything.

He made his way through the thick tangle of trees. The single Earth sun lowered in the distance, displaying a hint of glittering stars. Dante brought the hand Autumn permitted him to kiss up to his nostrils, still able to detect the faintest scent of her sweetness. He managed to pinpoint why he found her smell so appealing. Her scent reminded him of the warm summery air, he yearned to breathe back home.

It had to be a sign from the gods.

Autumn was *everything* he'd been searching for. Her demeanor was like grace itself.

While he walked, troubled by thoughts of her, he cast a deep, unwavering stare at the sky. He failed to recognize it was the night of the full Earth moon. His least favorite phase. Rage flooded through his veins. It was *too* late. He'd already seen it.

Falling to his knees, he cursed his only weakness, his vision scrambled into a thousand pieces before going black.

He woke the following morning, rays of golden orange sunlight glinting in his eyes. Dante laid on his back, branches scraping against his bare skin on the forest floor. He glanced around. Entire trees were felled, and deep claw marks marred the trunks of standing ones. His fists clenched. Next time, he'd have to be more mindful of the moon. For when he or any of the tailed members of his family glanced into the light of the full moon, *they shifted into beasts.* A natural born gene that had been used to conquer entire civilizations for centuries.

Worst of all, if Autumn had been with him, and discovered who and what he was capable of, it would have spelled disaster—maybe even death for her. No, he could never let that happen. He could never forgive himself.

When Dante rose to a stand, his clothes were nowhere in sight. Fortunately, he discovered his communicator beneath a tree and the device still functioned.

When he reached his ship, he strode through the door. As soon as he set foot on board, his cousins accosted him. They lingered and talked in the central corridor, blocking the stairway to his quarters. They needed a hobby, but while they were stranded on this planet, it was unlikely they'd find one.

He was their hobby.

"Looks like the full moon gotcha good, didn't it?" Armienti nudged him.

"Yeah, unless it was Autumn." Ronan winked.

Dante cleared his mind to prevent his cousin from probing his thoughts. He wanted to smash their heads together.

"She was delightful," he said curtly, choosing not to affirm or deny their activities together. It was none of their business, anyway.

Armienti brushed past Ronan and patted him on the back. "Well, it's about time."

Dante's mouth curved deceptively, and he ascended the stairs to his chamber when Armienti grabbed his shoulder.

"By the way, the Emperor sought an audience with you earlier."

Dante crossed his arms. "Which one? Our Emperor or the Grand Supreme?"

"Our Emperor."

"What the hell does he want?" The mention of the Emperor made his blood boil. How he despised him for being such an impressionable weakling.

"He wishes to discuss the status of our conquest and eagerly awaits an update from you."

"My update is there is *no* update," Dante hissed. "He can thank the pathetic pilot and useless tech who is still at bay for delaying our acquisition of Earth."

"And whose fault is that?" Ronan muttered.

"Excuse me?!" Dante snarled, grabbing Ronan by the collar of his uniform and slamming him against the steel wall. "I'm in charge here, and I dirtied my hands taking care of the pilot. The tech is on you, number three."

Ronan dislodged himself from the metal, his spiked hair frayed from the force of the impact. "Perhaps if you didn't spend your days pursuing pleasure, we wouldn't be in this predicament now, would we?"

"I could say the same for you," Dante snapped.

"Go put some clothes on, cousin. You look utterly absurd," Armienti interjected.

Dante clenched his teeth. He hated to admit his cousin was correct. He looked idiotic after an all-night bender. Curse the full-moon.

"I think not to begin our mission until our replacement ship arrives. I shall inform the Emperor *if* I muster up a spare moment."

He turned on his heel and went on his way.

He entered the loneliness of his private quarters. The room was dark except for the blue ceiling lights flickering on borrowed power. Hints of marmalade and golden sunlight shone through his only window, spraying across the metallic tiled floor.

He marched to the shower and scrubbed his body and nails clean from the unrecalled series of events that had occurred the previous night. In his mind, there was the present moment in the shower, a blank slate during his rampage, then came the memory of the last time he'd made the same foolish mistake of ignoring the moon.

* * *

Dante had been too young to lead a mission. But the greed of his superiors and the desire to control vast empires in the sky had put him to the test. At the tender age of eight he was shipped off to the higher Universes, crew in tow. He was their master and commander. A child warrior prince.

After laboring for weeks on end, conquering worlds, some larger than his own, he'd successfully completed his mission to nobody's surprise. He was a prodigy and his ability to transform proved to be useful. As well as his other natural born talents.

However, his own arrogance, like a thorn in his side, served as his downfall. Instead of simply conquering, he killed those who could have been useful, including his entire crew that was there in support of him and his cause all because he failed to monitor the phases of the moon as he had been taught. He'd been too caught up in his own success.

When he woke from his trance-like state he was surrounded by the death and chaos he had created.

Upon his return home, he wasn't scolded for his error but instead celebrated. And used to destroy until he had nothing left to give.

* * *

After he cleaned himself, he blow-dried his body, took a fluffy white towel and secured it around his waist. Pattering barefoot across the room in his natural form, he entered his private pantry area to rustle up some food. The selection was bland and limited, but the best there was on the ship.

He closed his eyes, thumbing through the freeze-dried packets, and selected one at random to make his meal more interesting. He added water to a bowl, grabbed a spoon, and ate.

It turned out to be soup, filled with brown meat and purple vegetable cubes. *What a surprise.* Not his first choice, but it beat starvation.

This was his life away from home.

Dante sipped and swallowed the remaining gelatinous pieces of his meal and wiped his mouth. Sitting in his chair, he glanced outside, stomach full.

There was one upside to being stranded on this miserable planet. One positive attribute on a distant world so far away from home. She was young and pretty, with wide eyes as brilliant and pale as the moon. Her cheeks were the shade of fresh pink roses, and her lips were satin soft against his own. At least that's how he imagined them. Dante's face warmed. And she was kind.

The thought of not seeing Autumn at least once more was inconceivable.

In the heat of the moment, he grabbed his cracked

communicator. There was one bar of life left before it was due for a charge. He could either call Autumn or discuss business with the Emperor.

Dante picked Autumn.

After thumbing her number against the screen, a familiar ring followed.

"Hey Dante!" Her voice crackled into the speaker. He could tell she smiled on the other end, based on the tone of her voice. He hoped it was because of him.

"Hello Autumn," he said. "I wanted to make sure you arrived home safely last night."

"Yeah, I did. Thanks."

"And I wanted to tell you I had a nice time."

"So did I."

"And also…" His throat ran mysteriously dry. "I want to know when you're free again. You mentioned next week, did you not?"

"Yeah." She paused for a long moment and his heart hammered in his chest. "Umm, how about Wednesday?"

"Wednesday. When is that?" He *honestly* didn't know.

"Dante, you crack me up. Four days from now."

To his relief, she found him amusing, but in actuality, he needed a better grasp of the human calendar.

"Yes, I'm free."

"Okay, great! You can meet me at my house. A group of us are going to the Castle and we can ride together." Autumn gave him her address, although he already had it memorized.

"Perfect, I'll be there." Dante was tempted to sigh, realizing they wouldn't be alone.

"See you then." She clicked off the phone.

Dante needed to see her again, and for the first time in a long while, he picked his own pleasure over duty, proving Ronan right.

Twenty-One

THE NIGHT before their trip to the Castle, Dante returned to visit Autumn while she slept. He maneuvered through her room, which was pitch black, except for a star lamp affixed to the wall, glowing gold. Kneeling by the bed, he watched her breastbone gently heave. Who was he kidding? *He was a creep.* Sneaking around like this was unacceptable, but try as he might, he couldn't stay away from her.

It ate away at him to where he could no longer sleep. To think he, Dante Martyne, pined after a young woman. All they ever did back home was beg him to cast a glance their way.

Dante brazenly twirled a loose coil of her hair around his fingertip before bringing it to his nostril. Autumn laid suspiciously still from what he understood was a normal sleeping pattern for her. She gasped suddenly and rose from her sleep. Limbs flailing, she tangled herself within the confines of her blanket. She landed in his lap with a soft thud, before rolling onto the floor.

Rising to his feet, he dashed behind the open closet door.

He stood there in the shadows, watching and waiting. Hoping she hadn't seen him.

Autumn stumbled to her feet and switched on the light. Squinting, she tiptoed.

"Dante?"

Twenty-Two

AUTUMN'S LEGS went limp as she maneuvered slowly toward her closet door, Eiffel Tower lamp flickering on her nightstand. Squinting, her eyes refocused. A man stood before her. One who resembled Dante, but different.

He looked inhuman.

She couldn't make out his features clearly, eyes still clouded with heavy sleep. When she blinked, he vanished without a trace.

Autumn peeked behind her closet door. The man disappeared. Rubbing her fists against her eyes, she trembled and yawned. She must have been sleepwalking—it wouldn't have been her first time.

The hairs on the back of her neck rose. She was too old to be afraid of the bogeyman. There was no such person. But why did once again her room smell of cinnamon? *Cinnamon,* she thought. It was the same scent she breathed in when Dante was with her.

Autumn puttered back to her bed and sighed. Never had she dreamed so vividly in all of her life. Quietly, she crawled beneath her comforter, careful this time around to leave her light on in case she suffered another night terror.

* * *

Autumn rose, stomach twisting and turning from the previous night. She'd hardly slept a wink. She climbed out of bed and went downstairs for breakfast.

Her dad sat at the kitchen table sipping a hot cup of coffee. As per usual, he pored over his laptop, engrossed in the morning news.

"Good morning." Her voice wavered as she grabbed a sesame bagel from the counter and smeared it with cream cheese before taking a bite.

Her dad finished the video he watched. "Good morning." He glanced from the screen. "Did you sleep well?"

"Yeah," she lied. Last night was one of the worst nights of sleep she'd suffered all summer.

Her dad shut down his computer and took a swig of coffee, staring at her in silence.

"Is everything all right?"

Her dad cleared his throat. "I know I promised, but I have another question about Dante."

"Okay?"

Her dad continued, "Have you been to his house yet and met his family?"

She shook her head. "Not yet, I'm sure he'll invite me over eventually."

"If I were you, I'd insist on meeting them. You can tell a lot about a person from his family. He could be keeping secrets from you."

"Stop it, Dad, he's not doing that!"

His eyes clouded with tears. "I'm your father, and I'll protect you until the day I die. We've been through enough, and I don't want to see you get hurt over this boy. The way Caleb hurt you—"

Ding dong.

"Are we expecting someone?"

She glanced at the clock on the stove. "My friends, but not until much later."

He stood from the table and ambled to the front door, opening it.

"Hello, Dante." Her dad's voice cracked. "Can I help you?"

Autumn's stomach fell to the floor. *Why was he here so early?* She took an emergency peek at herself on the screen of her phone. *What a disaster.*

As quickly as she could, she flattened her mess of hair, raking it into submission behind her ears, using her fingers as a comb. She pinched her cheeks, flushing them.

She *didn't* want Dante to see her like this.

In a last-ditch effort, she shot up from her chair to flee to her room to ready herself, but her foot became tangled between the legs of the chair, casting her onto the floor face first.

Crap. Dante and her dad strolled into the room together. Her cheeks heated as she attempted to free herself. They both stared at her; Dante with a mild look of amusement on his face, while her dad shook his head.

"Autumn." Dante regarded her with his piercing amber eyes. "I hope I didn't come too early for our Castle visit."

"No, not at all," she lied, struggling to even the tone of her voice.

"Well, it is a *little* early," her dad interjected.

Dante ignored his remark. "Can I speak to you for a moment?"

"Sure." She nodded.

Autumn stood from the table and led Dante upstairs to her room so they could speak in private.

Her dad shot her a look. "The door stays open. Thank you."

"I know," Autumn answered.

They entered her bedroom, and she closed the door slightly so her dad couldn't hear their conversation.

"Is everything okay?" She fidgeted her hands.

Dante analyzed her slowly from head to toe. "I don't know, you tell me. You suddenly appear nervous around me."

She had a flashback of the man she'd seen standing in her room the night before. The man she'd dreamed of. Sometimes she could no longer distinguish her dreams from reality.

"Sorry." Her voice jumped. "I'm a little on edge."

Before she could blink, he approached her with impossible speed. She took a step back and shuddered against the wall as he caressed her cheek with his black-gloved hand.

"Why?" he asked, his voice low and gruff.

"It's stupid, I shouldn't say."

"No, tell me."

She hesitated, then continued, "I had the most terrifying dream last night."

He walked closer. Warm body to body, he stared into her eyes. "Tell me. What did you dream?"

Autumn averted her gaze to the ground. He propped his fingers under her chin and moved her head up, lowering his face to hers. The smell of cinnamon consumed her, warm breath poured over her ear. "Tell me."

"I dreamt of an intruder," she breathed.

"Did you see a face?"

She nodded. "He looked like you, but *different*."

"Different how?"

"Just different." She shrugged.

The more she spoke, the more she realized how ridiculous she sounded. He stared at her quietly.

"I'm sorry, I sound stupid."

"No, you don't." His stare softened. "Sometimes our minds play tricks on us and make us unnecessarily afraid."

Her mouth bowed. He was probably right. With what had taken place over the summer, of course she was mentally fried.

"I'm sorry I went off on a tangent," she murmured. "What did you want to talk to me about?"

Dante leaned over, midnight hair brushing against her face. "I needed to see you sooner. I've been thinking about you non-stop. I wanted to ask you if it's all right if—"

"Autumn, your friends are downstairs!"

"We should get back," she said. "If we don't go down, they'll come upstairs. We can talk about this later. Okay?"

Dante stepped away and nodded, looking crestfallen.

Autumn discovered Lauren and Ellie seated at the table with her dad chatting his ear off as usual. Everyone fell silent and stared at them. Autumn's cheeks heated as their eyes darted between her and Dante, more than likely making assumptions.

"This house is turning into Grand Central Station." Her dad chuckled.

Lauren's sky-blue eyes glinted in the morning sunlight.

"Hey Autumn *and* Dante," she emphasized. "Are you ready to go rollerblading at the Castle?"

"Yes," Autumn said.

"Great!" Ellie's high ponytail swished against her neck. "We're going to have the best time."

"One minute, I need to change."

Autumn sprinted upstairs. Her mind sputtered out of control as she pondered what Dante had come over to ask her, but she supposed whatever it was could wait. Stumbling into her closet, she tossed on a black crew-neck t-shirt, a pair of white denim shorts, and her low top sneakers. She parted her hair in the center and braided it into two flat plaits. One swipe of her favorite watermelon lip gloss and she was ready to tackle the day. After grabbing her tan canvas crossbody bag, she reunited with her friends.

"I'm all set."

"Have fun," her dad said. "And ladies, please, please, *please*, be careful. I read two horrible stories recently about a man murdered during a carjacking right here in town, and a decapitated body discovered at Farrah Falls."

Ellie gasped. "That's disgusting."

Autumn's stomach knotted.

"Don't worry, Mr. Ramon, we'll be safe," Lauren promised.

Dante stared at everyone in silence, arms folded.

Autumn, her friends, and Dante left the house together. Sprinklers swirled and an ice cream truck played an off-key tune. The air smelled of freshly mowed grass and charcoal barbecues.

Lauren scanned the street like the nosy friend she was. "Where did *you* park, Dante?"

"I walked."

Lauren continued, "Really? You don't have a car?"

"Lauren," Autumn warned.

"Of course I have a car, but I prefer the exercise. If you like, I can retrieve it." He brushed against Autumn, twining his fingers in hers. She could barely breathe.

Lauren shrugged. "It's no problem, I can drive."

They piled into Lauren's silver Corolla. Ellie rode shotgun while Autumn occupied the backseat with Dante. She kicked aside several soda cups and empty French fry boxes to make space for her feet.

Lauren and Ellie clicked their seatbelts in place, but when

Autumn went to fasten hers, Dante reached over and buckled it for her instead.

She pulled him close, whispering into his ear. "Why did you do that?"

"I want to make sure you ride safely."

Autumn bit her cheeks. For a guy that wasn't her boyfriend, he was sure thoughtful. Maybe she misjudged him after all.

Lauren backed out of the driveway, and they drove off.

The car was silent, except for the low hum of the radio. Autumn stared out of her window. It was a picture-perfect day without a single cloud in the sky. Peeking over her shoulder, Dante did the same. They rode by sparse buildings that transformed into a dense stretch of dark evergreen forest.

Lauren cleared her throat, disturbing the silence. She peered through her rear-view mirror, watching them.

"Do you start college in September?" she asked Dante.

"No, I'm finished with school." He tensed. Autumn could tell he had little interest in engaging with her friends. She couldn't blame him, either, since Lauren was being relentless. Sometimes she was a lot to handle, whether she realized it or not.

Lauren laughed, eyes locked on him through the rearview mirror. "Oh, so you're a few years older, then? You didn't tell us that, Autumn." She winked.

Autumn shrugged, mortified Lauren would even discuss this topic. It was like being grilled by her dad *twice in one day*. "I didn't think it was important," she admitted.

"I see."

Ellie grinned. "Where are your friends? The ones you were with at Farrah Falls?"

Dante tightened his folded arms against his chest, his expression hardening. "They're not my friends, they're my cousins."

Lauren grinned. "Oh, wow. Good looks sure run in your family."

"Definitely," Ellie added. "If they don't have any plans today, tell them to come meet us."

She kicked Ellie's seat, and her best friend jutted forward. Autumn's fists clenched around her seatbelt; she could have throttled them. They were always so pushy.

"I guess it could be fun. The more the merrier," Autumn said sarcastically, hoping she wouldn't explode on her friends.

Smiling at Dante, she held her expression for a moment too long.

"Very well then." He pressed a strand of raven hair behind his ear. "I'll inform them of our destination."

A series of giggles erupted from the front seats. *How embarrassing*. Autumn wanted to shrivel up and disappear. Dante probably thought she, Lauren, and Ellie were too immature for him.

Autumn placed a finger in her mouth, gnawing at the cuticle. She glanced at Dante and wondered why he was texting while concealing his phone with his other hand. She recalled he wouldn't give her his phone even at Farrah Falls, which was customary when a girl gave a guy her number. At least where she was from.

"What kind of phone do you have?" She tried to catch a glimpse.

He took her hand, holding it instead. "You wouldn't recognize it, anyway."

Autumn laughed. "That old, huh? Don't feel bad, I have an older phone, too." She slid her phone from her back short's pocket. It was decorated with holographic rainbow butterfly stickers and a piece of packing tape holding the battery in place. The screen was cracked.

"Yours certainly is ancient," he mused.

She rolled her eyes. "At least I'm not afraid to use mine in public."

Dante blinked, long lashes fanning the peaks of his cheekbones. Autumn bit her bottom lip, admiring him. A single crisp beep interrupted her thoughts.

He discreetly read his message. "They'll join us."

"Great!" Ellie clapped her hands together in excitement.

"This should be fun," Lauren agreed.

"Interesting is more like it," Autumn muttered.

Dante stared straight ahead in silence.

Twenty-Three

FOR AN EARLY WEDNESDAY AFTERNOON, the Castle was slammed. Cars double parked, and a white and gray stone gatehouse was packed with people carrying brightly-hued golf clubs and balls. Dripping ice cream cones sat in the hands of screaming children with sticky mouths, and a forest-green dragon sang a jovial song, meaning someone had won a free game of miniature golf.

Lauren stalked a potential parking space. A navy blue mini van's reverse lights turned a bright off-white. The car pulled out, and she maneuvered into the spot.

Autumn and her friends exited the vehicle, followed by Dante. They stood together in a group, but Autumn noticed Dante was acting odd. Probably because her friends had been pushy and rude throughout the entire car ride over.

Dante crossed his arms, muscles appearing tense. His amber eyes scoured the premises, analyzing the area. He rolled his mouth in a scowl, seemingly unimpressed. Maybe this wasn't the *cool* way a twenty-year-old would choose to spend his afternoon.

Maybe their age difference was apparent after all.

Lauren and Ellie seemed blissfully unaware, texting away on their phones. All they noticed were cute guys.

"Are you all right?" Autumn asked as they sauntered toward the main entrance. It must have been too stressful for him to see her friends and dad over the course of a few hours. She hoped he didn't flake.

Not that she should care this much anyway.

"I'm fine." Dante snapped out of his daze. He flashed her a small tentative smile.

Then it occurred to her. "Have you ever been rollerblading before?"

"No."

Relief flooded through her as she pegged the source of his discomfort. He was probably worried again about impressing her. After all, he'd gone to such great lengths to capture her attention.

"You'll be okay." She tilted her head to the side, braided plaits brushing against her shoulders. "I can help you learn. It's a lot easier than it sounds."

"Don't worry about me." He chuckled. "I'm an exceptionally fast learner."

Autumn rolled her eyes. *Typical guy*, refusing everyone's help. She was positive he'd be sorry after his feet hit the rink floor.

When they passed through the main gate, Dante's cousins waited for them.

Weird. He'd only texted them minutes before.

Autumn figured they must have been in the area. *Or they moved at lightning speed.*

Her eyes fell upon Armienti, who had the same sour expression on his face Dante had earlier. His arms were folded, and the sun illuminated his golden hair. Armienti's crystal blue eyes narrowed when he beheld them.

The other cousin with brown spiky hair flanked him.

Autumn couldn't recall whether Dante had told her his name. His clover-green eyes rolled. He had a strong jaw and a beautifully sculpted face. Dante came from a gorgeous family from what she'd seen, but they must have been hot. *Literally.* They all wore a uniform of onyx long-sleeved shirts, pants, and *gloves,* even on a day like this one. Why the gloves? She'd been working up to ask him.

"We were summoned?" Armienti's scowl rolled into a pearly white grin. His eyes roved over Autumn and her friends. Dante's arm cinched tighter around her waist.

"Indeed," Dante said. "Since I'm well aware neither of you have any prior engagements, you'll be accompanying us rollerblading."

"What's rollerblading?" The spiky-haired cousin made a disgusted face.

Lauren's mouth fell ajar. "What planet are you from? How could you not know what rollerblading is?"

"Planet hotness," Ellie murmured.

Although Ellie spoke in little more than a whisper, they stared at her with amused expressions. Dante and his cousins must have heard her somehow.

"Who might you be, pretty speckled girl?" Armienti took hold of Ellie's hand, planting a kiss on her knuckles.

"I'm Ellie." Her freckled cheeks flushed bright red.

"Pleasure to meet you; I'm Armienti." Ellie's hand was still in his grasp. "I'm enthused you find us attractive, you have excellent taste, my dear." He ran his fingers through his golden hair. Autumn could've sworn Dante gagged.

"And who might you be, pretty girl with a mouth with slack jaw?" the other cousin said.

"I'm Lauren." Her cheeks flushed crimson.

"You have my permission to call me Ronan."

"Ha, your permission?" Lauren said. "What are you, a celebrity?"

Ronan ignored her question and continued, "Just because we haven't heard of this rollerblading phenomenon, doesn't mean we can't master it with little effort. We're not—"

Dante raised his palm, cutting Ronan off mid-sentence. "Enough. We're here to rollerblade, and we've made our introductions. Let's not keep these lovely ladies waiting any longer."

Ronan and Armienti nodded. Clearly, Dante called the shots in their group, like Lauren did in her own. Autumn wondered what Ronan planned to say before Dante interrupted him.

The rink itself was darkly lit and swarmed with people of all ages. The air was a cool contrast compared to the outside. Music blasted, making it difficult to speak at a normal level. A multi-colored sphere spun from the ceiling, spraying rainbow lights all over the floor and walls. In nearby rooms, children jumped into ball pits, climbed through tunnels, and played carefree games of laser tag.

When they approached the counter to rent inline skates, Ronan bent over the desk and smiled coyly at the rental clerk. The tall, slender clerk reciprocated, batting his dark-brown eyes, tousling his dyed strawberry blond hair with his fingertips. They chatted while Lauren stood watching them, a hand on her hip. She made a face, staring at Autumn in the darkness.

Autumn couldn't help but feel embarrassed Lauren was being ignored, but apparently Ronan preferred pretty guys to pretty girls. Ellie was also by herself.

A few feet over, Armienti engaged a girl with a pink pixie cut, who ran her hands over his corded, muscular arms. She scoffed; Dante had warned her about his cousins at the mall. *They were players.*

Her brow furrowed, she shouted into Dante's ear, which sounded more like whispering with the music pulsating.

"What's their deal?"

"I told you, did I not?"

Yeah, he did. Her poor friends. This is what they got for being so pushy. If only she'd warned them beforehand and insisted his cousins didn't come. Now she'd hear about it the entire way home.

"Don't pout; I'll have a word with them. I won't let them spoil your fun."

Dante strode over to his cousins, placed a palm on each of their shoulders, and led them to a private corner of the room. They huddled and conducted some sort of *meeting*. A minute later, Ronan and Armienti reemerged and stood by Lauren and Ellie in silence, arms folded. Autumn pondered what they discussed.

Afterwards, Autumn leaned her arm against the counter.

"What size skates do you need?" The olive-skinned clerk snapped his gum in her ear.

"Seven."

"I'll take care of the cost, and theirs as well." Dante handed the boy another one of his crisp one-hundred-dollar bills. They seemed to be never ending.

"Don't worry, I have my own money," she insisted.

"A simple thank you will suffice," Dante countered. "We've hung out a few times. Allow me to spoil you, for heaven's sake."

"Thank you," she muttered.

"You're welcome. Was that so difficult?" He winked.

Autumn laughed, figuring it wasn't worth arguing about anymore.

After they fastened their inline skates, everyone rolled onto the rink. Apparently, Dante and his cousins misrepresented their skating abilities. They zipped across the floor, sometimes on one foot. Autumn and her friends struggled to keep up, and they'd been skating since forever. All the while, the colorful twirling ball dimmed and flickered above their heads in rapid streaks. *Definitely* not a coincidence.

On Dante's third pass, Autumn caught him by his hand, and he slowed to match her speed.

"I thought you said you hadn't been skating before?"

"I haven't." He shrugged. "As I already informed you, I'm an exceptionally fast learner."

"Liar," Autumn hissed. Dante disappeared into the crowd. *So much for showing off.* Without fail, he left her in the dust.

A dark figure waved from the exterior sideline. She squinted, attempting to see who sought her attention.

"*Autumn, Autumn, over here!*" She could barely hear over the techno music.

When she rolled closer, her blood froze in her veins.

"Caleb, go away!"

"Autumn, I'm sorry." Caleb regarded her with his sapphire eyes. "I know I fucked up. I tried to call you to apologize. I left you text messages and voicemails."

"You're still blocked," she blurted.

"I figured as much." He stared at his feet before meeting her glower.

Autumn fled as quickly as she could, but Caleb followed, maneuvering his way through the crowd. People stared, and her cheeks heated with humiliation.

He pulled her toward him. "I was drunk and stupid at Tyler's party—and during prom, and everything that happened with Misty. It was a huge mis—"

"Enough!" She broke free from his grasp.

"What do you want from me? Do you want me to get down on my hands and knees and beg for your forgiveness? Do you want me to kiss your feet, clean your house for a year? I'd give anything to take back what I did. I never meant to hurt you."

Autumn skated to the center of the floor to avoid him,

gasping in horror after he hopped over the wall divider. He jogged after her, dodging skater traffic.

"If you can't forgive me right away, please at least allow me to explain myself. Maybe I can take you to Starbucks sometime?"

Autumn opened her mouth to retaliate when an arm cinched around her waist, pulling her against solid muscle.

"I'm afraid Autumn has no interest in the likes of you."

Caleb's brows knit together. He stared at Autumn, bemused.

"Who the fuck are you? Her boyfriend?" Caleb's chest puffed.

Dante remained quiet.

"I didn't think so." Caleb balled his fists. "She has a voice, and she can speak for herself. Do you know who I am?"

"You're nobody." The corners of Dante's mouth curled. He released Autumn from his grasp and flicked Caleb on the nose with such force he stumbled backwards. "I, however, am your worst nightmare. The darkness that lurks in the shadow of your dreams. Never in my life have I been addressed with such insolence. Nobody *dares* speak to me the way you have."

Caleb's complexion flushed purple. He quivered with fury. "Well, there's always a first time, isn't there, pretty boy?"

Dante knocked Caleb's red cap off his head, and clear across the room. "Show me what you've got, then. You talk a tough game, but can you back it up?"

Caleb assumed a fighting stance and launched a round-house kick toward Dante.

Dante caught his sneaker in his hand mid-flight, shoving him back. A giant crackling wave of fire ripped across the ceiling and the floor, inches from Caleb. Autumn screamed, her brow drenched with sweat.

Caleb whipped around and gasped. A stampede of fright-ened skaters headed to the exit of the rink. Autumn froze, staring at the hypnotizing blue and orange flames. She was unable to move, unable to think. She lost herself within the blaze. Dante took her hand, snapping her out of her trance and led her to safety.

Autumn's eyes darted around the room in search of her friends and Dante's cousins. When she didn't see them, she hyperventilated.

"Wait, we have to find the others," she struggled to catch her breath.

"I'm sure they're already outside." Dante was eerily calm. "Follow me, we'll find them."

He dragged her out.

She discovered her friends by Lauren's car trembling, eyes red-rimmed. Autumn squeezed them in a hug, grateful they were both alive.

"Are you guys okay?" Autumn's hands quivered.

Lauren nodded. "How about you?"

"I'm fine. Thankfully, Dante was with me."

"And thankfully, Caleb didn't kick his ass. We saw the whole ordeal," Lauren said. "He's desperate to get you back."

Apparently, they weren't watching closely, because it was the other way around. Dante had the upper hand. Autumn changed the subject.

"Where are Ronan and Armienti?"

Lauren pointed to the far end of the lot. Armienti stood at perfect attention, arms crossed. Ronan stood a few cars away, necking with the cute skate clerk from earlier.

"Eww get a room," Autumn muttered.

"It looks like he's doing the best out of all of us," Ellie said sarcastically. Autumn could imagine how disappointed her friends were in this dud of a hangout.

The Chester Fire Department arrived. Fire trucks rolled up, along with an array of other emergency vehicles with swirling lights and blaring sirens. On top of everything else,

Autumn caught Dante exchanging glares with Caleb, who stood with his own friends across the way. She still couldn't believe a fight erupted—*over her*.

She brushed her fingers over Dante's arm. "He's not worth it."

"In his mind, he believes otherwise."

Autumn sighed. There was no reasoning with either of them. Though she would never admit it out loud, she was strangely flattered that Dante was jealous of her ex.

About an hour later, Autumn and her friends were permitted back into the building to retrieve their belongings. They returned their skates and changed into their sneakers and flip-flops. Dante and his cousins pulled on their boots. It'd been a bizarre afternoon. They almost burned to death. So much drama, one week from college.

When they returned to the parking lot, Lauren said, "Are you riding home with us, Dante?"

"No."

Lauren shrugged. "Suit yourself." But Autumn suspected she wanted to say good riddance.

"I'll see you soon." Autumn waved at Dante and his cousins. They left on foot, and she and her friends drove back to Monroe.

The first few minutes of the ride were uncharacteristically silent.

Then, Lauren blurted, "What a *weird* family."

"I agree," Ellie concurred. "And Dante is rude. He barely said goodbye to you, and he couldn't be bothered with us."

"Yeah, he was kind of rude, wasn't he?" Lauren crinkled her nose.

"Maybe he was nervous," Autumn said, partially offended that her friends didn't like him. "He's never met you before, and he also had to deal with my dad. You know how he can be."

"True." Lauren cut the wheel onto Highway 17. "Maybe we'll give him the benefit of the doubt."

"That doesn't change the fact his cousins are scumbags," Ellie interjected, loosening her ponytail.

"What did you expect?" Lauren chortled. "They're hot guys, they can get anyone they want."

"Dante didn't ignore Autumn, though." Ellie pouted.

Autumn listened to her friends bicker from the backseat of the car. It was pointless. They'd leave next week and meet so many new guys they won't even be worried about these few.

Every time she closed her eyes, she was haunted by two memories. Her mom's face, the last time she saw her, and the wall of fire that erupted behind Caleb. She couldn't imagine where it'd come from, or how it'd started. It materialized out of thin air.

Her pocket buzzed with one new text from her dad. When she looked more closely, she realized he'd called her ten times in a row.

Are you okay? I just heard about the fire. I'm on my way.

Yeah, I'm fine. We're all okay. Don't worry, we're on our way home.

Good, I'm glad everyone is safe.

Do you know what started it?

No. It's still under investigation.

Twenty-Four

WHEN DANTE RETURNED to his ship, he had an inkling his cousins were displeased with him. Neither of them uttered a single word. On a typical afternoon, he couldn't shut either of them up. Similar to Autumn's friend Lauren, who he wanted to gag, rather than hear the useless stream of words that flowed from her ignorant human mouth. He couldn't get used to it, no matter how hard he tried.

What bothered him most of all about Lauren was he could tell she didn't like him. He feared she'd been poisoning Autumn's mind since the moment they departed from the Castle.

On their way to the common area, vibrant rays of sunlight spilled through the windows over the steel walls of the interior of the ship, creating light where otherwise there would've been darkness.

They sauntered toward a table, where the one-armed soldier who Dante had ordered punished stared out the window. Defeated and hopeless. There had been no other dead bodies discovered.

Once past the soldier, Dante's cousins cornered him.

"What transpired earlier?" Armienti asked. "Now we've been reduced to socializing with humans? They should be so fortunate."

Though he spoke ill of socialization, Armienti did plenty of it on his own free accord. Armienti ran a black-gloved hand through his gilded hair, glimpsing at himself in a mirrored panel of the wall. Dante resisted the urge to vomit.

"And since when is it any of your business who we choose to take pleasure with?" Ronan slammed his fist against the steel table. "This has never been an issue with you before."

Dante took a seat and propped his cheek on a fist. He inhaled deep, controlled breaths to relax himself before he spoke. "Whether you like it or not, it's well within my right to give you orders, and you're obliged to obey. I'm your superior, lest you forget."

Armienti rolled his eyes. "You remind us often enough."

Ronan erupted into a fit of boisterous laughter that eclipsed the chatter in the room. "Oh, great leader of ours, deliver us from this ridiculous planet," he said in a mocking tone.

"Bite your tongue." Dante's eyes shot open.

"He jests," Armienti said. "We're not asking you to do the impossible. It all makes perfect sense to us now."

"What does?"

"You haven't been thinking with your head since the night of the crash."

"And what exactly are you suggesting?" Dante narrowed his eyes, unsure of what Armienti was hinting at. Ronan snorted, probably probing through his mind.

"Cousin, how can you be so clever, yet so thick at the same time?" Armienti continued. "It's really quite clear, actually. You're falling for Autumn."

"Who, me?" Dante crossed his arms. "Don't be preposterous. I do admit I enjoy the company of a pretty girl, but she's a human, and it doesn't go beyond that. It *can't* go beyond that."

"Yet you wouldn't let Ronan speak the truth," Armienti added.

"I deemed it unnecessary under the circumstances," Dante said. "The humans here are unaware of life on other worlds, and I'd prefer to keep it that way for the time being. There will be fewer complications down the line."

"At the rate you're going, you'll have far greater issues to deal with than this." Armienti chuckled. "What are the Emperor and the Grand Supreme going to say when they find out you've neglected our mission for a human girl?"

"I've said it once, and I shall say it again." Dante slammed his palm against the table, denting it. "There is no mission until our replacement ship arrives. Once it's here, our great work will begin."

"Good, we look forward to it."

Dante stood from the table and turned on a heel, leaving his cousins to their own devices. On his way upstairs to his chambers, his chest ached with an indescribable tightness. There was so much truth in what Armienti said about the Emperor and the Grand Supreme being displeased. He'd sort out that matter later.

Thankfully, he persuaded his cousins his interest in Autumn was purely superficial, but he couldn't understand why he had so much difficulty convincing himself.

Why couldn't he kick his Autumn habit? She was like a drug. He was never satiated; she was utterly intoxicating. Dante craved her like he craved the air in his lungs. He could barely breathe in her absence.

To think he, Dante Martyne, had developed a soft spot for a human girl. What was wrong with him? *She was a human.*

And then there was *Caleb.*

When he discovered Autumn speaking to that despicable

boy, something latent inside of him snapped. He regretted not gutting him and adorning the interior walls of the Castle with his flesh. It would have been his pleasure.

Caleb thought in his wildest dreams he could lay claim to what already belonged to him. How he despised him.

He couldn't unwind until he took care of a pressing matter. It laid heavily on his mind and threatened to drive him mad. Instead of climbing the stairs like he'd planned, he sauntered into the cool night air with one destination in mind.

*　*　*

Autumn was relieved to be home after an unusual afternoon. Lauren and Ellie had gone home for the evening, and her dad sat downstairs watching television in the living room. It took her an hour to convince him she was okay after what occurred at the Castle. He offered to bring her to Urgent Care, but she declined, seeing as she wasn't injured, only frightened.

The fire had been really, really close. Close enough for her to see the embers of its blaze and feel the sheer magnitude of its heat against her skin.

Where did it come from? It was amazing how two major fires had broken out over the course of the summer. Summers in Orange County were quiet and uneventful. This had been the most action packed one so far in her life, and not in a good way.

Autumn's cheeks warmed against her will as she remembered how Dante remained level-headed and brave during the fire. How he'd guided her to safety.

Autumn laid in bed; unbound coils splashed over her pillow. Her Eiffel Tower lamp glowed as she read a long overdue paperback from the library.

A rap came to her window like knuckle to glass. The echo startled the book from her hands. Coming to all fours, she crawled to the window and popped a blind. Autumn's gaze met a pair of amber eyes.

Dante.

But what was he thinking? Climbing to the second story of her house, when her dad was home... He was lucky it wasn't garbage night.

"What are you doing out there?" She glanced at him, unable to imagine how he'd climbed up to the second level.

"I needed to see you."

She moved, making space for him on the bed. Dante crawled through with ease and sat next to her cross-legged.

"I needed to know you were okay after what happened earlier."

"How did you know this was my window?"

He shrugged. "Lucky guess."

"I'm fine," she said, "all things considered."

She paused for a moment, then continued, "I'm glad you were with me. It isn't every day you see a fire up close like that. Thank you for helping me. How are you doing, by the way?"

"Does fire frighten you?"

"I think fire frightens everyone, especially when it's uncontained. It reminded me of Farrah Falls. It happened out of nowhere."

"That was quite the night indeed," he mused, maintaining her gaze. "I saw the flames erupting from my door."

Her brows rose. "I didn't realize you lived so close."

He nodded.

Have you been to his house yet and met his family? Her dad's warning echoed through her head. A discussion for another time.

Dante drew closer and snatched a curl, twirling it around his fingers. Autumn became aware of every pore on her skin. Her internal temperature rose as shivers trickled down her spine. He leaned over, observing her. Cinnamon scent, filling her nostrils.

"What about Caleb?" Dante's gaze settled on her.

She scrunched her nose. "What about him?"

"How are you acquainted?"

"What's this sudden fascination you have with him? Are you feeling guilty for the fight?"

"No." He chuckled softly. "I assure you, if it had escalated, it wouldn't have been much of a fight."

For Caleb maybe. That thought, she kept to herself, but from what she'd seen, for the first time ever, Caleb had been surprised by an opponent. He had quite the reputation around the county and throughout the state for his taek-wondo skills. He was the reigning state champion and made sure everyone knew about it.

Dante leaned over and kissed her neck. She shuddered, her skin erupting in goosebumps. "Can you blame me?" He grazed his lips over her throat. "He tried stealing you from me."

Autumn regained her strength and stumbled to her feet. "Steal me?" she asked, half joking. "What's that supposed to mean? Are you asking me if I want to be official?"

Was that his strange way of asking her to be his girlfriend? She stared at him, and he appeared to be lost in deep thought. Maybe she had breached the topic too soon. She chewed her bottom lip, feeling foolish. They'd gone on two dates. If you could even call the second one a date. It was more like a disaster.

"Official?" Dante shrugged finally, after too long of a time.

"You know..." Her cheeks burned, embarrassed she was going to have to spell it out for him. Ellie was right: what planet was he from? "Are you telling me you want to be my boyfriend?"

He leaned over and tucked a fallen strand of hair behind her ear. Autumn's heart sped.

"I must admit, I'm not so used to this terminology." He ran a hand through his hair. "This is sort of a first for me."

Dante caressed her cheek with his black-gloved hand, sending goosebumps crashing through her limbs. Her eyes fluttered closed. He brought his soft lips to hers, warm cinnamon breath flowing against her skin. Their mouths and tongues joined as he ran his hand through her hair, pulling her in deeper and deeper until she lost herself in his gentle touch. Her pain and loneliness faded for the first time all summer. When their mouths separated, Autumn stared at him in a rose-colored daze. She trembled.

"I don't wish for you to see anyone else in an intimate scenario. In exchange, I'll extend the same courtesy."

"So we're boyfriend and girlfriend?"

Dante ran his fingers through her hair and kissed her again. "It's clear you find those titles pleasing. So yes. Yes, we are." He nuzzled his nose against hers. "I have one more request."

"Okay, what is it?"

Dante stared at her, his features drawn and serious. "I'd much prefer you don't see Caleb. I don't feel comfortable with you associating with the likes of him."

Autumn snorted. "Caleb again?"

He remained quiet.

"We dated in high school for a few years, but we've been broken up since the beginning of summer. We're not even friends anymore. Don't worry."

"Good." Dante pulled her close. "For if we don't have honesty in this arrangement of ours, we have nothing."

The Freshman

Twenty-Five

AUTUMN LAID in bed on the night of August thirty-first. The pale glow of the crescent moon shone through her blinds spraying across her lavender comforter. The shadowy leaves of the trees swayed in the midnight breeze. Her satin cloud shorts and white camisole brushed against the sheets. No matter what she did, she couldn't get comfortable. For once, it wasn't a result of the dreams that plagued her. They had long since passed. Instead, she feared the unknown.

College started bright and early in the morning.

As soon as her eyes shut, her phone alarm rattled her to the core, dancing along the edge of her wooden night table. On a day like today, she didn't have the luxury of sleeping in. Especially because she relied on getting a ride to college.

Once she finished pulling on a pair of dark wash jeans, a navy crew neck t-shirt, and her black canvas sneakers, her phone buzzed.

"Hello."

"I'm outside."

"Okay, I'll be right there," she said before hanging up.

She grabbed her galaxy-patterned backpack and headed

downstairs. Her dad sat at the kitchen table tinkering on his computer.

"Good luck," he said.

"Thanks, Dad." Autumn raced around the corner toward the front door.

"I'm proud of you."

"Thanks," she turned around and waved.

When she reached the front doorway, she stopped, her mouth falling wide open in disbelief. Even Queen Misty, with all the money and prestige she possessed, would be impressed.

A Ferrari sat in the driveway, complete with obsidian-tinted windows that matched its glittering exterior. Flecks of silver finish sparkled in the early morning sunlight.

A pair of gullwing doors soared toward the sky. Autumn wanted to jump up and down and scream with excitement, but refrained, trying her hardest to keep her cool in front of her new boyfriend.

She climbed inside and took hold of his black-gloved hand. "Nice ride."

"Thank you, it was a gift." He reached over her lap and grabbed her safety belt, clicking it into place.

She snorted. "You don't have to buckle my seatbelt every time, I never forget to wear one."

Dante tucked a stray strand of hair behind her ear. "My landcraft. My rules. If you take issue with that, feel free to find another ride."

Autumn chuckled. "Landcraft? I've never heard that term before."

Dante mumbled something incomprehensible under his breath, starting the car. The engine revved.

"Sorry, I didn't mean to be rude. You can call your car whatever you want. Thanks again for driving me."

He glanced at her with his brilliant amber eyes, mouth coiling.

A few minutes into their ride, she gripped the handle. *Holy crap*. Dante was the worst driver she'd ever ridden with in her life.

He slammed his foot on the petal, casting her against the seat. She was grateful she hadn't eaten breakfast, or else it would be splattered all over the windshield.

The speedometer read **220 mph**. No wonder he had concerns about her safety belt. But where the heck was his?

"Slow down and put on your seatbelt!"

He grinned. "This vehicle is incredibly slow. If I traveled any slower, we'd be rolling at a crawl. I assure you, even if I were to crash the landcraft at its maximum speed, I would emerge from the wreckage unscathed, with you in my arms in a heartbeat."

"I'm not in the mood for your jokes." Autumn slapped her palms against her thighs, teeth gritted. "I'd like to arrive at school alive."

The driver that hit her mom probably shared his mentality.

Autumn's gut twisted when she saw red and blue emergency lights; piercing sirens blared through her ears. Not one, but *two* New York State Troopers zoomed behind them in hot pursuit.

A nail automatically went into her mouth. "We're in trouble now. You have to pull over."

"Nonsense."

When Autumn glanced again, the cruisers did U-turns through the highway divider and sped in the opposite direction.

Dante shrugged then winked. "Apparently, they're after someone else. Don't worry."

They pulled onto campus. It was larger than she expected, based on the photos she'd seen online. They parked by the

Eugene Levy Fieldhouse. The building sported the name *Rockland Community College.*

She sat in silence, not believing this fateful day had finally arrived. She sucked in a breath, exhaling slowly.

Dante parked in the lot and turned to her. "We should go, I don't want you to be late."

Autumn glimpsed at the clock. Damn. He was right. She had fifteen minutes to spare before her first class, and she was entirely unfamiliar with this new campus. When she stepped out, a guy with plaited braids approached them, holding up a balled fist to her boyfriend. "Cool car, bro."

Dante raised his fist as if to strike him. Autumn pressed her fist to his instead.

"Thank you," she said warmly.

Dante stared the boy down as he walked away.

"He was paying you a compliment, not looking to start a fight," she explained. "I guess you've never heard of a fist bump?"

Dante winked. "I've bumped fists many times. It never ends well for the other party."

They made their way to the central courtyard. Students and faculty hustled along carrying textbooks, backpacks, and hot foam cups filled with coffee. Autumn inhaled, watching the chaos. Where was she supposed to go? She didn't know where her first class was.

She rustled through a folder in the main compartment of her bag for her schedule and map she'd printed the day before.

"Okay, my first class is Chemistry." She compared two pieces of paper side by side. "Where's Academic I?"

"Here." Dante pointed. Of course, he was right.

They walked to the Academic I building, hand in hand. The lights blinked and flickered as they made their way through the hall. Autumn wished she could understand why the lights danced in a frenzy every time he was around.

They arrived at a well-occupied lecture hall. A silver projector streamed light over a white scrolled screen.

"I have to go. Thanks again for bringing me."

"I'll see you later. I can't wait to hear all about your first day."

She pulled away slowly, waving goodbye, before slipping into the room. Autumn wished Dante could have accompanied her. Too bad he already graduated.

Entering the room was intimidating, and Autumn kept her eyes on the ground. Darkness set in, except for the projector displaying slides of the periodic table. When she scanned the room, she discovered a free seat in the center. Quietly, she unzipped her backpack and grabbed a marble notebook and a pen, preparing herself for the lesson.

Until—a tap on the shoulder startled her. She whipped around, mouth hanging open.

No, no, no! She resisted the urge to pack up her stuff and change her seat. The lesson had already begun. Dizziness set in, crushing her senses.

"What are you doing here?" she hissed.

"I could ask you the same question." Caleb's sapphire eyes gleamed in the shadows. "I thought you were accepted at UPenn?"

"That's none of your business."

He shrugged. "Have you decided on a major? Mine is Chem."

"Well, good for you." She turned back around until the hard cap of Caleb's pen dug into her shoulder, grazing against a pressure point. "Ouch."

"What's the deal with you and that brute, Dante? Is he your boyfriend?" People turned and stared at them.

"It's none of your business."

"Quiet!" the professor commanded.

Autumn whipped around and didn't move a muscle. Caleb snickered.

Stealthily, she rumbled through her backpack and turned on her phone, signing into the RCC website. There had to be another open Chemistry class. *No such luck.* All of them were full. She frowned, horrified to no end that they would be stuck together for the rest of the semester.

Trembling, she grabbed her pen and took scattered lecture notes, barely able to focus on the lesson. All she could hear was Caleb's breathing and the pull of his number two pencil against looseleaf. He reeked of cheap body spray that lingered with his every movement. She'd once found the smell appealing, but now it evoked nauseating memories.

She wanted to be rid of him forever.

Class continued for two and a half more torturous hours. Time came to a standstill. And this was only the first day. She had to survive a semester of this hell.

At the end of the session, when the lights came back on, she recalled little of the lesson. Inhaling a breath, she packed her belongings. This was going to be a long, horrible semester.

When four o'clock rolled around, Autumn was already outside sitting on a bench waiting for Dante. Day one went by in a whirlwind, and now she navigated through a steep pile of homework. She had no recollection of what she'd learned in Chemistry, Calculus, English, or Speech class, which was easily her least favorite course in the lineup. She cringed at the recollection of her stuttering and eating her words. All thanks to *Caleb* ruining her day.

Dante rolled up in his Ferrari, right on the dot. She climbed in, totally stressed out. At least she understood what college entailed. Now, she only had to worry about how she'd survive.

Twenty-Six

WHEN AUTUMN ARRIVED home with Dante, the windows of the house were dark, and her Neon was the only car parked in the driveway.

She headed inside, but Dante didn't follow.

"I'll be up in a minute," he said, sitting in the car. "I have a couple of calls to make."

Autumn nodded. She went into the kitchen, grabbed two bottles of water and granola bars, and headed upstairs to her room to complete her excessive amount of homework.

She sprawled on her bed with her Calculus textbook. Pressing a loose strand of hair behind her ear, she read the directions she'd scribbled down while half listening during class.

Within minutes, she realized computing limits *sucked*. Every question she attempted, she failed. Frustrated, she raked her fingers through her curls, ready to tear them from her pounding head. Why was this so difficult? Curse Caleb for being in her class.

She couldn't let this situation with Caleb get the best of

her. And worst of all, what would she tell Dante? Maybe she didn't have to mention him at all. It wasn't her fault, and she knew how uncomfortable Caleb made him.

In the middle of panicking, two heavy boots hit the floor. She looked up, shocked to see Dante standing in her room, when she never heard him enter.

"How did you get in here?"

His mouth fell crooked. "I climbed."

Autumn glanced and her window remained locked. Could he be that quiet? Or was she too preoccupied she didn't hear him arrive?

"I have a front door too, you know," she stated matter-of-factly. "It seems to work well enough for everyone else."

His amber eyes twinkled as he gave her a gaze of admiration that made her stop asking questions. "Are you all right?"

Autumn cyclically massaged her temples. "I'm fine," she lied, positive he wouldn't be able to handle the truth even if she told him.

"Just fine?" He raised a brow.

"Yeah."

A long pause hung in the air before he replied. "Well, I think you're lying."

Her stomach fell through the floor as he stripped her bare with his gaze. "Wha—"

"Don't bother to deny it, I consider myself an excellent judge of character." He caressed her cheek. "You've been acting bizarre the whole way home. You know you can talk to me, don't you? What's the issue?"

Autumn stared back at him. What gave her away? She didn't want to lie, but she knew full well she had to tell him *something*, because he wouldn't settle for nothing.

"Well..." She glanced at the bed before meeting his penetrating stare. "I'm having trouble with my homework." It was the best she could come up with, and it wasn't a lie. But even so, she felt foolish admitting it aloud. Dante graduated and had a career and real responsibilities. But he asked for her honesty, and this was partially true.

"Do you mind if I have a look?"

Autumn gave him her textbook. Dante snickered and shook his head. "You can't be serious? This is what they have you learning at that school of yours?"

Her blood pressure rose in her veins at his insensitive remark. How dare he imply she's *stupid!*

"What exactly are you hinting at?"

Dante stared at her with initial surprise. "This math is simplistic. I learned it ages ago when I was a small child."

"You think I'm an idiot?" She ripped the textbook from his hands. "And you're some kind of child prodigy?"

A neutral expression overtook his face. "Did you hear me *say* the word *idiot*?"

"No, but you implied it."

"Perhaps I implied your lesson seems rather basic."

Autumn's patience slipped. She shoved open her bedroom window, the sun setting in the distance. The full moon peaked beneath the clouds.

"Feel free to leave the way you came in!" Her voice echoed through the stillness of the front yard. An elderly neighbor taking the trash out stopped and stared. Autumn withdrew from the window, flushed with embarrassment.

"And what if I refuse to comply?" Dante tilted his head to the side.

"What are you doing?"

He moved so close the warmth of his breath flowed against her neck, giving her goosebumps. "What a feisty one you are."

"What are you talking about?" She made a face, nose wrinkled. "Stop being a jerk."

"I've never seen this side of you before." He grazed her hand. "I have to admit, you look even more beautiful when you're cross."

Dante leaned over and she fell flat against her comforter. Her book and pen landed on the floor. "I find you irresistible. Tell me once more you wish for me to leave."

When she opened her mouth to protest, he leaned down and kissed her. Autumn wrapped her legs around his waist, fingers clinging to the loose strands of his ink-black hair. The previous anger she'd experienced faded away. All she could focus on were his firm hands pressed against her hips, the satin smoothness of his lips, and their ragged breathing.

"Do you like that?" He dragged his lips and warm breath over her neck, skin pricking down the deepest depths of her spine.

Autumn bit her bottom lip hard. She didn't want him to hear just how much she did. But it was no use; noises slipped out against her will.

Dante ran his palm against her navel, reaching underneath her shirt. "Is it all right if I—"

"Yes."

Autumn kissed him while removing more clothing. His black-gloved hands caressed her body when suddenly he stopped. Dante pulled away, helping her to a seated position. She stared at him, her core and chest tightening.

"What's wrong?"

"Your father is here."

Autumn popped a blind, and sure enough, his vehicle was parked in the driveway. She was surprised Dante heard him roll up. How humiliating it would have been if her dad walked in on them. Not a conversation she wanted to have.

A series of hollow footsteps were followed by a knock at her door.

"Come in."

The door creaked open, and her dad popped his head inside with a smile that immediately faded.

"Autumn...and *Dante*. What are you up to?"

A cool breeze blew by. Crap, she forgot to pull her shirt over her stomach. It clung to the edge of her bra. Ears and neck burning, she freed the fabric.

"Dante's helping me study." Her palms sweat against the edge of her t-shirt. "He's great at Calculus."

"Is that so?"

"Yes," Dante interjected.

Based on Dante's one-word answer, Autumn could tell he sensed the awkwardness of the situation. Dante glanced several times at the window.

Her dad glowered at Dante before leaving the room but not before he muttered, "*and rounding second base.*"

When the door finally closed, Autumn's heart thrummed in her ears. *How mortifying*. She ran her fingers through her hair while Dante stared out the window.

"I'm sorry." She grimaced. When she went to touch his shoulder to reassure him all was well, he pulled away. Instead, he opened the window and jumped down two stories, landing upright on his feet. He climbed into his car and drove off, exhaust swirling. The full moon gleamed in the center of the sky.

Autumn blinked, unable to determine whether her imagination played tricks on her. Trembling, her heart clenched. She headed downstairs, wiping a stray tear from her cheek. Her dad sat on the couch sipping a glass of sangria.

"Dad, I hope you're happy." Autumn placed a hand on her hip. "Dante left."

Her dad shrugged, never bothering to look at her. "What a shame, I didn't hear him go. Was he too afraid to say goodbye to me, or is he just plain rude?"

"He jumped out the window. I didn't get a goodbye either..."

"Is that how he comes to see you?"

"No. I think he can tell that you don't like him—"

Her dad glanced at her. "I said it once, and I'll say it again. I don't trust him." He paused. "Has he had you over at his house yet? Have you met his family?"

Autumn shook her head, realizing she'd done neither. He'd only ever mentioned his cousins, Ronan and Armienti. But in his defense, she never asked.

"You were *never* like this when mom was alive." She sniffed. "She would've understood."

He grew quiet for a moment before continuing, "Also, I know you were *studying*, or whatever you want to call it. My only hope is that you two *studied* safely."

Her jaw fell open. This was humiliating on a whole other level. She never wanted to have *this* conversation with her dad.

She turned on her heel and left feet stomping.

She flopped on her bed, tears streaming, grabbing her phone. The end of another awful day. When she went to call her boyfriend to make sure he was okay, a text message landed in her inbox.

Autumn swiped up. It was her dad.

I'm tired of fighting with you about Dante. I love you too much to let him ruin our relationship. Invite him over for dinner one of these nights, and I promise I'll attempt to get to know him.

After reading his message, she was frustrated with herself for not thinking of the idea sooner.

Okay... but only if you promise.

A few minutes would pass before his reply came.

I promise.

This was her one chance to help her dad to realize how wonderful her boyfriend was. Maybe he was a little rough around the edges. Maybe he put his foot in his mouth and pulled stupid stunts to get her attention. But he was a good person, who listened to her thoughts and feelings. Who cared for her.

She wanted her dad to like him as much as she did. It was time to set him straight about her boyfriend once and for all.

Twenty-Seven

THAT WAS TOO CLOSE.

Dante arrived back at his ship mere moments before the full moon shined at its highest in the sky.

He was furious with himself—twice he failed to monitor the moon phases. However, this time was different. He posed a threat to Autumn's life.

Strangely, he'd always remembered to track them before, but he didn't want to miss any opportunity to see her. His *girlfriend*. Dante could still taste her on his lips and wanted nothing more than to hold her in his arms.

Striding through the central corridor, Dante seethed with anger and made no secret of it. He was enraged every second of every day, except for when he was with Autumn. Somehow, life became more bearable.

Now he was especially angry because he had an obligation to fulfill. One he had neglected since the crash.

He strode to the cockpit, still decorated with Ronan's handiwork. Pressing a faint admiral-blue glowing button, he sent out a silent signal. A speaker popped and crackled, followed by a series of inaudible whispers.

"XD2X, this is Dante Martyne." He crossed his arms. "Advise me on your scheduled arrival date." He'd been informed it would take one Earth year to acquire a replacement vessel, but he hoped the status had changed in the meantime.

"Greetings, Master Dante. Our anticipated arrival date is day 168 of the year 2024." Dante smoothed his palms roughly over his face. He still couldn't believe this had happened to him. He was marooned on an alien planet and a year behind schedule. He'd have to answer to the Grand Supreme for failure to produce his most prized conquest in a timely manner.

At this rate, he wouldn't see his home planet again for a long while yet.

"That's absolutely unacceptable!" Dante crashed his fist against the control counsel. "You had better step up your pace. I swear if you haven't arrived well before that date, there will be hell to pay."

The gasps and whispers of his inferiors became frantic on the other end before he hit disconnect. He sighed furiously, resting his head in his hands.

What had he done to deserve a life such as this one? Sometimes he felt like it would have been better if he hadn't been born at all. His crimes were innumerable and counting.

Dante's stomach tumbled with sickness, thoughts returning to Autumn. The way she shouted at him, commanding him around like a General. He had to admit, no one had ever challenged him before, not even Maeve. It was immensely exciting. His human girlfriend was filled with surprises.

What he implied was rude and hurtful, and honestly, he wasn't sure why he brought it up at all. It wasn't her fault her planet was woefully behind in both education and technology.

A vibration emanated from his pocket. His heart stopped. It was Autumn.

"Hello?"

"Hey," she said. "I just wanted to make sure you got home okay. And I want to apologize for the way my dad behaved. That was super awkward."

"I feel I owe you an apology as well." It was one of the few times in his life he needed to issue an apology. "I didn't mean to poke fun at your lesson."

"I know. I was already having a bad day."

"You can talk to me, Autumn. You know that, don't you?"

A long pause.

"I know. That's why I called. Are you free this Friday evening? You know, four days from now." She chuckled. Dante was glad she found some sort of humor in his inability to master the calendar.

"Yes, why?"

"I want you to come to dinner at my house, so you can get to know my dad better. He didn't mean what he said earlier."

"I'll be there."

"Okay, sounds cool. I'm glad you're all right. I'll see you then. Have a goodnight."

"Goodnight."

Dante stayed on long enough to hear her disconnect, enjoying the melody of her sweet voice.

A dinner party, how lovely. With a man who *loathed* him. A man he didn't particularly care for himself.

Twenty-Eight

DANTE WANTED to make an excellent impression and dressed to impress. Clean clothes, fresh gloves, and shining obsidian boots. As Friday progressed, he decided to surprise Autumn early, although she had never told him her schedule.

Dante experienced the overwhelming need to know where she was at all times, for safety reasons. Or so he convinced himself over the passing months.

The air was crisper than usual. The sun glowed high in the sky, casting long shadows through the walkway trees. Never did he think the day would come where he developed a fondness for a human servant. But he no longer cared, he was beyond reason.

After he entered the Monroe Diner, his stomach grumbled with false anticipation. They weren't scheduled to eat for at least a few more hours. If dinner tasted anything like the burgers and fries he ate at the Galleria, he needed all the room he could get.

He scoured the restaurant for his girlfriend. Autumn scrubbed away at a mountain of plates. Suds trickled onto her sunlit uniform. Dante couldn't understand why she'd insisted she was a *waitress* and not a *servant*. To him, the terms were interchangeable. Perhaps she was ashamed of her station, but with him, there was no need to be.

Marcela lorded over her like a taskmaster. She yelled, tossing endless dishes into the murky body of water, drenching Autumn repeatedly.

Dante thought to punish her for her insolence, but Autumn was in too close range. *There will be time later on.* Marcela glanced his way and passed through the swinging doors, leaving Autumn to labor.

Dante crossed his arms as Marcela walked over to him, menu in hand. She flashed a yellow-toothed grin. Bile rose from his stomach, biting against his esophagus at the smell of her.

"Can I help you, sir?" Marcela stared at him with her beady eyes.

"It's *sire,* actually," he emphasized.

Marcela stared at him blankly.

"Go fetch Autumn."

"And who are you?" Marcela scrunched her nose.

"I've asked you once, I will not ask you again." He snapped in her face. Other dining humans stared at him, but he didn't care if they disapproved of his behavior.

Marcela stuttered inaudibly. Good. His patience had grown paper thin.

Autumn reemerged with her moonlit, childlike gaze. Her uniform was soiled with remnants of food and wetness.

"Do you know this guy?" Marcela whispered in Autumn's ear.

"Yes, he's my boyfriend."

Marcela threw up her hands in the air in protest and waddled back through the door from which she came. Finally, *good riddance.*

"What are you doing here?" Autumn shifted her weight from side to side. "Dinner isn't for another few hours."

"I wished to surprise you." His mouth sat crooked. "I'm your boyfriend, isn't that reason enough?"

"You're right." She smiled tentatively. "I'm sorry. I'm a mess."

"You're beautiful." He reassured her, taking her hand in his. Her cheeks flushed. It was true. She was as lovely as any star in the sky. What made her lovelier still was her modesty.

"Thanks, well, you're right on time. Let me grab my stuff. My shift is over."

* * *

How did Dante know I had work? And better yet, how did he know my shift ended at exactly 3:15 p.m.? Autumn never provided him with her schedule.

She sucked in a breath as they walked together through the parking lot. It couldn't be a coincidence. There were too many oddities, and they didn't add up.

Dante led her home, but she redirected him.

"I need to go to the supermarket first."

They entered the store, where she grabbed a red shopping basket and a sticky note containing her shopping list. Autumn scanned the ingredients for the pizza she planned to make. It was one of the few meals she was confident would taste fine. She was no chef, but she still wanted to impress her boyfriend.

"Hmm." She scanned the list. "I need mozzarella cheese, basil, fresh dough, and pizza sauce."

When she glanced at Dante, he was acting odd.

He squinted into the fluorescent lights as they rapidly flickered above his head. It was more apparent because the supermarket was so bright. There was no earthly explanation for the phenomenon.

"There go the lights again," she said, but he ignored her remark.

Instead, he analyzed every product that occupied the shelves, distracted in a way she'd never seen before. She wondered if he suffered from social anxiety or, worse—someone was out to hurt him. Either way, he acted like it was his first time in a supermarket.

"Dante?" She raised her voice an octave.

He ignored her, holding a bag of potato chips away from his body like an active bomb. His eyes roved over the package repeatedly like he'd never seen chips before in his life. *Weird.* People stared at him as they walked by. Her cheeks heated from the attention.

"Dante!" She waved her hand in his face. He snapped out of his daze, snatching her palm and kissing it.

Autumn exhaled. "Is pizza okay?"

"What's that?"

Autumn gasped, her jaw falling to the floor. His response was confirmation. He had to be from some remote country, still undiscovered. Or else, he was an alien from outer space.

Now that she thought of it, she had no clue where he originated from. Dante had skillfully avoided her question like the plague. She was mad at herself for not pressing him harder, but now was neither the time nor the place to bring this up.

"You really don't know what pizza is?"

"I've honestly never heard of it."

"I promise you're in for a real treat. It's my specialty." She smiled uneasily.

Twenty-Nine

WHY DO *shelves have to be so high off the ground?* Autumn thought as she struggled to reach well over her head. Her fingertips scraped against a can of *Don Pepino* pizza sauce. When she glanced up, wondering why her six foot plus boyfriend neglected to help her, instead she saw Caleb stood next to her.

A wave of dizzying heat crashed through her body, leaving her weak. Desperate to cool down, she fanned her hand against her beading face.

"Do you need some help?" Caleb brushed past Dante and placed the can into her basket.

Stunned, she uttered, "Thank you." She so did *not* need this right now.

"Doing a little shopping, I see?" Caleb made small talk.

"Have you come to finish what you've started with me?" Dante's muscles tensed.

Caleb glimpsed at Dante. "Easy there, buddy. Autumn and I are old friends. Isn't that right?" He winked.

Autumn rolled her eyes.

"Get away from us."

"Geez, no need to overreact." Caleb twisted his red cap over his unruly ink-black curls. "I just wanted to say hi."

"Well, you've overstayed your welcome."

Caleb finally got Dante's not-so-subtle hint and walked toward the end of the aisle. Before he rounded the corner, he waved at her. "I'll see you in Chem."

As his words registered, Autumn's stomach plummeted. Dante narrowed his eyes. *If looks could kill, she'd already be dead.* Dante purposefully brushed past her. Autumn's hands shook at the realization she had betrayed him.

The air temperature stabilized as soon as Dante left.

* * *

Dante sat on the walkway outside, mind racing a million kilometers a second. His delicate pupils burned from the bright lights of the store and a migraine pounded in his skull from the entire ordeal. He couldn't believe Autumn *withheld* information from him, and that wretch Caleb had been in on it the entire time. His fists clenched. *How he wanted to kill him.*

He couldn't fathom why she would lie unless there was an unspoken bond between them she was hiding. Worse still, he was furious at himself for letting this human facade play out for so long. He'd been lying to her since the night they met. No matter how disappointed he was in her indiscretion, the illusion he created was unforgivable.

Before long, he sensed Autumn's life force. He stood abruptly and sauntered away.

"Dante, wait!" she shouted.

He ignored her, still processing the situation.

"Please wait!"

He doubled his speed.

"We need to talk about this." Desperation cracked through her voice.

He whipped around. Autumn caught her breath.

"You lied to me and broke our trust. You failed to mention Caleb goes to your school."

She frowned. "Can you blame me?"

Autumn turned and walked off. Dante experienced a brief wave of panic. He pursued her.

"What do you mean?" He matched her speed.

"Seriously?" She kept walking. Dante raced and stopped her dead in her tracks.

"No, tell me. Tell me what's wrong."

Her innocent gray eyes met his. "It's like you become a different person around him. You're angry and aggressive, and honestly, it scares me a little."

His chest tightened. "So you're afraid of me?" He sought further clarification, insecurities surfacing.

"I'm not afraid of you, but I don't like the person you turn into around him. I don't like Caleb either. But still..."

Autumn shrugged, brushing past him. Dante took the bag from her hands, palm resting on the small of her back.

"Well, that was never my intention. I never meant to frighten you. You're important to me, you know that don't you?"

Her rosy cheeks blossomed. "You're important to me, too. That's why I'm having you over for dinner. I want my dad to see how wonderful you are."

Wonderful, his lips bowed. Nobody had ever referred to him as *wonderful* before. Dante had been called many terms throughout the course of his young life. Brute, soulless demon, the devil incarnate. Essentially, every swear word in existence. Never once had anyone highlighted his positive attributes. And he had to admit, he rather liked the compliment. Especially because it came from Autumn's mouth. Her perception made him want to try to be a better man.

His chest warmed, another first for him. "Thank you. I find you wonderful as well."

They sauntered silently, then she said, "You know I was thinking, after dinner maybe I can come to your house and meet your parents."

Dammit. He knew this topic was bound to arise. Somehow, he didn't think it was the best course of action, considering the circumstances. Where would he ever find two humans to pose as his parents on such short notice? His gut twisted with anxiety, but he remained cool and collected on the outside.

"Actually, my home is in a state of disrepair. and my parents aren't home. But I promise you, if they were here, I'd gladly introduce you."

"Okay, we'll take a raincheck then."

He nodded, grateful to have her off his back for the time being. He knew he couldn't ignore the situation forever.

Thirty

WHEN THEY ARRIVED at Autumn's home, Dante was relieved her father's car was nowhere to be found. His presence only ever made matters worse. *They had all night long to suffer.*

Dante was intrigued by Autumn's living situation. It differed greatly from his own. Small and quaint, but not necessarily in a bad way.

While Autumn stood in the eating area unpacking her bag, he stumbled upon a dark brown wooden case containing ancient, withered books and cameras. Dante had only ever seen such primeval technology in manuscripts he'd studied back home.

"Those used to belong to my mom. She loved reading and photography. I think I got my love of reading from her."

"Fascinating."

Next, he wandered to a silver ice box. Pinned on the front sat an image of a female human baby with suspiciously poofy hair and bright gray eyes that smiled, although her expression was serious. She sat on a cushion half-clothed with a fluffy brown animal in hand.

"Is this you?"

"Yes." Her cheeks flushed crimson. "I asked my dad to take it down, but he never listens."

"I'm glad he didn't. You were magnificent even then."

For an unexpected second, Dante wondered what his and Autumn's children might look like. Without a doubt, they'd have beautiful eyes and full heads of hair. But other than that, he couldn't conceive of their likenesses. A mixture of his race and hers hadn't occurred in recent times.

Autumn punched the numbers **4-5-0** into a cooking device. A frequency hummed and rose. She took the tan malleable ball and kneaded it over a metal sheet.

"Do you cook?"

Dante bit his cheeks and willed away the intense urge to laugh. "Never would I ever cook, that's *woman's work*. But I do enjoy a sumptuous meal."

Autumn furrowed her brows. "Take off your gloves, you're going to help me."

Glancing sidelong, he wondered if someone else was in the room, But they were indeed alone. Groaning, he dragged his feet over to her. The way she stared at him with *those* eyes, he couldn't deny her request.

Fortunately, nobody could see him now. They'd laugh their asses off.

Dante reluctantly removed his gloves and spread the red liquid over the flattened ball. Autumn's lips curved, deriving joy from putting him to work. Dante hated to admit, but it wasn't as terrible as he thought.

When they finished, Autumn sliced the white ball into slivers. They arranged them over the liquid and placed the tray into the cooking device. She punched in the number **20** and left a pair of cushioned gloves on the table.

"I'm running upstairs to freshen up. Can you take the pizza out when the oven beeps if I'm not back?"

He nodded. Her directions were simplistic enough.

* * *

Woman's work? What was wrong with him? It was like he was from a different century. If he wanted to be with her, Dante was in for a rude awakening.

When she finished freshening up, she heard her phone buzzing away, but it was nowhere to be found. Autumn crawled on all fours and furiously searched until she found it beneath a pile of her laundry. Lauren was calling her on FaceTime.

Autumn answered.

"What's up, girl?" Lauren grinned, her hair glowing across the screen.

"I'm making dinner."

"Ooh fun! What are you having?"

"Pizza. How's college going?"

Lauren sighed. "It's good, I guess. It's just weird being away from home. You know?"

Autumn nodded, hearing the pizza buzzer in the background.

"I can imagine."

"And my dorm mate is such a slob!" Lauren whirled her phone around. There were bras and shoes thrown everywhere. Kind of like her own closet.

The buzzer continued. Why didn't Dante take the pizza out like she asked him to?

"Lauren, I'm sorry, can I call you back? Dante's here."

"Aww. You're making dinner for your boo."

"Call you back." Autumn ended the chat.

She sprinted downstairs and stopped dead, hands trembling. Autumn watched in horror as her boyfriend removed the pizza tray from the oven. *Gloveless.*

What an idiot.

Tears burned in the corners of her eyes. In a frenzy, she grabbed his hands, shoving them into the sink and turning on the ice-cold water.

"Why would you do something so stupid?" Autumn choked. She held him under, warm salty tears trickled down her cheeks.

Dante's facial expression remained painfully neutral.

"Let me see your hands." She prepared to dial 911.

Stopping the faucet, she braced herself for the sight of bloody, mangled skin. After all, if she was planning to be a doctor, she needed to be prepared. But—

His flesh was unscathed.

"I don't understand," she stuttered. Dante stared at her wordlessly.

A thought raced through her mind. Perhaps she'd forgotten to turn on the oven. That had to be the case. She opened the front door and met with a thick cloud of heat rushing into her face. The pizza bubbled, cooling in the pan.

"But I saw you. Didn't you just—"

"I should get going," he said abruptly and brushed past her.

"Wait!" she shouted, running after him. "How...I don't understand."

The front door opened from around the corner and slammed. When she went to pursue him, she collided with her dad.

Thirty-One

DINNER WAS SILENT. Autumn's eyes met with her dad's, and he shot her a look that screamed *Dante isn't worth your time*. She'd told him she and Dante had a "fight," and he left shortly before dinner. It was the quickest and most believable excuse she could come up with, considering the circumstances.

It was certainly better than explaining to him what really happened. She witnessed the impossible and couldn't think of any logical explanation. Dante reached into a burning oven bare handed and emerged unscathed. More unsettling, he'd disappeared into thin air without a trace.

Her mind raced with possibilities, but whatever the case, he'd clearly been keeping secrets from her all along. It was frustrating to admit her friends and dad picked up on it long before she did.

She could sit idly and wonder all night, but there was only one person who could answer her questions. She quietly excused herself, leaving her dad at the kitchen table.

Inside her bedroom, she scrolled through her recent calls,

attempting to reach Dante once, twice, *three* times. No answer. A pit twisted in her stomach.

Glancing at his phone number, [X] [X] [X] [X], she reprimanded herself for being so stupid. What kind of number was that? Why did she never question this before? There were so many inconsistencies she ignored because she liked him.

Who wore gloves 24/7 on the hottest of summer days? She picked up the pair of gloves he'd left behind. When she tried them on, she had to admit, weirdly, they were comfortable. Like an alien skin. A shiver rattled through her core.

* * *

The weekend flew by, and Dante never called. By Monday morning, Autumn had chewed her nails to nubs. She had a sinking feeling in her chest, and although her personal life fell apart, she still had college to contend with.

She didn't need to be late for class.

Autumn arrived on campus with time to spare. She climbed off the bus and began her trek across the courtyard to Academic 1. It was her first Chemistry lab after a week of lectures.

The lab room was typical, filled with rows of tables, silver metal stools, and a chalkboard with the periodic table of elements.

Autumn glanced around, searching for a spare seat. She spotted Caleb wearing his typical bright red cap, despite being taught *not* to do that in settings like this.

She tried to walk the other way when he waved, attracting everyone's attention. "Autumn, over here."

Autumn glowered, not wanting to make a scene.

"What?" she hissed.

A twenty-something year old teacher's aide entered the room, and she scrambled into the seat beside Caleb. Ignoring him, she dug through her backpack, pulling out a pen and notebook. Caleb's sapphire eyes burned through her. Why couldn't he ever just leave her be?

"I want to apologize to you."

"For?" She raised a brow. A simple sorry wouldn't do, even if he tried.

"I ruined our relationship."

Autumn removed the cap from her ballpoint pen. "It's fine. I'm over it."

"No, it's not." He tried to play footsie with her underneath the table. She moved to the far end of the stool.

"Stop it please, I don't want to talk about this anymore."

Caleb's long lashes grazed his cheeks. "Why didn't you tell your *boyfriend* we're in the same class?"

"Mind your own business."

While they bickered, the aide took attendance.

"You were afraid of what he would do if he found out we were together."

Autumn made a face. "Don't be ridiculous. I'm not afraid of him."

Caleb paused and said, "So you're aware, I could have kicked his ass at The Castle. He should've known better than going up against a state champion."

"And just so you're aware, I think you're an asshole," Autumn said. No one cared about his taekwondo "prowess." Caleb stared at the table frustratedly.

Autumn wrote the date on her paper while the aide rifled through his satchel. From the corner of her eye, she caught Caleb staring at her. *What now?*

"Autumn please," Caleb murmured. "We really need to talk. There's so much I need to tell you, and I'd prefer not to do it here."

"There's nothing to talk about," she snapped. "You made your decision, and I made mine."

"Autumn, Caleb," The teacher's aide addressed them, horn-rimmed glasses sliding to the edge of his burnished nose. They stopped talking and stared at the lab instructor. All eyes were on them. Autumn's cheeks heated with embarrassment. How loud were they speaking?

"You two seem well acquainted."

"Yeah, we graduated from high school together," Caleb announced.

"Perfect, I'm assigning you as lab partners for the rest of the semester."

Caleb grinned like a jackal, and a wave of nausea rolled through Autumn's gut. She would rather go to jail than have to endure partnering with him for the next *four* months.

He moved closer and subjected her to the sickening scent of his pungent body spray. There was a time when Autumn would have welcomed a situation like this, but high school had long since concluded. Hurtful words were exchanged, and Caleb showed his true colors. As far as she was concerned, he lost the right to be her friend.

Lab dragged on at a snail's pace, and every so often, Autumn sneaked a peek at her phone, hoping Dante tried to contact her. Every time she checked her heart sank further into her chest.

Maybe it was a tall order to expect he'd be more mature because he was a few years older. Being ghosted hurt, but secretly she wondered if he thought of her.

The conclusion of lab couldn't have come any faster. Caleb said goodbye, and she flat-out ignored him. She'd have to practice this technique for the remainder of the semester. She needed all the mental clarity she could muster for her next class.

Speech was in Academic II, and as soon as she walked through the doorway, her stomach plummeted. What she didn't need right now was to stand in front of a group of quiet, staring people and speak on the cliche subject of *world peace*. Placing a finger in her mouth, she chewed her nail.

The class filled quickly, with students who looked equally uncomfortable to be there. Some shook while reviewing their index cards, others turned suspiciously off color.

It was Autumn's rotten luck that she was selected first. But in her experience, bad events happened in threes. Dante, Caleb, and *this*. Life couldn't get much worse.

She navigated her way to the front of her class, fiddling with her note cards. Autumn stood there in complete silence, trying hard not to make eye contact.

The cards fell to the floor with a *slap!* She knelt to pick them up while a few kind people handed her the strays that had fallen beneath their desks. When Autumn stood up, her vision narrowed.

"I'm not feeling well," she told her professor.

He assessed her with his cerulean eyes. "Do you need someone to bring you to the nurse's office?"

"No, thank you. I'll walk myself."

Autumn gathered her belongings and left. As soon as she exited, she could breathe again.

She never went to the nurse's office. Instead, she sat on a bench in front of the library and enjoyed what little sunlight remained in the sky. A positive sign, perhaps.

She shot Dante another text. *Please call me back.*

As she feared, *Undeliverable* flashed in red.

Thirty-Two

DANTE WASN'T sure what had gotten into him on this planet. From the night of the crash forward, he neglected to make a single preparation for his conquest of Earth. A mission supported by his father and assigned to him by the Grand Supreme Emperor himself. He'd been selected over his superiors Keyserike and Valdez, the Grand Supreme's other two favorites, for his efficiency at his work.

He had a *slight* reputation throughout the twenty-four universes. Typically, when his distinctive ship landed on a planet, the inhabitants ran for cover.

At least the intelligent ones. The foolish ones challenged him, which to date, never resulted in their favor. Or they surrendered and gave him what he was after.

Earth was a different story altogether. It existed in the most remote of all the universes, Universe 1. Here, he was not someone of great accord, and traveled around under the radar. Though he yearned to go home, he rather enjoyed the freedom being stranded afforded him. He'd give anything to escape the Grand Supreme's influence if only for a year of his life. He'd been under his control for the last twenty.

On Earth, he suffered his first ever setback, and for good reason. Too bad it was impossible to resurrect the pilot and the tech from the dead. For if he could, he would thank them for their oversight.

Because of them, he'd discovered Autumn. Now, there were three problems.

One, he'd slipped up and revealed to Autumn he wasn't human in a less than ideal way. He was slowly working up to telling her the truth.

Two, he came to Earth on a mission he was expected to complete.

And three—

A fist cracked across his jaw, sending him airborne. Shadows and a stream of pale lights flooded his eyes before his body collided with a tree, demolishing the stretch of forest in its path.

Dante laid amidst the rubble, rasping to catch his breath. Red radiated across his vision. Warm, salty blood trickled down his chin. He slid his tongue over his teeth, fortunate they were still intact. He spit the metallic taste from his mouth, aching from head to toe.

"What on Earth has gotten into you, cousin?" Armienti yelled, a stream of white crescent moonlight shimmering through his golden hair. "Your technique is suddenly shoddy."

Dante ignored his cousin. From the ground, he admired the twinkling stars flitting around like embers from an open flame. A dream wide awake haunted him.

He turned his head and was met with a pair of luminescent gray eyes.

"Oh, Dante." Maeve traced her fingertip against his bicep. "Do you know what I'd like?"

"What?" Dante kissed her hand, concrete cool against his

back. Aircrafts zipped overhead, double crescent moons and stars peaking along the sparkling horizon.

"Never mind." She crossed her arms. "I can't tell you unless you promise to say yes."

He rested his head against her shoulder. "Well, I can't say yes unless you tell me what you want."

She giggled, curls falling on his face. "You already know."

"You know I'd give you anything, but not that."

"It's not fair I never get to go with you." Maeve stood up and marched over to the rooftop railing, pouting. "I'm tired of being left behind."

"I'm afraid it's out of the question. It's too dangerous." Dante followed and took her hand, but she pulled away.

"Just say yes this one time and I promise I'll never ask again."

He folded his arms, and she batted her eyes.

"Please, please."

"Okay, fine. Just this once."

While drifting in and out of thought, a faint vibration emanated from his communicator. It was Autumn.

He sighed and clicked decline. It was her every time he checked over the course of the last few days. What was he supposed to tell her?

Hello Autumn, I've been lying to you the entire time.

Dante pushed himself off the ground, wiping his bloody face against his arms. He resumed a fighting stance, charging Armienti head on, striking him square in the nose. Armienti's teeth ground together and he toppled into a series of jagged boulders.

BOOM! Rubble exploded, gravel and dust flying about.

Armienti pulled twigs and branches from his frazzled hair. "Ouch."

Dante chuckled. Oh, how he enjoyed one-upping his pretty younger cousin. While he reveled, his communicator shook again.

Armienti brushed himself off. "Are you going to answer your damn communicator already, or shall I?"

Dante once again identified the caller as Autumn for the *ninth* time that evening.

Hesitantly, he slid his finger over the answer, and the decline button. His cousin sauntered closer. Leaning over Dante's shoulder, he peeked at his communicator.

"What's the matter? Have you tired of your Earthen beauty already?" He chuckled. "I didn't see that one coming."

Dante pulled away and finally settled on the decline button. The safer of the two options.

Armienti continued, "She was a fun run, was she not? She certainly lasted longer than the others. Except for Maeve."

"I don't want to talk about this."

"Her eyes sure remind me of Maeve's."

Dante ignored Armienti and grabbed his chest plated uniform top from the muddy ground. He slung it over his shoulder and made his way through the maze of woodland.

"What, Dante? What is it?" Armienti jogged after him, boots crunching against the damp, fallen branches and leaves. "I'm sorry, Dante. I'm sorry." Suddenly, Armienti halted in his tracks. "You love her, don't you?"

He wasn't listening before, but Armienti's statement grabbed his attention this time around.

Dante whirled around, willing his features into a scowl. "I love only myself. Don't be preposterous."

"Save it," Armienti said. "You're not fooling anyone, for the walls of your cabin are thin. I hear the way you whisper sweet nothings into her ear until the earliest hours of the morning. The way you make arrangements together and disappear for unspecified amounts of time. You're at her beck and call. I never thought I'd see the day where you fell in love again, and with a *human*."

"It's none of your business what I choose to do and with whom."

"Maybe not." Armienti shrugged.

"No, absolutely not," Dante corrected.

"Have you at least thought enough to run this match of yours by the Grand Supreme, or at the very least, our Emperor?"

"It's none of their business. They can both rot for all I care."

"Of course it is. I would think to inform them before anyone else, if you have plans of permanency."

Dante scowled. "Whose side are you on, anyway?"

"Yours, obviously."

Dante narrowed his eyes. Armienti. Sneaky Armienti. Suddenly it occurred to him what this conversation of theirs was about.

"You think to take her from me." The ground trembled and cracked beneath his feet. Dante balled his fists. "But you're too late, cousin, I've already claimed her. She's mine."

Armienti folded his arms. "Stop getting all bent out of sorts. I wanted to bring to your attention, there's a definite possibility your match will be declined."

"I know."

"But even so, not only do you have the Emperors to contend with, but what will become of our mission? You can't expect to successfully complete it and keep Autumn's affection as well."

Dante stared at Armienti, and hated to admit he was right. How would he be able to look Autumn in the face after he conquered her world?

"Yes, I know."

Teeth clenched, Dante stormed through the forest. He

hated the way Armienti spoke the truth. He needed to figure out a way to navigate through the delicate situation he created.

He mulled over his options, when the third dilemma dawned on him. Could Autumn care for him if she knew he wasn't human, but an alien here to claim Earth?

Thirty-Three

AUTUMN READ an overdue library book on a crisp Saturday in October. Outside her window, leaves changed to vivid hues of crimson, mustard, and flaming-orange. The wind whirled stray leaves across her driveway, settling around the tires of her unused car.

She was frustrated with her life on so many different levels, but she finally stopped contacting Dante. He proved himself unworthy of her feelings.

At first, she'd admit she behaved desperately. However, after six weeks of failed attempts to reach him, she finally got the hint.

He didn't want her in his life.

Something was wrong with this picture, and she was too foolish to see there was a problem from the beginning. Instead, she chose her own happiness.

Autumn pondered the bizarre series of events. Although Dante laid predominantly on her mind, she had a worse issue to contend with.

She flunked her Calculus midterm and risked losing her scholarship.

Autumn ambled downstairs and found her dad frying eggs on the stove, while the television streamed the news. Another decapitated corpse had been discovered at Farrah Falls. She grimaced. What a way to ruin her appetite. The griddle popped and sizzled as he scraped their breakfast with a spatula.

"Dad." She watched as he filled two plates with food.

"Yes?"

Autumn silently debated the best approach to deliver the news. "I failed my Calculus midterm." The words spewed from her mouth, and she couldn't retract them.

Her dad stroked his whiskered chin. "Well, I don't understand, didn't you study?"

"Yeah," she admitted. The problem wasn't that she hadn't studied, she'd been distracted. Unable to sleep or think clearly after what'd happened. Not to mention Calculus bored her to death. She'd rather watch mold grow on a tree.

"Well, this is bad news all around. If you don't pick up your grades, you're going to lose your scholarship. And I can't afford to pay your college tuition."

It was true. He was still paying off her mom's funeral bills.

Autumn stood there quietly, confirming he was correct. Her poor performance had put her in somewhat of a sticky situation academically. And her dad was already under enough stress. She took responsibility for her failure.

"I'm going to quit my job at the diner to make more time to study. It's my number one priority."

"I think that's a great idea," her dad replied. "School comes first."

Autumn grew queasy. Working as a waitress was exhausting on top of being a full-time student, but she loved having the extra spending money in her pocket, as well as the independence it allowed her. Autumn hated relying on anyone. People were disappointing.

Her dad continued, "You know, I hate to admit it, but

your grades were a lot better when Dante was in the picture. Maybe there was an advantage to you studying with him after all."

It took every bit of self-control in her body not to roll her eyes. First, he hated him, and now he thought they made good study buddies? *Please.*

Autumn nodded mechanically and went upstairs to dress. She selected a burnt-orange sweater, dark wash jeans, and her black low-top canvas sneakers. She pressed a skinny black headband through her unruly curls and grabbed her crossbody bag, filling it with her belongings.

When she arrived in the kitchen, her dad said, "I'm sorry it had to come to this, but I think your decision is a blessing in disguise."

Outside, a cold gust of wind whipped through her hair. Autumn was her name, but she was the first to admit she preferred the heat of summer and the warmth and rebirth of spring. Unfortunately, all four seasons were mandatory in New York, and she couldn't escape them.

Goosebumps prickled over her skin as she headed to the diner for the last time.

When she arrived, her stomach tied itself in knots. Marcela's silver dented minivan sat in the lot. Autumn feared she'd have to address her directly.

Thirty seconds into her visit, she spotted Marcela, manning the register. Autumn and her soon to be ex-manager briefly locked eyes. Meanwhile, Autumn waited patiently by the door.

After Marcela finished tending to the last customer online, she sauntered to Autumn, her dark beady eyes narrowing.

"What are you doing here, Ramon?" Marcela's mouth fell flat. "I'm positive I gave you the day off. Did you forget to write your schedule down *again*?"

Autumn remained quiet. Cool and in control.

"Typical," Marcela hissed.

Autumn squared her shoulders, head held high. "You gave me the day off, but I need to speak to you about something else…"

"Can it wait?" Marcela asked. "We're really busy right now."

"No, it can't. It's now or never."

Her manager tapped a foot against the floor impatiently. Autumn supposed she was reciting her favorite motto in her head. *Time is money.*

"I quit." Autumn reached into her satchel and removed her sun-colored apron and laminated name tag, handing them to her ex-boss.

Marcela's eyes popped as she took hold of the crumpled uniform. "You're quitting on me, Ramon? I never pegged you as a quitter. May I ask the reason?"

"I need more time to focus on my schoolwork." She enjoyed having a job and the freedom it afforded her, but recognized keeping her scholarship was a priority.

Marcela chuckled. Autumn found the sound of her laughter frightening. "Oh, I assumed you were leaving because of me."

"Why would you think that?"

"Well, it's no secret you and I haven't always seen eye to eye."

That was certainly putting it lightly. Marcela had hounded her every hour of every shift since the beginning of summer. It was like she'd made it her personal mission to make her life a living nightmare.

"I know we've had our differences…" Marcela's voice was as sweet as gum drops. "…I can say you're an exceptionally hard worker."

"Thank you." Taken aback by her compliment, Autumn's lips tugged upward.

"But you move as slow as molasses, and you could never be on time if your life depended on it. Your time management skills are subpar."

"That's not fair." Autumn folded her arms. "You know what I've been through. I've always done my best."

"Sometimes, little girl, your best isn't good enough. If you ever hope to amount to anything in this life, college degree or not, you need to get your act together. Stop being so doe-eyed and timid, it's sickening."

Autumn's eyes wavered with anger, but she wouldn't give Marcela the satisfaction of making her cry.

"It was a pleasure working with you too." Autumn willed herself to be kind. It was her first job, and she might need a reference in the future.

Marcela sauntered away. Neither of them exchanged another word.

"*Good riddance*," she breathed.

When Autumn left the restaurant, relaxation numbed her body. She was finally free. Autumn took a financial hit, but not having to work with Marcela again comforted her. *Wicked witch*.

When she checked the time, it was 11:05 a.m. It was still relatively early, and she had one more stop to make.

The Monroe Free Library was conveniently located across the street from the diner. Many people her age would agree this was a pretty lame way to spend a picturesque Saturday, but to Autumn, there was no place she'd rather be. Any life was better than her own, and books created an escape that she desperately craved.

When Autumn entered the fluorescent lit building, she scanned the room. Surprisingly, single people and entire families alike read around tables and whispered quietly among themselves.

Autumn ambled to the new arrivals section and ran her fingertips over the spines, plastic creaking.

It didn't take her long to settle on a few interesting titles. *Dracula* and *The Wolfman*. Two books perfect for Halloween. She grabbed them and walked to the counter to check them out.

Autumn waited *forever* in line. When she finally reached the counter, after rifling through her bag and her wallet, she discovered her library card was missing. She sighed, recalling she last saw it in the front pocket of her backpack. *At home.*

Fortunately, the chipper, freckle-faced librarian agreed to hold her selections for her at the front desk. After graciously thanking her, Autumn went to leave—then hesitated.

Standing on the sidewalk, she spotted a familiar head of midnight-black hair. Amber eyes burning hot like the desert sun. The single white long-stemmed rose he held in his hand was a stark contrast against his all-onyx ensemble.

Thirty-Four

"**BEAUTIFUL ARE** you with eyes that gleam like the moon, sparkling beneath a sea of rippled darkness. Your purity, your spirit, your loveliness, your likeness, are mysteries to those who exist within the shadows of this world, but walk among the starlight. For yours is the touch that cures. A single glance from your moonlight makes kingdoms crumble, knees bend, wars wage, and fires burn. Autumn, a season of the Earth. Can you somehow find it in the kindness of your heart to forgive me?"

Dante placed the single white flower in Autumn's trembling hand. She watched him, gray eyes wavering.

"Are you going to speak?" His voice was soft and urgent, but she remained silent.

Dante sensed a stark shift in energy from her usual pleasant demeanor. She stared at him with uncertainty in her innocent eyes. Her normally rosy cheeks flushed the deep shade of scarlet, her delicate hands balled and shook. Perhaps she wanted to fight him.

He bit his cheeks, stifling the urge to laugh at her adorable attempt. Resisting, because he landed himself into far more trouble than he was already in.

Autumn had every right to be displeased with him. He disappeared from her life without a trace close to thirty-one suns and moons ago, not including half of the present day, which made it almost *thirty-two*. He had a lot of explaining to do. But where to begin?

Judging by her reaction to his arrival, it was going to be difficult for her to swallow. But at the very least, he had to try.

Being around Autumn inspired a different side of him, one he never knew existed. He cared, maybe a little too much. Armienti was right, and recognized this long before he did.

Autumn approached him quickly according to human standards, her brows furrowed.

Never in all of his life had he encountered such a darling and sensitive creature. One glance into her eyes, and he could see her pain; not just the pain he caused her.

"How do you always know exactly where to find me?"

For a split second he spaced, forgetting where he was, but never who he was speaking with. He was tempted to pull her into his arms and kiss her from head to toe right there on the walkway, but it was neither the time nor the place.

"And why didn't you call me back?" She folded her arms. "I called you over a *month* ago. You could have at least let me know you were alive."

"Well, clearly I'm not dead." He chuckled. Autumn looked even prettier than usual when she was angry, fearsome and fearless all at once.

She groaned, turning on her heel, loose curls flowing in a tornado of wind.

"Autumn, stop right there," he commanded.

She whipped around.

"I can explain," was all he could think to say to her so she'd remain there with him, if only for a moment longer.

"Okay, you can start by telling me why the lights always change when you're around. And why your skin didn't melt after you grabbed the pizza from my oven *bare handed*? And how you come and go as you please. I'm not stupid and I didn't imagine any of it. I'm tired of your lies and your secrets."

She looked around. Dante supposed she wanted to ensure no human ears listened. Autumn was modest; never wanted to make a scene. From what he gathered with his heightened senses, they were alone.

She sighed and walked away again. If it was an answer she required, it was an answer she'd receive.

Dante approached as swift and nimble as the night and pulled her into a darkly lit corridor, invisible from the travel way. Sides bricked tight with pink stones.

He moved closer, a stinking trash receptacle nearby. Dante imagined this moment being somewhat *different* and regretted the putrid, rotten food surrounding them. It was the quickest solution he could think of so they could speak uninterrupted.

"How did we move all the way over here?" She quivered uncontrollably.

"Don't demand the truth from me unless you yourself are prepared to handle it. You've made some fair observations. Now please do indulge me. How do these puzzle pieces you've assembled fit together in your mind?"

She cleared her throat. "Um..." she began quietly. "I was wondering if maybe, as impossible as it sounds, you're a superhero?"

Dante's brows rose. He had no clue what she was talking about. He chuckled in amusement at her supposition. Perhaps the clues she'd so carefully assembled for herself had flown over her own head.

"I'm not a hero, and I'm not in the habit of saving anyone other than myself."

"Then I don't understand."

"I hope you realize at the very least I'm not human."

"What do you mean you're *not* human?" She laughed, on the verge of hysterics. "You look and feel human enough to me." She ran her fingers over his lips and down the cleft of his chin.

"That's because this isn't my natural born form."

"What are you talking about Dante, you're scaring me!" Her voice trembled.

"I never intended to lie to you. I feel I owe you the truth after I ruined our dinner plans."

"Why did you wait so long?" Autumn asked. "I've been waiting to speak with you."

"I'm sorry Autumn." He took her hands in his. "It's complicated."

"Well, it doesn't have to be. Tell me what's going on and stop being weird and confusing about it."

Dante could've sworn he told her the truth a few moments ago, but apparently she hadn't been listening to a word he said. He inhaled, holding his breath for a moment too long before exhaling, figuring in a case like this, it was best to start from the beginning.

"Well," Dante began, "I'm not from Earth as you've probably gathered from all the incidents you've witnessed."

Her gray eyes widened.

"Hence the reason I'm not human. I was born give or take twenty years ago, on a substantial blue planet named Surge. It's located at the far end of Universe 13, and is approximately 100 billion light-years away from here—"

Midway through his sentence, she slipped under his arm and stumbled over a stinking bag on the ground. She turned around watching him with *those* eyes he'd grown so fond of.

"You know, there was an easier way to tell me you're not interested in me anymore." Her voice shook. "I should've gotten the hint when you didn't call me back, after *fifty* calls. I probably looked so desperate. Maybe I'm the crazy one. Maybe my imagination played tricks on me. Maybe I desperately wanted to believe there was magic in the world. But to stand here and tell me you're from a different planet is impossible. How could you think for one second I would believe such a crazy story?"

"I'm here to tell you you're neither crazy, nor did your imagination play tricks on you," he said. "There is indeed life beyond the stars. Intelligent life. Entire civilizations. Just because you haven't seen them doesn't mean they don't exist. For I assure you, they do. I am they."

Telekinetically, Dante swept Autumn from the ground. She gasped as he used the tiniest sliver of his energy so as not to mistakenly injure her. Dante placed her on her feet.

"How did you do that?" She cupped her hands over her mouth.

Dante was in disbelief; she continued to question him after everything she'd been told and seen. But if all else failed, there was one surefire way to convince her. It was the reason he'd been tasked with heading missions, the reason he was rarely home for longer than a few months at a time, a*nd the reason he'd secured a position as one of the Grand Supreme's top three favorite warriors.*

He removed his glove, holding his hand at a safe distance away from Autumn's face. Dante willed his pointer finger and the tip glowed bright red. A burning sensation singed through his crisping flesh, exposing an orange sparkling flame. Dante took great pains, stabilizing himself, allowing her to inspect him.

She flinched, followed by the faint flow of breath, silencing his flame. A fresh layer of skin regenerated, hardening in its place.

On the off chance she still doubted him, he ignited a blazing ball of fire for the second time, consuming the entirety of his hand. He effortlessly returned the flame back into his palm. A rough outer covering cracked in its place.

Dante experienced a twinge of pain every time he created and manipulated fire, but at this point in his life, he was more than accustomed to the uncomfortable sensation. He'd been generating fire since childhood, with a limitless threshold.

Autumn touched his palm, gazing into his eyes and said, "That was you at The Castle, wasn't it?"

He nodded.

"Why would you behave so selfishly and endanger all of those people?"

"I lost my temper," he said matter-of-factly, recognizing it was something he needed to work on.

She shook her head. "Wake me, I must be dreaming."

"I assure you, you're not. This is reality."

Autumn crossed her arms and said, "If you're an alien, how can you speak to me?"

"Excuse me?" He made a face. "I'm an alien? *You're* an alien."

She placed a hand on her hip. "You're on my planet, so you're the *alien*."

Touché. He couldn't argue with that. "I suppose you're right when you phrase it that way. I'm Elattion actually, if you want to get technical, and we can speak because I took great pains to learn your language. I was desperate to communicate with you."

The normal level of pink returned to her cheeks upon his admission.

"Seriously?"

"Yes. Is that all right with you?"

She nodded. "Why did you want to talk to me so badly?"

"Isn't it obvious?" He touched her cheek. Autumn tensed before relaxing into his caress. Dante sensed her fear by the racing of her heart.

"You don't have to worry, I have perfect control over my ability," he said. "I would never hurt you."

"I'm sorry." Autumn glanced away. "It's going to take some getting used to."

"I understand."

"Why did you come to Earth?" She wrapped her arms around his waist.

A dreadful question. One he didn't have a straightforward answer to. But, eventually, it needed to be addressed.

"Unfortunately, I'm not at liberty to say," he lied through his teeth. "I'm under oath. The reason for my visit is confidential."

Autumn's lips curved. A sign she accepted his poorly contrived excuse. But being well acquainted with her curious nature, he didn't have a doubt in his mind she was dying to know the truth. That, however, could wait. One matter at a time.

He rerouted their conversation to a lighter topic. "Please allow me to apologize for dodging your attempts to contact me. I want you to know there's nobody I've thought of more fondly than you in my absence. I needed time to consider our unique situation."

"What do you mean, *unique* situation?"

"Well, I never imagined I would fall for a human. This is kind of a first for me."

Autumn paused for a long while. "What happens now?"

Dante's communicator vibrated in his pocket. He peeked at the device. Ronan. Another soldier's body was discovered in the forest. *Mangled and headless.*

Dammit, another man down.

He rested his chin on her head, mind racing. "I'd like to come see you after dark. Will you perchance be home? I wish to continue this conversation." He could barely think straight as his anger boiled.

"Yes, I'll be home."

Perfect. The exact answer he anticipated. Autumn barely went anywhere. Either she was serving, reading in her bedchamber, or attending school. She was innocent, and above all, predictable. He enjoyed that about her. His life was typically in an uproar, and he craved stability.

"Wonderful, I shall see you then."

Taking a step back, he said, "Don't tarry, now. Your books await."

"Wait, how did you—" were the last words he heard her speak before he teleported away.

Thirty-Five

AUTUMN WAS ALONE ONCE MORE in a vacant alleyway. The sun lowered in the distance. Sparkling rays of violet and fuchsia reflected over the mirrored twin ponds in the center of town. The chilly fall air whisked through her burnt-orange cable-knit sweater, followed by the putrid scent of garbage.

If she wasn't in awe, she'd likely be sick to her stomach.

Autumn slid to a seated position. She closed her eyes and took deep, controlled breaths, unable to comprehend what she'd witnessed a few minutes prior.

Dante was an alien who could generate fire and whisk her through the air like a rag doll with his *mind*. More profound was his ability to disappear before her eyes and go who knows where. She'd never felt more insignificant in her life.

She exhaled, wondering how many times he had visited her over the course of the last few months. *Who knew at this point?*

More frightening still, she couldn't believe he fooled her into thinking he was human. Never once did she suspect otherwise.

The joke was on her, as *usual*.

Natural form. What exactly did he mean? Was he an animal? Or a *creature*? The possibility of him being a creepy crawler turned the contents of her stomach upside down. Not to mention—what was so confidential about his visit to Earth he couldn't talk about? Autumn's mind spun out of control with endless possibilities.

Amidst the chaos of her raging thoughts, it was strangely thrilling Dante chose her, of all people, to confide in, and terrifying yet exciting to find out he was an alien.

There was no one she could entrust this information with. Not her dad; *especially* not her friends. Though they were away at college, if they caught wind of the situation, they'd alert the entire internet, and the government would come knocking at her door. Dante would be hauled off to Area 51.

It had to remain their secret.

Autumn finally came to a stand. Grabbing her belongings, she grinned. Dante was exciting, and his romantic gestures were over the top. A poem and a rose. She only ever read about romance like this in fairytales. No human guy had ever treated her so well.

When Autumn left the alleyway, an even mixture of terror and excitement consumed her. She desperately needed a distraction until Dante came to see her later. She craved answers from him with every ounce of her being. There was still so much she didn't understand.

* * *

Dante stood with Ronan and Armienti in the cargo bay of his ship. The remaining twenty or so soldiers aligned against the wall in order of rank. He scowled, holding the severed head of the soldier he ordered maimed. Another man down. Their mission would be more difficult with so few soldiers left.

Perhaps he should've given the injured ones adequate time to heal. It was too late: he couldn't allow himself to second guess.

"Who did this?" Dante demanded.

One bald soldier stepped forth, clearing his throat. "Sire, have you considered the possibility he took his own life?"

"Did I grant you permission to question me?" Dante snapped. The soldier's jaw tightened, his eyes averted to the ground.

"He has a point," Armienti whispered in Dante's ear. "Perhaps he lost the will to live."

It made no sense. The soldier was discovered in the identical position as the first casualty. Back propped against a tree. Head in the crook of his remaining arm.

"From this point on, nobody leaves the ship without my permission. Not for food. Not for fresh air. You shall remain here. Is that crystal clear?"

Silence.

"I *asked you a question!* Is that crystal clear?"

Every person in the room nodded, trembling.

* * *

When Autumn arrived back home, she planned to locate her missing library card and spend the rest of the evening reading. It was the only way she'd be able to survive without losing her mind while she patiently waited for Dante's return.

Her dad occupied the kitchen, where she left him hours before. He stirred a pot of bubbling arroz con gandules with a wooden spoon. A whole chicken sizzled in the oven. "You were gone an awfully long time. I texted you three hours ago. How did your resignation go at the diner?"

Autumn checked her messages, seeing the one she missed. *Guess I was too engrossed with watching Dante generate fire with his hands.*

"Sorry," she croaked, trying not to arouse suspicion. "I completely lost track of time at the library. They got lots of new books over the last week."

A vertical line formed between his brows. "I thought you went to the diner to quit."

"I did," she blurted, forgetting to mention her resignation after the day she had. "Everything went fine. The manager was understanding." A lie, but it didn't matter anymore. Her former job was the last thing she was thinking about.

"Good, I'm glad," he said. "She has to understand you're a student and school comes first. I was worried you'd be upset, but I'm proud of you. You're taking charge and handling this situation like an adult."

Okay, okay, okay, whatever Dad. Autumn tapped her sneaker against the floor. She needed to return to the library ASAP; it was due to close in thirty minutes.

"You're right, school comes first." She forced a smile.

Her dad nodded, satisfied with her answer. Relief flooded through her. She could finally put their conversation to an end.

Autumn arrived back from the library, feeling foolish. It turned out her library card had been in her back jeans pocket the *entire* time. She sighed, books swinging in her crossbody bag. Her dad sat on the couch watching the news, and she sprinted to her bedroom for some privacy.

Her dad loved her and was only trying to help, but she couldn't handle another ounce of stress. There was already too much on her mind.

Climbing into bed, she grabbed *Dracula*. The book fit her current mood. A story about the undead. Someone inhuman who could never hope to be human. Someone different and frightening.

An alien, her mind drifted away from the story for a moment. *I can't believe Dante is an alien.*

A few chapters in, she gave up. It was an interesting read, but after every couple of words, she couldn't help but peek at her closet door. Hopeful that Dante finally arrived.

Every time, she grew increasingly disappointed. What was he doing and why was he taking so long? *An alien with an agenda.* All she could do was sit and wait, and waiting was beyond frustrating.

A few more hours passed, painfully, slowly.

The sun set for the evening. Twinkling stars shimmered through the blinds. Her stomach twisted and grumbled with hunger.

After fixing herself a bowl of arroz con gandules, she returned to her room, hoping to see Dante. But he wasn't there. She feared he had changed his mind or had gotten cold feet and wasn't coming at all. Autumn resisted the urge to call him, not wanting to appear desperate.

* * *

Half-past midnight came at a snail's pace, and Autumn was forced to cope with the reality Dante wasn't coming. One hour seamlessly drifted into the next. He ghosted her *again*, making her anxious and a little insecure. Grumbling, she changed into her pajamas and collapsed into bed.

Just after she closed her eyes, she felt something collide with her feet. Autumn stretched and her foot bumped against something soft at the far end of her mattress.

She yawned, running her palms over her eyes. "Dante?"

A long silence.

"Yes," he said, followed by a breathy whisper of laughter. "Did I fail to indicate to you I was coming? Or perhaps you were expecting someone else in my stead?"

"I thought you'd be here earlier. It's already half-past twelve."

"I do apologize for my tardiness. It's unacceptable, and to be honest, I wouldn't tolerate it myself. Please understand I came as soon as I could."

Autumn squinted, now fully alert but realized she couldn't see two inches in front of her face. All there was by way of light was the glow outside from the occasional passing car.

"It's fine." Her fingers slid against the switch of her lamp.

"Stop," he said abruptly.

"Why? What's wrong?"

"I'd like to gently ease into this."

A knot fastened itself in her stomach. "Ease into *what*?"

"I wish for you to see me how I truly am, without my human disguise."

Her mind went wild. *Human disguise.* She trembled, unable to fathom what one would look like if they weren't human.

"Maybe we should do this in the light."

"No." His black silhouette reached for her, grabbing hold of her hand. *At least he still had five fingers.* Dante guided her fingers along his arm, no longer wearing a long sleeve t-shirt. His skin was coated with a tight material, the same consistency as a bathing suit.

As she reached his jawline, he kissed her knuckles, and her body erupted in goosebumps. Rubbing her palms over his face, she encountered his angular cheekbones and cleft chin. Nothing felt amiss, but for whatever reason, he seemed reluctant.

"I don't understand why you're doing this."

When she reached his hair, he leaned close, crushing his lips to hers. They melted together. Her toes curled as he glided his mouth against her neck, realizing how much she missed him over the last month. He leisurely pulled away, leaving her craving more of him.

"Why did you stop?" She asked in a daze.

"I wished to steal from you one last kiss. In case everything doesn't go as planned. Nothing ever seems to go right between me and you. I'm nervous and clumsy in your presence. Listen to me, I'm babbling on like a fool."

Autumn felt the same way, but she was too shy to admit it.

"Turn on the light. There's no more delaying the inevitable."

Unsteadily, she stood from her bed, making her way across the floor. She clicked on her lamp, hesitating. Unable to bring herself to face him.

Perhaps she wasn't ready to relinquish the fairytale she'd been living in. The one where they recovered from a month-long misunderstanding, made up, and he was human.

Autumn's thoughts spiraled out of control. The springs popped on her bed, followed by the full weight of Dante's heavy boots. She hugged herself as he approached—then stopped, his body heaving against hers in silent breaths.

His arms cinched around waist, and she jumped from the pressure of his touch. Autumn turned around and saw the difference she couldn't detect in the darkness.

Thirty-Six

DANTE HAD PALE BLUE SKIN. Autumn's lips parted a touch, mesmerized by his ethereal allure. He wasn't a creature like she feared. Dante was beautiful. Beneath his raven-black hair, his ears came to soft points, resembling an elf's.

He wore an onyx bodysuit, long sleeves hugging his muscles. Pants secured by calf-high boots. On his right breast sat an embroidered emblem with a swirl of dark purple and silver stars and flames. Autumn realized what sat around her waist wasn't his arm, but a pointed, fleshy tail. It recoiled, wrapping around his waist like a belt.

Being an alien wasn't as bad as she feared. *Minus the tail*, which would take some getting used to. Staring at him, she chewed her bottom lip subconsciously.

"Are you frightened?"

This entire ordeal was a result of Dante caring about her opinion. She never saw him vulnerable before and had to admit she liked this side of him.

"No, of course not." She squeezed his hand.

Wrapping her arms around his waist, she said, "I don't care

that your skin is a different color than mine, or that you're not human. I think you're beautiful the way you are. More so now."

Autumn wasn't sure whether it was the way the light played off his cheeks, but they darkened with a hint of pink before shifting back to blue.

"I'm glad you find me pleasing, but your beauty Little Moonlight far exceeds mine."

Her cheeks singed from his compliment.

"Do all Elattions look like you?"

Dante chuckled, too white teeth glistening. "Am I not well-suited enough for you?"

She rolled her eyes. So *dramatic*.

"The vast majority of inhabitants on my planet have skin tones within the normal human spectrum. Only pure blood Elattions with refined psychic abilities share my hue."

"I see. Do you have any other abilities?" she asked. *Other than generating fire, disappearing at will, and moving objects without ever lifting a finger.* While she was normal.

"Besides the obvious...I can fly."

Autumn jumped into the air, almost knocking Dante onto the bed. "Wait, are you serious? You can fly?"

"I enjoy how easy you are to please." He took her hands in his. "You make me want to please you more and more. If you wish, I'll take you right now. We'll go anywhere in the world you wish to see."

Autumn was so excited, she could scream, but she reminded herself to be mindful of her dad one room down. There were so many places she wanted to visit. She'd always had dreams of traveling. The London Bridge, the Eiffel Tower, the Colosseum, the Pyramids of Giza. Her list was lengthy, considering she'd never gone anywhere before.

But there was one special place she and her parents visited as a family when her mom was still alive. Plus, she knew she had to be back before morning so her dad didn't worry about her more than he already did.

"Can we go to New York City?"

"Sure, do you know the coordinates off hand?"

Autumn grabbed her phone. Trembling with excitement, she got on the internet and searched. The city was huge, so she decided on a location she hadn't visited before. The Freedom Tower.

Handing Dante her phone, the coordinates read 40.7127°N, 74.0134°W.

Dante reached into his pocket and removed a slender, black and silver square object. Subtle cracks extended across the screen. It sat neatly in the palm of his hand.

"What is that?"

"A communicator. This is how we speak, and the reason we can't text each other. My device can't properly transmit to yours."

An alien smartphone. The technology appeared far more advanced than what they had on Earth.

When he finished, the black screen of his device flashed neon green. "It appears we're all set. Shall we?" He offered her his hand.

She clicked off the light, and he guided her toward the window.

Autumn crawled over her comforter, the sharp bite of the post-midnight air stinging her cheeks. When she glanced, Dante waited for her outside, floating. She couldn't believe he was *flying*.

She gulped, eyes gravitating toward the driveway. For the first time, it occurred to her how high off the ground the second story of her house was. Eyes flickering to Dante, she shot him a pleading look. Wordlessly, he glided over like a phantom in the night.

Hoisting her out of the window, he cradled her in his

arms. "I promise, you have nothing to fear. I would never allow harm to befall you."

Autumn fastened her grip as she and Dante rose higher and higher into the chilly, starlit sky. The pale half-moon beamed. Her home transformed into a microscopic speck. The rest of her neighborhood was flecked with golden lights, like flitting fireflies.

One blink, and they were gone.

Thirty-Seven

EARTH, overall, was an underwhelming planet filled with weak inhabitants. Humans were simple creatures, blissfully unaware of life on other worlds. Other worlds that were dangerous and unpredictable. Harmful to their existence.

Seeing Autumn's happiness helped Dante to forget his troubles. She was so innocent and pretty. Moon colored eyes affixed on the stars. Resting her head on his shoulder, she put all of her trust in him, which he thoroughly enjoyed.

There was a warm glow in his chest that hadn't been there previously. It was the first time in a long while he wasn't furious or anxious. Instead, he was complete.

As they soared, he securely clutched her to alleviate her fear, unwilling to risk spoiling their special time together.

He was pleasantly surprised she didn't mind his natural form. Although he knew he was a catch, he wasn't quite sure how Autumn would perceive his different appearance. His pale blue skin and *tail*, which he caught her staring at. The tail often caused more harm than good, and he didn't particularly want to have it either. Especially on nights where there was a full moon.

Dante spied a city approaching in the distance as they flew through dissipating clouds and soared by clunking Earth aircrafts. The metropolis sparkled like a radiant beacon in the night. This city was a mere shadow of the one he left back home. Perhaps even half a shadow. Overall, it was a disappointing spectacle, but Autumn was pleased. It was all that mattered.

His communicator beeped, indicating their arrival. They descended from the sky, landing on a building with a silver pointed spire. Mirrored glass coated all four sides, reflecting the surrounding light. They sat at the base of the pinnacle, and he propped Autumn onto his lap, to ensure she wouldn't fall.

"This is amazing." She rested her head against his shoulder. "I can't believe a little while ago we were in my bedroom, and now we're in the city."

"It was no trouble at all." His cheeks warmed. "Really."

Flying was as easy as breathing. It came naturally. However, he was pleased she was impressed. Autumn was unphased by money and flattery. It was life's simplicities that mattered most to her, and family. That was perhaps her most appealing trait.

"Do they have cities like this on Surge?"

He nodded. "Girildinia is tremendous and overpopulated. It spans much of the planet."

Girildinia was *fifty* times the size of her miniscule New York City. In fact, this city was one of the tiniest he encountered during any of his travels.

"I love the city." Her moonlit gaze met his. "I bet yours is a beautiful place to visit."

"That it is."

Autumn moved closer, and he wrapped his tail around her waist.

"Why did you come to Earth?"

He caressed her cheek before kissing her, unprepared to

shatter her with the truth. Not when they made so much progress. He fed her the tiniest bit of information to satiate her curious nature.

"Well," he began, "as I indicated to you earlier, I've sworn an oath. What I can divulge is I had pressing matters to attend to in Universe 2."

"What do you mean by Universe 2?" Autumn asked. "I thought there was only one universe."

"No, I'm afraid you're mistaken," he gently corrected her. "There are 24 Universes code named 1 through 24."

"Wow, I had no idea." Her brows rose. "Is Earth in Universe 2?"

"No, Earth is actually located in Universe 1. In any case, my mission in Universe 2 was a complete success, as I fully anticipated. However, whilst on my way to Earth to complete a secondary mission, my team and I crashed."

"You're stranded here?"

"Yes, my replacement ship is on its way as we speak. It's scheduled to arrive midway through next year."

Autumn glanced away; eyes glassy. "You're not staying?"

Dante could tell he upset her. She wasn't as skilled at hiding her emotions as he was.

"No." He took her hand in his. "I'm afraid I can't. I've been out in deep space for well over a year. It's time for me to go home. I have a family and obligations."

"I understand," she said quietly. "You must miss them. That's a long time to be away from your family."

He traced his fingers through her palm and continued, "Although I must leave, it doesn't mean I don't care for you."

Autumn stood up and circled the steeple. He followed her, unsure of how to remedy the situation. There was no way he could successfully complete his mission and still maintain her respect. At least no way he'd thought of yet. If he didn't protect her, no one else could.

Autumn stopped suddenly, breathing in steady white puffs. "What if we have a long- distance relationship? That way, we don't have to break up when you leave?"

"I'm afraid that wouldn't work," he said. "I live too far away. A little over one of your Earth years."

She took his hands in hers. "What if I go with you? Then we can be together."

Dante wasn't sure that was the best option either, or how to breach the topic. In his wildest dreams, he considered bringing her with him. Could she still care for him after she saw what he was capable of? Somehow, he doubted it.

"No, I'm afraid that's not an option either."

"Why not? Don't tell me you have a girlfriend waiting for you back home. Or even worse, a wife," she crossed her arms. "I can't stand cheaters."

What was she talking about? Wife? Another term he was unfamiliar with, and clearly it made her upset. To his surprise, the human language system never got any easier.

Dante researched the term on his communicator, and she rolled her eyes.

As she made a move to approach him, Autumn's foot slipped over the ledge, and she free fell. Her shrill voice echoed through the chilly night air.

He leapt, catching her instantaneously. Trembling, she buried her face against his chest. This time he sat her in his lap, tail secured around her waist. Unable to trust her in this erratic state.

"Sorry..." Her voice wavered. "I overreacted a bit. Thanks for saving me."

"It's okay," he said calmly.

Sometimes, Autumn impressed him with her maturity, other times *not* so much. She still had a lot of growing up to do.

"Ah, here we go." His communicator finally yielded results. Autumn wanted to know if he had a mate.

"Let me be honest with you. There was somebody a long time ago, but she passed away."

Maeve. And he'd been out of control ever since. Traveling as often as he had didn't make matters any easier.

"To answer your question, no. I don't have a girlfriend, nor am I married."

"I'm sorry I didn't mean to—"

"You have nothing to be sorry for."

* * *

The flight home was silent. Autumn sat in his arms; attention cast elsewhere. Dante wished Maeve hadn't come up in conversation. The mere mention of her name was like raising the dead. She was gone; slipped through his fingers like stardust.

When they reached her home, the Earth sun peeked its golden rays beyond the horizon. They descended from the sky and entered her bedchamber. Sitting on her bed, Autumn rested her head on his shoulder. Clearly, she had enough adventure for one night.

"What happens now?" she said, voice raspy from lack of sleep.

"We rest." Dante traced his fingers through her curls. "There's no sense in worrying about what can't be changed."

"I know what you mean."

"How so?"

She shrugged. "Never mind."

"Obviously it's bothering you or you wouldn't have mentioned it."

"It's silly, really." She yawned.

Dante's interest piqued. "Tell me."

"Well, um…" Autumn began, "It's stupid, and I probably shouldn't have said anything. It's about Caleb."

A flash of red crossed his vision. "What happened?"

"While you were gone, we kind of got assigned as lab partners. We're stuck together for the rest of the semester. Don't worry. Nothing to worry about."

Autumn rolled over, drifting off to sleep. Dante sat there seething with jealousy.

Thirty-Eight

A WEEK HAD PASSED since Dante revealed his alien nature. It was one of the weirdest weeks of Autumn's life. Not only was she dating a confirmed extraterrestrial, but he hadn't left her side, except for school, meals, and family obligations.

She figured Dante's change in attitude had to do with Caleb. It was amazing what jealousy could do, even if she didn't cause it intentionally. *Or did she?*

Secretly, she wanted him to experience the urgency of what it would be like to lose her. The way she felt since he told her he would leave next year. With each passing day, she was terrified of losing him to the stars. She lost everything she ever loved. First Caleb, then her mom, and now—

No matter how many times she wrapped her head around the situation, she couldn't figure out his reluctance to bring her back to Surge with him. If only for a visit. In the meantime: midterms.

At 11:00 p.m. on a Sunday in mid-November, Autumn's head spun off its axis. Equations, equations, and *more* equations. Why did Chemistry have to be so frustrating? Not to mention the added pressure of acing this exam. Her scholarship was still on the line. At this rate, she'd have no hope of *ever* becoming a doctor.

Autumn sprawled over her comforter. There were countless crumpled looseleaf papers littered with failed computations.

She was going to fail. She buried her head in her palms, in disbelief she had a midterm bright and early in the morning. And where the heck was Dante? She desperately needed caffeine to fuel her all nighter and had sent him to *Dunkin'* over an hour ago. Amidst her wallowing, a faint tap came to her window.

Finally...

Drawing the blinds, she discovered her boyfriend floating in his flawlessly contrived human disguise. Grinning and carrying a cardboard holder with four large coffees and a box of munchkins. *Why four coffees?*

Suddenly, two sets of heavy boots hit the floor. She whirled around, mouth falling open. "Armienti, Ronan, what are you doing here?"

Dante materialized on the bed, handing her the coffee she ordered. Pumpkin spice, light and sweet, her absolute favorite. Armienti cocked his head to the side.

"A pleasure as always to see you, Autumn."

Armienti pressed his lips against her knuckles. Autumn's cheeks heated from a combination of shock and embarrassment. Dante shot his cousin a look before passing him a coffee.

Ronan, on the other hand, seized this opportunity to explore her room. His clover-green eyes were fixated on her impressive snow globe collection. Snatching her favorite globe from *Alice and Wonderland,* he smirked. "Catch."

Ronan pelted her precious globe through the air at Dante. The last gift her mom gave her before she died. Autumn's heart plummeted as it headed toward the floor.

At the last second, Dante flicked his wrist, stopping the globe in mid-air. It floated, landing back on the shelf in its previous position.

Autumn shot to her feet and marched over to Ronan, fists balled. He grabbed another globe, filled with a bright red cardinal perched on a snow-laden branch.

"Stop it," she hissed, grabbing the globe from his hand. "You're welcome in my room but please stop messing with my stuff."

Ronan folded his arms. "Who exactly do you think you're speaking to, human?"

"Do as she says," Dante commanded in a voice that demanded respect. He reached over and handed a coffee to Ronan.

"This is delicious," Armienti murmured while sipping his own coffee, inviting himself into her closet to explore her mess. Ronan joined Dante on the bed.

Autumn plopped on the floor and massaged her temples, taking deep controlled breaths. She was so stressed out; she could barely see straight. *Failure seemed inevitable.*

It appeared Armienti grew bored with exploring her closet as he exited the area almost as soon as he had entered. *What a surprise*, all that was inside were coats and dirty laundry. He stared at her, blue eyes blazing, and took a swig of his beverage.

"Aww, why the long face? Are you fretting over your silly globes?"

"They're not silly," she muttered, watching Armienti suspend all eighteen of them simultaneously from her shelf and inspect them individually. When he was through, he placed them back neatly in a whirlwind.

Armienti cocked his head to the side. "Why are these globes so important to you?"

Autumn smoothed her hands against her pajama pants.

"They feel safe and remind me of home. Each one is like its own little universe. So please, treat them with care."

"If one of your globes broke, it would be easy enough to fix, *especially* for one of us." Ronan popped a powdered munchkin into his mouth, chewing before swallowing.

Dante and Armienti each shot him a disapproving look.

Autumn glowered. She should've known. She walked over to Dante, placing a hand on her hip. "I need to speak to you. *Alone.*"

Armienti chuckled from the far corner of her room. "Come now, brother, I smell a lover's quarrel."

A lover's quarrel? Neither of them had ever used the term before. Although the idea of love frightened her, she wanted to experience it wholly.

"Enjoy yourself, cousin." Ronan winked.

Both cousins faded into the air. Coffees in hand.

"It was you?" She pointed a finger. "You repaired my snow globes? What were you doing in my room *on* the night we met?"

Now she would officially *fail her midterm.*

"How fascinating you ask." He tousled his raven hair, his human disguise fading to pale blue. "I don't recall repairing any snow globes, though." He stared at her strangely.

"I don't believe you." Autumn folded her arms. "I'm waiting for an answer."

Dante blinked, long lashes grazing his hollow cheekbones. "You know I find you attractive."

"That's *not* going to help you now."

His tail thrashed softly. "The night of the crash when I first saw you, I could barely think straight. Not because of the crash itself, but because I'd never seen such a beautiful girl in my entire life. Yes, I followed you home. Many, *many* times. My inclinations turned into a habit; one I made no effort to break. I found watching you sleep calming, because during the waking hours you shot down my advances and never cast a second glance my way."

Autumn stared at him, not knowing whether she should be more creeped out or flattered. Nothing surprised her about him anymore. Not that he was an alien, or that his home planet was located universes away. Now she discovered he'd been following around her the entire time.

"The dreams?"

"They were from me." He smiled.

Autumn pulled away, face and neck burning. Overcome with shame at how much she enjoyed those dreams.

"Why would you do that?" Her breath hitched in her throat.

"Isn't it obvious, my sweet, sweet Autumn?" His lips grazed against her lobe. "I wanted to torture you the way you torture me with your moonlit eyes and candied lips. Before, I could only dream of kissing. Now they're mine."

"I didn't mean to torture anyone." She trembled, the caffeine from her coffee finally kicked in.

"You don't have to try."

Autumn fell onto her bed, straddling him. Dante placed his mouth against her ear, hot breath pouring over her skin.

"Are you okay?" he asked.

"Yes." Autumn bit her cheeks, desperate not to wake her dad.

Pulling his top off, she ran her fingers across his chest. His abs were as ripped as she imagined. But his body was riddled with two deep jagged scars. An X mark crossed his right breast, and a long vertical gash extended from his rib cage to his hip. When she went to touch them, he snatched her hand and brought it to his lips.

"What happened?"

"Don't worry about it."

Autumn tangled her fingers in his hair as he kissed her,

strong hands against her hips, not knowing how to ask for what she wanted. He moved lower, and lower, her skin erupting in goosebumps. His fingers grazed her thighs when he stopped.

Autumn stared at him dazed as his lips played into a smile.

"We should study. I've distracted you enough."

Thirty-Nine

STUDYING WITH DANTE WAS INTENSE.

While they reviewed her Chemistry material, Autumn couldn't keep her eyes from drifting to his lips. Unable to prevent herself from imagining them pressed against her skin. Chewing her bottom lip, she willed herself to pay attention to a lesson even he couldn't make interesting. Chem was boring, but she was in crisis mode. If she failed one more midterm, she would lose her scholarship.

Occasionally, their gazes met, and her cheeks smoldered. Deep down, she wanted to go all the way with him. But subconsciously, a nagging voice in the back of her head made her reluctant. *He was an alien.* How did she fall for an alien? Did they love like humans? Or make love in the same way? There were so many questions plaguing her while she was supposed to be studying. And to make matters worse, he had plans to leave next year, regardless.

"Autumn, does that make sense?"

She nodded, unsure of what she agreed to.

He continued reviewing the chapters. Zoning in and out,

she traced her fingers through the smooth strands of his hair, grabbing his attention.

Snatching her hand mid-stroke, he kissed her. "Careful, or you might get me started again. I told you, you're my torturer."

Maybe he was right. Who knew anymore? She was so exhausted she could hardly keep up.

By 3:00 a.m. Autumn's brain was fried like a scrambled egg. Hopefully, she retained at least some of the information they studied. The only problem was she couldn't sleep. A smile crept across her lips.

Laying in Dante's arms, tail wound around her waist, she tossed and turned, unable to get comfortable.

"Tell me a story." She felt childish asking, but it always worked in the past. Her parents, and sometimes even Caleb, would tell her a story when she felt restless or uneasy. Caleb's stories were usually no frills about his martial arts accomplishments.

"I don't know any." His eyes shifted.

"How could you not know a single story in all your travels?"

He shrugged. "How about I show you something instead? Something dear to me."

"Show me, how?"

"I can plant dream-like visions in your mind, but surely you're aware now." He chuckled softly.

She rolled her eyes. "Okay, what do I have to do?"

"Relax." Dante moved closer, and she detected a tingling sensation at the base of her skull. It was neither painful nor uncomfortable. Her eyelids grew heavy, fluttering closed. The rest of her body felt heavy like it was covered by a million pounds of wet sand. Muscles slackening, she was unable to fight the powerful sensation.

"I feel funny." Her speech slurred, thoughts racing faster than they left her mouth.

Gently, Dante's fingers connected with her temples, massaging cyclically. Electrical waves spiked in her brain as he applied pressure, moving them deeper, and deeper, and deeper.

"Focus on the sound of my voice as I peel back the layers of your mind," he whispered.

Her body became limber. It was pointless to fight sleep any longer. Autumn fell out cold to the melodic caress of his voice.

An internal suctioning sensation came, like her soul was plucked from her body. When she opened her eyes, she floated toward the ceiling of her bedroom. Her sleeping form lay peacefully in Dante's arms.

She zipped around, light as a feather. A cool wind blew, gusting her up, up, up through the roof of her bi-level home. Monroe twinkled with microscopic lights beneath her.

She drew further still into the starlit sky, past clouds and silent planes. Weightless, she ascended higher into the atmosphere, through a rainbow barrier and into outer space.

It was pitch quiet. Earth rotated in all its cerulean and emerald magnificence. Gravity was nonexistent.

A powerful pull yanked her away into the great unknown. Past the solar system, she knew, until it was indistinguishable from the billions upon billions of blazing stars of the Universe, *or* Universes, as Dante would have affectionately corrected her.

Sparking shooting stars raced. All the while, Dante's voice urged her onward, speaking at an impossible speed.

Autumn traveled a great distance for what felt like forever, eventually reaching an enormous planet that mirrored Earth, only fifty times the size, with a stunning cobalt-blue hue. Not one, but two volcanic suns and pale white moons orbited around it.

Dante's home planet Surge. The one he was destined to return to. She descended through the dense colorless atmosphere to the ground, landing gracefully in a field of dewy cobalt grass.

To her left was a tremendous cityscape extending as far as her eyes could see, filled with futuristic, densely packed buildings, and whizzing aircrafts. Eons ahead of the technology on Earth.

But on the far end of the field stood a dark forest filled with crooked evergreen trees. A force deep inside beckoned, and she could no longer hear Dante's voice as her guide.

"*Autumn*," the trees whispered in a scramble of a thousand voices at once. She followed the caress of her name, leaving the blue meadow behind.

The trees became darker, blocking out the suns and sapphire sky. Autumn fought her way through them, snapping spindly branches.

Before long, she came upon a stark clearing, and descended a hill toward a glass still body of water. By the time she reached the bottom, she was drenched from head to toe with sweat. The temperature was hotter than a scorching summer day. Desperately needing to cool off, she dove into the cool, crisp water.

Autumn swam without a care in the world. When suddenly, she flinched. She was not alone. She glanced over her shoulder, her heart jumping through her throat. A hunchbacked figure draped in a thick onyx cloak waded through the water, mumbling in circles to itself. Autumn retreated, but a suctioning sensation brought her toward the form.

She trembled. "Who are you?"

It hung its head in absolute silence, never bothering to answer. They were in such proximity its wet, saturated covering brushed against her skin. Pulse quickening when it turned in crooked, uneven motions.

Breath escaped her lungs as it bent over, dripping salty water into her mouth, bearing the metallic taste of blood. A scraping sensation ripped over her arm, causing her eyes to well up with tears. A long razor-sharp talon protruded from a lumpy pink-vomit-hued finger followed by a long bumpy tongue that snapped out. Stumbling backwards, it caught her, nails like razor blades.

It repositioned its hood. Autumn's eyes widened as she timidly peered inside. A shiver of fear rolled through her essence. Its icy breath poured over her face in a visible white mist, bearing the rank scent of death.

"*Aaaaaaahh!*" She kicked and screamed, fighting with all her strength, but it was too strong. Several feline slit, red-rimmed eyes blinked before darkness consumed her.

When Autumn woke, her room was black, and Dante was fast asleep beside her in the bed. She grabbed her arm and winced. Her fingers trembled as they ran down the length over deep jagged scratches from where the monster attacked her. A gooey substance remained that burned like fire to the touch.

Forty

"I DON'T KNOW what you're talking about," Dante insisted while Autumn packed her bag for school. He was trying his best to be an understanding boyfriend and see the issue from her point of view.

"Stop it, you know what you did." Autumn extended her arm, skin smooth, which made her claims more outrageous.

"There's nothing there," Dante examined her.

"There was, I'm telling you."

"You think I hurt you?"

She remained quiet for a long moment, then said, "No, I didn't say that. I think maybe you were trying to be funny or scare me. I know what I saw... But I'm exhausted and I don't have time for this, I have a midterm to take."

Point well received. Autumn wasn't in her right mind. He never planted a pink, lumpy monster in her dreams. Although, the description reminded him of a disgusting pig he knew who resided in Universe 24. Keyserike. He would no sooner lift a finger to perform any measure of labor or wipe his own ass, that was always Dante's job.

This was the thanks he got for trying to be nice to his girlfriend. Dante wanted to end the evening with beautiful visions of starlight and his planet. No matter how hard he tried, he always messed up.

"You're driving me, right?" Autumn slung her bag over her shoulder.

"Yes."

"You should get your car. I can't be late."

* * *

Autumn hurried downstairs, flustered and frustrated. Dante *really* pissed her off.

To think he didn't believe her. She knew she wasn't crazy.

Autumn bumped into her dad, who donned a crisp navy-blue suit for the first time in forever. She assumed he was going to the office.

Her dad stood at the kitchen countertop, filling a thermos with coffee. "Did you find a friend to carpool with, or are you planning to take the bus?"

"No... Dante and I are back together. He'll be driving me."

She waited for the nuclear bomb to settle.

Her dad furrowed his brows. "How long has this been going on?"

"A few weeks."

"I can't say I'm thrilled about this, especially after what happened last time. Please promise me you'll be careful. I don't want to see you get hurt again."

She nodded. "You don't have to worry about me."

No sooner had they finished their conversation did her pocket vibrate. Autumn slid her smartphone out of her jeans. Dante called her.

She leaned over and kissed his cheek. "I have to go; I'm going to miss my test. Love you, Dad."

Autumn left the house, flanked by her dad, his laptop bag slung over his shoulder.

Dante's Ferrari shimmered in the driveway and her dad stopped dead. "Where did your boyfriend get a *two-hundred-thousand-dollar car*?" He folded his arms. "Did he steal it off a lot?"

"Dad," she hissed. "Of course not. It was a gift."

"You know, this car looks a lot like the one that was hijacked in town over the summer. A man was killed, and they never found his murderer."

A knot fastened itself in her stomach. A coincidence. Dante was *not* a murderer, and she trusted him.

Forty-One

WHEN DANTE ROLLED up to Autumn's home, her meddlesome father trailed her. *Just the person he didn't want to see.* Like his own father, who he never agreed with.

Dante stood and stretched his legs. He took Autumn's school bag and placed it into the land craft. Autumn sat in the front passenger's seat, and the door sealed vacuum tight. Her father looked like he wanted to speak with him in private.

"Sir," Dante said.

Mr. Ramon's mouth twisted, eyes gravitating toward the landcraft.

"This is the car you choose to drive my only daughter to school in?"

"I know not what you speak of. But I have no other means of transportation, unless, of course, you would prefer for us to fly."

Mr. Ramon's eyes narrowed to razor thin slits. Little did he realize it wasn't a jest.

"Maybe my daughter is impressed by your facade," Mr. Ramon said. "But I'm onto you."

"I don't care what you think of me." Dante squared his shoulders.

Mr. Ramon's face flushed a deep shade of crimson. He opened his mouth to respond when Autumn pushed the buzzer, the window rolling down.

"My test!" She threw her arms in the air.

"Don't worry. We'll arrive with plenty of time to spare," Dante assured her.

"Who are you really?" Mr. Ramon asked. "Where are you from? Where are your parents? And why are you *never* at work? I was told you have two jobs."

"It's none of your business."

"It is if you want to continue seeing Autumn."

Dante snorted. "Who's going to stop me, *you?* Don't make me laugh."

"Listen here you little punk, you don't get to waltz in and out of her life whenever you feel like it—"

Dante opened and slammed the door of the car, cutting him off at the pass. The expression on Mr. Ramon's face was priceless. A combination of fury and defeat. Dante bit his cheeks.

He turned toward Autumn, and she took hold of his hand. "I have to ask you a question and you have to promise to tell me the truth."

"Of course, I promise."

"You told me this car was a gift. You didn't steal it, did you?"

"Where would you get an idea like that?" Dante paused. "Was it your father?"

She glanced away, an indication he was correct. He suspected as much.

"Don't listen to him." He planted a kiss on her forehead. "You know he despises me and aims to pull us apart. You know me by now, don't you?"

She nodded.

"Then you know I would never ever steal a car, nor would I plant a monster in your dreams. I swear it. I swear on my life."

"Okay, fine, I believe you."

Dante kissed her knuckles. "Good."

* * *

They arrived on time after another high-speed chase with the authorities Dante diffused with his mind. When would the humans ever learn they were no match for him, and their efforts were futile?

Wrapping his arm around Autumn's waist, he walked her to class. Upon entering the facility, Autumn's curious moonlit eyes wandered toward the rapidly flickering lights.

"Tell me, what's the deal with the lights already?"

"Well, it's rather simple, you see. I have boundless amounts of energy within my body, and it interacts with your world's weak electrical current."

Her lips curved in approval. *Mystery solved.* When they reached the class, he hugged her and wished her good luck. Suddenly, his hair stood on end. He spotted Caleb with his strange red headgear and a smug expression on his face.

Forty-Two

WHEN AUTUMN PULLED AWAY from Dante's tender embrace, she realized his attention drifted over her shoulder. She turned. *Caleb.* She should have guessed. He sauntered down the hallway whistling, without a care in the world.

Caleb's statement red cap sat sideways over his shining ebony curls, backpack hanging from his shoulder.

Autumn fanned the sheen of sweat that erupted on her face. Her breathing shallowed.

"Hey," her throat tightened like someone choked her.

Caleb's eyes sparkled, and he moved his mouth as if to speak.

"Here he is, the man of the hour," Dante interjected. "State the nature of your business."

Caleb's features contorted. "Wait, is he serious? This must be some kind of joke."

Autumn disintegrated. She was hotter than she'd ever been in her life. Raising her arm, she wiped her moist brow against her sleeve.

Caleb continued, "Don't you have a job or somewhere else to be? You *obviously* don't go to this school."

Dante's lips coiled. "My job is watching you, imbecile."

Caleb tossed his backpack onto the ground, the impact echoing over the cold tiled floor. Fluorescent lights danced in the ceiling.

"Okay pretty boy." Caleb stretched his legs and limbered his arms. "Fight me."

Dante's fists balled. Autumn rolled her eyes. *Stupid guys.*

Drenched with sweat, she threw her body between them, creating a barrier. "Cut it out. This is ridiculous!"

They backed off, hatred simmering in their eyes. Holding her backpack, she headed into class, followed by Caleb, who glowered at Dante.

Dante remained in the hallway, watching and waiting. Autumn shook her head. It was somewhat flattering they were willing to come to blows over her, even if she would never admit it. She certainly didn't need this before her test.

Autumn unpacked her backpack and sucked in a breath. *Here goes nothing.* Being away from all the nonsense, her body temperature stabilized.

Her snowy-haired professor distributed the midterm.

"Begin."

A pit settled in her stomach. The moment she dreaded had finally come to fruition. Cracking open her exam, Autumn heard the rustling of pens scratching against paper, and the shuffle of sleeves over the wooden laminated desks.

Relief washed over her when she glanced at the first page. Not only were the questions familiar, but she completed them in a timely manner.

About an hour into the exam, the noise in the room died down with everyone wrapped up their midterms. Autumn had been done for a few minutes, and double-checked her work, eager to do well.

The scraping came out of nowhere. She dropped her pencil and glanced around. It was insanely distracting.

Everyone around her tuned in to the same strange noise. Their eyes wandered curiously around the room in search of the source. Her ancient professor, who sat at the head of the class, tossed his pen on top of a pile of papers.

"Ahhh!!" Autumn startled to the core. Heart pounding in her chest, she whipped around and stared at the rows behind her. All eyes were on *Caleb.*

Caleb twisted and turned in his seat, ripping off layer after layer of clothing. Instantly, his red cap collided with his desk, and he cast his hoodie onto the floor. He unbuttoned his white-collared shirt, revealing his toned, drenched body.

"Is anyone else burning up?" he slurred.

Autumn's heart pounded. Crap. There was only one explanation. Glancing at the door, she saw Dante grinning in the hallway like a jackal. What the heck was he doing?

The professor shot up from his desk and stormed over to Caleb.

"What's the issue, Mr. Cortez?"

"I'm sorry." Caleb's sapphire eyes widened. "Suddenly I was feeling *HOOOTTTT!!!*"

Caleb screamed, his voice carrying even higher than before. Several bouts of laughter erupted from different areas of the lecture hall. Autumn bit her cheeks and fidgeted her hands nervously. He was her boyfriend once, and Dante was hurting him.

"This isn't a place of antics, Mr. Cortez. It's a place of learning."

The professor snatched Caleb's examination and tore it in half. "I'm afraid you've earned yourself an *F* on the midterm."

"But I, I, I—"

"Leave, so my serious students can finish up their tests."

Face beet-red, Caleb accepted his punishment and sheepishly gathered his belongings. Shirt still unbuttoned, he left the class, mumbling under his breath.

Shaking, Autumn finished reviewing her test. She delivered it to her professor. Hopefully, her answers were correct.

Autumn reunited with Dante in the hallway, unsure of how to act. Although Dante's prank was funny, she felt terrible for laughing.

"Caleb is probably going to fail Chem," she muttered.

"That's really none of my concern." Dante rested his palm against the small of her back. "He needs to learn his place. I assure you there's plenty more suffering where that came from if he threatens me again."

They made their way to the lot where Dante's Ferrari was parked. Her stomach churned.

Someone in town was murdered during a carjacking. Her dad's words rang through her head. But there was no way he was right. Dante was hot around the collar, but he didn't have it in him to be a *murderer*.

Autumn hoped Dante had been truthful. She didn't need the cops materializing at her front door.

Footsteps scraped against gravel as Autumn stood with Dante. She glanced into the reflection of the Ferrari at Caleb charging full force. *What the heck did he want?*

Autumn turned around to demand to know what his problem was and gasped as Caleb's balled fist flew toward her. She tripped backwards over her own feet to avoid his blow and skinned her palms wide open. Blood and rock trickled into her sleeves.

For a split second, Autumn locked eyes with Dante before he moved aside gracefully. Caleb's fist crashed into the driver's side door, leaving an indentation. His flying shoe kicked the mirror clear off the car.

Dante whipped around, folding his arms. "You like to fight dirty, do you now?"

Caleb rubbed his bloody knuckles against his jeans and stood at a ready fighting stance.

"Hit me asshole. Hit me!"

"You were *warned*."

Forty-Three

FURY SEETHED through Dante's veins along with a heavy dose of bloodlust. Autumn sat on the ground, head resting against the car, trying to pick the pebbles out of her wounded hands. Nobody dared attack him, or worse, hurt his girl. He was going to kill him.

Dante clenched his fist and experienced pure satisfaction as he cracked Caleb square in the nose. He fell onto his back, fabric tearing against gravel, ruby-red blood trickling from his nostrils. Caleb kipped-up, landing on his feet, launching a roundhouse kick. Dante blocked his attempt, exerting little effort, and launched him across the pavement. Caleb sputtered backwards into someone else's car, shattering the windshield.

Caleb climbed out, picking the glass from his hair. "You're a martial artist?"

Dante loomed. "I'm far more skilled than that."

"I don't recognize your technique." Caleb crouched. "You're a freak and you fight like one, too. I've been taking it easy. Now, I'm going to show you the true power and technique of a state champion."

"Stop it, what are you guys doing?" Autumn groaned, still seated on the ground.

Dante's ears pricked. Autumn. He turned to check on her but heard the whizzing of wind as Caleb's fist flew toward his face. Enough already. The time had come for Dante to end him. It was long overdue.

Scattered groups of humans gathered around to watch, and Autumn, sweet, innocent Autumn, stared at him with her oversized moonlit eyes. Wider than usual with uncertainty.

Dante caught Caleb's left fist and squeezed it less than gently. Caleb whimpered, his complexion fading to a ghostlike hue. Dante jerked Caleb toward him, head whip lashing.

"Where's this power you speak of?" Breath flowed from Dante's mouth in a visible white mist. "All I see is a weak boy with a big mouth. You asked for this."

The glass of the lamps surrounding the land crafts shattered. A violent wave of fire ripped across the pebbled ground. Spectators screamed and retreated.

Dante crushed Caleb's hand. Bones cracked and tendons popped in conjunction with shrieks. Nobody bothered to interfere. Tears sprouted from Caleb's eyes before Dante shoved him to the ground. Caleb howled like an animal in heat as he cradled his broken hand.

"Quit crying like a little bitch and show some dignity." Dante hocked saliva in his mouth and spat on the ground.

Dante went to walk away but stopped. Succumbing to innate warrior tendencies, he rammed the heel of his boot into Caleb's left shoulder, dislocating it with a single strike. Caleb wailed through the parking lot. The crowd remained silent.

Dante attracted more than his share of unwanted attention, and even worse, Autumn witnessed the entire ordeal. Leaving Caleb to suffer publicly as people swarmed all around him, Dante assisted Autumn to her feet. She stared into his eyes, trembling. The fire continued to smoke in a thick black cloud.

* * *

Dizzy and weak, Autumn shook so violently, she feared her legs might give out. Dante embraced her and helped her steady herself. She was shocked and disgusted he could be so cruel.

Caleb's cries echoed while a fire truck and an ambulance rolled up, to transport him to Nyack Hospital. *She was torn.* Should she check on him? Or leave? Her skinned palm didn't compare to Caleb's injuries.

"Are you all right?" Dante asked, but it took a second for her to register his words.

"Yeah, I'm fine." But she wasn't, she was horrified. So horrified she couldn't look away from the ongoing scene. Caleb was strapped to a stretcher. Security guards pointed their way.

"Don't lie to me, you're bleeding." Dante ripped fabric from his shirt. He fastened a bow around each palm and opened the passenger seat car door.

Autumn stepped inside, unthinking, as EMTs loaded Caleb into the ambulance. She watched as it drove off. Autumn sat there quietly while Dante fastened her seatbelt, too stunned to protest.

They pulled out of the parking lot. Autumn could still see the lights of the ambulance swirling in the rearview mirror. Suddenly, recouping her senses, she unbuckled her harness.

Something wasn't right. Her gut screamed.

Autumn needed to get away. Needed to go anywhere but here.

At the stoplight, Autumn flung open the door. She jumped out of the car, sneakers skidding against the icy blades of grass as she ran away as fast as she could.

With tears streaming down her cheeks, frozen upon impact, she peered over her shoulder to see if Dante followed her. But he didn't. The car sat on the side of the road with the blinkers flashing.

When she turned around, he stood there. She slammed into him full force, the breath leaving her lungs with a sharp pull. Airborne, she headed straight toward a tree, when she stopped mid-air. A cool tingling sensation freezing over her body.

He gently placed her back on her feet. Legs wobbling, she fell to the ground, but Dante caught her by the arm before she made impact.

"Stay away from me." She pushed his hand away.

"Tell me what's wrong." He ignored her warning. "You're upset."

Was he serious?

"Where's all of this coming from?"

"Why did you hurt Caleb?" She pounded her fists against his chest, wincing on impact.

Autumn fell to her knees, burying her face in her stinging palms.

"Well, answer me this," Dante said. "How do you feel I should've handled the situation? Should I have turned my cheek and allowed him to strike me? Let him blacken an eye or take out a tooth? Lest you forget, he attacked me first."

"Oh, please. Don't pretend you didn't want to fight him." The wind howled, Caleb's phantom screams still ringing in her ears.

Dante's mouth fell into a tight flat line. "Autumn, he hurt you. I know he did, and that enrages me to no end. To think he believes you'd be willing to reconcile with him."

"How do you know that?"

"How do you not?"

Air whipped through her unbound coils.

"Autumn, I can't stand the way he looks at you, the way he gives himself false hope, and that he's human and I'm not." There was a long pause. Her heart accelerated. "Life can never be normal between us. The difference between me and Caleb is that I love you. And I would never hurt you."

Autumn's cheeks warmed. He loved her. Even Caleb never told her he loved her before. Still, she couldn't allow herself to fully enjoy the moment after what he did.

Dante tucked a stray strand of hair behind her ear. "I've loved you since the first moment I saw you, but you never answered my question. How do you feel I should have behaved differently?"

"I ummm..." She hesitated, at a complete loss for words.

"Maybe I should've allowed him to publicly torment me, and trip me while I was performing my station."

A quiet gasp escaped her. *That was him, too.* In her opinion, Misty and Hazel deserved what happened a little more than Caleb did. They were cruel without reason and tortured her through four solid years of high school.

"Thank you," she stammered. "You didn't have to."

"Oh, but I did," he said. "Because you refused. I can't handle seeing you disrespected. The thought of anyone hurting you makes me angrier than you could ever imagine."

"What you did was excessive. There are peaceful ways to make the same point."

"Where I'm from, strength is the only way to acquire respect. The Universes are man eat man. It's kill or be killed. Dominate or be dominated. Conquer or be conquered. I'm afraid there's no way around it. If you don't protect yourself, others will walk all over you and stake their claim. It's their nature to test, and your duty to set them straight."

"Dante, promise me this won't happen again. I understand you're from a different world, but violence is not okay."

Kneeling, he wiped away her tears and kissed her softly. Pulling away, he gazed at her.

"Okay, I promise."

Forty-Four

DANTE MADE a promise he could *never* hope to keep. How would he train? Manage a restless crew? Serve the Emperor or the Grand Supreme? Perform his duty? No, there was no hope for a peaceful existence. Fighting was ingrained into his very being. It was the Elattion way to fight. Dante had a reputation to maintain. But he wanted to please Autumn, desperately.

He didn't want to risk losing her. As it was, the clock on their time together was ticking.

To his everlasting disappointment, she never returned his *I love you*. He wasn't sure how he wound up slipping up and admitting it in the first place. it bothered him that she never reciprocated. It'd been so long since anyone told him they loved him and meant what they said. Maeve. *Was he truly unlovable?* She was probably laughing at him from beyond the grave.

Presently, his focus was on human troubles, and Autumn had more than most. If she wasn't fretting about school, her friends, running into Caleb again, which he admitted was *mostly* his fault, and her family, she worried about her driving test.

To redeem himself, he vowed to make it up to her the only way he knew how.

Ten suns and moons after his public brawl, he and Autumn traveled to a destination of her choosing bearing coordinates 67.04393 °N, -79.86402 °E. Her driving test was scheduled for the following morning, and like a wonderful boyfriend, he promised to help her.

The crisp air bore the relaxing scent of burning wood. He kept the Ferrari's heat at a firm eighty-five degrees. Else, Autumn shivered. Being human, she couldn't handle the harsh elements like he could. He felt no difference between the hottest of days to the most frigid.

Autumn gnawed away at her nails. This was her natural response to fear and anxiety, although he couldn't fathom why she'd be afraid.

Unless it was of him. Which, if that was the case, he wouldn't be proud.

When she went to place her hand into her mouth again, he snatched it mid-air and softly kissed her knuckles.

"You'll be fine."

She glanced at him, steel-gray eyes twinkling in the shadows. "How do you know? Can you predict the future?"

"No, unfortunately I can't." He chuckled. "But when have I ever failed you before? Look at your Chemistry exam. You earned a ninety, which is well above failing. You have much to be proud of."

Her cheeks shifted the color of roses. He noticed Autumn blushed often and deeply. He admired her, face warming.

They arrived at a chain link barrier reading, *Gonzaga Park.* Autumn's face lit up for a split second before she frowned.

"What's the problem?" He squeezed her hand. "Is this the incorrect location?"

"No. They're closed for the season."

He exited the vehicle, breath flowing visibly through the chilly night air. Millions of stars winked in the sky. The moon, however, hid from plain sight.

"What are you doing?"

"Getting us inside."

He severed the chain and tossed the metal links into the woods.

"That's illegal."

"According to who?" He winked.

"The Town of Monroe."

Dante flashed a small smile. A trivial worry.

"Let us hurry then, so nobody sees," he feigned concern, throwing his hand over his forehead.

Autumn sprinted back to the car while he ambled leisurely. What a silly girl. No matter how hard he tried, he couldn't get enough of her.

They rolled through the entrance, and with a flick of his wrist, the gate closed behind them.

The park itself was dark and deserted, with crumbling stone pillars and weathered monumental structures. Barren trees bent with frost dipped tips.

Dante drove the car to the opposite end of the travel way, cast in part by shadow by the surrounding forest. He placed the keys in her palm. After they switched stations, she made the appropriate adjustments.

She went to press the gas pedal. "Aren't you forgetting something?"

He chuckled, fastening her safety belt. *Autumn knew him all too well.* An inexplicable sense of relief overtook him, knowing she was safe.

When she pressed the pedal, her lack of experience became apparent. They accelerated in uneven spurts. Her knuckles paled as she gripped the wheel with intense ferocity.

"Are you nervous?" he asked, certain she was. Either that or she exaggerated her inexperience.

"Very." She stopped the car, glancing at him. "Sometimes I can drive, and other times my mind wanders to my mom. Although I wasn't with her when she died, I can't help but think about her last moments. How alone and scared she must have been." She wiped a few stray tears with the edge of her sleeve. "It's hard. My dad and I can barely function without her."

He stared at her. No words would comfort her or ease her pain. He was too familiar with the agony of loss himself.

"I'm sorry."

"You don't have to apologize."

"For your loss, I mean."

"Thank you."

"I think your mother would be proud of you if she was still alive. I think she would want you to spread your wings and roll."

Autumn revved up the car again and snorted wetly. "I think you mean drive."

Dante was not one used to being corrected, but he took it in stride.

"Fine, drive." He smiled, about to give up on the English language entirely. No matter how hard he tried, certain terms escaped him.

When Autumn attempted a second time, the result was more controlled. She pressed the petal in even strokes, convincing Dante her block was of a mental nature.

"Excellent. Let's try backwards."

Autumn placed the gears in reverse, and to his surprise, she was more skilled driving in this direction. They successfully drove in a complete circle.

"Stop. Have we covered every element of the test?"

"Yes, all except for parallel parking."

"What's that?"

"I need to park our car between two vertically parked cars. But obviously there are none."

He could manage. Conjuring an illusion with his mind, he projected two cars only they could detect. They were glowing white, in the darkness. He placed them to the right and left enough space between them for their vehicle.

Autumn did a double take. "That's amazing. Is there anything you can't do?"

He opened his mouth to respond, but hesitated. She'd asked a loaded question. Sure, he was young, attractive, and had the Universes at his fingertips. More than accustomed to getting what he wanted. And that was all fine and well, but what did any of it matter? If he had nobody to share his success with.

"Thank you," he said in a delayed response.

"There's no need to thank me. It's the truth." She smiled.

Autumn backed up and attempted to maneuver the car between the two vehicles. It was impossible to fail anymore miserably than she had. He simulated the sensation of metal crunching against metal.

"Sorry."

"It's no matter." He squeezed her shoulder. "Try once more. Don't give up so easily."

To his delight, she was successful after his encouragement. Autumn clapped her hands together, jumping up and down in her seat.

"I did it!"

Dante grinned, never doubting her ability for a minute.

They practiced for many consecutive hours. By the end of their session, he was more than confident in her ability to pass her test. But she didn't seem content. Instead, she was unusually quiet. Autumn stared ahead, bottom lip quivering. Cheeks slicked wet with warm, salty tears.

"Why are you crying?"

Ignoring him, she threw open the door and walked into the chilly night air. First slowly, followed by quickening steps. A cloud of white breath flowed through the wind.

Forty-Five

NOT AGAIN. Dante floated, phantom like in grace.

"What did I do?" His voice echoed through the silent field. "Tell me what's the matter?"

Autumn finally stopped, crouching, burying her face in her hands. Bitter sobs escaped her mouth. Gradually, she glanced at him with glistening eyes.

"I'm sorry." Her mouth quivered. "I'm not sure what got into me."

"What's the problem?" He guided her to her feet. "I want you to speak freely with me."

Autumn hesitated, staring at him.

"Autumn please," he said, voice soft and urgent.

"I know this sounds selfish, but I don't want you to leave. I don't want to be alone again."

Autumn spoke of selfishness, when he knew he was the selfish one. The mess of feelings he created. Sometimes he wondered if life would be simpler if he never met her at all.

But he did. Dante discovered her, pursued her, and wanted her all for himself. *He loved her.* Honestly, he didn't want to leave her either. But there was no alternative option. Duty summoned.

"Unfortunately, staying is not an option. I have to return whether I like it or not."

"I know, I always knew. I was dreaming again, hoping for a different answer."

"Dreams do come true, you know."

Autumn squeezed out a smile, painful to behold. Tears trickled down her cheeks.

"Not this one apparently," she said. "None of mine do. I can't help but wonder what it would've been like to know you longer. I wish my first kiss belonged to you."

Dante tucked a fallen strand of hair behind her ear and she continued. "Maybe high school would've been easier. I wish we could've met a year earlier. At least then I would have had a date for prom."

"What's prom?"

"It doesn't matter." She averted her eyes. "Never mind."

He could always tell when she wasn't being truthful. It was written all over her face. Apparently, prom was a matter of great importance, or else she wouldn't have mentioned it.

"Tell me, what is it?" he insisted.

Smoke poured from their mouths, mingling together through the crisp night air.

"Prom is a special dance that takes place in junior and senior year of high school. It starts with a promposal where a girlfriend or a boyfriend asks their significant other in an elaborate way if they'd like to go to prom. Friends can ask friends, too. Girls wear fancy dresses and guys wear tuxedos. And the party lasts all night long."

What Autumn described resembled a ball, and he'd attended quite a few on various occasions.

"Why didn't you have a date?" Her story didn't add up. Instinct suggested she'd eliminated an important detail. Why would a girl with such beauty and charm be made to attend alone?

"Well..." Her shoes crunched against the frozen greenery. "Nobody asked me after—"

"After what?"

"When Caleb and I were still together, he asked me to prom. My mom had already bought my dress and shoes. And then he broke up with me out of nowhere, slept with Misty, and took her instead. I guess I should've seen it coming. They were studying together, doing some kind of class project. She's cool, rich, popular, and beautiful. Any guy would've made the same decision. I was nobody special then, and I'm still not."

With every ounce of his being, he fought to hold his tongue. What the hell was wrong with Caleb? No manners. No consideration. Dante despised him before, but Autumn's admission brought his hatred for the boy to a new, unfathomable level. He regretted not murdering him during their fight.

"I would've taken you in an instant. Follow me." He gestured.

* * *

Dante gently walked Autumn through the soccer field at Gonzaga Park. Blades of frozen grass slipped against the soles of her Converse.

The sky was overrun with millions of glittering stars, and the moon drifted behind the clouds.

Dante fell on one knee and she gasped, unsure what he was up to.

"Will you be my date to prom?"

Her cheeks burned, instantly becoming the warmest part of her body.

"What are you talking about?" she asked skeptically. "How are we supposed to have prom here?"

There was no venue, DJ, students, or refreshments. The time for prom had long since passed. Barren trees swayed in the howling wind.

"Close your eyes and visualize the dress you wish to wear."

Her pulse thundered in her ears. "This isn't another dream with a scary pink monster, right?" She'd been terrified since that night to close her eyes.

"No, I assure you it's not." Relief flooded through her body.

Dante snatched her hand from her teeth and twined his fingers in hers. Autumn inhaled and closed her eyes. Still longing for the dress she should've worn the first time to prom, she visualized a champagne tulle skirt, with a fitted bodice laying horizontal across her chest. It was secured by two spaghetti straps, and adorned in its entirety with golden foiled stars.

Around her wrist, she wore a corsage of four white roses and a fresh sprig of baby's breath, secured by a coordinating satin bow.

"Now open them."

She opened her eyes tentatively, and grinned with sheer delight. A circle of netted tulle puffed around her, and crinkled foiled stars rested against her palms.

"This is amazing."

"You look beautiful."

They rose together hand in hand, to the sky. Autumn did her best not to look down, being deathly afraid of heights, but she wanted to remember every detail.

Dante took her hand in his and placed his other palm on the small of her back. Butterflies flitted through her stomach when she realized what came next.

"I'm a terrible dancer." She gulped.

He chuckled softly. "With me as your guide you'll be fine."

Dante bowed, and she automatically curtseyed. In the background, she heard the faint strumming of a harp. Haunting and of foreign origin.

Taking hold of her hand, he whisked her through the night sky. Autumn twirled as she moved her body close to his. She gazed into Dante's eyes and they drifted like duel fading spirits through the night sky. In the distance, a quaint ember of a town sparkled and shined along the blackened horizon.

"Do you dance a lot?"

"No, not since I've been away from home. It's been a few years since I've attended a celebration at the Capital."

"Where's the Capital?" Dante lifted her and spun her above his head. Autumn landed delicately onto her feet, and they glided through the air.

"Surge."

"How could Surge be the Capital of itself? Earth isn't the Capital of Earth."

"Surge is the head of the territories controlled by my Emperor."

"That must be so exciting to be around royalty." For a split second, Autumn was envious. His life sounded thrilling. Dante partied with royals at the other end of the Universes, and all she had to look forward to was passing her road test. *If she even passed.*

Dante shrugged. "I suppose many would find it appealing."

"What's the royal family like?"

"Like any other family, I suppose," he said. "They have their quirks. The Empress, though, reminds me a lot of you. She charms everyone she comes in contact with. Including the miserable man she's bound to."

"The Emperor."

Dante nodded. "Many despise him, including myself."

"Your Emperor sounds like a real jerk. What's the matter with everyone?"

"How so?"

"People prey on the vulnerable. You know bullies. I don't understand. Outer space sounds no different than Earth."

"Outer space is far worse, Autumn," Dante said. "I know those two girls at the diner left a bitter taste in your mouth, among other people."

"Well," Autumn tentatively began, aware of how protective he was of her, "Hazel actually apologized, but Misty is a different story."

A vein twitched across Dante's forehead.

"Please promise me you won't hurt them. You can't hurt anyone else because of me ever again."

Dante's amber eyes twinkled with sincerity. "Okay, I'm confident justice will dispense itself another way."

Forty-Six

WHEN THEY LANDED, Autumn's magnificent dress faded before her eyes. Glitter and tulle blew through the surrounding forest with the passing wind. In the heat of the moment, Autumn decided she wanted to have a new experience. Something she'd never done before and had thought of often but was too afraid to act on.

When Dante took her by the hand, she stopped and said, "Uh one second, I have to use the bathroom." It was the quickest and most believable excuse she could concoct.

He stood by the car, giving her privacy.

Autumn crouched behind a bush and pulled lipstick and mascara out of her peacoat pocket. She'd been carrying around makeup she'd found in her mom's top drawer. *In case the opportunity presented itself again.* Shaking, she quickly used the selfie camera on her phone and swiped her lips and lashes, guided only by a silver stream of moonlight peeking from beneath the clouds.

She never wore makeup before, but from what she heard from her friends, guys liked it. More so for an occasion like *this* one.

She sprinted back, grabbing hold of Dante's hand.

"Are you all right?"

"Yes, um, I've been doing a lot of thinking and there's something I'm hoping we can try together if you feel up for it." The words were surreal coming from her mouth, especially because she knew he was leaving next year, regardless.

"Okay. What do you have in mind?" He tucked a stray strand of hair behind her ear. Too shy to answer, she grabbed his hand, and pulled him onto the backseat.

Trembling, she straddled and kissed him. Softly at first, but then more deeply.

She pulled away slowly. "I—"

Dante's eyes traveled along her face. "You seem different."

Her heart thundered. *He noticed.*

Dante ran his fingertips over her lips and lash lines. "You're wearing cosmetics. Autumn, you didn't have to do all of this for me."

"Do you like it at least?"

"I think you're beautiful," he mused. "You're beautiful on the inside and outside, and you never needed any of this to prove it."

Her mouth bowed. "Dante, I love you too. I should've told you sooner, but I was afraid of—"

"Afraid?"

"Of getting hurt again," she admitted. And falling in love with a guy who'd be leaving next year, but she left the last part unsaid.

"Oh Autumn." His lips crashed against hers before he pulled away, trembling. "Are you sure this is what you want and you've thought it through? What you're looking to give me you can never get back."

"Yes, I want you," she said, barely able to breathe with the excitement building inside of her. His tail wound around her thigh, and warm breath poured over her neck before he kissed her again.

"Wait, I almost forgot."

Reaching to the front seat, she dug inside her bag, and found a foiled wrapper she'd purchased from the drugstore.

She handed it to him. "This is a—"

"I'm sure I can figure it out."

She unbuttoned her wool peacoat and tossed it to the floor along with her shirt. Dante unfastened her bra, casting her a look of admiration that made her insides smolder. Autumn grasped his hard muscles as soft noises escaped her mouth from his tender touch.

Dante moved lower to where she desperately wanted him before he hesitated. "Perhaps we should slow down. Maybe this isn't the best idea after all."

Her heart slammed against her ribcage. "What? But you just? I don't under—"

"I'm aware of what I said." He froze. Every muscle in his body went taut.

"What's wrong?" she stammered.

But Dante didn't answer. He stared into the dark woodland. He pushed her off his lap and frantically dressed himself.

Heart racing, she said, "I'm sorry. Did I offend you?"

"Stay here." He leapt out of the car. Slivers of full moonlight illuminated his flowing hair.

* * *

There was an entity here, only a moment ago, *watching them.* Dante could detect its raw, untapped power. But where did it go?

He closed his eyes and inhaled, his senses heightened.

"Dante, where are you going?" Autumn stumbled toward the forest.

"Autumn, go back to the car!" he shouted.

"What's going on? We need to talk." She folded her arms.

"Right now!"

Autumn stopped, apparently hearing him this time, and sprinted back to the Ferrari.

Continuing to survey the area, he met with a pair of familiar blue eyes. He exhaled. "Armienti, what are you doing out here? Did you follow me?"

"It's a free forest, is it not?" Armienti ambled leisurely, smoothing his golden tresses with his black-gloved palm.

Dante scrunched his nose. "Where's Ronan? Who's watching the ship?"

Armienti shrugged. "How should I know? Isn't that supposed to be your station, princeling?"

"Your pardon?"

His cousin peered over his shoulder. "Who's the girl?"

Dante made a face. "Are you drunk? Have you been dipping into my stash of wine *again?*"

"A simple question."

Dante's vision scrambled. Shit, the full moon. *And Autumn.*

Armienti grinned through the shadows as strange lights danced before Dante's eyes and his world faded to black.

Forty-Seven

AUTUMN BALLED HER FISTS, warm tears rolling down her cheeks. What an idiot she was. How could she be so stupid? Spilling her guts to Dante, only to have him run off on her. She planned to make love to him for the first time.

Either he was a complete coward, or he lied to her about his feelings.

Why did she have to tell him she loved him? It was too late to retract her words.

Hours passed, and she was stranded in a perfectly good car *without* a license, so she couldn't drive herself home.

Shivering in the dead of night, she walked to the main road and called an Uber. Autumn concluded he ditched her and wasn't coming back. She'd never felt so foolish in her entire life.

When she arrived home, she was fortunate her dad was asleep. She wasn't in the mood to explain to him how she got home and why she'd been out so late.

But Autumn had a bigger problem. Who would take her to her road test after Dante flaked?

When the morning arrived, she'd have to ask her *dad* for a ride, and *dreaded* the awkward conversation. She'd been so adamant about her boyfriend and vouched for him.

When she climbed out of bed, it occurred to her, *really* occurred to her for the first time, that Dante had a ship somewhere. A ship he'd never mentioned, and she'd never seen. Autumn couldn't help but wonder why he never talked about it and *what* he could be hiding? Perhaps it was where he ran off to.

After freshening up, she walked downstairs wearing a light-blue sweater, with a silver butterfly barrette securing her hair. Her dad sat in the kitchen, dressed casually, which meant he planned to work from home. Hopefully, he had time to drive her.

"Hey Dad," she said, taking a strawberry sprinkled donut from the counter.

His mouth rolled to the side. What now? She sighed.

"I'd like to have a talk with you about your boyfriend," he said. "I think he's disrespectful, and he's not being entirely truthful with you."

"I know, I know, I know. Stop it Dad, you're driving me crazy! I can't take any more stress! I have my road test!" She raked her fingers through her hair and paused. "I need a ride to the test site and to school after."

"I thought he was bringing you?"

"Dad, now!"

Her vision split before her pocket vibrated. She peeked, and Dante's number flashed across her screen.

"Hello?"

"I'm outside."

Click.

"Never mind. Bye, Dad, I have to go."

Autumn left her house in a thunderous rage, slamming

the front door. She marched to the Ferrari, wind whistling through her coils. The sky was overcast with thick, dark-gray clouds.

She climbed inside and her boyfriend fiddled with the heat controls, making the car warm enough for her, which on any other occasion would've been thoughtful. His hair was disheveled, dirt streaking the high planes of his cheeks. Muddy branches laid by his boots on the floor.

"Where were you?"

"I was preoccupied," he said nonchalantly.

"You look like you were rolling through the mud like an animal. You left me last night to freeze and find my way home! You really have some freaking nerve!"

"Well, I'm here now, aren't I?"

Autumn ground her teeth as he leaned over to buckle her in. She batted him away, fastening her own safety belt. That's all he had to say? No sorry? *Screw him.*

"Well, that's not good enough."

"What do you want from me?"

"*We need to talk.*"

Dante stared at her. "If you don't stop complaining, we'll be late." She hugged herself, forehead twitching. They pulled away, driving to the test site.

Not long into their ride, she sensed his eyes on her. Calculating.

"What's on your mind?" he asked smoothly. He forgot their previous conversation. Or else he purposely ignored the issue.

"Well, for starters, you abandoned me." She crossed her arms. "You left me naked in your car when I was ready to sleep with you. I think you're hiding something from me."

"Oh really, what do you suppose I'm hiding?"

Autumn continued, "I want to see your ship. I think we've

been dating long enough. You should've invited me over a while ago. And I know your parents are back on Surge, but have you at least told them about me?"

"What's this sudden fascination you have with my ship and my family?"

She squeezed his hand. "I love you. Why is that so difficult for you to believe? I'm not sure how it is on Surge, but here on Earth you're supposed to invite your girlfriend over to your house and introduce her to your family. It's kind of a rule."

"Who makes these rules you're always talking about?"

She rolled her eyes. "They're common knowledge."

"I see."

* * *

Dante was ready to pull his hair out of his scalp between the horrific night he had and Autumn's incessant questioning. Dante was horrified, catching a glimpse of himself in the mirror. He smoothed his frazzled tresses. Not to mention he couldn't get Armienti's sickening expression out of his mind. He planned to have a word with him upon his return. What he'd done was an act of defiance, and they needed to present a unified front.

But Autumn had a point. He felt more guilty than ever, leaving her to wonder about his whereabouts. Especially when it was supposed to be their first time together, and he ruined *everything*.

Autumn deserved so much better.

Upon their arrival, his communicator bore the coordinates, 41.40159°N, -74. 32150°E.

"Are you ready?"

"As ready as I'll ever be." She gulped.

Several cars lined up along the travel way, filled with

humans waiting to be tested. A middle-aged female with a sallow complexion motioned for them to move forward. She exchanged pleasantries with Autumn. Afterwards, Dante left the car, handing his girlfriend the keys.

"Wish me luck." Autumn's lips trembled slightly.

"You won't need it."

Autumn rolled off with the woman in tow. Sauntering along the side of the travel way, he kicked stones with the tip of his boot, gritting his teeth.

After everything he'd done for her, she doubted him. Between the rides to school, the late-night study sessions, and dedicating every waking hour to meeting *her* needs. The more he dwelled on it, the more he realized he was essentially at her beck and call.

And strangely, he didn't mind.

Maybe he was a fool after all. A fool for the Earth girl named Autumn. All rationality was lost on her.

When Autumn returned, she beamed from ear to ear.

"I passed!" She jumped into his arms. "Thanks again for helping me." Her long lashes fanned against her soft rosy cheeks.

"Congratulations. I never doubted you for a second."

Dante took the control seat, and she resumed her previous position in the passenger's seat. He preferred this arrangement for the time being. Not that he didn't trust her skill, but he was confident his was superior.

Dante also had a *specific* detour planned. One, only he knew how to navigate.

"I have an idea." His mouth curved. "I've been thinking and you're right. It's high time I bring you to my Earth dwelling."

"Right now? But I have class," she protested.

He stared at her features straightening. She was never

pleased. It seemed she loved the sound of herself complaining. "I don't care, Little Moonlight. Perhaps you should've thought twice about taking issue with me."

"But..."

Ignoring her pleas, they pulled away with one destination in mind.

Forty-Eight

AUTUMN STOOD WITH DANTE, *shivering* in the cold wintry morning light. Snowflakes trickled from the sky in a white glittering whirlwind. They were not in a neighborhood, but at the head of the Farrah Falls hiking trail. The forest was dense and dark, wind gusting clear through her light-blue sweatshirt.

"*This* is where you live?" she asked through numb lips. White smoke poured from her mouth.

Dante appeared unphased by the elements. Not a single raised hair or goosebump was visible on his skin.

"Follow me."

Autumn walked, but halfway through entering the forest, Dante halted. Sneakers sliding against the slush, she collided with him. Her breath was ripped from her lungs, and she was reminded of his strength and how totally human she was in comparison.

He caught her by the arm. "Breathe."

Turning, he waved his hand through the air. The Ferrari's onyx metallic finish faded.

Autumn approached the spot where the car was. With awe

and wonder, she extended her fingertips, only feeling the icy wind.

She gasped when her feet left the ground, a familiar cool tingling sensation flooding through her limbs. She rested, cradled in Dante's capable arms.

"I can walk on my own," she insisted.

"Settle down and enjoy the ride. The terrain is slick and rugged, and we can cover ground faster this way."

As usual, he was right. The snow settled around the rocks. And in some places, ice had formed. From the many occasions they'd spent together, she already gathered there was no changing his mind when he believed he was right. He was *pigheaded*. To keep the peace, she opted to remain quiet for the duration of the trip.

When they crossed the footbridge, a layer of thick, sparkling ice solidified the water that flowed freely over the summer. The sun peeked its face shyly through the barren tree tops, offering little to no warmth on such a brisk day.

Dante had solid hiking skills. Never once did he rest or catch his breath. All the while, she dangled impatiently like a baby kangaroo, ready to kick at a moment's notice.

A few minutes into their trip, they arrived at the crystallized waterfall where the "incident" took place. Autumn's cheeks boiled with the passing memory. He glanced at her, lips flickering. Quickly, she averted her eyes to ease the awkwardness.

They came upon a vast, circular clearing in the center of the forest. She had never hiked out this far before, and it looked out of place in comparison to the neighboring landscape.

The ground was lined with hundreds of fallen crisscrossed trees. The standing trees were halved to stumps and singed black at their bases, causing her to believe they'd been severed at a singular point in time.

He stopped walking and placed her back on her feet. Autumn stretched her arms and legs as they stared over a graveyard of trees. Squirrels scratched their way up trunks as snowflakes twirled through the breeze.

"Is this it?" She scanned the clearing.

"Yes."

She found it difficult to believe he'd been living all the way out here for months on end. Disappointment flooded through her. She expected to see a ship. Not a decaying pile of trees.

"Are you sure this is the right place?"

The wind howled and whipped over her skin, she wanted to be inside. Somewhere warm, preferably with central heating and a cup of hot pumpkin spiced coffee in hand.

"Patience is a virtue."

Autumn laughed to herself. Easy for him to say. He was a walking, talking fire generator.

Suddenly, the faintest layer of white smoke misted and condensed above the grounded trunks. It swirled cyclically in a counterclockwise direction and rose well above the tallest standing trees. As the fog dissipated, an obsidian chrome structure came into clear view, resembling an angular slice of cake. There were three distinct levels divided by rows of stacked windows. The structure exceeded the height of the tallest tree in the forest.

A side door opened and fell to the ground with a thud. Hissing seeped out, reminding her of a cobra ready to strike. Gray smoke poured from the interior and melded with the howling wind.

Autumn grasped Dante's hand so tightly her knuckles popped. She had been adamant about seeing his ship. But now, she got an ominous vibe from the entire situation.

"Is this not what you wanted?" His voice was soothing and even. "Or have you changed your mind?"

She hesitated. "It is. But I didn't realize your ship would be so scary..."

He chuckled. "I assure you, there's nothing to fear. If a tour is still of interest to you, I must ask you to pick up your pace. Lest the force-field expires, we only have moments remaining."

They entered, the door suctioned closed with a whoosh. Autumn's heart sped so rapidly she feared she might faint.

Forty-Nine

DANTE MORPHED BACK into his natural form, golden olive skin fading to pale blue. Autumn couldn't help but admire his inhuman handsomeness. She chewed her bottom lip.

Figures stirred in the shadows, catching her attention. Two towering bodies stood in absolute silence, clothed in onyx uniforms with rounded helmets concealing their features. They held oversized chromatic guns resembling rocket launchers.

"Who are they?" She stuttered, wrapping her arms around Dante's waist.

"They're guards," he said nonchalantly. "There's no need to be alarmed."

"*Malafec te und,*" he said, in a voice that commanded respect and expected to be obeyed.

The guards knelt, placing their weapons at their feet.

"What did you say?" She had never heard him speak *alien* before.

"At ease in my native Ivarkian."

Offhand, she noticed the lights faded and flickered, which

wasn't out of the ordinary. But it was apparent the ship ran on a borrowed power source. And could go dark any day.

Three levels of winding steel steps led from one floor to the next. She followed close behind and they descended to the base of the ship.

They entered a room filled with silver rectangular tables. A series of horizontal stainless- steel pods with clear curved tops sat on the right. On the opposite wall were dozens of free-standing metal cabinets above sinks. The air stank of vinegar, and the room itself had a sterile vibe.

"What is this place?"

"A medical ward. All of our more substantial ships have one."

"And those?" She pointed toward the strange beds.

"Ah, yes." He smiled, brilliant white teeth twinkling. "Those containers are what's commonly known as sleep chambers. A vast majority of our voyages are months or years at a time. It's not unheard of for warriors to experience bouts of madness, being confined to a small place for such an extended period. These pods offer them the option of sleep until we reach our destination."

"Have you ever used one before?"

"No, but plenty of others do. I prefer to use my precious travel time to dream. It's the only peace and quiet I ever truly have."

Dante's life seemed lonely. Traveling so often had to take its toll. It must've been tiring after a while, constantly being so far away from home.

BANG, BANG, BANG, "*AAAAH!!*" echoed from a distant room. Her adrenaline spiked, trickling through her limbs.

Someone sounded like they were in trouble. The screaming continued while they stood there together. A vein twitched along Dante's forehead.

"What's going on?"

Dante shook his head, ignoring her question.

Placing his palms on her shoulders, he said, "Follow me and remain behind me at all times."

They climbed the stairs in rapid steps, making their way onto the main floor. She ambled through the hallway, her short legs working twice as hard to keep up with Dante's stride. A pit hardened in her stomach.

This level resembled a dormitory with compact stacks of cots on either side of the steel walls. How many Elattions were stranded here?

She spotted a substantial gathering of twenty or so guys. They towered above her head, some taller than Dante. Their skin ranged from the darkest blue to the palest, and their eyes and hair were within the natural spectrum. They all wore pitch-black bodysuits and appeared to be in their early twenties.

They formed a circle of spectators and in the center was a man with a fire-red ponytail bound shirtless to a pole. His body was littered with black and purple bruises. A second man with a bald head loomed over him and cracked his back with a metal rod. Autumn's ears were assaulted with screams and smacking flesh. *Holy crap.*

Everyone laughed and jeered. Dante did *not* look impressed.

For a split second, she thought about running away. But her legs wouldn't cooperate.

Dante stormed over to the guy with the pole and ripped in from his grasp. The man turned around, color fading when he laid eyes on Dante. He dropped to his knees. The entire room fell silent except for labored breathing.

* * *

Dante was beyond *mortified*. Of all the days, his crew behaved like a pack of wild beasts. *Autumn had to be with him.*

"What the hell is going on here?" he shouted in his native tongue.

"Your—" The soldier spoke between chattering teeth.

"Silence," Dante roared. "This is how you choose to conduct yourselves in my absence?"

Everyone remained quiet.

"What is the meaning of this?"

"This man stands accused of a crime," one soldier said. "He stole my daily rations."

"Whether this may or may not be true, who granted you the authority to administer his punishment?" Dante slapped the rod against his open palm. "Was it Master Armienti or Ronan?"

Neither of them were present. *It figured.*

The soldier stayed quiet. He should've known better, but he was a fool.

"Soldier, remove your armor. I promise I won't be as gentle as you were."

Dante raised the rod to strike him when he remembered. *Autumn.*

She stood there, shaking. Eyes wide with terror. Recalling the agreement he made with her, he lowered the pole.

"Upon second thought. I don't want to be rude to my guest."

Folding his arms, he stared at the terrified man on the ground. "Soldier, you're in luck. Your punishment has been delayed. Use these next few hours to think about what you've done and where your allegiance lies."

The soldier trembled. He tossed the bar to the ground and rejoined his girlfriend.

* * *

There was so much yelling in Dante's alien language, Autumn's ears ached. A fight had broken out, and Dante intervened. The gathering dispersed, and there were two half-dressed blue aliens bound by their hands to a pole.

"What happened?"

"I apologize you were forced to bear witness to that. My men are often restless. They have little to occupy their time."

"What's going to happen to them?" The words left her mouth in slow motion.

"I intend to discipline them." He crossed his arms. "On my ship, nobody bends the rules. And if they do, they're punished."

"Your ship?"

"Precisely. I'm captain of this ship." He flashed a twinkling grin.

"Captain?" She wrinkled her nose.

Dante chuckled. "Are you aware you're repeating yourself, Autumn Ramon?"

"Aren't you kind of young to be a captain?"

"Age is irrelevant."

They walked to a stairwell leading to the highest level.

"How come you never mentioned this to me before?"

"Well, I suppose the topic never came up in conversation."

No, it didn't. Secrets, more secrets. Her forehead pulsated.

"I know this experience must be jarring for you compared to what you're used to." He wrapped his tail around her waist. "But there's still one more floor to see if you're feeling up to it. If not, I can take you to school a faster way than driving."

Although the tour had been overwhelming, she wanted to see what existed on the final floor.

They continued to the bottom of a dark stairwell. After what she just witnessed, she wasn't sure what to expect. She also discovered Dante was a captain. *Another detail he omitted.*

They were met with a substantial dark metal door. On the

right hung a scanner enclosed by a thick sheet of glass. Dante removed his glove and pressed his thumb. A blinding green light flashed before they were granted access.

This area was smaller than the previous floors. The walls were ivory and lined with three sealed metallic doors. Dante banged his fist against the first door, followed by a series of footsteps. She stood as still as a statue.

Autumn gawked when Armienti emerged from the room. Golden hair sopping wet against his blue skin, with a white fluffy towel secured around his waist. Steam flowed overhead.

"To what do I owe this tremendous pleasure?" The question played off Armienti's lips.

His sky-blue eyes gravitated to her. "What's Autumn doing on board?"

Dante rolled his eyes. "Suddenly you recollect her name."

"How could I possibly forget such a pretty face?"

Dante shot him a puzzled look.

"He's taking me on a tour of the ship," she offered.

"And how do you find it?"

"It's beautiful," she said politely. But in reality, what happened earlier rattled her to the core.

"I'm glad to hear." Armienti smiled. "I'm sure it's nowhere near as lovely as you are though." Taking her hand, he placed a kiss on her knuckles.

Dante cinched his tail tighter around her waist. "We're not here for flattery."

"Oh," Armienti said. "Have you finally brought her here to tell her the truth?"

The truth? She glanced at Dante for a sign.

"I haven't a clue what you're talking about. But I've come to inform you that a mutiny erupted on board a little while ago."

"I'm aware of no such occurrence. As you can clearly see, I'm busy." Mist from his room seeped into the hallway.

"If you weren't out all night, you'd have been dressed ages ago."

Armienti furrowed his brow. "What? I stayed here exactly as I was instructed—"

"Stop playing a fool. I'm in no mood. Where's Ronan?" Dante folded his arms.

"He's still asleep."

"Not anymore."

Dante kicked the opposite side door in, crashing it into the room. He stormed inside, grabbing his other cousin by his spiky hair. He dragged him thrashing into the hallway and tossed him onto the floor.

"Seriously, Dante?" Ronan yelled.

Autumn's cheeks heated, Ronan laid there blue and stark naked. She'd never seen a naked guy before.

"How nice of you to finally join us." Dante's voice oozed with sarcasm.

Ronan came to a stand. "What's Autumn doing here?"

"We already covered that," Dante snapped. "Perhaps you should take better care to wake your lazy ass up at a reasonable hour. I'm sure you're also blissfully unaware of the mutiny that took place."

"What mutiny?"

"*Exactly* my point."

"I do apologize," Ronan said. "I was out late, and I have more important matters to attend to than supervising those hooligans downstairs. That's your station. Perhaps if you weren't so busy all the time with your human girl, you would've been there to stop it."

"Ronan, you shall do what's required of you. I instructed you both to remain on this ship. Or at the very least, one of you to supervise the crew while I'm not around."

Dante pressed his fingers through his raven tresses. "I shall consult both of you later. This nonsense has eaten up far too much of my valuable time."

Dante gently took her by the hand and led her to the third and final door.

He whispered under his breath in his native tongue. *Probably obscenities.* He pressed his thumb onto another glass covered access pad and the door slid open.

Inside, was an all-inclusive suite with a circular bed topped with numerous royal-purple pillows. On the left was a bathroom with a standing shower. On the opposite side sat a crystal- clear propane size tank holding water. There was a pantry with hundreds of white oatmeal sized packets next to a round metal table with chairs. On the back wall shone a single source of light, a long rectangular window.

She walked over and discovered the window offered a scenic view of the Farrah Falls hiking trail. A group of hikers wandered through the forest, unaware of the massive extraterrestrial vessel sitting mere feet from them.

This is how Dante went undetected for all of these months.

"I'm assuming this is your room?"

His tail wrapped around her waist. "You never fail to impress me with your perceptivity, Autumn Ramon."

She brushed him away, taking a seat on the windowsill. "Not so fast. You have a lot of explaining to do. And you can start by telling me where you were last night. And what was more important than being with me?"

"Nothing is more important than you." He twined her fingers in his. "I've dreamed of someone like you my entire life."

"Then where were you, really? Tell me the truth."

Dante buried his head in his palms.

"What am I not good enough for you?" She rolled her eyes. "You can't imagine sleeping with a human?"

"Is that all you think this is about for me? Sex? Are you

sore because I didn't screw you last night?" Dante's mouth slanted.

Her ears and neck burned. She'd find her own way home. She stood up, but Dante shot to his feet, blocking the exit.

"Move." She tried to pull him aside, but his strength far surpassed hers.

"Maybe I think you deserve better."

"Well, that isn't your choice to make."

"I want to give you everything. Everything you've ever dreamed of and more. Everything you deserve."

Autumn needed to leave. Perhaps she'd jump from the window instead and hope to land in a tree. She sprinted, but once again, Dante eclipsed her with his inhuman speed.

Taking her hand, he fell to one knee. "I want you to come back with me. Not as my girlfriend. I want us to share a life together. This one, the next one, and the one after that."

She took a step back. "Are you asking me to marry you?"

"If that's your human term for lifelong commitment, yes. Yes, I am." He smiled. "But first, I owe you the truth about last night."

He stood up and sighed. "There's a gene that runs rampant in my family. And it takes effect when we look directly into the light of the full moon."

"What happens?" she asked, head spinning with thoughts of werewolves and other creatures of the night.

"We shift into another form, and our strength amplifies one hundred fold. Most nights, I can't recall the finer details. All I know is the shift is painful, and I have no control over it."

Autumn sat on the sill. "Why did you wait so long to tell me?"

"I didn't want to frighten you. There are already so many differences between us."

She sat there, contemplating. One full moon a month didn't seem like a deal breaker.

"Thanks for finally being honest with me," she said. "But I'm confused. Why do you want me to come back with you suddenly when you were reluctant before?"

"I love you more than anything, Autumn, and I don't want to imagine my life without you."

She glanced through the glass at the flurries of snow dancing in the passing wind. He placed his palm on her cheek. "I can understand if you need some time to think this over. It's a colossal commitment. We'd reside in Universe 13."

Her lips met his. "I need a few days to think about it." She had school, her friends, and her dad to consider. She wasn't sure how she'd break the news to him. She felt selfish thinking of her own happiness when they'd already lost so much.

A knock came.

* * *

Spellbound by Autumn, and her potential answer to his proposition, Dante was in no mood for an interruption. Nonetheless, the knocking persisted. He marched over to the door, sliding it open. His cousin Ronan stood there, arms folded. *Thankfully, fully clothed this time around.* He didn't need an encore performance.

"What's going on?" Dante spoke in his native tongue.

"Two more bodies were discovered."

"Where?"

"Downstairs bound to a pole."

"Where's Armienti?"

"Still in his room, I believe."

Dante strode around the corner and knocked on Armienti's door, but there was *no* answer.

Autumn approached. "What's going on?"

He pressed his lips to her forehead. "Nothing for you to worry about."

Fifty

THE FOLLOWING MORNING, Autumn noticed a shift in Dante's demeanor. He'd been acting off since his conversation with Ronan.

Alien drama.

She figured it had to do with the outburst on the ship. She couldn't help but wonder what happened to those men.

They rode in the Ferrari, her stomach twisting and turning. Dante drove as usual, and although she had her license, she didn't protest. Her thoughts were a million miles away.

An eighteen-year-old getting *married*. How would she explain this to her dad, and her friends? Could they attend their wedding in Universe 13? She loved Dante but wanted to be sure of her decision. As sure as he was about her.

They arrived on campus early, which didn't surprise her, considering the lightning speed they traveled. Standing outside of the Chemistry lab, she traced the cracks on the floor tiles with the toe of her Converse. Dante lounged against the wall; arms crossed.

Caleb limped, left arm secured in a hard cast hanging from

an L-shaped sling. When Autumn glimpsed him, Caleb averted his gaze.

Although she pitied him, she didn't need this right now. Her thoughts spun out of control with potential marriage and space travel.

When Dante spotted him, a smile played across his lips. She found his reaction annoying, but she couldn't stop it. A smile didn't breach their agreement.

"It appears someone has finally learned his lesson," Dante said, louder than necessary, attracting attention.

Muscles flinching before slackening, Caleb entered the laboratory and took his seat. Autumn wished their altercation had never happened.

Most of all, she pitied herself, because she was stuck sitting next to him for the rest of the semester.

Life just became way more complicated.

Nerves heightened, she said, "I have to go inside."

"I'll be right here waiting for you."

She left Dante in the hallway. He watched her like a hawk.

With extreme caution, Autumn approached the table. She pulled out a stool and unpacked her bag. Caleb sat there unmoving, eyes on the floor.

The lab instructor arrived a few minutes late and announced they'd be synthesizing aspirin for the day's experiment.

She grabbed a pair of plastic safety goggles and wrapped the band around her head. Caleb struggled with his arm, pulling and snapping the rubber band of his goggles.

"Do you need help?" she asked, momentarily disregarding the awkwardness of the situation.

Caleb's eyes narrowed. "No."

She watched him become tangled in the safety equipment. Band wound around his cast. He sat there pulling, unable to free his injured arm.

Enough *already*.

Frustrated, Autumn snagged the goggles from his hands and slapped the band across his forehead. Caleb stared at her, flabbergasted.

"I told you I don't need your help," he snarled.

"That isn't what it looks like to me," she countered. "You have no right to be angry at anyone. You're the one who started the fight. If it'd been the other way around, I'd be the one pissed off at you."

"Shut up, Autumn. Dante behaved like a wild animal. You were there. You saw for yourself."

She couldn't deny what Dante did was *excessive*. But like he said, what was he supposed to do, stand there and get his ass kicked?

Caleb sighed and continued, "I'm a state champion, the best in New York. I never lose a fight. And now I'm going to miss Nationals."

"Maybe you should think twice next time about picking a fight. It's one thing to use your words, and another to use your fists."

"Autumn, he's been itching to kick my ass since the moment we met. You have no clue what you're talking about. Shut up."

"No, you shut up."

The rest of the class had already started. Autumn grabbed an Erlenmeyer flask and weighed out 2.027 grams of salicylic acid and poured the contents inside, mixing it with several drops of sulfuric acid and acetic anhydride. She conducted the experiment alone, because Caleb was *useless* in his condition.

Shaking his head, Caleb glowered in silence.

"Don't you ever talk to me like that again," she snapped. "You can't be the best all the time. Maybe you've finally met your match, or maybe it's karma. Have you ever thought of that?"

Caleb blinked. "Not a day goes by where I don't think about how I hurt you. It was stupid and selfish. I regret it every day. I wish I could take back what I did with Misty. I wish you'd forgive me."

"Well, I can't."

Caleb paused for a long while, then continued, "I don't know how to ask this, but Dante seems violent, like he has anger issues. Has he ever hit you?"

"No, of course not," she shook her head. "He's always so sweet. Mind your own business."

"Friends look after friends though, remember?" Caleb insisted.

"Yeah, but we're not friends anymore. And you're talking crap about my fiancé."

Caleb's brows rose. "Your fiancé? Are you—"

"Yeah, I'm engaged."

He gawked at her, skin paling.

"Seriously *him*? Have you thought this through? Have you told your dad? You're only eighteen."

"You sound like an old man. I can pop your worry wart for you." She paused. "My dad doesn't know, but I'm telling him tonight after class. *Not* that it's any of your concern."

As the lab finished up, Autumn gathered her belongings. When she stood up to leave, Caleb pulled her arm with his uninjured hand. "Don't do this. You're going to regret it. You have your whole life ahead of you."

She rolled her eyes and left him sitting there alone. It was his loss.

Fifty-One

THE *NERVE* of Caleb second guessing her decision.

"What a jerk," Autumn mumbled. The answer to Dante's proposal dawned on her while she spoke with him. Dante was more of a man than he'd ever be. At least he knew how to be *faithful* and keep his hands off of Misty Beckett.

Dante stood in the hallway, arms crossed, lounging against the wall. A gloriously bored look on his face.

She embraced him warmly. "My answer is yes. I want to marry you."

Dante pressed his mouth to hers in a feverish kiss, followed by books splattering all over the floor and the clang of a metal thermos crashing against hard tile. It was Caleb, and he was on the ground. A group of classmates assisted him to his feet.

An arm cinched around her waist. "I'm going to make you so happy. You'll never want for anything again."

She opened her mouth to respond, attention affixed on Caleb.

"Is there an issue?"

Autumn exhaled. "No, it's nothing."

"What's wrong? Did something happen earlier?"

"No. Caleb's being annoying."

"Shall I set him straight for you?" Her ex finally came to his feet, bag slung over his functional arm.

She sighed. "No, please don't." Unfortunately, she had to deal with this problem on her own.

Bzzz. Autumn's pocket vibrated. One missed call from her dad, followed by a text reading, *Call me.*

Autumn called back immediately, but she was directed straight to voicemail.

When she arrived at her next class, she and her dad had played phone tag several times. She sighed, on the verge of giving up, and texted him. *What's up? I tried calling you.*

She couldn't afford to dwell on what her dad needed. She had a speech to give. Waiting for her class to start, she wrung her fingers together. This was one class she'd *not* miss at the end of the semester.

"What's the problem?" Dante asked. "Don't tell me that imbecile is in this class of yours as well."

"No," she laughed nervously. "I get anxious speaking in front of large groups of people."

Dante peered into her classroom. "This is hardly a crowd. There's only twenty or so humans."

"Yeah, but still. It's hard to explain." She gnawed away at a cuticle.

"Well, as someone who's done this a time or two, allow me to offer you a word of advice. In order to give an effective speech, confidence is key. Quit your slouching and don't forget to *annunciate* yourself. That's the best way to command the respect and attention of those around you."

"Thanks." Her hands quivered. "I need all the help I can get. I didn't realize you were an expert on speeches, too."

"Sure." He winked.

"I wish you could give my speech for me."

"No, Autumn. I know if you put your mind to it, you can rise to any occasion."

She reluctantly entered the room, smartphone buzzing in her pocket. She immediately silenced it. *Her dad.* She'd text him later.

As she took her seat, a pit solidified in her stomach. Sighing, she was relieved not to be up first, which hadn't been her previous stroke of luck.

While her classmates went one by one like logs on the chopping block, she chewed her nails.

Before she realized, well over half of the class had flown by. And she still hadn't been selected by her professor. It wasn't until ten minutes prior to the end, her luck came to a screeching halt.

"Autumn Ramon, you're up."

She navigated her way to the front of the room. Dante flashed an encouraging grin.

Perfect. He'd be there to witness the humiliation sure to follow. She organized her scrambled thoughts, trying her best to make sense of the pointers he'd given her. If he believed in her, she'd at least try to have some faith in herself.

She straightened her spine. Elevating her voice, she spoke on the persuasive topic of recycling, and how it could save the Earth. By some miracle, she maintained consistent eye contact, rather than staring at the floor like she usually did.

It wasn't until she heard the roaring round of applause that her concentration broke. Thank goodness, seven minutes of pure torture had concluded. Her professor called her over and revealed she received an A. It took every ounce of self-control she had not to jump up and down and scream with joy.

She grinned when she reunited with Dante.

"Glorious," he said. "I knew you were more than capable of seeing the task through to completion."

"Thanks, I couldn't have done it without you."

"Not a problem, you're a natural born leader if I ever saw one." He paused for a long moment. "I found the topic you discussed to be curious though."

"Why?"

"Do humans truly think their planet will be safe because of the phenomenon known as recycling?"

She paused. "What are you trying to say?"

He twisted his mouth. "The Universes are a dangerous place filled with vultures that prey on other people's worlds. And I don't feel recycling is a defense against them."

Her pocket vibrated. Her dad. She took out her phone.

"Hello?" she said.

"Where are you?"

"At school."

"Are you alone?"

"No, Dante is with me."

He gasped. "I'll come get you right now."

"Dad it's fine, I'm coming straight home."

Fifty-Two

AS SOON AS Autumn told Dante about her dad, they didn't bother to take the car. Panicked and trembling, she wondered what her dad possibly needed that was so urgent he couldn't divulge the details to her over the phone? She grew weak in the knees from Dante's last statement as well;

The Universes are a dangerous place filled with vultures that prey on other people's worlds.

No matter how hard she tried, she couldn't wrap her head around his words.

Smack dead center in the hallway, he held her close. Her eyes were overwhelmed with swirling colors. Whipping wind tore through the fabric of her clothing.

Instantaneously, they stood in her driveway, sun setting in the distance. Cerulean and marmalade rays of glow sank deep into the sky.

"Should I?"

"No, I don't think it's a good idea."

Autumn anticipated her dad wouldn't take the news of her engagement well. She'd break it to him softly.

Dante kissed her and disappeared, fading through the passing wind. As soon as her front door sealed shut, and she turned the lock, her dad sped over.

"Autumn, we need to talk."

Fifty-Three

"AUTUMN, WHERE IS HE?" Her dad peered through the peephole of the door.

Autumn shook her head. Her dad was acting *weirder* than ever. The conversation promised to be even more difficult than she expected.

"Dad, I know you don't like Dante, but you're being ridiculous. You had me worried. And I missed my last class for this. Seriously, get a grip."

She slid off her black canvas sneakers and dropped her backpack on the floor. She walked over to the living room, taking a seat on the couch. Her dad rushed over to her.

"I need to talk to you too, it's really important," she said. If she didn't tell him now, she feared she'd lose her resolve.

"Dante and I—"

"He's a murderer."

She sprang to her feet at his serious accusation.

"I can't take any more of this." She raked her fingers through her curls. "I know you don't like him, but stop spreading outrageous rumors. It's not fair, I wish mom was here!"

"It's true."

Her heart thundered. "Well, we're getting married. So you're going to have to stop this."

"Like hell you are," her dad shouted.

"No matter what you say, you can't change my mind. I'm eighteen. I love him and he loves me." She turned to walk upstairs, salty tears burning in her eyes.

"There's a surveillance video."

Water streamed down her cheeks. "What?"

"One of my friends down at the station told me there's a surveillance video that was uncovered from the day of the Ferrari jacking. Every morning, the same car has been seen traveling along I-287. A man was found dead and the physical description of the assailant sounds suspiciously like Dante. Tall, well-built, tan skin, black hair, and dressed in that bizarre long-sleeved shirt and pants he always wears. And his hands were concealed by gloves, explaining no fingerprints on the body."

"Did you actually watch the video?" Her lips quivered.

Her dad shook his head. So it was all speculation. The doorbell echoed. Two cops trudged through the door, hand-cuffs jingling from their belts.

"Where is he?" A gangly cop with sandy hair asked her dad, hand hovering over his gun.

"I thought he would be here, but he left."

"You called the police to come arrest him?" she croaked, vision blurring.

"For questioning."

"What's his address?" the cop asked. Her mind slowed to a fog.

"Umm..." she stammered. She needed to clear this up. There had to be some kind of mistake. "I don't—"

"Autumn, don't lie to them. You're interfering with an ongoing investigation."

"I..." Her jaw locked up, knees trembling. "He lives past Farrah Falls."

"Which development?"

"In the woods."

The cops exchanged looks. "There was another body discovered in the same location not too long ago."

Her legs buckled, and she collapsed on the floor, vision scrambling to black and white interference before her world went dark.

* * *

Dante re-emerged inside his ship, relieved Autumn would be accompanying him home as his mate. He grinned before retaining his composure. Even if this mission was a complete and utter failure from the start, at least it wasn't in vain.

He needed to speak with the Emperor. Correspondence was long overdue. If the setbacks he suffered on this planet had brought him to this point, it was well worth the trouble.

He descended the steps to the cockpit of his ship, surrounded by shadows. The room that once bustled with blinking lights and gauges was pitch black, said for the 3D projector unit emitting a hologram from the control counsel. A pale-green light reflected against the silver tiles of the ceiling and radiantly splayed across the floor. Within its ghostlike rays stood a man who he despised more than anyone in the Universes. A man responsible for his misery.

Back turned, his crimson cape dusted the floor of the dais. Legs affixed like two mighty trunks. He spoke with someone, paying Dante no mind. He huffed a breath, waiting to be acknowledged.

It wasn't out of the ordinary.

He cleared his throat. "Sire."

What could possibly be more important than speaking with him?

He sank into a waist bend bow, and the Emperor ceased his conversation.

"How thoughtful of you to finally reach out to me after all of these months. Or wait, has it been an entire year now?" The Emperor stroked his obsidian goatee. "How does it feel to be ignored?"

"I've grown quite accustomed to it, actually."

"Silence, boy. Enough of your smart remarks."

"How may I be of service to you?"

"Cut the shit." The Emperor sneered. "I need a progress update from you. The Grand Supreme has been badgering me daily."

"Ah, yes," his mouth curved. "The entirety of Universe 2 has been secured in both of your godly names."

The Emperor cracked his knuckles. "Excellent, and what of Universe 1 and of Earth?"

"As I'm sure you're aware" —Dante squared his shoulders — "I suffered a devastating setback to my Earth assignment. Might I add, the guilty parties have been punished."

"How unfortunate for you to be stranded on such a filthy world."

"It's cleaner than one might imagine," he corrected, not minding Earth at all anymore. It was the home world of his future wife.

"This pathetic oversight has cost the Grand Supreme a great deal of money, so *I'm* out a great deal of money, Dante. And with Keyserike and Valdez—"

"Understood, Sire."

"Perhaps you need to tighten the reins around your crew. I trust you're making up for lost time."

"Indeed I am. I've used my extended stay on this planet wisely."

A lie. He'd yet to survey the land and perform a thorough analysis of the population. But the Emperor didn't need to know, nor did the Grand Supreme. *For now.*

"Excellent. I trust I shall hear from you shortly with a progress report."

"Indeed you shall."

A long pause. Dante knew he promised to discuss another topic at his earliest convenience. One of the greatest importance.

"What is it?" the Emperor asked. "Do you have further issue to take up with me? Is it your salary? I feel fifty million rubies is more than a generous sum for securing Universe 2. And Earth is worth two million. It's only one planet after all, although I'm aware the Grand Supreme placed special emphasis on it."

"It's a fair price," he paused. "I wish to inform you I've selected a mate."

The Emperor blinked. "I never thought I'd see the day. Knowing your taste, I'd wager she's exquisite. What does she bring to the table? Wealth? Power? A fleet, perhaps?"

"Actually, she's a servant," Dante corrected. "I mean, a student from Earth."

Suddenly, the Emperor's pale-blue face shifted ruby-red. Veins protruded along his neck as he gripped the arms of his steel throne. Dante glowered.

"Is this a jest?" The Emperor struggled to catch his breath. His scarlet cape slithered across his lap. "That's the most preposterous proposition I've ever heard."

"No, I'm quite serious."

The Emperor emitted a deep belly laugh, palms slapping against his knees. "I cannot allow this."

"I don't recall asking your permission."

"I care not for your insolent tone." The Emperor's voice boomed. "We're running an operation here, and this girl is a human. For me to allow you to take this lower life-form nothing as your mate would be a great disservice. Your precious abilities would dissolve when mixed with her inferior blood. I cannot permit that to happen. There's so much wealth within arm's reach. And the four century-long agreement we've had in place with the Grand Supreme would risk being nullified."

He picked at his gloves before meeting the Emperor's gaze. "This conversation has grown dull."

The Emperor's face flushed.

"While you're there sitting on your ass playing monarch, I've been working my hands raw, growing stronger by the day. I very much look forward to my return to Surge." Dante winked. "Send my absolute allegiance and kindest regards to the Grand Supreme."

The Emperor opened his mouth to respond, but Dante clicked the projector off before he could get a word in otherwise. What a wretched man. He was in for a rude awakening. The Grand Supreme, however, was on a whole different level.

Fifty-Four

AUTUMN'S EYES fluttered open like two broken butterfly wings. A sweating, ice cold compress draped across her brow. Glancing from her pillow, her dad sat reading a *National Geographic* magazine. She went to rise, but he stopped her.

"How long was I out?"

"An hour." He placed the magazine on the floor.

She recalled what had happened. Her stomach churned. Holy crap. She came to a shaking stand. "Where did the cops go?"

"Autumn, lay down, you need to rest."

"No, where are they?"

Her dad's whiskers twitched. "They went to the forest to search for Dante."

She had to warn him. Had to tell him the cops were out to arrest him. And it was *all* her fault. She crumbled under pressure.

She had betrayed him in the most terrible way.

Her fiancé. She needed to speak with him. Needed to clear this whole mess up. There had to be a logical explanation for whatever her dad thought he'd seen. It couldn't be true, it just couldn't be.

She tried to maneuver around him, but he ushered her back to her bed. "Please let me go. I need to talk to him."

"I'm sorry, but I can't allow it."

"Dad, why? Why would you do this?" Her voice quaked.

"To protect you, Autumn. Dante is only trouble."

"He's innocent, though. He's innocent," she pleaded.

"Let the cops do their job, sweetheart. They'll determine whether he committed the crime. And if he's as innocent as you claim, I'll apologize to his face."

Her dad rose and headed toward the door. "Dinner is cooking and I put on a kettle of your favorite tea. Let's wait this out as a family."

She nodded mechanically as the door closed. She searched for her phone frantically, but it was in her backpack. *All the way downstairs.*

Autumn sprinted to the window and glanced at the driveway. It was high up, the fall wouldn't be dangerous. Heart pounding, she concocted a plan. If she were to jump, she could land in one of the evergreen bushes. From the top drawer of her night table, she collected her Neon car keys.

She opened the window carefully. Trembling, she lowered herself from the window, and fell splat into a bush. Crap. Branches and greenery bit against her skin through the frigid night air. She came to a shaking stand, fumbling with the keys in her hands.

She managed to open the car door. And after a rough rumbling start, she backed out of the driveway and drove to Farrah Falls.

When she arrived at the vast stretch of forest, Autumn wasn't surprised to see several Monroe cop cars and trooper cruisers. She parked further down in order to avoid being discovered. It was full dark, but the waning quarter moon allowed her enough light to navigate.

Rather than enter at the trailhead, she slipped between the trees.

The howling wind stung her cheeks. Teeth chattering, her eyes streamed with tears. But she didn't care, and she didn't let it stop her. This entire ordeal was all her fault. If only she'd been thinking straight, and her Dad wasn't so overprotective.

Covered in goosebumps, she slid over slick rocks and frozen patches. She fumbled, losing her balance often, but pressed onward. Every once in a while, a golden stream of light flashed through the trees from the search party.

About halfway through her trek, Autumn struggled to catch her breath. Her cheeks burned from the whipping elements. Heavy snowflakes danced from the sky, affixing themselves to her messy array of curls.

After another half an hour, dizziness set in. Through frozen lips, her breathing slowed. Icicles settled along her lashes. Tempted to turn around and give up altogether, she ceased taking a seat on a rock, burying her face in her palms. Mustering her strength, she rose and continued.

It took hours for her to reach the graveyard of fallen trees where Dante's ship laid.

With difficulty, she waded through the pile of logs, her denim jeans scraping against the crackling bark. Exhausted, she persisted. Snow accumulated on the ground more than she would have liked it to. Heavy flakes gusted in a whirlwind of white.

When Autumn stopped in the middle of the ring, the silence was so deafening it pierced through her ears. Trembling, she outstretched her hand, but only bitter wind blew by.

Stomping her shoe against the frozen earth, she winced.

"Dante, I know you're out here!"

Folding her arms, she stared at the sky, convinced he could see her from his invisible window. Voices approached from the forest, and she spotted the swirl of flashlights in hand.

Heart pounding, she yelled, "Dante, Dante, Dante, Dante!"

When she turned around, he stood there. "Autumn." He cupped her frozen cheek with his palm. "What are you doing out here?"

Fifty-Five

"THERE'S a search party looking for you and it's all my fault. I'm so sorry." She buried her face against his chest, tears streaming. "They think you killed somebody. Allegedly there's a video surveillance tape with you and the Ferrari. If only you could talk to them and tell them it's some kind of mistake."

The sound of crunching leaves and snow sliding underneath boots amplified. Dante remained eerily quiet.

She hugged him with all her might.

"How did you get all the way out here?

"I drove, then hiked."

"I'll take you back, you're going to catch your death."

When she blinked, wind whipped around them, followed by a blinding swirl of radiant color. They teleported to the front seats of her parked Neon. White, glittering snow coated the street at a furious pace.

"Where are the keys?"

With icicle coated fingertips, she pulled them from her jeans. The car groaned to a start. Heat blew, thawing her frozen skin.

Dante stared at her with his penetrating amber eyes.

"Autumn, I don't ever want you to do that again. You could get sick or hurt out here in these conditions, you're my entire world." He pressed his warm mouth against her cold lips.

She blinked, lashes clinging together. "I didn't want to see you get in trouble for something I know you could never do."

Dante remained quiet, then spoke. "How can you be so sure I didn't do it, Autumn?"

"I know you could never kill anyone. I'm so sorry I put you through all this. And embarrassed my dad created such a terrible rumor. He wants to break us up."

He glanced out the windshield, snow still falling in a blanket of white. "I love you more than life itself Autumn, you deserve to know the truth."

A tear sparkled down Dante's cheek. "It was an accident, the man got in my way. I desperately wanted to impress you by seeming human. He had something I wanted, and I took it from him. I wish I could undo my mistake, but I can't."

A pit formed in her stomach.

"I should have been the one to tell you first, but I was afraid you'd think less of me." Dante stared at his hands. "Can you ever forgive me?"

The sight of Dante twisted her insides into a cruel knot. She squared her shoulders. "What right did you have to take his life away? What's wrong with you?"

His features straightened when she didn't accept his apology.

"He had a family, friends, and maybe even children who will never see him again because of your selfishness." She clenched her fists. "Did you ever consider any of that?"

She breathed and continued, "Get away from me." Tears streamed down her cheeks. "Get out of my car. I never want to see you again. You're a liar. I don't know you anymore."

Dante's shoulders tightened before slackening. "I'll respect your wishes for *now,* I know you're upset. But don't forget you made a promise to me."

"There is no promise. We're over. Stay away from me! *Stay away from me!*"

"Well, I'm afraid I can't comply. Your promise was a binding one." Dante vanished before her eyes.

Autumn opened her door, vomit splattering all over the ground.

When she arrived home after a white knuckled drive through the storm, her eyes stung from crying so hard. Her dad paced the driveway.

Sliding into the car, he hugged her, and she wept in his arms. "Dad, you were right about him all along."

A ring came from his pocket, and her dad answered. There were a few inaudible words and his phone slid from his hand and landed in the snow.

"What happened?" Autumn's eyes widened.

He wiped the flakes from his silver spectacles. "All of Farrah Falls is gone. Another forest fire."

"Please tell me you're not going." Her heart leapt to her throat.

"There's no fire to put out."

For her own safety, Autumn remained cloistered in her home for the following week, on false pretense she had period cramps and a migraine. She reemerged when it was time for finals and never revealed to her dad what transpired between her and Dante. He already had his share of worries, and didn't need one more.

When she arrived on campus for her Chemistry final, she took a series of deep therapeutic breaths while sitting in her car. Every shadow and gust of wind triggered a fearful out-of-body experience.

As she waited in the hallway for class to begin, Caleb walked by. Autumn glanced away to avoid making eye contact.

He stopped, walking over tentatively. She assumed he expected to see Dante.

"Where's your fiancé?" He adjusted his backpack. "Did he finally let you off your leash?"

Autumn stared at him, eyes gritty and swollen.

"Have you been crying?"

She snapped out of her daze. "What do you care?"

"Believe it or not, Autumn, I *do* care."

She crossed her arms defensively. "Who are you trying to fool? You're only here to gloat. Do me a favor and spare me your false concern."

"He made you cry, didn't he?"

The mere thought of him caused a single tear to roll down her cheek. Not of sadness, but rage.

"What did that asshole do to you?" He paused. "He dumped you, didn't he? I can see it in your eyes. Don't lie to me."

"Mind your own business," she hissed. "I actually broke up with him."

"I warned you, he has issues. He's aggressive. A girl like you deserves the world."

"Oh, please, Caleb, save it." She rolled her eyes. "You're not innocent."

"I never made you cry."

"You made me cry plenty. I'm done with you, and I'm done with this conversation." She folded her arms.

"It wasn't all bad, you know."

She remained silent.

"People grow and they change. They realize the mistakes they've made. If you gave me another chance. I promise I'll never hurt you again."

Autumn stared at him. She'd heard it all before. She would no longer allow herself to be lied to or deceived. She was so *done.*

* * *

Dante stood in his cabin window, staring through his reflection at the burnt trees, the remains of the forest that once surrounded his ship. Black ash floated in a passing gust of wind.

He formed a ball of fire in his hand and threw the flame, melting glass and steel, leveling ash to dust. About every half an hour, a new fiery sphere glowed from his palm and he whirled it wherever it fell. Sometimes the roar of emergency vehicles followed.

Dante fell to his knees, losing control of himself.

What occurred between him and Autumn was *inevitable. Eventually,* she would've found out who he was and what he's capable of. His warrior nature had been ingrained in him since birth.

That was the excuse he gave himself. But he wished he'd handled the situation differently. Begged her forgiveness. Instead, he behaved like a fool.

For now, though, he'd allow her space. Time to enjoy Earth as she knew it, because once he was through, mankind would never be the same.

PART THREE

Nineteen

Fifty-Six

OVER A MONTH PASSED since fall semester concluded, and Autumn couldn't believe the predicament she got herself into. Worst of all, there was nobody she could confide in. And if she could trust someone, they couldn't help her, anyway.

Autumn *Martyne*. The words made the hairs on the back of her neck stand on end.

The day was January fifth. Her birthday. For if it hadn't been, it would've blended in with the countless days she'd been in hiding. None of which had a beginning or an end. Her chest ached, making it difficult to breathe. No matter how hard she tried, the pain wouldn't go away.

A firm knock hit the door. Her heart skittered. But she remembered, if it was Dante there to seize her, he wouldn't have to knock. He hadn't knocked since *ever*. When and if he came for her, she wouldn't give up without a fight.

She sighed, not prepared to deal with any of this.

Autumn sat up, wearing satin cloud pajama shorts and a white cami tank top. "Come in."

The door creaked open. Her dad peeked into her room

with a toothy grin. He held a sprinkled vanilla cupcake with a flickering candle. A brown paper package tied with a plain white string sat in the crook of his arm.

"Happy Birthday!" He sang.

"Thanks," she muttered, somewhat self-conscious, not wanting her dad to see her like this *again.*

He took a seat on her bed, handing her the baked good. She closed her eyes and wished Dante would leave her in peace. She blew out the candle with a single gust of breath.

"I hate seeing you like this," his eyes glinted with concern beneath his simple silver frames. "This isn't healthy, normal behavior for a nineteen-year-old young woman. You should be out enjoying your life and spending time with your friends. I'm running out of excuses everytime Lauren and Ellie come to the door looking for you."

"Bu—"

"I know you're worried about running into Dante, but the authorities will find him, and justice will prevail. I promise." Her dad didn't know the half of it, but it was better this way. He'd never believe her in a million years.

"I'm fine, dad," she forced a smile. "Really."

"No, you're not. All this hiding and moping around has gone on long enough. It's time to move on. Your mom wouldn't have wanted this."

"I know, I don't want to talk about this right now." She fell onto her pillow, folding her arms.

"As much as you would like to, you can't stay cooped up in here forever. You have to understand heartbreak is a part of life. Dante was the first—"

"Second," she corrected him.

"Okay. The second boyfriend you've ever had, and I promise there's a better guy out there worthy of your love."

She exhaled, throwing her head back. Her dad left her room, closing the door.

Autumn rolled over and grabbed the package, fingers crinkling over the brown paper. She carefully untied the string and shredded the package apart. As expected, a beautiful snow globe with swirling glitter sat inside. A smile hinted across her lips until she realized the scene displayed New York City. Tears welled in the corners of her eyes and her mouth fell flat.

She spent the rest of the afternoon lounging in bed on the phone, scrolling through social media and looking at pictures of everyone else's exciting winter breaks. Around 4:00 p.m., she heard a ping. *One new message.*

A single text from Lauren read, *Hey Birthday Girl!! What are we doing tonight? P.S. Ellie is coming too! :)*

Crap.

Only so much time could pass until her friends reached out again. Both Lauren and Ellie had been back in Monroe for a few weeks, on winter break. Somehow, she dodged them at every turn.

Unfortunately, she had no excuse. If she didn't oblige, they'd surely force their way through the door and find her like *this. Not a good look.* But at the same time, she didn't want to risk seeing Dante. She supposed, though, one hang out couldn't hurt. It was her birthday after all.

With trembling fingers, she typed, *How about we meet for cosmic bowling at the Colonial Lanes in Chester. Is 9 okay?*

Lauren immediately replied. *Perfect! We'll see you then! :)*

Her stomach flip-flopped. She was committed to an outing. Hopefully, she could avoid discussing the intimate details of her life. Although she knew it was highly unlikely.

After dark, she drove to the bowling alley to meet her friends. Snow filled shadows danced through the trees, and the half-moon cast pale light against the blacktop guiding her way.

Tonight marked a historic night for Autumn. Not only was it the first night the three friends had traveled in separate vehicles, but the first time she had her license.

As she pulled into the parking lot, she spotted Lauren's car. Despite her initial reluctance, she grew excited to see her friends.

When she entered the building, she did a double take, eyes widening. Lauren stood in the doorway, her previously cascading gilded locks styled in a tidy lob with a side part. A pair of faint cat eyes were painted delicately onto her lids. An air of sophistication emanated from her. A young woman aged by a single semester away at college.

When Autumn turned around, Ellie stood there beaming, as radiant as morning sunlight. Her long chestnut tresses draped her shoulders. A noticeable change from her usual high ponytail. Her makeup was perfect as always.

Autumn felt plain Jane in their presence, not having bothered with makeup, only her usual swatch of sheer watermelon pink lip gloss. Plus, the first and last time she bothered to apply makeup had been a complete *disaster*.

The three friends hugged and giggled. After they rented their bowling shoes, they headed to the lanes. Bowling balls crashed against pins, and a neon-blue light shined, casting parts of the alleyway in shadow.

"Autumn, what's new with you? I'm dying to know," Lauren asked. "The three times we came to visit we were told you had a cold, the flu, and vertigo? And you haven't answered any of our texts."

Her stomach churned as her best friend started with an intense question-and-answer session. Lauren may have matured, but she remained as bubbly and nosey as ever. People never really changed, she supposed.

"Yeah, sorry, I've been sick, but I finally passed my road test." Autumn offered the first tidbit of information, hoping to avoid subsequent questions.

"Awesome," Ellie said. "I knew you could do it all along."

"For a while, I wasn't so sure," she admitted. But in reality, she thought she would never pass.

"Nice try, Autumn." Lauren winked. "You're not getting off that easily. What's going on between you and Dante?" She batted her eyes.

Her breath caught in her throat. As usual, Lauren saw right through her facade. But she could never admit the truth to her, the truth she'd been painfully made aware of.

She'd been dating an alien murderer.

"No," Autumn fidgeted, her hands. "You guys first. I'm sure your stories are better than mine." An outright lie. *Her tale was unmatched.*

"Well," Ellie began, "I have a boyfriend, and his name is Noah. And we've been going steady all semester long. He's a Sophomore." She placed her hand over her mouth. "We went all the way."

Lauren snorted. "Good for you. How was it?"

"Satisfying." Ellie's freckled cheeks hinted at pink. "We did it in his dorm room while his roommate was at a frat party. How about you?"

"I have a boyfriend too," Lauren said. "His name is Matt, and he's a little older."

"How much older?" Ellie's mouth fell open.

"21."

"Lauren!" Ellie gasped.

"He's an engineering student, and let's just say skill improves with age." Lauren winked.

Sensing her turn arrived, Autumn fled to the bathroom. "I'll be right back." She jogged off, hopeful they'd think she had to pee.

Standing in front of the mirror, she took deep, controlled breaths to calm her nerves. She splashed iced cold water over her face. Okay, she could do this, she reassured herself.

On the way back to her friends, Autumn spotted an unwelcome face. Her stomach plummeted.

Fifty-Seven

A GIRL STOOD BESIDE CALEB. One she'd never seen before. Autumn's eyes widened as she inspected her. It was like staring into a funhouse mirror at her own likeness. The girl's eyes differed, however, they largely resembled her own, but were dark-brown.

Autumn approached with extreme caution. When Caleb laid eyes on her, his face lit up like Times Square on a Saturday night. Autumn tensed as he gave her a hug that lingered a little too long. Lauren and Ellie snorted softly.

"Long time no see." Caleb twisted his signature red cap. "Don't think I forgot it's your birthday."

"Yeah," Autumn flashed an uneasy smile. "You didn't have to come out because of me. You could've sent me a text or wished me Happy Birthday online."

"You blocked me. Remember?" He murmured. Yes, she recalled, and he deserved the cold treatment.

"Anyway, happy nineteenth. Welcome to the club."

"Thanks." Autumn affixed her attention to the girl.

Caleb suddenly remembered her. "Oh yeah, there's someone I want you to meet. This is my girlfriend, Brianna."

"Nice to meet you."

"You too." Brianna eyed her strangely. Autumn assumed Brianna's thoughts were in line with her own. *How creepy.* Who knew how long they'd been dating. Caleb had been known to keep secrets and hadn't mentioned Brianna all semester long.

"Well, we're going to get back to our lane. I'll see you in school." Caleb waved. "I'm sorry again about what happened with your fiancé."

"See you." Autumn flinched as they walked away. In an instant, Lauren and Ellie were on her.

"You were engaged?" Lauren whispered, eyes widening.

"And who's the freak show Caleb's with?" Ellie interjected. "I can barely tell you apart."

"It's a long story, you guys."

"Trust me. We're good for it."

She finally caved and unloaded select pieces of the lengthy saga between her, Caleb, and Dante. It was satisfying to unburden herself to her friends. It helped to talk about her problems rather than keep them bottled up inside like she had a tendency to do.

What she failed to mention, though, were Dante's true intentions. He was wanted by the police, and most important of all, he was an *alien* set on marrying her, even though she broke the engagement off. If only her life had been uncomplicated like theirs were. Normal human guy, normal college experience, and both parents still alive. Not a worry in the world.

But life could never be the same. She already knew more than she ever dreamed of knowing, and there was no going back.

The end of the night came all too soon. She hugged her friends, bidding them both goodbye, unsure of when she'd see them again.

When she began her quiet drive home, she squinted, trying to decipher where the lines were on the road. She yawned and slapped her cheek. With all the sleep she'd gotten over the previous month, it surprised her she felt tired at all.

Instead of pulling over to rest, she lowered the windows. Icy air whipped against her skin. The thought of laying in her own bed carried her onward.

A shadow swept across the street. Autumn jammed on the brakes and the car screeched into a one hundred and eighty-degree turn before coming to a full stop. Shaking, she peered through the windshield.

Hearing a rustle, she glanced in the rearview mirror, breath catching in her throat. Two crystal blue eyes stared back at her.

Fifty-Eight

LITTLE EXCITED ARMIENTI since the night of the crash. The food tasted bland and underwhelming. And the area bored him, with no nightlife to speak of. He *yearned* for the comforts and extravagance of home.

On top of these negative aspects, they were hopelessly off schedule. Which he certainly didn't have to answer for. But if all went according to plan, his time served on this planet would be over with.

The girls, however, represented Earth's sole asset. They were absolutely stunning.

Armienti knew better, but he couldn't resist. Since Dante took a leave of absence, he acted on his instincts. Sure, it went against protocol to leave the ship without his cousin's permission, but this was a first-time offense and the risk was worth it.

Although he didn't find Autumn to be traditionally attractive according to Elattion standards, her features were far from plain. *However*, her eyes sealed the deal for him. They were far too large for her face, and the unique hue of pale moonglow. He'd only seen that distinctive shade on one other female before.

Maeve. Oh, how he loved her from afar, although it was wrong. His cousin always secured all the best women.

"Maeve, psst, hey Maeve." He sauntered through the hallway, purple evening sky shimmering through the high windows.

Maeve turned around and smiled. His entire body warmed.

"Sorry, Armienti, were you calling me? I must have been daydreaming." She tilted her head to the side, curls falling against her rosy cheeks.

Armienti's hand trembled. "Yes, um, I think you dropped something."

He pulled a silver necklace out of his pocket with two crescent moons and a star.

Maeve clutched her delicate throat. "Oh, thank you. I was so distracted I mustn't have felt it fall off."

"Here, allow me," he undid the clasp. Maeve lifted her hair, and he secured the necklace around her neck.

He admired her. "You look—"

"There you are." Dante's boots clicked against the marble floor. "I've been searching everywhere for you. We're leaving in under an hour."

Dante wound his tail around Maeve's waist, fingers catching in her hair. Armienti took two steps back, his chest aching like he was punched.

Dante looked Armienti up and down. "And you cousin, you're not even in uniform. What are you waiting for?"

"Sorry, I'll change now."

"Good, we can't be late."

"Thanks again," Maeve muttered, running her fingers against the chain of her necklace.

Dante glanced at him for a moment too long before they rounded the corner.

. . .

Autumn stared at him, trembling. Timid, yet beautiful.

"Armienti, why are you here?" Her voice quaked. "Did Dante send you?"

"No, of course not. That's utterly absurd."

Autumn blinked. "I don't understand."

"I heard from a reliable source it's your name day." Which meant he'd been lingering around since first light undetected.

Her gray gaze met his. "I don't think I ever told you or Dante when my birthday is."

Armienti shook his head.

"Then how did you—"

"I have a present for you."

He held a globe, similar to the globes he'd seen on Autumn's shelf in her home. Inside sat a silver castle with four towering spires. Sparkling flakes drifted in a whirlwind. A circle of glittering jagged rocks filled the bottom. It reminded him of the snow he'd seen for the first time on Earth during the ongoing cold season, making him feel less alone.

He presented his masterpiece to her.

Autumn gently inspected his present, gray eyes magnified through the glass.

"This is beautiful. Where did you get it from?" A smile flickered across her full pink lips.

"I made it for you. It's one of a kind."

"Did you really?" she said and paused. "Why?"

"A simple thank you will suffice." His cheeks heated. Human girls talked too much, especially this one. Instead of speaking, he much preferred for her to admire it in silence.

"Um, sorry. Thank you."

"I should get going. My presence will be missed."

"If you're going back to the forest, I can take you. I'm

headed in that direction regardless and it's only a few extra miles."

"Thank you. That would be lovely."

Armienti took a seat beside her, although he could've easily transported himself.

Every once in a while, over the course of their trip, the moon struck Autumn's face and twinkled through the dark strands of her hair. Its pale rays emphasized her delicate silhouette. He couldn't help but admire her.

"Are you all right?" she asked. "Is there something on my face?"

If only she could see what he saw. She'd be staring as well.

"No, sorry. It's just I can see why Dante cares so much for you. You're a rather intriguing girl."

Autumn stared at him in silence. "I don't want to talk about him. I never want to see him again."

* * *

They reached Farrah Falls, and the trees were all halved and blackened. Ash particles blew through the air and mixed with the falling snowflakes in a gray whirlwind.

When Autumn stopped the vehicle, her shoulders tensed as she beheld the desecration. "I don't understand why he destroyed the forest."

"I'm sorry I can't be of more assistance. He's notoriously private with his feelings. Some would wonder if he has any at all."

"Don't be ridiculous. Everyone has feelings, even if they're a raging jerk. Tell him I said so. I don't care."

"As long as I have your permission," he snorted. "If I had a girl as charming as you are, I would never have put her through any of this. Dante, on the other hand, abides by a different set of standards altogether."

Armienti reached for the door.

"Wait," she said, "what do you mean?"

Armienti turned. "Dante has killed on many occasions."

"What?"

Armienti disappeared into the passing wind, his golden locks fading to shadow. The beautiful snow globe he created sat on the front passenger seat in his place, swirling.

She drove all this way and didn't get any answers. Crap. She failed to understand Dante's true intentions. This may have been her one and only chance.

Pressing the gas pedal, she stared at what remained of Farrah Falls. What a horrible shame. She'd grown up here. Hiked here on countless occasions. And it was gone, all thanks to *Dante* and his selfishness.

Squinting into the blackened brush and fallen trees, her eyes fixated on *someone*. A gangly, limbed boy wandered along the side of the road barefoot in the snow. Spine hunched and clothed in tattered attire. He looked to be her age.

Against her better instincts, she slowed the car, and cracked the window.

"Do you need some help?" she asked.

He stopped walking, turning her way. The hairs on the back of her neck stood on end as he sprinted to the open window and pressed his hands against the glass.

Autumn stared into his feral eyes. Golden like butterscotch, beneath a mop of short inky hair. Try as she might, she couldn't turn away.

"You're the girl everyone is talking about."

She watched him, a lump fastening itself in her throat. "I—"

"You are. I've seen you before. Don't think I haven't noticed you, Autumn."

"I'm sorry," she said, "I don't know who you are. I've never seen you before in my life." The hair on the back of her neck pricked when she realized he addressed her by her *first* name.

Her inner voice urged her to drive. But she remained, hypnotized to stay put. Electric waves caressed her brain.

The boy inhaled deeply, closing his eyes before exhaling. "You smell pretty. Like the flower fields at Zym."

"Thank you." She trembled.

"I bet you're delectable as well."

She jumped as a long, frog-like tongue flicked from his mouth through the cracked widow grazing the side of her cheek, leaving a gooey residue. It sizzled as she frantically wiped her burning skin.

She screamed, throwing herself against the opposite door. He pulled away, satisfied. "You're sweeter than I could've ever possibly imagined," he mused. "Perhaps your flavor will be more favorable after you've been charred to dust and bone."

Autumn jammed her foot against the gas pedal and sped away. She glanced in the rearview mirror and the boy walked in a complete circle until he too faded through the winter wind.

Fifty-Nine

DANTE HAS KILLED *on many occasions.*

Over the rest of winter break, those words haunted Autumn's dreams. To think Dante had been a murderer *all* along. How could she have no idea? How could she have been stupid enough to fall for him?

But the boy she'd seen induced terror in her bones. The gross sensation of his slippery, bumpy tongue against her cheek. And the burn spot that took weeks to fade. She shivered at the recollection. None of it made any sense.

Even Armienti and the globe he presented her with. His gift had been so unexpected and extravagant she almost returned it. Why wouldn't the aliens leave her alone and go peacefully back to their planet?

When spring semester began, Autumn sat in the Chemistry 102 lecture hall, dwelling on her many problems. Tormented, she was ready to give up on college altogether, and go home. Safe from aliens and weird boys with long disgusting tongues.

Perhaps she should've taken the semester off, but she

feared for her scholarship. She needed to press on whether she liked it or not.

Instead of focusing on the lecture, she people watched, surrounded by students with high hopes and aspirations like she used to have. Everyone was intelligent and focused. While she sat there, worried and obsessed.

Glancing a few rows over, she spotted Caleb. He twisted his red baseball cap, avidly taking notes. *There was no escaping him either.* It figured they'd have another class in common, *two semesters in a row.* Autumn didn't want to spend the next thirteen weeks staring at him and her weird doppelganger, but she had no choice.

For some reason, she missed Caleb a little. Although he was a selfish jerk. It would've been nice to have someone normal and human to confide in.

The end of the lecture couldn't have come any faster. She grabbed her belongings and raced out the door. With a four-hour gap between classes, she went to the cafeteria for lunch.

She peered around the room and selected an empty table, chair squeaking momentarily. Everyone glanced over, before returning to their conversations. Cheeks heating, Autumn pulled a book from her backpack and ate her peanut butter and jelly sandwich in silence.

About a quarter into the story, a throat cleared, distracting her. She glimpsed up from her book, half expecting to see an *alien stalker,* but she was pleasantly surprised. Her face and neck warmed as she made eye contact. A guy stood beside her with a glowing burnished complexion and deep almond eyes. The tips of his short curly hair were frosted like sparkling starlight. A shy smile tilted across his soft lips as they formed words.

"Your name is Autumn, right?"

She stared at him quizzically, trying to figure out how he knew her name. She'd never seen him a day in her life.

"Yes," she said regardless. "Can I help you?"

"Is anyone sitting here?" He pointed to the chair, biting back a smile. His dimples protruded, cheeks shifting to pink.

She hesitated.

His chair screeched as well. People glanced over at them before returning to their meals. Her face felt hot as the breath caught in her throat. What was wrong with this table? It seriously couldn't have been any louder if it tried. She didn't need this right now.

He folded his long fingers and stared at her. Autumn felt the urge to gather her belongings and walk away, but it wasn't in her nature to be rude. Plus, she'd just gotten to the juiciest part of her book. Crap.

"I'm Iain Smith, by the way." He extended his hand. She reluctantly shook it, his warm soft palm sat against hers.

"Nice to meet you," she muttered. "Do I know you from somewhere?"

He flashed a warm smile. "I'm in Chem and English with you."

Funny. She couldn't recall seeing him in *either* class, and the semester had been in session for two weeks. She suspected he was lying. Every other guy she'd met so far turned out to be a liar.

"Okay, do you need my help with homework or something?"

Iain grinned, the dimpled apples of his cheeks glowed beneath the fluorescent lights. "No. I wanted to introduce myself."

She stared at him with an unreadable expression. "Um, okay. Nice to meet you."

"Nice to finally meet you, too." Iain glanced coyly at the table before meeting her gaze and holding it for a moment too long.

"Okay, then—"

"You should smile more often. You always look so sad," Iain said.

"Maybe it's because I *am* sad," she admitted, somewhat uncomfortable discussing her feelings with a random guy she'd just met. "I broke up with my boyfriend a few months ago, and I guess I'm still not over it."

"I'm sorry to hear."

"Yeah..."

"You have a pretty smile," he murmured, lips curving. "I hope I get to see it more often."

He rested his navy-blue backpack against his shoulder. "See you in class."

Autumn sat there, speechless. She could only imagine how long Iain had been plotting their interlude. *Two entire weeks.* She couldn't believe she didn't recognize him from either class. But Iain had an unspoken charm about him worth investigating.

Sixty

LATER ON THAT AFTERNOON, Autumn entered her English 102 class, with her anxiety spiking through the roof. She stared at the floor demurely, a majority of the seats were occupied.

After she settled, she peered over her shoulder, searching for any sign of Iain, not immediately noticing him. But soon enough, they locked eyes. She breathed a deep sigh of relief when she realized he told her the *truth*.

When Iain waved, her heart accelerated. Flashing him a small smile, she turned around and focused on the lecture as best she could.

As time passed, her body flushed with heat. Autumn could sense his gaze piercing into her. And when other students raised their hands to contribute, she didn't dare look. Autumn couldn't pinpoint the source of her anxiety, but she became increasingly jittery.

At the conclusion of the lesson, everyone filed out the door. She did the same, when her eyes gravitated to Iain, who took his sweet time packing his bag.

Her muscles tensed. He must have been biding his time to

leave with her. As she made her way toward the door, Iain sprinted her way, like a lost puppy. Her lips parted in suspense.

"Where are you headed to now?" Iain asked.

"Home."

"Where's home?"

"Monroe. Where do you live?"

"Suffern." Iain slung his backpack over his shoulder before shuffling his feet. "It's a ten-minute drive from here. I'll walk you to your car if you like."

Autumn reluctantly agreed, not wanting to hurt his feelings, but Iain came off as *intense*. Sure, he was cute with his dimpled cheeks and sweet smile, but it was too much too *soon*.

On the way to the car, Iain glanced at her, cheeks reddening. *Obviously,* he was into her.

She couldn't help but sympathize. More than anyone, she understood what it was like to fall head over heels for a guy she barely knew. From now on, she planned to be more careful to whom she gave her heart to.

In the corner of her eye, she spotted Caleb, Brianna, and *Misty Beckett,* texting on the hood of her white Audi A8. *What was Misty doing here?* Autumn could've sworn she got accepted to some fancy University in England she could barely pronounce.

Balling her hands into fists, she crushed her fingers to conceal her growing discomfort. If only there was a way she could escape, but they already made eye contact, and she refused to retreat. She was left with no other choice but to say hi.

Caleb grinned, enthusiasm fading when he saw Iain.

"Long time no see." Caleb's attention gravitated toward Iain. Twisting his mouth to the side, he not so subtly assessed him.

"This is Iain," Autumn introduced her new friend.

Caleb gave Iain a rough shake. Apparently, his bones healed up well.

"Nice to meet you," Caleb muttered. "How is it you know each other again?"

"We're in the same class." Iain smiled warmly. "Well, two classes. English and Chem."

"Funny, I don't recall seeing you," Caleb mumbled.

Autumn couldn't believe Caleb gauged their non-existent relationship, especially with his new girlfriend in earshot. She waved to Brianna, but, as usual, she was an afterthought.

Brianna may have physically resembled Autumn with her dark coiled hair and oversized eyes, but she was a girl of few words. How could she have been so blind as to not notice her own boyfriend's rudeness?

Misty twisted her fingers through the strands of her honey-blonde hair, to the point of tying them into knots. Previously, Autumn had been terrified of her, but Misty no longer held a candle to what she witnessed over the last few months.

"What brings you here?" Autumn said. "I thought you were London bound?"

Misty contorted her full pink lips. "Who wants to know?"

Autumn stared at her, arms folded.

"I flunked out," Misty finally admitted. "I partied too hard and lost my four-year scholarship."

It turned out her royal highness was human after all. Autumn hated to admit there was a sense of satisfaction she experienced watching Misty get *exactly* what she deserved for once.

"Shame." Autumn shrugged. "Welcome to RCC."

Misty's jaw tightened. It served her right. Autumn no longer desired an apology from her. This was payback enough.

Caleb tapped Autumn on her shoulder, interrupting her gloating. "Where are you guys headed to?"

"Nowhere, home." Autumn crossed her arms.

"We should all get together sometime," Caleb suggested. "How about Friday? We could double date. You can come too if you want, Misty."

"Rain check," Misty said curtly, texting again. Her hot pink gel set clicked against the glass.

Autumn couldn't believe Caleb put her in this position with a brand-new guy she barely knew. But she didn't want to hurt Iain's feelings.

"Sure, sounds fun."

Iain's cheeks flushed again, dimples emphasized.

"Okay, I'll see you guys later." Autumn waved goodbye.

A surprisingly painless conversation, *with a catch.*

Iain walked her to her car, fiddling with his hands in silence as he stood next to her. Frustrated, she dug through her backpack in search of her key. Nothing was ever where she left it.

"Um..." Iain muttered.

Autumn stopped and turned around mid-search.

"Can I have your number?"

Heart stammering, she gave it to him, instantly second-guessing her decision.

* * *

Dante soared through the sky, lazer in hand. Pink streaks cut through the white fluffy clouds and scraped across the ground below. He needed to prepare for his mission, anything to keep himself distracted from the problems he created. And the first step was obtaining accurate measurements of Earth's terrain.

His gut twisted as the beam zapped through Monroe. He started as close to his ship as possible, in case another situation arose. But he'd have to leave the area sooner or later. Earth was a small planet but it still required his attention.

Brilliant rays grazed across the roofs of the library, human eatery, and the green. When he reached Autumn's quaint little home, her car was missing. His heart pounded.

Although she didn't want to see him, he worried about her. Hoped she was driving safely and wearing her seatbelt now that he was giving her space. *How he hated giving her space.*

He didn't blame her. If only he'd been forthcoming about his mistake.

Now she saw him like everyone else did. A monster.

He checked the time, tempted to teleport to make sure she got to school safely but stopped himself. She wouldn't like it. It would do more harm than good if he ran into her, he convinced himself. For now, it was better this way.

But there was no denying the magnetic pull he experienced to be close to her at all times.

After a few hours of calculations and other monotonous tasks, he returned to the ship. With the sour way events had been unfolding lately, he had no clue what kind of state he would find it in.

For the first time in the daylight he witnessed the desecration he'd caused in the forest. Shame assaulted him at the realization he'd destroyed one of Autumn's favorite places. He needed to learn to hold his temper but when it came to her, he succumbed to his emotions.

Dante sighed on his way inside and at the last moment caved to his curiosity and decided to check in on her. Only, he wished he hadn't. He quickly sped back like a hollow punch to his chest at the sight of her standing with another guy.

Sixty-One

OVER THE FOLLOWING WEEK, Autumn existed on pins and needles, seeing Iain in class. By the time Friday rolled around, she worked herself into a tizzy.

After her last lecture of the day, she paced the campus bathroom, gnawing away at her fingernails. A nasty habit she'd yet to break, but it calmed her during periods of extreme anxiety. And this situation certainly qualified.

In less than twenty minutes, she had a double date, having agreed to meet with Caleb, Brianna, and Iain at the Lafayette Theater in Suffern.

Once again, she couldn't figure out whether it was a date or a hangout.

Autumn sighed. The idea of putting herself out there again after the drama between her and Dante seemed overwhelming.

Sure, she looked pretty enough, dark curls secured half up with a barrette. Tendrils framing her heart-shaped face in a wild yet controlled way. Oversized gray eyes.

On the outside, she feigned having her life together, but on the inside, she was ready to crumble at a moment's notice.

She was terrified Dante would keep his word any day now, and come to ruin her life.

When she made her way to the student parking lot, drizzle trickled against her skin. The sun sank low into the sky, and street lamps flickered like fireflies shimmering their tangerine rays over the slick blacktop.

Although somewhat apprehensive, she found the scheduled feature film exciting. She and Brianna had selected a documentary about Mary Queen of Scots. Apparently, Brianna was a history major, and Autumn was fascinated by the subject. She always found the fashion and intrigue of court life exciting.

Thankfully, the theater was located only minutes away. What she didn't count on was hitting *every single stoplight*.

When she arrived, her group of friends were already standing outside beneath the canopy of the lit mezzanine. A line of people filed into the building to grab refreshments and take their seats.

Her stomach bubbled and churned upon the sight of the available parking spots. On the street she'd have to pull out. She struggled with parallel parking the most. After botching two consecutive attempts, horns buzzed. Some impatient people even sped around her car. Autumn's knuckles clenched the steering wheel. Although she mastered this technique with Dante, she'd yet to use it in a real-world scenario. Cheeks flushed with embarrassment, she buried her face in her palms.

Iain dashed across the street, dodging traffic. He leaned over the window, flashing Autumn a sympathetic smile.

"Having trouble?" Apparently, he knew the answer to his own question.

Cars honked, but he shrugged them off, impressing Autumn with his confidence.

"Isn't it obvious?" She sank into her chair.

Autumn climbed through to the passenger's seat and Iain

took the driver's seat, struggling to squeeze into the car without making adjustments. He was tall and lean, with large feet. In one full swoop, he maneuvered the vehicle into the impossible space.

"Thank you."

"No problem, it's a small price to pay for a night out with such a beautiful lady." He raised an eyebrow.

Autumn's cheeks heated, confirming her worst fear. She was on a *date again.*

When they reached the theater, Caleb snorted. "I think someone needs to go back to driver's ed."

Autumn rolled her eyes. *What an ass.*

"Yeah, thanks for all your help," she said.

Caleb leaned over and hugged her. Tensing, she pulled away. Brianna noticed this time, glowering at her.

"We should go inside." Iain placed his hand on Autumn's shoulder. "We're going to be late for the show."

Autumn went to the counter to buy her ticket, when Iain conveniently pulled one out of his pocket, placing it into her palm instead.

"Thanks, you didn't have to buy my ticket." She reached into her bag to grab her wallet.

Autumn wanted to make it clear she was more than capable of taking care of herself. Why did every guy treat her like she was helpless? It infuriated her.

"No, don't worry about it." He stared at the floor bashfully.

"I'll pay for the refreshments," she insisted.

In the corner of her eye, she caught Caleb and Brianna standing on the concession line. Caleb glanced her way while Brianna nestled her head against his shoulder. Autumn wondered what his true motives were.

When she turned to Iain, a sheen of sweat slicked his brow. Quivering, Iain brushed his hand against hers, palms moist and warm. Autumn shifted uneasily. There was no mistaking how he felt about her, but she couldn't deal.

When they reached the counter, Autumn was greeted by the delicious scent of freshly popped corn drowned in butter. She purchased a large bucket for them to share. Iain ordered a *Coke*, but promptly spilled it in a rush of bubbles and ice all over her shoes. Iain's face flushed crimson as he blotted her sneakers with a napkin and apologized profusely.

Autumn's feet squished as they made their way into the theater. She moved through the darkness, as a reel of previews rolled. To her dismay, she was sandwiched between Iain and Caleb. Brianna glared at her over Caleb's shoulder, and she subtly shrugged.

Autumn shrunk into her chair; there was no escape in sight. She wished she could make alternative seating arrangements. Who knew this many people on a Friday night would be fascinated by a sixteenth century Queen?

While she ate her popcorn, Autumn chewed with her mouth closed. Iain, on the other hand, ate like a *barbarian*, crunching loudly in her ear.

Absolutely disgusting. And one of her biggest pet peeves.

After a while, her clothing became covered with half eaten kernels of corn. Grease stains seeped into her white cotton shirt. And worse still—Iain tried to caress her hand with his slippery, butter-stained palm.

She held onto his hand for a moment before patting it away and wiping the grease onto her jeans. Oddly enough, whenever their skin brushed, memories of Dante flooded her mind. But she couldn't in good conscience allow herself to miss him.

Unable to process her emotions, she wanted to scream and cry and run away all at once, but she sat as still as a chess piece, willing her feelings away.

Fed up with Iain's attempts, she twined her fingers in her lap. On her opposite side, Caleb's sapphire eyes sparkled.

Unable to take anymore of this nonsense, she stumbled from her seat and climbed over Iain after informing him she needed to use the ladies' room. By the time she reached the hallway, she glimpsed over her shoulder. A messy head of curls bounced furiously in her peripheral vision.

Brianna stormed in like rapid fire. No sooner did Autumn enter the bathroom, did a bout of hysterical sobbing erupt.

"Are you okay?" Autumn's eyes widened.

"I know there's something going on between you and Caleb," Brianna's cheeks were slicked with tears. "Don't think I haven't noticed the way he looks at you."

This entire time, she was positive Brianna was clueless. Maybe she was more perceptive than she gave her credit for.

"Nothing is going on between us," Autumn reassured her.

Brianna's bottom lip quivered. "I'm sorry. I love him and I'm terrified of losing him. He told me you went to high school together, and I assumed you had history."

"We're just friends," Autumn said. "Acquaintances. Don't worry."

Obviously, Brianna was distressed, so Autumn purposely neglected to tell her about their dating history. How they were childhood friends and each other's first kiss. How they had a relationship all throughout high school until senior year came and Misty seduced him.

If anyone needed to speak with Brianna, Caleb did. She hoped she'd made the right decision keeping this information from his girlfriend but she didn't want to see Brianna get burned the way she'd been.

She embraced Brianna, patting her on the back, suspecting Caleb would have some explaining to do in the not-so-distant future.

After relieving herself, she went back to the theater.

Iain leaned over and whispered, "Is everything okay?"

"Yeah," she reassured him, although every ounce of her being was itching to leave the theater. The night had been a total bust.

By the end of the film she barely enjoyed, both of the guys snored like roaring freight trains. She poked Iain awake, not wanting to touch him any more than necessary. Iain stretched and yawned before he came to.

Caleb's eyes opened, and he cast her a lazy blink. "Where's Brianna?"

Autumn glanced, realizing she'd never returned to her seat. "The last time I saw her was in the bathroom."

The guys followed her to the ladies' room and waited outside. When she entered, the sink ran. Thick steam fogged the mirrors in white puffs. She turned the faucet off and glanced around. *Drip, drip, drip.* The hairs on the back of her neck stood at perfect attention. Her stomach flipped.

"Brianna, are you here?"

Nobody answered. She was assaulted by the sound of silence. Autumn went from door to door to door peeking through the cracks and then underneath the stalls but she was nowhere to be found. How strange. After everything that had happened, she must've gone home.

Caleb and Iain approached her as soon as she left the restroom. "Where is she?" Caleb's brows furrowed.

"Not in the bathroom." Autumn shrugged. "Maybe you should text her."

Caleb pulled out his smartphone and called her instead, but he was directed to voicemail.

"Brianna mentioned not feeling well earlier, she probably went home. That has to be where she went. I'll see you guys later." Caleb waved, texting on his smartphone.

When Iain walked Autumn across the street to her car, her

legs swayed. She fumbled through her pocket for her keys, needing to leave ASAP.

Deep in her gut, she had an inkling of what was coming next.

"I had a really great night." Iain grinned.

"Same here," she said, trying her best to be polite, unable to rip her mind away from Brianna's disappearance.

He leaned over and continued. "We should definitely do this again soon."

Iain lowered his face, and Autumn's muscles tensed. His eyes shut, and lips puckered. At the last second, she turned her head, derailing his attempt. His lips slid against her cheek.

Iain stepped back and jumbled his words as Autumn pulled away. His face shifted tomato-red. Unfortunately, there was no other way.

"Listen, Iain..." Autumn jingled the keys in her hand. "I think you're a great guy and all, but right now, I think I need a friend more than a boyfriend."

Iain's mouth twisted to the side, and the lamplight danced overhead and faded before going dark.

"Okay." Disappointment hummed through his voice. "We can take it slow. I know you're still hurt."

"Yeah," she said. "Thanks again for the movie and the fun night out."

She hugged Iain before climbing into her Neon. He ambled away, head hung low. She didn't want to hurt him, but she couldn't return his feelings.

She arrived home completely exhausted, yawning as she pulled into her driveway. All the lights were out. She kicked off her shoes and trudged upstairs to her room. Collapsing in bed, she drifted off to sleep. When she opened her eyes, she found herself in an all too familiar dreamscape. The same clinical room she'd dreamt off all summer long. She squinted in the blinding white light. The neatly made bed sat behind her. And the lone silver door was closed tight, offering her a foggy reflection of herself. *No, no, no, this couldn't be happening.*

Walking around, she shivered as cool steam particles blew beneath the door, misting around her feet. She knew what would happen next. Her heart pounded in anticipation. The door slid open with a vengeance, colliding with the frame. She stood her ground, trembling fists balled at her sides. She refused to be intimidated.

"Stay away from me." She took two steps backwards, stumbling.

Dante folded his arms. "I just wanted to check in."

Her brows knitted. "I want absolutely nothing to do with you, Dante. I told you, we're over."

"You gave me your word, and where I'm from, words are a binding agreement." His long lashes grazed his sharp cheekbones.

"Get away from me, you're a liar and a murderer."

"You have every right to be upset. I should have been more careful and considerate."

A pit settled in her stomach. "Well what you did was evil and selfish."

Dante ignored her statement. "I know I promised you space for the time being, but I had to see you," he paused. "Who's this Iain Smith you've been spending time with?"

Her limbs exploded with pins and needles. "Nobody, just a friend, and you can't control who I spend my time with."

Dante's white teeth gleamed. "How fascinating, he doesn't seem like just a friend to me. You have three months remaining."

Autumn shot up from her sleep. She didn't know whether she was more frightened Dante came to visit her in her dreams, or that he was in her room while she slept. All that remained of him was the lingering scent of cinnamon.

She hoped Dante didn't plan to hurt Iain. Her heart sped. She couldn't stand the thought of him hurting more innocent people because of her.

Sixty-Two

THE FIRST WEEK of March arrived, and the Monday after the double date gone wrong, promised to be a difficult one. Autumn needed to check on her friend and somehow warn him he was possibly in danger. She imagined the conversation unfolding like: *Hey Iain, my alien ex-fiancé is out to kill you*, which she didn't imagine would go over well...

But she at least had to try.

When Autumn arrived at the Chemistry lecture hall, class had commenced, so she didn't have a chance to seek him out. She took a seat, uncharacteristically close to the projector. She met Caleb's gaze from a neighboring row. He sat, shifting his signature red cap over his shining raven curls. Autumn's eyes flickered around. Brianna was *absent*. Her heart leapt to her throat before she threw a nail in her mouth, chewing the cuticle down to a nub. She hoped she was all right. She was a mess the last time she saw her and prayed she didn't do anything drastic to keep Caleb's attention. She'd left their double date so suddenly.

Brianna was an emotional wreck and Caleb was a cheater.

For Brianna's sake, Autumn hoped she realized this sooner

rather than later. She sighed, reminding herself she had bigger problems to deal with and didn't need to get caught up in their drama. *Mainly Iain's safety.*

Chemistry class dragged on and on and Autumn's mind wandered. She'd never realized how boring the subject was. Too many equations and definitions.

By the time the lecture ended, Autumn gathered her belongings in one full swoop. But when she turned around, she realized—

Iain.

Wasn't.

There.

In a panic, she raced over to Caleb. He was packing up his stuff and stopped when Autumn approached him.

"Hey!" Autumn's voice jumped a bit. "Did you notice if Iain was in class?"

Caleb blinked. "I bet he's avoiding you. That date was a little weird. And get this, Brianna never answered my texts or calls, so I went to her apartment in Nyack and it was completely cleaned out."

"Wait, are you serious?"

"Yes, I feel like such a loser. I guess it serves me right getting dumped." He zipped up his backpack. "You can laugh if you want."

Autumn didn't understand. She stared at him wide-eyed, recalling Brianna's confession.

"She was always a little unstable and never knew what she wanted, unlike you." Caleb admitted. "She mentioned traveling cross-country a few months ago, and I guess she finally acted on it."

She turned to walk away, and Caleb grabbed hold of her arm. She stared into his sapphire eyes.

"I'm sure Iain will call."

Autumn pulled away abruptly, making her way to the door.

Later on in English class, she scoured the room for any sign of Iain.

But he failed the attendance check. She was terrified, her worst fears confirmed. *Iain was in trouble.*

Sixty-Three

NEW YORK CITY *would be conquered first.*

Followed by all of North and South America, Africa, Europe, Asia, Australia, and Antarctica, the frozen wasteland. Dante had taken the time to tour the rest of the globe, and knew it was lacking both technologically and militarily.

In as little as three months, Earth would have its first planet-wide ruler. A miniscule job that would take forty-eight, maybe seventy-two hours at most, depending on how diligently he worked his crew. Dante was more than eager to complete this mission and go back home.

But at the same time, the thought of performing his duty was dreadful.

His thoughts were interrupted by a young woman who had been watching him all night long. Sparkling diamonds adorned her ears. Her cascading hair resembled the rich shade of Mars. *Somehow, he found her irritating.*

"Hello, handsome." She stumbled, reeking of wine.

The humans and their inability to hold their drink in a social setting. How pathetic.

"Hi." Dante folded his arms, glancing at his cousins who

had acclimated themselves to the party. Dancing lights flickered wildly overhead.

"I didn't imagine someone with such strong arms and the cutest cleft on his chin would be this shy." She ran a red-taloned finger along his arm. "If you'd like, we could go somewhere private."

Dante lounged against the wall, waving a hand. "I'm not interested, make your leave."

She stared at him exasperated and turned on a spiked heel, clicking away with a fury. A shudder of embarrassment rattled through him when he recollected his initial behavior around Autumn. He never deserved her, still didn't. She no longer wanted him in her life.

Dante sighed, knowing it was a matter of time, anyway. If she despised him for killing one human, he could only imagine what she'd say after he completed his mission. She'd probably spit in his face.

The time on his communicator read 0100 hours. Crashing the party at 40.7794°N, 73.9632°W was not his idea, although it was more in line with the parties he was accustomed to. It was filled with well-dressed humans of high rank. They spun around in their gowns and finery. Clinking their glasses and laughing without a care in the world.

All this for Ronan's nineteenth name day, or it should've been if they were back on Surge. As soon as Dante let it slip New York City was nearby, Ronan jumped on the opportunity to celebrate.

Armienti circled the room with a girl hanging from his arm. They laughed and kissed as they danced amidst a row of twirling humans. Ronan stood by a table of refreshments, exchanging pleasantries with a male servant, or waiter, as Autumn would have corrected him.

What was the allure with servants and his family on this planet? They couldn't resist them.

For the rest of the celebration, Dante kept to himself. Girls approached, but he ignored them, mind fixated on Autumn. Staring into space, he heard his name shouted from somewhere in the room. As he glanced across the way, Armienti waved him down. The girl from earlier vanished; he now had two more hanging on his arms with lively brown eyes and tawny complexions.

"*Not again*." Dante sighed and reluctantly approached.

"Cousin, meet my new friends." Armienti smoothed his hair away from his black satin eye mask. "Candice and Lexy."

Dante watched them in silence.

"They're twins." An obvious observation, unless Armienti thought him dense.

"Enough, I'm leaving." Dante brushed past them.

Armienti jogged after him, catching him by the arm. "What's wrong?"

"What are we doing here, truly?"

"Celebrating Ronan's name day and having a little fun. You should lighten up and quit behaving like you have one foot in the grave. It's a party."

Armienti smiled at the girls, and they giggled in return.

"I know, but how many women does one need in a lifetime? A hundred, a thousand? Why not choose one to share your life with?"

"Cousin, you sound like a love-struck fool, you're youthful yet. I know you're still hung up on Autumn, but believe me when I say she *doesn't* think highly of you."

Dante blinked. How would he know? *It all made perfect sense.* Armienti had been to see her in his absence, but for what purpose?

"Tell me." The stone floor cracked beneath their feet. Windows smashed in a spray of colorful glass, and people ran away screaming. "When did you see her?"

Ronan approached nonchalantly. "What's going on here?"

Fire crisped through Dante's flesh, and he threw the flames at Armienti, who dodged them. Flames singed the wall, leaving black streaks. Alarms screamed, and water sprinkled from the ceiling.

"I ran into her on her name day a few months back."

"Twice you've defied my orders. *Twice*," Dante said. "I'm beginning to question your loyalty."

"This was the first time, I swear. I needed some fresh air."

"Don't you dare lie to me." Dante crossed his arms. "I saw you in the forest on a separate occasion *after* my orders were issued."

"No, I would never—"

"You need to relax, Dante," Ronan interjected. "Your mind plays tricks on you."

Dante snapped in Armienti's face. "On your knees."

Armienti hesitantly fell to his knees. Dante massaged his temples before speaking. "This has been a horrible experience for all of us, but what infuriates me the most is the dwindling level of trust between us. Without loyalty and trust, we can no longer function as a unit. I'll give you one last chance. Swear your allegiance to me and we'll put this whole mess behind us."

Armienti remained silent.

"I won't extend this courtesy to you again, cousin."

"I swear." Armienti averted his gaze to Dante's feet. "My allegiance belongs to you."

Sixty-Four

AUTUMN SAT ON HER BED, fingertips hovering over Iain's number. *Should I call or text him*? Another week passed, and still no sign of him *anywhere*. She should've contacted him earlier, but was terrified of facing the truth.

Iain disappeared without a trace, missing both the Chemistry and English midterms. Her gut told her he was in trouble, and somehow, *Dante* was responsible.

Trembling, she texted him. "*Hey Iain, I noticed you haven't been in class. Are you okay?*"

Her stomach knotted as she hit send. Not a minute later, her phone rang, and tentatively, she answered.

"Iain?"

"Hey Autumn, how have you been?" He sounded as normal as ever.

A wave of relief washed through her. "I'm good. Um, I noticed you haven't been in class, and you didn't show up for the midterms. I wanted to make sure you're okay."

He chuckled. "I'm surprised you noticed. I thought after our date you didn't want anything to do with me."

Autumn hesitated. "That's not true." But deep down she knew, it was.

"I'm sorry I didn't contact you earlier. I've been overwhelmed with taking care of my sick dad and helping with Silver Spoons, our catering company. I'm taking the rest of the semester off."

Her heart clenched as she thought about what she would do if her own dad was ill, especially after her mom's passing.

"I'm sorry to hear that," she said. "If you ever need help, let me know, I used to work as a waitress."

"Thanks, Autumn. There are a few positions open and the tips are excellent. It's mostly weekend work."

"Sounds good."

"Thanks again for checking in, I appreciate your concern. Have a goodnight." *Click*. He hung up on her.

Autumn sat on her bed, relieved, suddenly missing Iain. Sure, he was a nice enough guy, and down to earth. A messy eater maybe, but more than likely nervous. Or maybe she created this situation because she was afraid to make a new friend. Ever since Iain stopped coming to class, she secretly wondered about him.

Maybe a little too much.

Autumn was beyond grateful Dante didn't harm him. Iain deserved better.

Sixty-Five

OVER THE COURSE of the next few weeks, Autumn invented reasons to speak with Iain. First, she checked in on him, and then admittedly, she enjoyed hearing his soothing voice over the phone.

She racked her brain for a reason to see him. And it occurred to her.

Perfect.

The sky assumed a dull gray hue and crystallized snowflakes trickled in on the passing wind. Little by little, one by one, they coated the driveway in a dusting of white. It wasn't uncommon for it to snow in Orange County, NY until the early days of spring, and this morning wasn't an exception.

Autumn chewed her nails while sitting in her car, engine humming. She was eager to see Iain, having planned to meet him at a cafe in Suffern, on the *pretense* of discussing a job.

Her plan was flawless. Chemistry had been canceled, but English would take place right on schedule, leaving her morning *wide open*.

She was eager to explore her growing feelings for him and wanted to determine whether he was boyfriend material.

Bundled in her baby-blue puffer coat, she checked her phone. It had been buzzing all morning long.

Misty posted a photo online in her brand-new forest-green Range Rover. As soon as Lauren saw the car, the gossip column started. Misty was entitled, vain, a princess, and a bitch—all facts Autumn had known long before. Her parents didn't have the wherewithal to punish her after she flunked out of her fancy college. Did Autumn particularly care?

No. She had enough of her own problems.

As her best friend, Autumn tolerated Lauren's ranting and raving. That's what friends were for, even if it was obvious Lauren was a little jealous. Misty had that effect on everyone. The world revolved around her no matter the circumstance.

As Autumn backed up, the driveway was slick, and so were the roads.

When she merged onto I-287, it was smooth sailing, with light traffic. So light that while she rode in the traveling lane, she grabbed her phone and placed it onto her lap. The conversation started getting juicy. Ellie talked about Hazel and how she looked pregnant. With one eye on the road, Autumn went back online to check.

Her eyes widened. Ellie hadn't been kidding. Hazel seemed different, but it didn't look like a pregnancy. Perhaps she put on the dreaded freshman fifteen.

Mid-text, clear as day, she spotted the gangly limbed boy who had assaulted her with his tongue back in January, trudging along the highway. His mouth and tattered clothes were stained red. His neck cracked and straightened in an unnatural direction.

She couldn't look away, frozen with fear. It had to be her imagination. Her trembling fingers touched her cheek, caressing her phantom scar. When she refocused on the road, she was met with a swirling flash of color.

CRASH.

The car spun in a three-hundred-and-sixty-degree turn. Tires screeched. A van smashed into her front headlight, crunching the hood like an accordion. She flew forward, choked by her seatbelt, the airbag ripping against her face.

BOOM.

The car collided with the guardrail and stopped rolling. Gray and white steam hissed from the hood, and Autumn laid there, vision blurred. She trembled and attempted to sit up. But her muscles slackened.

It hurt to move, to even think. Eyes closing, she was met face to face with her mom before her world went dark.

* * *

When Autumn woke, EMTs sat on either side of her wearing navy-blue uniforms. As she went to reposition herself, she realized her body was bound to a board. Panic ripped through her limbs.

"Where am I?" Her throat rasped.

"You were in an accident," one EMT said. "We're on our way to Nyack Hospital."

Holy crap. She tried her best to sit up, but the restraints did their job.

Her quaking hands roamed the pockets of her jeans.

"Where's my phone? I need to text my dad."

"You can have it when we get there."

And Iain. *No, no, no, no, no.* She needed to tell him she couldn't make it. Autumn frowned, hoping he hadn't been waiting too long, but by now, he probably thought she stood him up.

When they arrived at Nyack Hospital, she was promptly rolled to the ER. Her heart pounded the entire way. Doctors filled out charts, nurses raced, and sterile air assaulted her senses. It was somewhat reminiscent of being back on Dante's spaceship. Not to mention, kind of creepy.

She was placed in an observation room. Nurses greeted her, and with a single prick, hooked her up to an IV drip. She winced as the cold, hard metal pierced her vein. After her initial screening, one nurse finally returned her phone.

Exhausted, she texted her dad, followed by Iain. While she laid there in shock and disbelief, she messaged her friends as well.

Huge mistake.

In a matter of minutes, they posted worried statuses all over social media and a fundraising campaign. Worst of all, they told *everyone* her exact location. She was mortified.

Stiff, sore, and overwhelmed, she closed her eyes.

Mid-slumber, a palm smoothed across her forehead. When she opened her eyes again, she saw her dad, eyes wavering with concern beneath his simple silver frames.

"How are you feeling?" Her dad's eyes pooled with tears. Horizontal creases crept across his forehead.

"Sore," she adjusted herself, muscles screaming in agony. "What happened to my car?"

"It's totaled," she nodded, wide-eyed. All she could think of was the weird boy plodding along the highway.

"You have a visitor," her dad announced, interrupting her thoughts.

Iain stood in the doorway, cute and doe eyed, light reflecting off of the golden strands of his curls. Wound around his wrist was a blue and silver balloon that said *Get Well Soon.*

Her dad glimpsed speculatively at her and at him.

"This is my friend Iain."

Iain walked through the doorway, balloon floating, and extended a hand. "Nice to meet you, Mr. Ramon."

"Nice to meet you, too." Her dad shook Iain's hand. He left and went to the hallway to speak to the nurse.

"I came as soon as I heard." Iain tied the balloon to the head of her bed.

"I wasn't expecting you."

"Well, always expect the unexpected, I guess." He smiled, dimples protruding against his cheeks. "How are you feeling?"

"I'm sorry you have to see me like this." She could only imagine what Iain thought of her. An incompetent driver and a hot mess.

"I'm glad you're alive," he reassured her. "We'll have to make plans soon. I'd really like to get together again under better circumstances. My offer still stands."

She nodded. "Ouch."

"Don't move." Iain leaned down and gently kissed her on the cheek.

Autumn twined her fingers in his. "You missed."

Slowly, Iain pressed his lips to hers, and she wound his soft curls around her fingertips. As he pulled away, a throat cleared in the doorway.

Caleb stood there, holding a pink and gold balloon that read *It's a Girl.* What the heck?

Autumn snorted.

"I heard you had a car accident."

Thanks a lot, Lauren and Ellie. She sighed. Mortified, she watched Caleb fasten his balloon next to Iain's.

Caleb's cheeks reddened. "It's all they had left at the gift shop."

"Thanks."

"You seriously need to go back to driver's ed." Caleb snickered.

"Okay everyone, my daughter needs her rest." Her dad came back into the room.

"Dad." She frowned.

Getting the hint, Caleb and Iain waved goodbye.

She rubbed her fingers against her lips. If she ever needed

confirmation this was it—she liked Iain a lot. Drifting off to cloud nine, she yearned to see him again.

Autumn stayed overnight for observation. Her dad slept at the edge of her bed keeping her company.

* * *

When morning arrived, they rolled her out in a wheelchair, balloons fluttering in tow. Her dad loaded her into his Jeep.

On the ride home, her dad glanced at her several times, appearing as if he wanted to speak.

"I don't want to frighten you, but I need to talk to you."

"What's wrong?"

She struggled to reposition her head. Stiffness and sharp pain radiated through her cervical spine.

"Last night, I had the strangest dream." Her dad turned the wheel of the car. "Dante came to visit you. And the way the light reflected off his skin, he appeared blue. It was half-past three when I noticed him by your bedside. I blinked, and he disappeared into thin air," he paused. "I know it sounds silly. It had to be a dream but it seemed so real."

"Did he speak?" Her lips trembled. "In your dream I mean."

"No, but he looked distressed. Seeing him again was more like a nightmare. He's a murderer, and I'm sure justice will be served."

A cool chill trickled down her spine and Autumn stared outside in silence. They rode the long stretch of highway. Why did he continue to visit her? She made her point, but apparently it hadn't been received. And why couldn't she shake the creepy long-tongued boy from her mind?

Sixty-Six

THE CREW HAD BEEN WHITTLED DOWN DRAMATICALLY since the night of the crash. Eighteen soldiers, a tech and a pilot, all gone. Twenty-one men remained. Twenty-one men split into three even units of seven, manned by himself and his cousins, would secure Earth. That was more than enough, and *admittedly, he could do it by himself*.

Dante smashed his fist against the steel table while he reviewed the tactical plans with his crew. The green light of the projector featuring a 3D holographic image of Earth rotated.

Ronan and Armienti glowered at him after what happened at the masked ball. But Dante didn't care. Armienti needed to be reminded of who made the rules, and insubordination would get him *nowhere*. Ronan was a different story altogether and did what his older brother asked him to. Which Dante couldn't fault him for.

He desired to put this entire ordeal behind him. But his mind was plagued by thoughts of Autumn and their uncertain future. Seeing her battered body in the infirmary filled him with an indefinable rage. If only he'd been there to protect her, but he was too busy respecting her wishes to be left alone. All he wanted was for them to be together.

He wished he'd been injured in her stead. Or better yet, he yearned to be dead. The cool darkness of death would be as just a punishment for his crimes as any. They were *never* ending. But somehow, this one stung the most. *He failed again.*

After three hours of reviewing tactical plans, he released his crew for the evening. They filed out of the room, and he remained, staring at his reflection through the cracked glass.

Another Earth evening arrived, as lonely as ever. Heavy droplets of rain water streamed against the exterior of the ship. A flash of silver caught his attention from a side compartment near the control panel. Curious, he opened it, and discovered a half empty flask of wine. But not just any wine, contraband from the orchards of Universe 24 available *only* to the super elite.

It all made perfect sense.

The pilot was a thief, who was intoxicated at the time of the crash. That's why he failed to notice the ailing crystal liquid fuel line. Drunk flying, especially from a wine of this potency, offered with it a stiff punishment back on Surge. *Death.* But justice had already been served.

It was a sin to waste good wine, and his personal stash had long since been drained. Popping open the cap, he took a swig, savoring its warm, rich, salty flavor. He laid in the control seat and closed his eyes, rolling the fluid in his mouth before swallowing.

Midway through his unwinding, a soft reluctant knock hit the door. Dante tilted his head to see who sought his attention. A soldier stood there.

"Yes?" The room tilted slightly. He blinked and his vision focused.

The man bowed. "Master Dante, the Emperor wishes to

speak with you. I'm here to request your permission to transfer his call through to the control room."

He waved his black-gloved hand, and the soldier left.

The room fell pitch black. For a moment, Dante sat alone in the darkness, accompanied by his steady breaths. The hologram light flickered pale green, and the Emperor stared back at him. Their amber stares united.

Dante lounged in the seat, eyes closed, flashing a toothy grin.

"What's gotten into you? Is this how you choose to address me now?"

"How foolish of me, Sire." Dante stumbled over his own boots to a stand, and fell into a mocking bow.

"You're drunk." The Emperor scrunched his nose. "Your mouth is tinted blood shade."

Dante rolled his eyes and flopped into the chair. The Emperor was a fine one to talk. It seemed the more time he spent on this planet, the more human he became. He didn't bother to deny his drunkenness. How hypocritical.

The Emperor smoothed a black-gloved hand over his obsidian tresses. "Well, this is just perfect. I need to have a serious conversation with you. I can clearly see your maturity level is as low as your tolerance for wine. What has Earth done to you?"

Dante dismissed his insult. "Speak, then. Don't be a fool to think I'm incoherent. I've done far more during this voyage than you've done over the course of your lifetime."

The Emperor's eyes widened. "What's the status of the Earth mission? Has it been successful?"

"It's still a work in progress."

"*That's what you told me last time.* You'd better hurry the hell up about it. The Grand Supreme has been relentless. Calling me day and night, inquiring about his acquisition. He's eager to stake his claim over Universe 1."

"How is any of this my problem?" Dante leaned back and folded his arms. "It will be ready when it's ready. Lest you forget the reason I've been selected to lead these missions all these years over yourself. I'm the strongest our kind has ever known."

The Emperor's face flushed crimson, mouth twisting to the side.

"What?" Dante smiled.

"Tread carefully, boy."

"Or what? What more will you do to me that hasn't already been done?"

"Enough," the Emperor snapped. "Where is this rebelliousness coming from? Has your human whore been whispering sweet nothings into your ear? Surely you're not that impressionable."

"Don't you dare speak about her with such disrespect. You have no clue what you're talking about."

The Emperor's obsidian whiskers twitched. "I'll tell you what, Dante, you do a thorough job, and I'll allow you to keep your human girl."

"Allow me? First off, she's not an object to be traded and second, I never needed your permission to begin with."

The Emperor continued, "A little motivation and a thank you for your service. Your failure could put us all in very real danger. The treaty has been in place for centuries. You need to get to work, unless you'd prefer to take issue with the Grand Supreme directly, and explain to him how you've been spending your time on his ruby. I'm certain he won't be as understanding as I am."

Dante rolled his eyes.

"I thought not."

"Well, you're mistaken. If you're searching for a coward and a weakling, perhaps you should look no further than the mirror. All these years you've crumbled at his every whim."

"Bite your tongue. Every difficult decision I've made, including delivering you to him, I made for the prosperity of the realm."

"I'm sure that's what you tell yourself so you can sleep at night, but I know the truth." Dante clicked the hologram projector unit off, unable to tolerate another lie that came out of *that* man's mouth. He took deep, controlled breaths. Even the wine couldn't calm him now.

Sixty–Seven

DANTE'S POST-MIDNIGHT visit had been a false alarm. Autumn hadn't heard from him since the night her dad caught him visiting her. But she didn't dwell on it, or breach the barrier of no contact. Three months had passed since they last spoke a word to each other, and she intended to maintain her distance. She also hadn't seen any more of the strange boy.

Other than the emotional trauma she suffered, her injuries from the car accident had healed.

The problem was, she needed a ride to finish out the rest of the semester. She didn't want to inconvenience her dad. Not to mention it would be humiliating having him drive his *nineteen*-year-old daughter to college.

Although he offered to help her purchase a new car, she declined. She could take care of herself. She'd use the insurance check as a down payment and work off the rest.

There was only one other option, and clearly the most convenient. He lived a mere fifteen minutes away from her and was more than willing to be her ride.

* * *

Autumn stood at the edge of the driveway on a bright, breezy spring day in May. Her cosmic backpack rested over her shoulder. Caleb's midnight-blue Volkswagen pulled up with an incredibly oversized spoiler and a loose muffler that roared. Heavy metal music blasted loud enough to wake the dead.

Autumn couldn't believe she was really about to go through with this. But she was *desperate*, or she never would've considered traveling with him. She climbed inside, immediately accosted by smoke. Coughing, she lowered the volume on the radio.

"Hey, I was listening to that." Caleb's sapphire eyes flickered with annoyance.

"It's giving me a headache." Autumn massaged her pounding temples. "I thought you quit smoking a while ago."

"Stop being such an old lady." Caleb rolled his eyes. "I'm planning to quit. I'll vape instead if it'll make you more comfortable."

She buckled her seatbelt. Although Caleb referred to her as an old lady, he suddenly drove like an elderly man. She'd never ridden in a car with a more cautious driver. They missed every green light by a mile.

"You can step it up any day now." She rested her head against the seat and closed her eyes.

"Listen to you. First, you invite yourself into my car, and now you're telling me how to drive. If I remember correctly, you're the one without a car, and I'm the one doing you a *huge* favor."

"Sorry." Autumn bit her tongue. "You're right, and thanks again. I'd be up a creek without you."

"Damn straight you would." Caleb tilted his red baseball cap. "I don't normally drive like this, you know. I wasn't sure how you were feeling after your accident. I can only imagine how scary it must be driving in a car again."

She hated to admit it, but Caleb was actually being considerate for once. It was unlike him to think of anyone other than himself.

They arrived on campus and Caleb parked his roaring Volkswagen in the student lot. As he pulled the key from the ignition, he paused. "I really like this, you know. I don't mind being your personal chauffeur, it's like old times again."

"Yeah." She snatched her backpack, gut telling her where this conversation was headed. Another pathetic trip down memory lane.

"Do you ever wonder what it would be like if we had stayed together?"

"Do you mean if you didn't cheat on me—"

Knock. Knock. Knock.

Autumn glanced outside and Iain stood there, grinning. She returned his smile, and Caleb sighed, mumbling incoherently to himself.

She and Iain were official. Closer than ever after her accident. And it was she who, surprisingly, asked him to be her boyfriend.

She leapt from the car, jumping into Iain's arms. "What are you doing here?"

"Registering for summer session." Iain glanced at Caleb. "Thanks again for taking such good care of Autumn. If I lived closer, I would gladly drive her myself."

Caleb climbed out of the car and pulled on his backpack. "No problem," he muttered.

Iain slung her bag over his shoulder, resting his hand in her back jeans pocket. They strolled. Caleb trailed not far behind them. It was his turn to be a third wheel for once.

The sun danced overhead. Spring was a time of endless possibilities and fresh new beginnings.

She fidgeted her hands. "I need a favor from you."

"Of course, babe, anything."

"Is the catering position you mentioned still available?"

she asked hopefully. She needed the money to save up for a replacement car. Riding with Caleb was convenient for now, but she couldn't rely on him for weekend trips to the library and the mall. Plus, traveling with her ex sent all the wrong signals. She didn't want to risk sabotaging her blossoming relationship.

They stopped in the central courtyard. Caleb waited with them as well.

"Babe, your timing couldn't be any better. There's a wedding in Tappan this Saturday with a whopping five hundred guests. Although we're staffed, there's always room for one more."

"Is there room for two?" Caleb interjected. "I was fired from my construction job, and I need the gas money. Plus, I'm guessing Autumn needs a ride."

Crap, he was right.

"Sure, two is great." Iain smiled. "Just so you both know, for this wedding, the dress code is strict. Black shoes, no sneakers. Black slacks, a crisp long sleeved white button-down shirt with no wrinkles, a red bow tie, and a black button vest."

"I think I can manage," Autumn said.

"Same."

"Perfect, I'll see you both at 6:00 p.m. on Saturday."

Lord of Blood and Shadows

Sixty-Eight

AUTUMN WIPED the beading sweat from her brow. Of all the days for Caleb's car air conditioning to crap out. They'd been sitting in traffic for *forty-five* minutes and counting, waiting in line for clearance to enter the wedding venue. Apparently, Iain remembered the intricate details of the dress code, but *failed* to tell them they were working the wedding of some New York senator's daughter. Her future husband was a famous lawyer.

The line of cars extended forever. BMWs, Cadillacs, Audis, and the occasional Maserati. They rolled up a foot. *Finally.*

Sweat pooled beneath her pits. Thankfully, she remembered to wear deodorant. Her bow tie choked her, she could barely breathe. But Autumn could understand why the dress code was so strict. People waltzed around in jeweled headbands, peacock feathers, and gilded hair combs. Jewel tone ball gowns glinted, and tuxedos sparkled beneath the setting sun.

Caleb cursed, hand hovering over the horn of his car. A vape hung from his bottom lip, which Autumn kept quiet about. She was grateful for the ride.

They passed through a metal gate, and were stopped by guards in a booth. Sunglasses and caps concealing their faces.

"State your business."

"We're working the wedding." Caleb removed the vape from his mouth.

The guard gestured for them to stand. They were patted down, and Caleb's trunk was searched before they were permitted entrance.

On either side of the long gravel driveway were rows of shady weeping willow trees. In the distance sat a gray stone mansion with eggshell-white shutters. It was fairytale-esque with two jutting wings and a ten-vehicle garage.

In the center of the wrap around driveway sat a silver fountain with cherubs hovering over clouds. Fairy lights lit the tennis court, and behind it was a pool house ten times the size of her own home, coated with lush wisteria.

A bus boy handed Caleb a paper ticket, and he parked next to a white van that donned Silver Spoons. Autumn grabbed her phone, planning to take plenty of pictures. Lauren and Ellie would *never* believe any of this.

A butler ushered them through a dense crowd to the pool house. Sweat beaded along Autumn's upper lip. Five hundred people were present, and with the catering company, at least fifty more.

Iain waved cordially as Autumn fanned her face.

"Thank you again for helping out." He handed Autumn and Caleb each a headset.

"If it gets to be too overwhelming, let me know, I know you're still recovering." Iain placed a hand on her shoulder.

"I'm fine," she lied, perspiring more than ever. "Where should I start?" Iain pointed to an iced jug of water. She grabbed the handle and left through the patio door.

The venue was *no* Monroe Diner. Autumn glanced around, star-struck by singers and celebrities. Even a few prima ballerinas ambled gracefully through the crowd. Champagne poured from every bottle, and plates of caviar sat on white linen-draped tables. All of high society was present.

She held her breath, overwhelmed by the sheer volume of people. She struggled to keep glasses filled and made several trips back and forth to the kitchen to ensure she completed her task correctly.

Next, she was saddled with the unimaginable chore of tracking the entrees. There were four; chicken, beef, fish, and vegetarian. Easy enough to keep straight, if not for the crowd and the humidity. With a notepad and pencil in hand, she traveled to every table, doing her best to document the orders accurately.

She spotted a familiar head of honey blonde hair, romantically curled over tan, sculpted shoulders. A golden sequin fitted single strap dress hugged her flawless curves.

Misty looked like an Empress. Although they *never* and would *never* hang out, Autumn knew this was her crowd.

As soon as Misty's sky-blue eyes locked with Autumn's, her lips flickered with amusement. Her fancy friends followed suit, briefly staring at Autumn before returning to their fabulous conversations.

"Well, well, well, what do we have here? I knew it was only a matter of time until you waited on me again, hand and foot." Misty chuckled, pinching Autumn's toe with her diamond encrusted spiked heel. "It's bad enough I have to see you at RCC."

"Well, that sounds like a *you* problem." Autumn kicked Misty's foot aside. "If you didn't flunk out of Oxford, you wouldn't be their latest transfer student."

Misty's cheeks flushed dark-burgundy because her friends were within earshot. She gracefully came to a stand, the train of her gilded gown flowed against the concrete patio.

She stared at Autumn, breasts puffed. At a second glance,

they were as fake as her spray tan. Her long lashes were coated with heavy black mascara. Her breath smelled of champagne. "The difference between you and me is, I *always* win, and I always come out on top. I may be down, but I'm never out. So if you haven't realized already, you're a little out of your league, always have been, always will be."

"Stop being a bitch," Autumn huffed. "Nobody gives a crap about your money, your perfect life, or your stupid new car. Just tell me what your order is so I can finish my rounds."

"If you had more than five cents in your bank account and a brain in your head, you'd be surprised how far money can go. And what it can make people do." Misty squared her shoulders. "I think Caleb can attest to that."

Autumn stared at Misty, fists trembling. "What are you talking about?"

Misty turned to walk away, then hiccuped. The corners of her eyes crinkled. "How do you think I got him to take me to prom?" She flipped her tresses over her shoulders and leaned in close. "How do you think I took his virginity?"

She continued, mouth winding in a smile. "A little money can buy anyone off. I think if I offered Iain enough money, I could get him to dump you as well." She laughed, straight white teeth glinting.

Misty grabbed a flute of champagne from a passing tray.

Autumn's subconscious slipped into the great unknown. Red clouded her vision.

Misty took a casual sip. "What? Don't tell me he never told you?"

Autumn stood there, struggling to breathe.

"It's no matter." Misty gulped the rest of her beverage down. "We community college girls have to stick together, right? Feel free to take my order anytime now."

Misty pushed the empty flute of champagne in Autumn's hand. It slipped onto the ground shattering.

"Screw you." Autumn pelted her pad and pen into Misty's face, and she stumbled, high heels scraping, and landed in the lap of another seated guest.

"Did you see? Did you see what she did?"

Autumn stormed off, surrounded by gasps and whispers. Tears burned and erupted in her eyes.

Sixty-Nine

AUTUMN SPRINTED TO THE KITCHEN, terrified to face Iain and admit what she'd done. *Assault.* She assaulted Misty in front of numerous witnesses. And worst of all, she embarrassed her new boyfriend, as a representative of his father's company.

All because Misty paid Caleb off. She never wanted to see Caleb again, she'd rather *hitchhike* home. Autumn stumbled into a bathroom, sealed the door, and sobbed her heart out. This *seriously* couldn't be happening.

Hours passed, and Autumn sat propped against the golden flecked wall of the lavatory. She'd since turned off her headset. The entire catering party searched for her *non-stop.* She texted Lauren and Ellie, and they both recommended she make a run for it. They were equally disgusted by Caleb and Misty's actions, more so now than ever before. Autumn couldn't have asked for more supportive friends. She could always rely on them.

This explained everything. One day, she and Caleb were hopelessly in love, and the next, he dumped her like a piece of garbage. *How much was her broken heart worth?*

After another hour of self-pity, a firm knock came to the door. Autumn ignored it, face buried against her palms, flowing tears slicking her cheeks.

"Somebody's in here." Her voice cracked, nostrils rolling with snot.

The knocking persisted.

"Dammit, I'm busy." Autumn's entire body quivered. Some people were so *rude*. Couldn't they see the door was locked?

"It's me." A breathy murmur passed through the crack of the door.

Autumn recognized Caleb's voice. "Stay away from me."

Hearing an unwelcome sound, she sprang to her feet. Autumn held on to the doorknob with all her might as Caleb slid a credit card over the latch.

But her strength was no match for him. The door flung open, and she was thrown against the wall. Caleb entered and closed the door behind him.

"Everyone is searching for you." Caleb slid his card back into his wallet. "The police are here, along with security. Misty claims you attacked her, and there are several witnesses."

She squared her shoulders. "You slept with Misty for money?" She ignored every other word that left his unfaithful mouth. "Why would you do that? How could you do that to me?" She shoved him against the door.

Autumn trembled and continued, "What did you need more stupid concert tickets? Clothing? Shoes? A car? Another ridiculous hat or a fucking vaporizer? Tuition? What the hell was more important than me?"

She slammed her fists against his chest. Caleb didn't bother to defend himself, even with years of martial arts training. Instead, he fell silent and accepted her blows, staring at his feet. "You were *never* supposed to find out."

"Well, I did."

Autumn tried to push him aside and leave the bathroom, but he grabbed her wrists, and pinned her against the wall. "Let me out! Let me out!" she screamed, trying to escape.

Her eyes narrowed into his rich, sapphire gaze. "I did it for my family, Autumn, my family. Do you think I wanted to break up with you? Do you think I wanted to hurt you like I did? Do you seriously think I wanted to sleep with *Misty Beckett*?"

Autumn paused, gathering her thoughts. This wasn't the explanation she expected. She figured Misty brought Caleb's entire family on an all-expense-paid vacation to one of her luxurious estates in Bermuda in exchange for her suffering.

"What do you mean?"

Caleb hesitated before speaking. "My parents fell behind on the mortgage payments. I overheard them one night. My mom was crying and my dad did his best to console her. He lost his job. A few days later, I found an opened foreclosure letter on the kitchen table." He paused. "When Misty came to me and asked me out to prom, I flat out rejected her. I told her we were together, and you were my girlfriend. But when she offered me enough money to help my parents out, I caved. I told them I won it from a scratch off. I'm so sorry, Autumn." Tears streamed down his cheeks.

Autumn's anger began to dissipate. She could breathe again. What he claimed made sense she supposed. He accepted money and slept with Misty to help his family. She'd do anything to help her own family no matter the cost. How selfless of him to put the needs of his family before his own.

Her lips quivered. "You and Misty—"

"I slept with her under the same arrangement. My first time should've been with you, but I can't take it back. I'm so sorry." He hugged her. "Can you ever forgive me?"

She knew more than anyone about making difficult decisions. She would go to the greatest lengths for her family, including sacrificing her dream college to look after her dad. Autumn loved her family most of all.

"I love you, Autumn. Always have, always will."

Her entire body ached for him. She couldn't help herself. She wanted him again, to hold him in her arms after all of these months apart. After all she'd been through. The choice was hers. Their mouths crashed together in a swell of red-hot emotion. Lips and tongue and broken breaths. Caleb's hands tugged at her hips and they slid to the floor, trembling. Caleb sat her on his lap, running his fingers through her hair. She pulled him in close, heart racing.

The creak of the bathroom door interrupted their reconciliation. Like an idiot, Caleb neglected to lock it, and Autumn never bothered to check. Two burly security guards entered. She stuttered, "*holy crap.*"

The security guards grabbed her roughly by the arms and escorted her out of the bathroom. They slapped cold metal handcuffs on her wrists. Autumn shot Caleb a pleading look.

Iain intercepted them. "Don't worry, babe, I'll find a way to get you out of this. I'll meet you down at the station" Autumn could barely make eye contact with Iain. *She knew they needed to talk after what had taken place.*

Security escorted her to the door of the pool house, when a loud static frequency ripped across their headsets. Everyone froze and stared. The security guards whipped their guns from their holsters and sprinted outside. What the heck was going on? Autumn tried to pull her wrists from the cuffs, but they cut against her skin, creating red marks.

Seventy

WHEN AUTUMN WENT OUTSIDE with Caleb and Iain to see what all the commotion was about, the wedding was at a standstill. No music played from the DJ booth, and the bride and groom clutched each other for dear life on the dance floor. Everyone focused their attention on eight men, clothed in onyx plated uniforms. Round tinted helmets concealed their faces.

They all carried metallic rocket launchers, minus the central figure with a purple and silver flames and stars crest, glinting beneath the flickering fairy lights.

Autumn's stomach flipped. *Oh no, what is Dante doing here?* A shiver rippled down her spine.

"At this point in time, I'd like to ask Autumn Ramon to step forth." She stumbled backwards, colliding with Caleb, who wrapped his arms protectively around her. Iain shot them a wide-eyed look.

"Finally, some justice." Misty strode over like a true, all American princess. She yanked Autumn by her cuffed arm, pinching a nerve.

"Ouch." Autumn glowered at her.

"She's over here," Misty chirped. "I hope you give her the harshest punishment in the book for assaulting a Beckett. Maybe a few months in jail will do her some good."

"Misty," Caleb hissed. "I don't think they're cops."

Dante removed his helmet, revealing his natural born features. "Autumn, you need to come with me at once."

Everyone gasped. Autumn had no plans to go *anywhere*. Especially not with a cold- blooded murderer. Misty's legs wobbled, and she fainted dead weight into the grass. Nobody bothered to help her.

"Drop your weapons." A gathering of gun clad security guards and cops shouted from beyond a row of shrubs. Their weapons aimed at him.

When Dante didn't budge, they opened fire.

Dante never broke his gaze from her. Instead, he lifted two fingers in the air and pointed toward the group of men. One helmeted figure flanking him aimed his weapon. A stream of radiant blue static energy twirled and rippled through the air. All that remained was a pile of black smoking dust. The smell of burning flesh lingered.

Everyone ran and screamed, shoving each other out of the way. Dante cocked his head to the side, while he and his soldiers remained eerily silent amidst the chaos. *Monster.*

She made her way through the oncoming stampede, hands bound. Caleb trailed close behind.

"Autumn, wait." Caleb tried to hold her, but she pulled away.

"Stop, please, we have to leave."

She didn't hesitate, neither was she afraid. She was sick to death of living in fear every second of every day. First when she and Caleb broke up, then after her mom's death, and now *this*. She intended to give Dante a piece of her mind. Her teeth clenched.

Dante approached when Autumn did exactly as he asked.

But when he saw Caleb, his mouth sharpened. Iain retreated with the rest of the crowd, screaming and waving his hands through the air.

"What a pathetic coward, but at least he has a seed of common sense. What's your excuse, Caleb?" Dante tugged against Autumn's cuffs. "Shouldn't you be playing warrior somewhere?"

Dante threw Autumn a concerned look before snapping her chain between his black-gloved fingers. "Are you okay? What happened?"

"Exactly what I wanted."

Dante inhaled. "You have his scent, did you and Caleb—"

"Don't you dare hurt her, you sick alien freak!" Caleb shouted, trying to disguise his terror. "I always knew you were trouble."

"*Kwiveq stott tot ayy um,*" Dante uttered in his native tongue. The men sprinted around Caleb who clearly wasn't their target.

"What did you say to them?" Autumn asked, but Dante didn't answer her question.

"Have you forgotten our last encounter?" Dante asked Caleb, tail thrashing with a fury.

Caleb assumed a fighting stance and charged. Autumn gasped as he was whisked from his feet and suspended mid-air. Panic was apparent in his eyes. He dangled like a fly in a web.

Dante walked a full circle around him, hands twined behind his back. "Whatever shall I do with you, Caleb? You never seem to learn your lesson. Well, perhaps you'll remember this; keep your filthy hands off Autumn."

Caleb's arms and legs splayed in opposite directions. His face paled, covered with spidery veins. "*Stay away from her.*"

Caleb's limbs stretched, and he screamed, tears sprouting from his eyes. Smoke poured from his ears in white puffs as Dante telepathically melted him from the inside out.

"Dante, please stop! You're hurting him." Autumn's resolve caved.

"If you beg for my forgiveness, perhaps I'll allow you to keep your life." Dante's lips flickered with amusement.

When Caleb didn't speak, Dante stretched his limbs until they cracked. Joints separated and bones shattered. Caleb's shrieks of agony echoed above the commotion.

"You're a worthless weakling."

Unable to take any more of this torture, Autumn stormed over to Dante. With all her might, she smacked him in the face, using the full force of her body. Dante's cheek shifted and flushed, and Caleb fell unconscious on the grass.

A jolt of sharp pain traveled up Autumn's arm like lightning, bringing her to her knees. She grit her teeth to prevent herself from screaming. Dante knelt, worried about her wellbeing.

"Don't you dare touch me," she came to her feet, stumbling backwards. " You're a monster. Look what you've done."

Dante remained quiet before saying, "Autumn, please forgive me."

"Stay away from me. Don't come any closer."

Scrambling to a nearby rock garden, she knelt and filled her hands with smooth, porous stones. In a fit of terror, she pelted them at Dante, crouching and throwing as quickly as she could. But she stopped, realizing none of them struck his body. Instead, they hovered weightless in a cloud.

Fearing retaliation, she bolted, shoes kicking up piles of dust over Caleb's unconscious body. But Misty was *missing*. Crap.

She glanced over her shoulder to gauge his distance, but he was *nowhere* to be found.

A warm gust of wind swept her higher, higher, higher into the starlit sky. She stopped suddenly, suspended thousands of feet in the air. She found herself in Dante's arms, *with nowhere to run and nowhere to hide.*

Horrified, she clung to him for safety. Below, streams of zapping blue light electrified through sleepy suburban neighborhoods. Fires blazed, and screams echoed through the warm evening air. But Caleb's shrieks of pain were forever etched into her memory.

"I admire your fierce spirit, Autumn. You're a true fighter, and your heart is always in the right place," Dante said. "You always keep me in check."

She bared her teeth at him furiously.

"Now I shall speak and you shall listen. No more outbursts or distractions." A cool night breeze blew through the strands of his onyx hair. She buried her head against his chest, seething that he'd cornered her.

Seventy-One

"I HATE YOU." Autumn breathed.

"I know." Dante stared at the impending chaos, unable to make eye contact. "How could you not despise the man who came to conquer your world?"

A pit formulated in her stomach. "But why? I don't understand," she clenched her fists. "Tell me the truth for once, I'm sick of your secrets."

"There is a need to provide living space for overpopulated worlds. Higher life-forms specifically. My master has placed a great deal of importance on Earth and selected it, to stake his claim over Universe 1."

She gulped. "What will happen to all of the people living here?"

"Most will be utilized to rebuild the planet according to his specifications. Others will be sent to distant worlds to harvest natural resources."

"So, he's looking for space? Why not tell him to go after Mars or Pluto, where no one lives? He'd rather ruin this planet and take everyone as slaves?"

She needed to get away. Far, far away from him. All she

could think about was whether Caleb was still alive. And if her friends were injured. And most importantly her *Dad*.

All she wanted to do was have her normal life back and put this entire nightmare behind her. If only she could rewind the clock.

"I never had a choice in the matter," Dante admitted. "I've been conquering planets for as long as I can remember."

"Well, you're wrong, there's always a choice if you're strong enough to make the right one. You could make a change right now." She stared at the dark smoke churning in the distance.

"I'm prepared to make a change."

Autumn swallowed hard. "What do you plan to do with me?"

"Devote my life to keeping you safe, and making sure you're cared for. I want you to come home with me as my wife."

"Never." She slipped from his grasp, but he caught her by her wrists, pulling her back into his arms. "My answer is no, Armienti already told me what you're like. I refuse to love and support a monster."

Dante mumbled incomprehensibly under his breath before raising a palm over his head. A flush of pure heat erupted against Autumn's skin. Blinding orange, blue, and silver rays swirled before her eyes. The collection of flames swelled to a size, both unwieldy and unimaginable.

Dante held the flame steady, staring into her eyes. "Upon further reflection I'll make a deal with you."

"I don't make deals with the devil."

"There are far worse villains out there than me, Autumn, and I can help you. You'd be wise to consider what I have to offer."

She had no other choice, not with the massive ball of fire crackling in his palm.

"If you agree to accompany me home to be my wife, what you've witnessed will be the last bit of devastation your planet ever suffers. I swear it. Deny me, and it becomes impossible for me to protect your planet. I will, however, provide you with safe passage to a nearby colony in Universe 2, where you can live out the remainder of your life as you see fit."

She carefully weighed her options. They were both terrible and permanent. Option one forced her to marry a monster and go home with him, to live on his faraway planet. *But at least Earth would be safe.* One life in exchange for eight billion. With option two, Dante's ironic take on freedom, the world would suffer because of her selfishness.

She buried her face in her palms, *all out of options.*

"Before I make my decision, you need to promise me my friends and family are safe."

"I assure you they're well and will continue to be if you make the right choice."

She sucked in a deep trembling breath after receiving the answer she needed to hear. "I'll go with you, but *only* to save my planet," she said, "But just so we're clear, I can never love you, and *I'll never ever forgive you for this.*"

"Consider this a wedding present from me to you." Dante retracted the flame into the palm of his hand.

She crossed her arms. "I have a wedding gift for you as well. I promise to make every day of your life from here on out a living hell."

"I look forward to it." He pressed his lips to her forehead.

Overwhelmed with debilitating sorrow, Autumn closed her eyes and succumbed to the darkness.

Seventy-Two

AUTUMN TOSSED *and turned in a fitful sleep. Fire, screams, and churning smoke. Dante overseeing the chaos. Caleb's pale features and lifeless eyes. Iain running for his life. Her mom's body on Lakes Road, broken, drenched, and bloodied. Her friends and dad in danger.*

She rolled over, white starched shirt rubbing against the base of her sore neck. Her patent black Mary Jane shoes were still bucked to her feet. Her too tight bowtie was strangling her. Autumn fell asleep in her catering uniform, but she couldn't remember when.

Drenched, she sat up slowly, wiping her brow. As she blinked hard, her vision came to. She was in the peaceful darkness of her own bedroom, unable to recall the fine details of the ride home.

There was the wedding, Caleb, Iain, swirled stars, and smoke. *Caleb?* Her heart thundered. *Oh, my goodness, Caleb.*

She discovered her phone in her back pants pocket and dialed his number.

It went straight to voicemail.

"Oh, Caleb, I hope you're okay."

She texted him desperately. *Please call me.*

"Do you love him?" A tall, upright shadow lurked behind the door.

She hesitated and then spoke, "Yes, for as long as I can remember."

Dante went quiet and continued, "His pulse is weak, but he's receiving the necessary medical treatment. He'll live."

"You broke your promise to me," Autumn added.

Dante watched her in silence before speaking. "I know, I'm sorry."

For a split second, she wondered why they were in her room, and not on his ship drifting somewhere through space. She hoped upon hope by some miracle; he had second thoughts about bringing her.

His wife. Autumn's stomach bubbled over.

"Have you changed your mind about me?" she dared ask.

A stupid question perhaps, but she had to know if there was any way she could sever their arrangement. All she wanted to do was stay home and have a normal life again. Not to travel to some planet in some far-off universe.

"Our agreement still stands."

She nodded, her thoughts drifting off to her dad. "Can my dad come with me at least?"

Dante scrunched his nose. "No, unfortunately he can't."

Her heart shattered. What was he supposed to do without her? He'd be all alone, left to fend for himself. Overwhelmed and devastated, she buried her face in her palms. An explosion of tears followed, and she wept for the hundredth time in less than a year.

Dante placed his hand on her shoulder, and she pushed it away, face streaked with wetness.

"I thought you could use this time to say your goodbyes and get your affairs in order."

"Screw you."

"Or we can forget it and leave right now."

She grew quiet, wiping her nose and mouth against her sleeve.

She nodded mechanically. He'd hardly left her with any time at all to say goodbye to her family and friends and pack her belongings. It was a daunting task on such short notice.

"I'll return to collect you in twenty-four hours." She blinked, and he vanished.

The contents of her stomach rose. She sprinted into the bathroom. Falling to her knees, she emptied her guts into the toilet. Slowly, she wiped her mouth. She didn't have time for sadness and self-pity. Every tick of the clock was one second closer to leaving Earth—

Forever.

First things first. Autumn needed to pack her belongings. She sprinted to the closet and located her backpack, tossing out textbooks, notebooks, and pens. She stuffed it chock full of clothing and overdue library books. Finally, she packed two boxes of thirty-six count tampons in her favorite crossbody bag.

The thought of being caught under prepared for her period on a ship of warriors was *beyond* mortifying. Maybe worse than being abducted.

She climbed into bed and never bothered to change, although she reeked of vomit. She watched the shadows dance across the ceiling, shuddering at each unnatural movement. A few times when she stared long enough, she could have sworn she saw her mom's deep brown eyes watching her.

Seventy-Three

AUTUMN SOAKED in the details of her last day on Earth. The way the golden rays of the sun shyly peeked through the blinds of her bedside window. The hum of the central air, and the scent of chocolate chip pancakes wafting up the stairs from the kitchen.

It was a typical Sunday. A peaceful Sunday at the end of May. But with it came a dark and terrible secret. One she could *never* reveal to her dad. It would be their final hours together, and she didn't want to waste them sending him into a panic.

After showering and washing off the sweat, grime, and never-ending tears, she put on her best face and joined him in the kitchen. He stood there, blissfully unaware, sprinkling chocolate chips into the simmering batter. Two glasses of orange juice sat on the counter, near a single scarlet-red rose with baby's breath. She hugged him with all her might. Her dad placed the spatula on the counter and held her, kissing her hair.

"What did I do to deserve this?" He laughed.

She was afraid if she spoke, she'd burst into tears. Somehow, she managed to squeeze out a convincing smile.

"I love you, that's all."

"Autumn, are you feeling okay?" He placed his hand over her forehead, checking her temperature.

She nodded rather than answering and took a seat. *Lying wasn't her specialty.*

"I didn't hear you come in last night, but I'm glad you're all right." He returned to the stove and flipped the pancakes. "I heard there was a terrible fire in Rockland County. It made headlines."

Autumn's muscles tensed. "I had no idea," she lied, taking a sip from her glass. The beverage trickled into her unsettled stomach.

"Two-hundred people were injured along with a few deaths," he said solemnly. "God rest their souls."

He brought over the plate of pancakes and a bottle of maple syrup. "What's the agenda for today? Are you seeing Iain? He seems like a nice guy. Not like the *others* you've spent time with."

"We broke up," she said flatly.

"I'm sorry to hear. I liked him for you."

So did she for a brief while, but Iain was in the past, and there was no sense in dwelling on what couldn't be changed.

"I'm thinking of walking around the ponds, do you want to come with me?" she asked, scarcely able to enjoy her food.

Her dad accepted her invitation.

When they arrived at the Monroe Ponds, the bright blue sky had shifted gray. Dark, dense clouds sprinkled water, dampening her face and pink jelly sandals. But Autumn insisted they walk, even after her dad informed her he saw severe thunderstorms in the forecast.

It was her one last chance to visit her favorite place in town, and she wouldn't let the weather spoil it. Fortunately, she remembered a compact umbrella.

As they walked, she noted the natural beauty of the ponds. The way the Canadian Geese waded with their brown and yellow goslings through the water. The way the blades of grass gathered raindrops, and the sway of the mighty weeping willow tree.

She and her dad were the only two people walking, and for good reason. Even with an umbrella, their clothing became soaked. But Autumn refused to let it ruin her final day on Earth.

"Have you ever thought of moving on after mom?" she asked as pelting raindrops skidded against the umbrella. She expressed her deepest and most desperate wish. Her dad needed someone to take care of him in her absence.

"Your mom left large shoes to fill. It would be difficult for me to find anyone who remotely compares." He peered at her through his droplet covered glasses.

Her heart clenched. As she feared, he wasn't ready to put himself out there again.

"I think you should at least try." She picked up her pace.

"I loved your mom until the day she died, and I still love her. I'll always love her."

"All I'm saying is don't give up so easily." She felt like a hypocrite, giving him advice she couldn't take. "You're a wonderful man and an amazing dad. Any woman would be lucky to have you in her life."

"I'm proud of you, Autumn." He hugged her tightly. "I'm proud to call you my daughter. You've blossomed into a beautiful young lady. Your mom would be proud of you, too. When and if the right woman comes around, you'll be the first to know."

The rain turned torrential, and lightning crackled through the sky. They found a boba tea shop and waited out the storm. After ordering two teas, they sat in the window, watching the sky pour.

"How are you?" he asked, taking a sip of tea. "You've been acting strange since this morning."

She debated whether she should divulge any information, but figured what more damage could it do than had already been done. "Dante contacted me."

"I should've guessed." He rolled his eyes. "We need to call the police. It sounds like my dream was a premonition."

Or a *nightmare*.

"I agree. We'll call tomorrow." She sipped her tea, staring out the window at the pouring rain.

"I'm glad you were honest and told me. Do me a favor and stay away from him. He's dangerous."

She nodded, too little, too late. If only it were possible. She was destined for danger.

After a period, the heavy rain clouds passed, and a glimmer of sunlight seeped from the sky, reflecting over the mirrored ponds. A faded rainbow shone through the clouds. They left the shop and walked around town in their sopping wet clothes.

Feet sliding around in her rubber jellies, her dad laughed hysterically at the squeaking. Even her dad could crack a smile; now if only she could remember how.

The day slipped into nightfall. Stars peeked through the clouds, and rays of sunlight dulled to full darkness. They ordered takeout sushi from Plum House. When they arrived home, Autumn grabbed her phone. She hadn't touched it the entire day, and she needed to reach out to her friends to say goodbye.

Once she was in her bedroom, she grabbed her phone and sent as many messages as possible. She told Lauren and Ellie she'd be studying abroad for a summer session in Paris. It seemed like a logical explanation for her absence. At least for the time being. But what would happen in a few days when her dad realized she was missing? She couldn't focus on that right now.

One last time, she asked Caleb how he was feeling and checked in on Iain, who was probably traumatized.

Neither replied.

As she locked the screen of her phone, the opposite end of the bed sank low with a creak. Her stomach knotted. Dante had come to collect her.

Seventy-Four

AUTUMN SHUDDERED at the sight of Dante. The corners of his lips flickered.

"Twenty-four hours are up. My replacement ship is ready for takeoff."

"I'm not ready to go," Autumn said, sounding more like a plea than a statement. "I have dinner downstairs, and my dad and I are planning to watch a movie. I won't see my dad again for I don't know how long. I owe him a proper goodbye."

Dante grew quiet, considering her request. "How long is a movie?"

She wished she could say *forever*, but she was honest. It was the first time she'd been honest all day. "An hour and a half."

"Okay, I'll allot you *an hour and a half more*. But we need to leave as soon as possible."

"Thanks," she murmured, tempted to run and scream. But she didn't want to alarm her dad and ruin their last evening together.

She rose and raced out the door.

"I'll be right here waiting for you when you're done." Dante's words pierced through her heart like knives.

When she joined her dad in the living room, the movie streamed, and her dinner sat on the coffee table. She noticed her dad drank a glass of sangria and reached for it.

"Autumn." He shot her a disapproving look.

"I need to relax. Guy stuff."

Her dad sighed and grabbed a second glass, pouring her root beer instead.

After sipping her beverage, she barely touched her food. The movie droned on in a blur.

She spent the entire time listening to her dad emit deep belly laughs. This is how she wanted to remember him. Content and full of life. And most importantly, proud of her. Her chest warmed; she would miss him more than anything.

Her eyes clouded with tears when the credits rolled. It was her cue to say goodnight. *Forever.*

Hugging him as tight as she could, she said. "Goodnight, I love you, dad."

She stood from the couch, making her way to the stairwell.

"I love you too."

She sprinted back over, giving him one last hug, squeezing him with all her might.

"I'm not sure what's gotten into you." He embraced her, glasses askew on his whiskered face. "I'll see you in the morning, sweetheart. Pleasant dreams."

"You too."

But what she really wanted to say was, "no dad, you *won't.*"

Seventy-Five

AUTUMN STOOD at the top of the stairwell. The cozy light from her room dimmed and flickered beneath the bedroom door. Trembling, she turned the knob to find Dante lounging on the bed with his communicator, as promised. He met her gaze as she entered the room.

"Did you enjoy the movie?" He stood up, slipping the sleek device into his pocket.

She ignored him and walked to the closet to collect her pre-packed bags. Kneeling, she grabbed her cosmic backpack and her cross-body satchel, slinging them over her shoulder.

"Let me help you." Dante extended a hand.

"Don't you dare touch me," she hissed.

Struggling under the weight of her belongings, she rustled through a zippered compartment of her backpack she failed to clean, and found a piece of looseleaf and a pen. She scribbled a note and placed it on her bed. A single tear rolled down her cheek, but she wiped it before Dante could see.

Glancing one last time around the room, she realized she'd forgotten something.

Her snow globe collection. She couldn't bear to travel without it. She juggled one ball, then two, but when she reached for a third, Dante placed his palm over her wrist.

"We don't have room for all this. Travel can be turbulent and unpredictable," he said. "I swear, upon our arrival, you can have as many globes as you like."

Autumn narrowed her eyes. His promises were empty.

"How is it fair you get to steal other people's planets and I can't keep any of my globes?"

Dante's eyes widened for a split second, and he huffed. "I suppose we can manage the two in your hands."

"Good." Autumn took her *Alice in Wonderland* globe and the silver spired castle Armienti crafted for her birthday. Which *wasn't* any of Dante's business.

"I'm ready," she muttered.

Wordlessly, Dante swept her into his arms. When she went to protest, they already teleported into time and space.

They arrived at Farrah Falls, at the familiar clearing of trees, halved to blackened ash. He placed Autumn on her feet, and she watched and waited for smoke and debris to form. *Only,* it didn't come from the ground, where the graveyard of trees laid still and silent.

In the sky above the clearing, dark steam seeped and sprayed in a cyclical formation, revealing a ship twice the size of the previous one. Identical in cake slice shape. Its onyx metallic exterior glimmered beneath the crescent moonlight.

A door opened, and bright rays of light illuminated the dark forest. Autumn clutched her bags as Dante swept her into his arms and floated into the night sky.

He set her down inside, and they were greeted by two blue Elattion women dressed in white bodysuits. A stark difference from the shadowy attire Dante and his crew typically wore.

They sank into deep curtseys and led her and Dante

onboard the ship. The lights of the replacement vessel were bright, and the halls were clean and smelled of flowers rather than body odor.

They were led down a flight of stairs to the bottom of the ship, where brutish Elattion warriors sat strapped and sardined on either end of the cargo bay.

One woman removed Autumn's bags.

"Wait—" she said before the globes were snatched from her hands as well.

"You can have your belongings back after takeoff."

She nodded. *Takeoff into outer space.*

Legs swaying, she followed Dante into another room covered from the floor to the ceiling with blinking buttons and beeping gauges. On the left were rows of spacious seating.

She did a double take when she noticed Ronan and Armienti already buckled in. Ronan was busy snapping alien selfies with his communicator, while Armienti rested his head against the window. Dante buckled her in although she was tempted to scratch his eyes out. Her forehead pulsated.

The room was silent and suffocating until Dante opened his mouth and spoke in his brutal-toned native Ivarkian to two helmeted men at the control panel.

As the ship trembled and revved, she accidentally brushed her hand against his, but quickly recoiled. He glanced at her momentarily. She never wanted to touch him again if she could help it.

Takeoff wasn't like she imagined, compared to the rocket ships she'd seen on television. Instead of dizzying pressure and a blast off, they ascended higher and higher like an elevator rising to the top floor of a skyscraper. They passed by planes and through clouds at an unimaginable speed. Before she realized, they infiltrated the layers of the atmosphere. Rich rainbow hues glinted against the glass of the windshield.

They came to a complete stop, followed by the pop of her

ears. Earth orbited in all of its blue and green, magnificent glory. Satellites bumbled clumsily. The level of gravity was nonexistent. The ship turned one-hundred-and-eighty-degrees, and soared off into a sea of stars. She watched in silent horror as the Earth disappeared into nothingness.

413

Seventy-Six

AFTER WHAT FELT LIKE HOURS, the ride stabilized. Ronan and Armienti were the first to stand and leave the cabin, followed by the pilots. Autumn remained with Dante; the silence so thick it screamed.

"So what do you think of outer space?"

She couldn't stand anymore of his small talk and phony concern. He single-handedly destroyed her life, and all he could think about was the *scenery*.

"I'm tired," she changed the subject. "It's late and I want to get to sleep." In reality, she wasn't sleepy. She needed privacy to cry her eyes out and shriek into a pillow until her vocal chords disintegrated.

"How rude of me," he offered her a hand. "I'll show you to your quarters."

Autumn brushed past, ignoring him. The sooner she escaped him, the better.

The new ship bustled with life. Men and women wandered the hallways, going about their evening. They curtseyed and bowed as Autumn and Dante made their way by.

Her face and neck burned; she never had this much attention in her life. Dante walked around with his usual swagger. *Arrogant jerk*. She wanted to smack the smug look off his face.

They arrived at a steel sliding door. She yawned and stretched, eager to start her crying session. Dante pressed his finger against the side panel scanner, and they were permitted access.

Her belongings were neatly assembled on the bed, but her jaw dropped when Dante entered the room as well. The door sealed behind them.

"What are you doing?" She gasped.

"Same as you." His amber eyes glinted. "Preparing for sleep."

"But I thought—"

"All the other rooms are occupied. Unless, of course, you'd like to sleep in the dormitory."

"I hate you." She stormed into the bathroom and slammed the door shut.

When she reemerged, Dante laid lounging on the bed, half undressed. Rippled abs and muscles gleaming, scars and all. Running a hand through his obsidian hair, he glanced her way.

Autumn rolled her eyes as she climbed into bed. "You better keep your hands to yourself."

Dante inched closer, a smile playing across his lips. "Do you really think I'm some kind of monster?"

"From what I've seen, yes. I think you're worse than a monster."

"Maybe you don't know me as well as you think you do. Have you ever considered—"

"I know you plenty," she interrupted. "I've seen you in action. And if you know what's good for you, you'll keep to your side of the bed. I'm so *not* in the mood for this."

Dante moved closer. She could feel the warmth of his body against her back. "You know, four hundred days can feel like a lifetime when you have no one to talk to. I thought at least we'd have each other."

Her jaw dropped. *Four hundred days?* They were going to be stuck together for four hundred days! She shot up and grabbed pillows from the head of the bed, and shoved them between their bodies, creating a barricade.

"Well, you thought wrong." She rested her head on her pillow, tears streaming down her cheeks. "I hate you, and I'll never forgive you for this."

Dante withdrew and stuck to his side of the bed, finally getting the hint. A long while passed before she drifted off to sleep. Her mind wandered to her dad and how lonely he would be without her. And whether her friends bought her story.

* * *

Autumn awoke, surrounded by an endless stream of black night and stars whizzing by the window. The bathroom door was shut, and thick gray steam seeped from underneath. Water poured furiously.

Squinting and reaching for her backpack on the floor, she grabbed her phone out of habit. It read 11:05 a.m. with no service. Her heart thumped as panic set in. Her dad knew she was missing by now. And what had he done after discovering her note?

The tears flowed uncontrollably. She cried and choked at the edge of the bed. Her Dad was all alone and there wasn't anything she could do about it.

A squeak came from the bathroom before the water stopped. A pair of feet hit the floor, and the door opened casually. Dante reemerged with a plain white towel wrapped around his waist. His blue skin gleamed in the artificial light. Steam flowed overhead.

"Oh good, you're awake. Are you hungry?"

Autumn wiped her face and pushed past him. She slammed the bathroom door, slid to the floor and wept uncontrollably.

Seventy-Seven

DANTE DRESSED AND ATE, keeping a watchful eye on the wash closet door, hoping Autumn would reemerge. But after two hours, there was still no sign of her.

Listening, he detected her miserable sobs. Autumn *despised* him, and he didn't blame her. Especially after coming clean about the true nature of his mission. Perhaps he should've told her the truth earlier.

Everything he'd done and everything he would ever do would be to keep her safe. Even if she didn't realize it yet.

Once again, he should've begged for her forgiveness, but pride had always been his greatest downfall.

He rose from the table, pushing the chair in place. He set out eating utensils, a glass of water, and a single packet of food.

"I'm stepping out for a bit," he muttered through the door. "If you get hungry, pour water into the contents of the packet. Mix and eat."

No answer came, nor did he expect one.

When Dante arrived downstairs, the common area bustled with a newfound life. He discovered his cousins huddled around a table in a corner of the room. They were almost as antisocial as he was. Now that Dante thought of it, he didn't have any friends to speak of. *He didn't need them anyway.* Or so he had convinced himself throughout the years.

Armienti flashed him a hesitant smile, and Ronan propped his chin on a fist as Dante approached.

"Where's your blushing mate to be?" Ronan stretched his neck.

Dante picked at his gloves. "She's having some difficulty adjusting to her new life."

Armienti snorted. "Seriously? What did you expect?"

Dante narrowed his eyes. "What is that supposed to mean? Please do indulge me."

"Well, you stole the poor girl away from her world, the world we almost conquered. You terrorized her friends and didn't have the common courtesy to provide her with her own accommodations. Do you really think this will make her want to reconcile with you?"

True, all true. He behaved like a fool and hated Armienti for picking up on it. *How could his cousin be more perceptive than he is?*

In the middle of their conversation, two soldiers burst through the door, approached the table and bowed. "Permission to speak, Sire," the taller of the two said.

"Permission granted."

"A wanted criminal was discovered hiding in the cargo bay."

"Wanted for what?" Dante folded his arms.

"He's responsible for the year-long delay of our mission—"

Dante waved a hand, dismissing them, and turned his attention to Ronan. He ground his teeth in his mouth.

"I thought I tasked you with punishing the other responsible party."

Ronan glanced at the table. "I was unable to locate him. I assumed he would meet his own demise; he was weaker and scrawnier than most."

"That's even more pathetic." Dante rose. "He should've been easy game. It seems if you want something done correctly around here you have to do it yourself."

Dante cracked his knuckles in preparation to slay him, and headed to the cargo bay when he was struck with an idea. Maybe it wasn't necessary to end him. Punish him, yes, but show him mercy, which he was admittedly unused to doing. Maybe Autumn could see he had redeeming qualities.

He turned around and smiled. "On second thought, Armienti go collect Autumn for me, and accompany her to the cargo bay. I'd like for her to join us."

Armienti stood up and nodded.

* * *

Autumn emerged from the bathroom with raw, burning eyes. Thankfully, Dante had left her alone. Weak and tired from crying so hard, she glanced out the window into the abyss of shadows and stars. There was no telling where they were, and no way for her to reach anyone back home.

Her stomach grumbled, as it had a habit of doing when she skipped two meals in a row. Ambling over to the kitchen area, she discovered a single white packet reminiscent of oatmeal, a glass of water, and eating utensils.

Just add water, she recalled Dante telling her. She tore open the packet and sniffed it. It smelled like pure sugar cane. She poured it into the bowl allowing the dust to settle, before adding a few drops of water. Instantly, it bubbled and slithered, forming black miniature serpents. Autumn screamed and jumped to her feet, toppling the chair backwards. The snakes leapt from the bowl, landing on the table.

When she looked up again, Armienti stood in the room. He chuckled white teeth sparkling. "They're lively, you're supposed to eat them as quickly as you can."

"They're disgusting." She stuck her tongue out. "I'd rather starve to death than eat them."

"They're a delicacy." He smoothed a hand through his gilded locks. "And I don't believe that for a second. You'd be surprised what you'd eat if you were truly starving."

"Why are you here? Is Dante too chicken shit to face me after what he did?"

Armienti shook his head. "I've been sent to collect you—"

"What, you're his errand boy now?"

Armienti pursed his lips. "Your presence is expected downstairs *immediately*."

She placed a hand on her hip. "Well, I'm not going anywhere."

"I'm afraid it's non-negotiable."

Autumn sprinted toward the bathroom, but he cut her off in the blink of an eye. "You either get dressed and behave yourself like a good little human or I swear I'll sling you over my shoulder and carry you the entire way."

"I told you already, I'm not go—"

Armienti reached over and flung her over his shoulder. She kicked and screamed and punched his back as he transported her through floors and down three flights of stairs, like he promised.

When they reached the bottom floor of the ship, Armienti set her down on the ground, exhausted and out of breath. The cold floor stung the bare soles of her feet. She shivered, crossing her arms, still in her satin cloud pajamas. So far, in her experience, outer space had been *miserable* and *freezing*.

Armienti led her into the bay. Soldiers in onyx uniforms gathered in a circle. Everyone stopped talking and stared at her as she entered. Although quiet in this room, in a nearby one, she could have sworn she heard uncontrollable sobbing. She erupted in a cold sweat.

"Sweetheart, there you are." Dante gestured for her to join him.

She hesitated, but in her head, she heard like a whisper of breath. "*Do as he says.*"

Autumn realized the words didn't come from Armienti, but from Ronan, who watched her from across the bay. She made her way through the crowd to where Dante sat, the chair next to him she supposed was hers.

Dante took her hand and pressed his vile lips to her knuckles as he guided her into her seat. Her heart thundered in her ears.

"What's going on?" she asked.

Dante ignored her and instead gestured to Ronan, who left the room. When he reemerged, Autumn gasped, blood running cold in her veins. She cupped her hands tightly over her mouth to prevent herself from screaming at the sight of her dad.

Seventy-Eight

"THIS TIME you've taken it too far." Autumn shouted at Dante and sprang to her feet. She ran over to help her dad, whose hands were bound in chains. Autumn pushed Ronan back, and he stared at her wide-eyed.

"Did they hurt you? Are you okay?" She leapt into his arms, tears streaming down her cheeks.

Her dad trembled, umber-brown eyes wavering beneath his plain silver frames. "This is *all* Dante's doing."

Autumn turned and scowled, but Dante sat there in silence. Unmoving.

"We're going to get out of here. I'm going to take you back home. Everything will be okay, you'll see."

The energy in the room shifted hot, like hell fire. Dante's face assumed the deepest shade of crimson. He rose and strode over, grabbing her dad by his collar. She screamed and pulled at Dante's bulging, muscular arms.

"Let go, you're hurting him!"

"How dare you speak with such familiarity to her, slave."

"Dante please. You'll kill him! You'll kill him!"

* * *

Dante stared down at the scrawny tech whose spine he couldn't wait to snap. The deal was off. How dare he put his hands all over his mate. But Autumn clawed and fought with all of her human might to separate them. And he still couldn't understand any of it.

"Get off my dad! Get off him!" She screamed.

But when he blinked again, it wasn't the tech's ruddy face he saw but Maeve's. Her youthful complexion, rosy cheeks, obsidian curls, and moonlit eyes. Maeve, who'd been dead these last *five* years. Eyes bulging, he took a step in retreat.

"Don't worry, Dante, I'll be right here waiting for you." Maeve twirled a curl around her fingertip.

"Autumn, stay away." He pushed her behind him, kicking and screaming. Maeve erupted in a fit of piercing laughter.

* * *

Autumn stared at her dad, laughing his head off. What in the world could possibly be so funny? It was like he was possessed.

Trembling from head to toe, she said, "Dad, are you okay?"

"That's not your father." Dante blocked her with his arm. But she pushed his hand aside to get a closer look.

"Dante, stop it, let me through." She struggled against his might.

Her dad blinked and two cat-like slits cut through his pupils, followed by a simmering wave of pink electricity. It rippled in a whirlwind of lightning across his form.

Seventy-Nine

THE CREATURE BORN amidst the storm of swirling light and electricity was monstrous. Autumn didn't know whether she should faint or run away. Although in her experience, she never gained more than a few steps on any of the alien beings. But this one was different. She could feel his unseen hatred seeping through the air, cutting through her like a sword.

The frightening being stood approximately Dante's height with lumpy pink-vomit-hued skin, a hairless head, and horizontal folds along his forehead filled with slit, blood-shot eyes. There were two on his face as well, eight like a spider. He had a thick veiny neck with bulging muscles, and a softer midsection. He dressed in the same uniform as Dante, black as midnight. Minus the crest.

"Your Imperial Highness." The creature fell into a mocking bow, the rolls of his stomach creasing.

Her heart skipped. "You're a prince? Why did you never bother to tell me?"

Dante glanced at her and crossed his arms, before directing

his attention back at the creature. "General Keyserike, what brings you aboard this voyage?"

After he spoke, everyone in the room except for Dante and his cousins fell to one knee. Autumn balled her fists furiously. Dante had admitted yet another important detail and she prayed to whoever would listen that her dad was still alive.

"A random quality check I assigned myself on, to see if the Grand Supreme's favorite Elattion pet prince has been upholding his vision around the Universes. It's been rather tasty thus far." Keyserike licked his salmon lips with his boiled tongue. The bile singed Autumn's esophagus.

"And how do you find the quality of my work, General?" Dante cocked his head to the side.

"Excellent as per usual, until you reached Universe 1."

Keyserike smiled. The edges of his teeth were jagged and yellow. "You've always been good for a laugh, but this is a new all-time low for you. You were sent on the most simplistic of missions I could've done with one hand tied behind my back," he said. "And most disturbing of all, it seems you've brought the vermin you were assigned to conquer back with you, planning to take it as your mate."

"If you could've completed this mission so easily, why is it you didn't volunteer, General?" Dante crossed his arms. "I suspect you were too much of a coward, hiding behind your master. Afraid to dirty your soft useless hands."

"Our master." Keyserike corrected before narrowing all eight eyes.

Autumn watched in horror as his tongue flicked from his mouth and elongated, wrapping around a nearby soldier's waist, who kicked and screamed. His mouth stretched open to an unnatural width, and he ate him alive, chewing loudly, crunching on bones, tendons, and sinew jaw dribbling with warm bubbling blood. He belched so loudly, Autumn covered her ears, and the mangled head flew out of his mouth coated with slime, sliding across the floor against her bare foot.

Her knees knocked together, and Dante made a face of disgust.

Keyserike grinned at her and looked back at Dante. "I'll make a deal with you, Martyne. You give me Autumn as a snack, and we turn the ship around and go back to Earth to finish what you should've. Then I shall make the Grand Supreme none the wiser of your indiscretion." He licked his lips.

Dante glanced at Autumn, smiled, and looked back to Keyserike. "Deal."

"But, I, I, I..." She trembled as Dante took her by the arm and moved her in front of him. She wanted to kick him in the groin. Why bring her at all and put her through any of this hell only to feed her to a monster? *Unless it was his plan all along.*

Dante glanced over his shoulder. "Ronan, Armienti, make sure nobody leaves the bay." They nodded and stood guard by the doors.

Eighty

AUTUMN'S INSIDES CHURNED. She looked around desperately for some type of escape. She had to get out of there, or else she'd wind up as Keyserike's next *meal*. Her stomach twisted when they walked by the head of the decapitated soldier, who Keyserike had eaten instantaneously. The sound of crunching bones still haunted her ears.

The doors were all so far away, but Ronan and Armienti carefully guarded them. And if by some miracle she squeezed around them, they were still in deep space, and she had no idea which way home was located.

"Well, Dante, give her to me." Keyserike extended a clawed hand. Autumn moved as far back into Dante as she could, trembling so hard her teeth chattered.

She shook her head, grabbing against Dante's thighs. "You don't really want to eat me. I can't imagine I taste good. I'm mostly bone."

"Actually, I can't get your taste off my mind. Yours is the sweetest flesh I've ever sampled in my life." Keyserike licked his lips, boiled tongue scraping over his flesh. The breath caught in her throat. "I intended to devour you sooner, but I'll admit even I make mistakes. Flavor wise, this girl was a close second."

Keyserike reached into a side pocket and pulled out a head of tangled dark-brown hair. Autumn screamed against Dante as he popped out an eye and ate it. *Brianna.*

"Here, enjoy." Dante pushed her toward him. But when Keyserike reached, Dante grabbed him by the wrist, flipped him around, and kicked him in the back, sending him flying belly first into the nearest wall with a hollow BOOM that echoed through the bay.

She made a break for it, heart racing, but Armienti stopped her at the door and wouldn't let her leave, no matter how hard she tried to pull him aside.

"On second thought…" Dante crossed his arms, smirking. "Why don't you fight me for her and for Earth? Unless, of course, you've forgotten how."

Keyserike pushed himself up and brushed the metal shards from his uniform, face scratched and bleeding. "You've made a fatal error, boy."

* * *

Adrenaline crashed through Dante's body. The time had *finally* come. For years he suffered at Keyserike's hands. The beatings, starvation, and the constant threats. All to ensure the Grand Supreme's vision. A vision his father caved to at Dante's expense and had been enacted for the last four-hundred years. He'd been tortured, brutalized, and over-worked since childhood. All leading up to this moment.

Keyserike flicked his tongue, and it coiled around Dante's arm, sizzling through the fabric of his uniform, singing his skin with an acidic bite. He cringed and threw a ball of crackling fire at Keyserike's face, melting off part of his tongue. Keyserike grabbed his mouth, stumbling backwards.

Dante laughed and wiped the acid saliva from his sleeve. "What's wrong? Had enough already?"

Keyserike's eight eyes bulged as he charged into him, making the whole bay shake with the weight of his stride. Keyserike opened his mouth, vomiting acid all over the floor in an explosion of saliva, melting through steel. Dante easily dodged him, again and again, as he chased him around the room in circles.

He stood there chuckling as Keyserike struggled to catch his breath. "Surely this isn't the best you've got. I have to admit, I'm rather disappointed. I remember you being so much stronger. I suppose this is the price you pay for sitting on your ass day in and day out, doing absolutely nothing as number three."

Keyserike suddenly grinned at Dante's challenge, yellow jagged teeth gleaming, and turned his attention elsewhere.

* * *

Autumn clawed desperately at Armienti's arm, attempting to slip past him, but he wouldn't budge, no matter how hard she tried.

"Come on, Armienti, please, move, you have to let me leave!"

But he paid her no mind, eyes glued on Dante and Keyserike's scuffle.

She had to get out of here and at least try to hide. But when she turned around a second time to check on the ensuing fight, her jaw hit the floor.

It had been a year since she'd last seen her face. Luminous olive skin, deep child-like chestnut-brown eyes, and golden highlighted curls.

Tears welled up in Autumn's eyes. "Mom."

"Autumn, no, don't let him deceive you." She heard

Dante's voice shouting from across the room. She ignored the warning. It was difficult, impossible not to stare. She needed to get closer to get a better look. She walked without consideration, all her logic disappeared.

Her mom's face glowed as she drew closer. Chest welling up, Autumn reached out to embrace her, and the flash of razor-sharp teeth came and chomped around her left wrist.

She screamed and screamed, falling to her knees as her flesh pierced wide open and burned like it was melting in a liquid fire. Tears rolled down her cheeks.

A deep growl sent chills down her spine. When she looked again, she couldn't believe her eyes.

Eighty-One

AN ANIMAL ENTERED THE BAY, one that was strangely human-esque. It stood on two legs, at over eight feet high, and was covered with a coat of thick, shiny black fur. Twisted ribbed horns sprouted from its forehead, and its eyes were feral and obsidian. It slashed its elongated talons at Keyserike, sending him sliding across the floor face first. He collided with a wall, pink skin fading to a paler shade of gray. The entire cargo bay shook from the force of his impact. Soldiers scrambled in the opposite direction, trying to make their escape.

Autumn crawled backward, the blood from her mangled wrist leaked all over the floor tiles in a wet stream of crimson. She caught sight of a passing full moon through a nearby window.

Dante transformed into a monster. She shivered as she rose to her feet, dizziness overtaking her. She wanted to give in. The agony that ripped through her after losing her mom a *second* time was unbearable. She had fallen foolishly for another one of Keyserike's mind tricks. The pain in her wrist didn't compare to the all-consuming sense of loss she experienced and the horror of Brianna's death.

The beast opened his mouth and shot a stream of fire, singing Keyserike's face to a blackened crisp. Keyserike screamed, tongue whipping out of his mouth, frantically trying to hit the beast. But the monster sank his dagger-like fangs into Keyserike's neck, followed by gurgling and the scent of metallic blood.

But, as Keyserike lost his balance, he ripped his arms around the monster's tail, severing it clear from his body with a rough yank. A piercing roar echoed through the room, and Keyserike fell to the ground, laying still, neck bubbling with warm, ruby-red blood.

The beast fell on his knees, followed by all fours, fur vanishing into every pore, body shrinking back to his regular frame. Dante breathed deeply, his tail now *gone*. All that remained was a raw circular scar above his buttocks where the appendage once hung.

"Bravo." Keyserike choked from the ground. "You've come a long way since last we've met. It seems you weren't all talk after all."

Dante slowly rose to his feet, stark naked, and spat on the ground, amber eyes wily with rage. "Speak your final words or forever hold your peace."

"Somebody has seen. And somebody will remember what you've done here today, princeling. Don't think your indiscretion will go unpunished."

"Perhaps." Dante's lips curved. "Until then, see you in the afterlife."

Dante took his heel and crushed Keyserike's windpipe. He wheezed, eight eyes rolling back into his skull. Shuddering violently, before he lay still. Dante lit his body ablaze.

Autumn stumbled to her feet and tried once more to slip

past Armienti, her wrist dripping. But Dante swept her into his arms before she hit the door.

"Continue to watch the bay. I'll be but a few minutes," Dante said to Armienti.

Armienti nodded, and they disappeared.

Eighty-Two

WHEN AUTUMN OPENED HER EYES, after briefly teleporting through time and space, she found herself with Dante in a cool, dark corridor somewhere on the ship. The slow drip of water hit metal, and the air smelled of sterile cleaning products.

"Where are you taking me?" Her voice quaked.

"I should've done this to begin with." Dante sauntered toward a doorway. A sliver of bright light shined through the crack. Her stomach knotted.

When they entered, she squinted, eyes taking a moment to adjust to the change in lighting. Her throat was so dry and scratchy, if she wanted to, she couldn't muster up a scream.

The bite of ice-cold metal stung her legs as he set her down on a table. Dante knelt, rummaging through a drawer, still naked as the day he was born. Autumn gulped.

When he reemerged, he held a bandage in his hand. He wrapped the cloth tightly around her bleeding wrist, stopping the constant flow of blood. She struggled with his constant personality shifting. One minute, he battled an eight eyed freak, and the next he tended to her wounds with a most gentle touch.

"Is Earth safe?" she said, afraid to ask.

Dante finished putting the final touches on her wrist bow. "I made a promise to you, and as you'll come to realize, I'm a man of my word."

She nodded slowly. "But I don't understand any of this, who was Keyserike, and why—"

"A distant memory, or better yet, a figment of your imagination. It's safer if you don't remember him at all."

She shook her head. "And you're really a prince?"

Dante smiled. "I'm the only prince who matters in my realm."

He leaned in close, staring into her eyes. "When you wake, all of this will seem like a bad dream."

A sharp pinch pierced her elbow pit. Autumn flinched, then looked down. Dante was holding a syringe.

"What are you doing?" Her words slurred, vision blurring at the sides. He carried her toward a long, oval, white capsule. But she was too weak to protest, limbs falling like they were filled with wet sand.

Dante pushed a button, and the clear glass top opened slowly. He placed her inside the brightly lit chamber. White smoke flowed from the interior in rhythmic puffs.

"I hate you. I hate you so much." She tried to pry her way out, but the last of her strength had vanished.

"This is for your health and relaxation." He pressed his lips to her forehead. She went to swat him away, but her vision split in half.

"And the safest course of action."

"But it's not fair—" Autumn's lips numbed, tongue falling slack in her mouth.

"Life's not fair," Dante said, before the capsule shut

airtight. "I'll see you in four hundred days, my love." White smoke swirled in a tornado, engulfing her. Autumn's eyelids fluttered closed and she drifted off into a peaceful, coma-like slumber.

Eighty-Three

DANTE RETURNED TO HIS QUARTERS, fortunate not to be seen by anyone as he ambled nude and barefoot through the maze of hallways. A shudder of disgrace from his mutilated body overtook him as he entered the room, but he didn't have time to dwell on it.

His eyes roved, there were remnants of Autumn everywhere. Her bags sat on the floor beside the bed, instantly reminding him of the awkward night they spent together, and how she despised him. Good food was spilled along the wall, and continued to slither across the floor in black slimy lines, and on the windowsill sat the two globes swirling with glitter and light she insisted on bringing.

He walked over and held them in his hands, inspecting them with care, knowing their great importance to her. They were beautiful by Earth standards, but nowhere near as beautiful as the gifts he planned to give her upon their arrival. Autumn deserved a good life. The best for the sacrifice she'd made.

Dante shook his head, snapping out of his own rose-colored fantasy. He still had a *nightmare* to deal with. As quickly as he could, he washed the chunks of gore and blood of his nemesis from his hair, scrubbed the filth from beneath his nails, and tended to his missing tail. Dante winced, cauterizing the burning raw spot with his hand.

He pulled on a fresh obsidian uniform from his closet, but instead of wearing it casually as he'd done throughout his stay on Earth, he clipped a royal-purple cape over his shoulders, which he typically wore back home, to disguise his missing tail. Smoothing a gloved palm through his midnight locks, he left the room, making his way back to the cargo bay.

When Dante arrived, the room was at a standstill, soldiers ambling around aimlessly. Most, however, fixated their attention on Keyserike's deceased body. *Or at least what was left of it*. Ashes and charred bone.

Ronan and Armienti were exactly where he ordered them to wait, keeping a watchful eye on the doors. Dante cleared his throat, and the room fell silent. All eyes fixated on him.

"Thank you all for your years of diligent service to myself and my father. But I'm here to inform you your service is no longer needed."

There were murmurs all around the room, and one soldier bowed and stepped forth. "Permission to speak, your Imperial Highness."

"Permission granted."

"Does this mean we're free?" Hopefulness flashed through his cerulean eyes.

Dante nodded. "As free as birds."

Smiles broke out among the crowd.

He gestured for Ronan and Armienti to follow him. And they did, leaving their posts unmanned. They left through the main entrance, and Dante sealed the door airtight. Casual talking erupted into a series of frantic gasps. And then came the knocking and the kicking from the other end of the door in fits of hysteria.

Dante stood there, arms folded, staring at his cousins. They looked at him, assessing. He put his hand over a lever beside the door and pulled it. Screams echoed through the chamber until all was quiet, but the whisper of an endless vacuum leading into the pitch silence of space. He flipped the lever back and the droning of the ship continued as if nothing had happened.

As far as he was concerned, what he did was necessary. He protected not only his family and realm, but the people of Earth.

"What you both witnessed here today was a terrible accident. Another oversight by the crew." Dante paused and continued, "We're family, and family looks out for one another. And as you're both aware, loyalty is supreme in my father's realm, one day to be mine. If either of you ever discuss or even so much as think about what occurred during this unfortunate situation, there's no saving you. We'll all be dead men. Do you understand?"

His cousins nodded. Dante knew he did the unthinkable. Murdered his superior. Number three to the Grand Supreme. He risked his station, his reputation, his life, and the safety of his realm, all for his love of Autumn, who slumbered peacefully in the medical bay.

As he walked away, leaving his cousins, Keyserike's final words sent a chill ripping through his spine. Perhaps a premonition. *Somebody has seen. And somebody will remember what you've done here today, princeling. Don't think your indiscretion will go unpunished.*

The only thought more terrifying than this was whether Autumn could ever love him again after what he put her through. It would be the longest and loneliest four hundred days of his life. But at least Earth was finally safe, and for the first time ever, Dante was a hero.

www.ingramcontent.com/pod-product-compliance
Lightning Source LLC
Chambersburg PA
CBHW022021300726

48970CB00003B/982